Sea Horses

Cheryll Snow

Cover photograph "Melancholy" by Tom Way
(tomwayphotography.co.uk)

Printed in the United States of America

ISBN-13: 9781794115255

Disclaimer: This is a work of fiction. Names, characters, businesses, places, events and incidents are either the products of the author's imagination or used in a fictitious manner. Any resemblance to actual persons, living or dead, or actual events is purely coincidental.

In memory of my mom,
Carol Janice Miller
(1944-1994)

1

Jack had gotten in the habit of ignoring everyday sounds, the way he might tune out the chirp of crickets or the neighbors' TV or the roar of a jet plane overhead.

But that day, Jack listened.

The warbling of a wren in a nearby tree. The soft purr of downtown traffic. A garbage truck rumbling down the block. The neighborhood slowly coming to life.

As he shuffled to the bathroom, his bare feet cold on the hardwood floor, old age creaked in his bones, especially his back and knees.

Cursed arthritis.

It wasn't as bad in the summer, when the heat and humidity provided temporary relief to his inflamed joints. But over the past few weeks, the familiar ache had settled in, more accurate than any barometer. Winter would be here soon.

He went about his daily routine of shaving, showering, and getting dressed. Despite his throbbing knees and the crisp weather outside, he felt an added energy in his movements, renewed in a way he never would have thought possible.

In planning his death he had learned to live again.

At the breakfast table, he pulled out the list he had started a week before. Jack had always been a list-maker. He didn't like to admit it, but it helped spark his memory concerning those everyday tasks which slipped his mind so easily, like forgetting to buy toothpaste, or the time he neglected to pay the light bill. His eighty-first birthday was next month. The occasional memory lapse was inevitable.

1

He reviewed the completed tasks. He had cancelled a December dental appointment. He called Munden Dairy to stop his weekly delivery of two half-gallons of skim milk and one pint of cream. His electricity and telephone would be turned off tomorrow. He told them he was moving.

In a way, it was true.

Two days ago, he had called his cleaning lady to inform her he no longer needed her twice-monthly services. He hadn't offered an explanation, and Jack could tell by the tone of her voice he had hurt her feelings. He knew she needed the money. But he couldn't do anything about it now. She would soon learn the real reason.

Jack rubbed his hands together in anticipation of the day's activities. Two items left on the list. Time to get busy. He took his jacket and hat from the coat closet in the foyer and patted the right breast pocket to ensure the envelope was still there. Then he went down the hall and opened the door at the end.

Norma's room.

At one time this airy, light-filled space was their master bedroom. He looked at the rose-patterned wallpaper and cherry wood furnishings as if seeing them for the first time. For the last few months of Norma's life, as she waged her battle against cancer, the space was transformed into a makeshift hospital room. With Norma as its focal point, Jack felt his presence was insignificant, as if he didn't belong among the pill vials and bedpans and other items that accompany the dying. Even after her death, the feeling lingered. Jack couldn't sleep a single night there.

Crossing the room to an antique dresser, he picked up a small brass-framed photograph and gazed at the youthful, smiling image looking back at him. A fresh arrow of pain pierced something vital inside his chest. This was his Norma, his bride, the woman who had shared his life for more than half a century.

The four-poster bed drew his attention. He remembered Norma's slight form huddled beneath the covers, her ashen face slick with sweat and agony. The final few weeks were especially difficult. Before she slipped into a deep coma, Norma was confused and racked with pain, despite the large doses of morphine. He could only keep vigil at her bedside, talking softly and clumsily patting her hand, utterly helpless. There was nothing he could do for her.

Jack closed his eyes and shook his head. No sense dwelling on the past. He'd done enough of that in the eight months and twelve days since she died. Besides, today was a very special day. Their sixtieth wedding anniversary. He pocketed the picture frame and left the apartment.

He took the elevator like always, the three flights of stairs to the lobby too intimidating to consider. But outside his building he didn't have a choice, so he grasped the metal railing with one hand, his cane in the other, and carefully walked down the concrete steps to the sidewalk.

Only half a block to Doumar's. He should be able to make it there in time and still catch the bus. He crossed Granby Street, the main artery leading straight into the heart of downtown Norfolk, so absorbed in his thoughts he didn't see the oncoming car until the driver blared his horn.

"You need to watch where you're going, old man," a male voice reprimanded as the car sped away. Jack ignored him.

Nearly all the details were in place. All he had left to do was say goodbye to Norma and give the envelope to Frank, his neighbor on the second floor.

He stopped. He had forgotten to make sure Frank was home.

Turning around in the middle of the sidewalk, he saw Frank's late-model Ford truck parked at the curb. His gaze traveled upward to a set of windows on the far side of the building. The shades were drawn, which meant Frank was home, asleep. He continued on his way.

He bought a newspaper at the corner drugstore and then slid into his favorite booth by the window at Doumar's. Business was brisk. A young girl dressed in low-cut jeans and a red apron approached his table.

"Having your usual, Mr. Dozier?"

"Not today." Jack looked at her nametag. *Carla.* He never could remember. She was pleasant enough, but he had hoped Betty was working today. "Where's Betty?"

"New grandbaby," she said. "That makes number four. She's in Phoenix with her daughter. She'll be back next week."

Oh, well. He ordered a large blueberry muffin, his favorite, and a pot of gourmet hazelnut coffee, the house specialty. He didn't usually splurge on such items, but today he felt entitled to make exceptions.

Basking in the warmth of the sun's rays streaming through the bay window, he read the headlines and chuckled over the antics of Snoopy and Hagar as the conversations of the other patrons flowed around him. He skipped the business and entertainment sections. Tomorrow's stock predictions and ads for the weekend's movie premieres were of no interest to him.

Finished with his reading and his breakfast, he leaned back and drank his coffee. Outside, a cluster of autumn leaves skittered across the sidewalk and into the street, where a gust of wind carried them off to places unknown. Above the half-naked branches of the towering pin oaks lining the streets, the sky was the color of faded denim with a few wispy brushstrokes of clouds. Jack couldn't remember when a day was any finer.

His knees were a cluster of bee stings by the time he reached the bus depot. He eased his tall, wiry frame onto a bench. A young black girl dressed in white scrubs sat at the opposite end, reading a book. Within minutes, the HRT bus rounded the corner. Jack glanced at his watch. 10:22. Right on time.

The driver, a portly woman with brassy blonde hair beneath her navy-blue driver's cap, greeted him as he boarded the bus. "Haven't seen you in a while."

Jack acknowledged her with a nod. She waited until he had taken his seat and placed his cane across his lap before she pulled away from the curb.

Jack looked out his window. The tinted glass was coated in a thick film of dirt and grime. Caught within the square metal frames, the passing landscape looked like a depressing series of overexposed Polaroid snapshots. After a mile or so the once-familiar sites blurred into places he no longer recognized. Jack turned away.

At his destination, he got off the bus and walked the short distance to Rosewood Memorial Gardens. He paused and looked up at the black wrought-iron arch spanning the entrance. Today would be the last time he would make this trip.

As he wound his way through the vast maze of narrow cobblestone paths, he passed row after row of headstones and grave markers. Some of the stones were more than a hundred years old, as were the massive oaks and maples towering above him, their thick trunks and gnarled branches bent and bleached with age. When he reached Norma's plot, he took the picture from his coat pocket and

4

set it on top of the marble headstone. He sat down on a nearby bench and removed his hat. "Hello, sweetheart."

The grainy black-and-white photo was from 1940, when she had been Norma Comstock, a vibrant twenty-year-old college student who had moved from a small town in Kentucky to Virginia to pursue a teaching degree. Jack was twenty-one.

They met at a dance hall in Norfolk when he was in the Navy. Norma's easy smile and striking features drew him irresistibly. When the band slowed things down with Gershwin's "Summertime," they danced. The minute he circled his arm around her waist and took her hand in his, he knew he never wanted to dance with another woman as long as he lived.

They were married a year later, and on their wedding night Jack had tenderly taken her to their marriage bed. She was his first and only.

Except for that one time, in South Korea.

He considered himself a good husband, despite the indiscretion, and he could honestly say their bond had grown richer with each passing year.

Their two-year stint in Hawaii was a joy, with white sandy beaches and flower-strewn paths and a mesh hammock strung between two palm trees in their backyard. Jack could still recall the sounds of the exotic birds and Norma's sighs of approval as he ran his fingers through the mahogany silk of her hair.

Jack smiled. "Those were good times, weren't they, sweetheart?"

They never had children.

Not because they hadn't tried. But it wasn't meant to be. "I'm so sorry, sweetheart." His voice cracked on the last syllable. A sudden gust of wind rustled the stiff, dead leaves overhead. Behind him, Jack could barely make out the muffled incantations of a priest as he spoke to a group of people standing around a raised casket.

Ignoring the other gathering, he continued his conversation with Norma, making sporadic comments about remembrances they had once shared.

The funeral ceremony drew to an end and mourners trickled past, paying no mind to Jack as he carried on his one-sided conversation with his deceased wife.

He was alone again. He rose and held his hat in his soft, veined hands. "I have to be going now." He fumbled for his next words.

How could he say he wouldn't be seeing her again, because he wouldn't be alive after today? There wasn't an adequate way to explain it.

A heavy sigh escaped him. "I won't be coming back."

Tears filmed his eyes as he brought Norma's photograph to his lips and kissed it. "Happy anniversary, sweetheart. You were the best part of me." He placed the frame on the headstone and walked away.

Back at his apartment building, Jack leaned an ear to the closed door of apartment 212 and listened. No sound of anyone bustling around or the mindless jingle of television commercials. Frank was still asleep.

Being a creature of habit himself, Jack had long since memorized the comings and goings of the building residents. Officer Frank DeMarco, a sergeant with the Norfolk Police Department, worked ten-hour shifts four nights a week. Tuesday night was a regular work night for him, so he would sleep until late afternoon.

By then, it would all be over.

Confident no one inside was awake, he pulled the envelope from his coat pocket. Frank's name was written across the front of it. Inside were several documents. The first was a note telling Frank where to find Jack's body and which funeral home to contact. No relatives or friends needed to be called. The remaining documents spelled out his burial arrangements.

Before Norma's passing, a longtime friend suggested he start making plans for her funeral. At the funeral home, the dour-faced mortician helped select Norma's casket, flowers, and headstone. Ever the shrewd businessman, he then deftly steered the grieving Jack to thoughts of his own "time of passing."

"Wouldn't it be simpler for everyone," he suggested, "if you made those arrangements now?"

A couple of hours and several thousand dollars later, Jack left with his and Norma's burial plots paid for and preparations made for his future demise. He would be buried next to Norma, in military fashion, with a simple oak casket and marble headstone. The only things he wanted inscribed on his marker were the dates of his birth and death and a small American flag.

Lifting the narrow metal flap of Frank's mail slot, Jack hesitated before pushing the envelope through, fully aware he stood on the opposite shore of his own Rubicon. There was no turning back. He shoved the last third of the envelope through the slot.

Inside his apartment, he left the door unlocked and turned off the security alarm. He went to his bedroom and removed his shoes and socks. He felt a pang of hunger as he padded down the hallway in his bare feet. He had purposely eaten a light breakfast for fear he might become ill from a sudden attack of nerves. But surprisingly, he felt nothing as he opened a cabinet drawer in the kitchen and pulled out the rope.

Jack had spent weeks debating the easiest way to pull this off. Pills took too long. So did slitting his wrists or ingesting something poisonous. He finally concluded hanging was the best way to go about it. A gunshot to the head would be quicker, but Jack wasn't a gambler by nature. Bullets carried too many variables. And the carnage left behind was far too messy. Frank was a good friend. He wouldn't do that to him.

So ... hanging it was. No noise. No mess.

At least he hoped not. He had heard stories of how people sometimes lose control of their bowels and bladder during the final stage of asphyxiation. But he figured that particular cleaning chore was far less offensive then scraping bits of his brain off the walls.

He tilted his head back. The cathedral ceiling loomed twenty feet above him, with a pair of skylights, one on each side, set into the slanted plaster. Below the level of the windows, a row of solid oak beams spanned the entire width of the room, roughly ten feet above his head.

In a far corner of the living room, a wrought-iron spiral staircase led to the roof. Only the larger units on the top floor offered this amenity. Before his arthritis had gotten too bad, he and Norma would climb the narrow stairs to the rooftop and tend their herbs and flowers and vegetable garden. Jack hadn't gone up there in months. The last time he did, he was so dismayed by the sight of the empty flowerpots and patch of gray lifeless dirt, he vowed never to return.

An unbidden memory of Norma came to him then, of her kneeling in front of a clay pot brimming with red geraniums, her nimble hands clad in a pair of pink cotton gardening gloves as she lovingly cradled the plants into their new home. He closed his eyes. He could almost smell the lavender and oregano and basil, their fragrant aromas adrift on an early summer breeze. Norma hummed to herself as she worked. Less than a month later, she was diagnosed with cancer.

Jack opened his eyes.

No. No more pain.

Selecting a beam at random, he held onto the noose and tossed the other end of the rope toward the ceiling. On the third try, the rope arced over the beam and tumbled down the other side. He fashioned a simple but sturdy slipknot and pulled the rope taut until the knot rested snugly against the beam.

He gave the rope a tug. Both the beam and rope stood fast. He grasped the noose with both hands and pulled. The muscles of his back and shoulders cried out in protest with the effort, but the beam didn't budge. The rope and beam would hold his weight.

He took a chair from the dining room and placed it beneath the rope. He stood back to survey the angle and height. Then he fished his list and a pen from his shirt pocket and drew a line through the last two entries.

Now he was ready.

A flicker of anxiety made his heart skip a beat. Using the back of the chair for balance, he carefully pulled himself up. His knees erupted in a starburst of pain. He waited for the sting to subside. His bare feet gripped the wooden seat of the chair as he reached for the noose. After a few minor adjustments, he had the loop of rope cinched around his neck.

Jack's heart beat faster now. But he felt no remorse or fear, only a deep sadness that things had turned out this way. He supposed he was somewhat hesitant about what lay ahead for him. He had never been an overly spiritual man. He wasn't sure he believed in a literal Hell. He did believe in some form of Heaven away from this life. Whether or not he was headed there, he couldn't say.

He took a final look out through the living room windows. Norma had loved this view. From this angle however, everything looked different. The skyscrapers didn't seem as tall, nor the blue-green ribbon of the Elizabeth River as wide. Beyond the downtown area, a gunmetal gray destroyer sat in dry dock at the Norfolk shipyard. Most of the vessel's interior was gutted, giving it the appearance of a prize fish ready for market.

Jack turned away. Random, mundane thoughts tumbled around. He thought of his parents and his younger brother, Charles, all long gone. Of a grade-school teacher, Mrs. Boaz, who had encouraged him with his math. Of the first time he walked across the deck of a naval ship at sea and smelled the salty air. Of an old hound he used to have as a child. What was his name? Spanky? No, Sparky. That was it. Why in the world had he given him that name?

He thought of moving vans and the first elementary school Norma had taught at and Christmases and holidays spent with their families and the time Norma's younger sister nearly burned their kitchen down when she came to stay after finals for Thanksgiving one year and insisted on cooking the holiday feast.

Should have seen that one coming, he thought wryly. The poor girl could barely boil water.

Is this all that life comes down to in the end? To be left with only memories having no value except to the person who embodies them? He wondered what Norma had experienced in her last hours, deep within the clutches of her coma. Had her dying mind conjured up comforting images to accompany her through that dark valley? Had she thought of him? Of anything?

A wave of sorrow passed over him. Jack pushed it away.

Enough.

Should he pray? He didn't know what to pray for. Words escaped his throat before he realized he'd said them.

"I'm sorry," he croaked. He wasn't sure to whom or for what he was apologizing. He took a final deep breath and then started to step down into thin air.

The phone ringing startled him so badly he nearly fell. He cursed out loud as he flailed his arms in an effort to regain his balance. Finally, he righted himself on the chair.

The phone rang a second time.

It's okay. His heart raced. *It's okay.*

Jack was determined to do this thing on *his* terms. A phone jangling in his ear as he hung from a rafter had no part in his plans.

He'd wait for the answering machine to pick up and then he'd be done with it. He closed his eyes and concentrated on his breathing.

In and out. In and out.

The bleating of the phone continued, his anxiety mounting with each ring. After the sixth ring, the recorded playback of his own voice resounded throughout the apartment, telling the caller he wasn't available right now and would they please leave a message. A shrill tone sounded. Then a woman's voice came on the line.

"Mr. Dozier? My name is Karen Price-Cochran. I'm an attorney from New York." There was a long pause. "I'm your granddaughter."

2

During her flight from JFK to Norfolk, Karen rehearsed what she wanted to say, going over the imaginary conversation in her mind, discarding lines and editing new ones until she felt confident the scenario she presented would be enough to convince this man she had never met to make a three-hour trek with her to the Outer Banks of North Carolina. So much was riding on the outcome.

After she retrieved her luggage from baggage claim, she found a quiet area next to a bank of pay phones to make her call. Her stomach felt sour. She almost hung up when Jack Dozier's recorded voice came on the line. But she forged on and began her speech.

She chose her words carefully, using the clear, concise tone she routinely adopted in the courtroom when presenting a case—cool, confident, self-assured. But then her resolve suddenly abandoned her, like a herd of gazelles at the discovery of a lion crouched in the grass. She fumbled her way through the rest of the message.

She snapped the cover of her cell phone closed and headed out in search of a rental car agency. *He probably thinks I'm a babbling idiot.* Less than five minutes later, Jack had called her back. She hadn't expected him to return her call so quickly.

He wasted no time. "I'm not your grandfather."

"Let me explain— "

"I'm sorry, miss. I can't help you."

"I need to speak with you," she said. "But I don't think this is something we should discuss over the phone." She fumbled for pen and paper in her purse. "May I come by and talk to you? I promise I won't take long."

11

"I'm sorry," he repeated. "I really can't help you. Now if you'll excuse me, I have an appointment."

She delivered her pitch. "You were stationed in South Korea in the summer of 1952."

There was silence on the other end of the line. "Yes… I was," he finally replied. "But what does that have to do with you?"

"I have proof." The statement wasn't entirely true. But he didn't know that.

"Proof of what?"

"That I'm your granddaughter."

"That's not possible."

"I know you live in the Norfolk area. I'm at the airport now. I can be at your place in fifteen minutes."

"How do you know where I live?"

"I'll explain when I get there."

"I don't see—"

"I know this is unexpected," she said. "Please. Ten minutes is all I'm asking."

There was a long pause, and for a moment Karen thought he had hung up. "Mr. Dozier? Are you there?"

She heard him mumble something then, words she couldn't make out. Then the line went silent again.

"Mr. Dozier?" she repeated. "Are you still there?"

"I don't know why I'm doing this," he replied. "I'm not your grandfather. But maybe I can help you find who you're looking for."

Karen would take whatever opportunity she was given. "Thank you."

"Ten minutes, miss," he barked. "That's it. I have an appointment this afternoon—a very important one."

"I understand. I promise I'll be brief."

Jack gave her directions, and she wrote them down in her daily planner.

After tossing her suitcase and overnight bag into the trunk of her rental car, she followed the signs to the freeway. Watchful for local law enforcement as she drove twenty-five miles per hour over the posted speed limit, she took the exit onto Brambleton Avenue and quickly got lost in the maze of one-way streets and narrow roads of downtown Norfolk.

12

She finally spotted Jack's apartment building on Dundaff Street. She had to circle the block twice before she found a parking space along the curb. She looked at her watch. Cutting it close. She checked her lipstick and hair in the rearview mirror. Then she took a deep breath and slowly blew it out. "I'll do my best, Mom."

As she hurried along the sidewalk, she took in the building and surrounding area. Constructed of stone and red brick, the sprawling three-story apartment complex sat back from the road, with a large atrium and dark green cloth awnings over the windows. The name *Crestwood* was etched in stone above the lobby doors. Mulched flowerbeds and mature trees of ash and crape myrtle were scattered across the grounds.

When she reached the atrium, she searched the directory and pressed the button for Dozier, J. After a brief wait, Jack's throaty voice came over the intercom, and he buzzed her through.

Karen let out another nervous breath as she opened the heavy glass door. "Here we go," she whispered.

Jack paced the kitchen floor as he waited for Karen to arrive. He glanced at the clock on the stove. Only a few minutes after two. He still had time. Frank didn't usually wake up until after three. If he could send this person on her way in a timely manner like they had agreed, he would still be able to complete what he needed to do. He hoped she didn't ask him for a cup of coffee. It would take too much time. His hands felt heavy, warm. He raised his palms and found them slick with sweat.

This is all just a misunderstanding. It's not possible.

He went to the sink and ran cold water over his hands. Why was he even doing this? Maybe the hint of desperation in the young woman's voice had lured him in. But Jack knew there was another reason why he had agreed to meet with her. The real reason.

South Korea. The mention lit a spark deep within Jack's memory, a flicker which grew into a burning ember, then a raging flame. She was right. He *was* there in the summer of '52, at the height of the Korean War.

How had she known?

A series of memories flashed through his mind like slides projected onto a screen, shining an unwelcome light into the hidden turns and passages of his recollection.

A crowded, smoke-filled bar in the seaport town of Inch'ŏn …

The sounds of shouting and raucous laughter …

A sea of empty shot glasses …

Watching through bleary eyes as a young girl approached him …

Jack dried his hands and discarded the paper towel into a wastebasket under the sink. He slammed the cabinet door shut. "It was fifty years ago," he muttered. "It was only one night."

He went into the living room to wait. He stopped midstride at what he saw there. He had forgotten to take down the noose.

Cursing under his breath, he stood on the chair, but he couldn't reach the slipknot. He raked back a flop of silver-gray hair from his forehead. What to do now? Then he remembered the stepladder in the kitchen storage closet and went to get it.

Beads of perspiration broke out along his hairline as he made his slow, careful ascent up the ladder. She would be here any minute. He worked at the knot.

Jack's doorbell rang, startling him. He continued to work at the rope. It loosened. The doorbell rang again.

"Just a minute," he called. There was a muffled reply from the other side of the door. Finally, he freed the knot. He climbed down and stuffed the length of rope into a kitchen drawer. He took a moment to collect himself before he answered the door.

The sight of Karen Price-Cochran took Jack by surprise. He didn't know what he had expected, but it wasn't this. Petite and fine-boned, the young woman standing before him couldn't be more than five feet tall, dressed in a dark tailored suit with minimal jewelry. The effect was further accented by the tight chignon of dark, auburn-tinged hair at the nape of her neck.

She smiled and extended her hand. "Mr. Dozier? I'm Karen."

He shook her hand and invited her inside. As she walked past him into the apartment, he caught her staring at him with a concerned look on her face.

"Are you all right?" she asked.

Jack realized he was still out of breath. "Yes, I'm fine." He took a handkerchief from his pocket and mopped his brow. He glanced at his watch and led the way to the living room. She stopped short when she saw the stepladder in the middle of the floor.

"I um ... I was dusting for spider webs on the beams." He immediately regretted the lie. Anyone could plainly see there was no way he could reach them, even with a higher ladder. He indicated a chair, and Karen took a seat while he settled on the sofa across from her.

"Your home is lovely," she said. "Have you lived here long?"

Jack was irritated by all this small talk. He wished she would say what she had to say and get this over with. He saw the list and pen he had left on the coffee table. He picked them up and slid the items into his pocket. "We've lived here ten years."

She glanced at his ring finger. "Is your wife home?"

Jack followed her gaze to the thin band of gold. "No, she's not." He looked away as he absently stroked his wedding band with his thumb.

"I'm sorry, Mr. Dozier. Did I say something— "

"My wife is dead."

An uneasy silence fell between them. "I'm sorry for your loss."

Jack looked up to find an obligatory mask of concern etched on her face. What an odd dance, the spoken words of condolences between strangers. This woman had never even known Norma existed, and yet here she was apologizing for her death. This whole scenario was ridiculous, and he didn't wish to continue.

He stood up. "I'm sorry, but I'm having second thoughts. I'm sorry you've come all this way, and I know I offered to help you find who you're looking for, but this isn't any of my business and I'd like you to leave."

Jack had expected some kind of rebuttal, but instead she studied his face a moment, as if trying to decide something. Then she nodded once and looked away.

"I can understand that," she replied. "In fact, I probably wouldn't talk to me either if I were you and confronted out of the blue with something like this."

Jack was taken aback by her honesty. She made no move to leave, however, and the moment grew awkward. "I'm sorry, I ... Can I call you a cab?"

She shook her head. "No, I have a car." She started to get up, but then she sat back down and looked at him. "On the phone, you said you'd give me ten minutes. If at the end of ten minutes you still want me to leave, I'll go and never bother you again. I promise."

Jack could see the earnestness in her dark eyes and felt his resolve slipping.

"Please," she added.

He sighed and sat down on the sofa. "I'm afraid you've come a long way for nothing, Ms. Cochran. I'm not your grandfather."

"I have evidence to prove otherwise."

He shook his head. "You don't understand. It boils down to simple logic. I can't possibly be your grandfather because my wife and I never had any children."

Karen fixed her gaze on him. "But you *do* have a child, Mr. Dozier. A daughter. Her name is Helen Price."

She dug through her pocketbook and pulled out a snapshot of herself and another woman standing on a beach. Their arms hooked around one another's waists, they smiled broadly for the camera as the wind whipped Karen's long dark hair into a makeshift halo around her head.

"My mother," she said softly.

Jack pulled his reading glasses from his shirt pocket and studied the picture. His mouth went dry. Helen Price appeared to be several inches taller than Karen, with the same high cheekbones and aquiline nose he saw every morning in his bathroom mirror. Even the smile was the same—a little crooked, with the left side higher than the right—and her hairline at the crest of her forehead came together in a deep widow's peak. Just like his.

This can't be. It can't!

He brought the photograph closer, taking note of the woman's almond-shaped eyes and tint of olive in her flawless complexion.

"My mother is Korean-American," Karen said. "She immigrated to the States with her adoptive parents in 1959."

Jack laid the picture on the coffee table. He opened his mouth to say something, but he stopped short when Karen pulled out a small, rectangular object from her purse.

"I believe this is yours," she said. He made no move to take it from her. She laid the item on top of the photograph.

It was a wallet. Jack's brow furrowed as he picked it up and turned it over in his hands. The faded brown leather was cracked and worn,

16

and he didn't recognize it at first. Then he opened it and looked inside.

There was his social security card, tucked behind a plastic window clouded with age, and a driver's license for the state of California, expiration date 1953. The billfold section was devoid of currency. From another compartment, he pulled out his old military ID. His picture, rank, and military ID number were emblazoned on the front. The renewal date was 1952.

"How—how did you find this?" he stammered.

She started to answer, but he cut her off. "What do you want from me? Are you trying to extort money from me or something? Is that why you're here?"

"I assure you, Mr. Dozier, neither my mother nor anyone else in our family mean to cause you any trouble."

He held out his hands in front of him. "Then why *are* you here?"

Before she could respond, Jack stood up again and crossed over to a row of windows along the back wall. He removed his glasses and stuffed his hands into his pockets. He was silent for a long time.

"She was a—" He shook his head. "I barely even remember what happened that night."

"I understand."

Jack whirled around. "No, you *don't* understand! I had never been unfaithful to my wife. *Never.*" He stopped short, surprised at his sudden outburst. It wasn't like him to share something so personal with a complete stranger.

He ran a hand down the length of his face. A dull headache formed at the base of his skull. "I was only one of what could have been a dozen or more men."

"That's true," Karen replied. "But I have to wonder about one thing. Why was your wallet the only one this woman saved out of the countless others she could have kept as well?"

Jack held up his hands in a feeble show of surrender. "I can't answer that."

He started to turn back to the window when a thought occurred to him. He spun back around. "Is this woman still alive?"

"We have no way of knowing. My mother was left on the doorstep of a South Korean missionary when she was only a few days old. They tried to find who the baby belonged to, but they didn't have any luck." Looking down at her lap, she smoothed a hand over her skirt. "Apparently, this type of thing happened rather frequently during that time."

Jack could barely control his indignation. "I can assure you, if I had known anything about this, I would have done the right thing."

"I believe you," she replied. "I didn't mean to insinuate otherwise."

He came back to the living room and sat down. "You haven't told me how my wallet came to be in your mother's possession."

"When my mother's adoptive father discovered her on his doorstep, your wallet was found sewn into the lining of her diaper."

A sudden image filled Jack's mind, one which smacked of both chance and desperation: a young Korean girl, her belly swollen with her unborn child as she wielded a needle and thread, sewing a wallet into the folds of a rag diaper in the hopes someone would find it and contact the child's father.

If he was the father. No one could argue Helen Price was of mixed heritage. But it didn't mean he was the one responsible. "Your mother's story is very poignant, but it still doesn't prove anything."

"You're right. Only a blood test can prove whether or not you're my mother's biological father. But no one is asking you to do that." She looked away. "There wouldn't be enough time even if we wanted to."

"I don't understand."

She looked back at him. "My mother is dying, Mr. Dozier."

Now it was Jack's turn to offer inept words of condolence. He looked at the photograph. "The two of you appear to be very close."

Karen's eyes filled with tears. "We are. We always have been." She took a tissue from her purse and dabbed at her lashes. She soon regained her composure. "My mother has a few months at most to live. And I'm here now because I have a favor to ask of you."

Jack waited for her next words.

"My mother wants to meet you before she dies. She's in the Outer Banks, in Hatteras. She has a request for you, but I'll leave that to her." Her dark eyes were imploring. "Will you come with me, Mr. Dozier? Please?"

Jack couldn't believe what he was hearing. Today was supposed to be the day he would end it all, not start a whole new chapter in his life. He suppressed an urge to laugh out loud. Perched on the edge of the sofa with his elbows on his knees, he covered his face with his hands. "I can't believe this is happening."

"I'm sure this has been a shock—"

Jack quickly rose from the sofa. The sudden change of position made his head swim. He staggered backward a step as he looked at his watch. It was five minutes before three.

"Is something wrong?"

"I—there's something I need to take care of."

"What's wrong, Mr. Dozier?"

Jack didn't answer. He went to the kitchen and dialed Frank's number. It rang once, twice, three times. After the fourth ring, the answering machine kicked in. He hoped it meant Frank was still asleep. He hung up without leaving a message.

"I'll be right back." He left the door to the apartment open.

Inside the elevator, he realized he had forgotten his cane. The car's descent to the second floor inched along. By the time he reached Frank's door, his knees were throbbing.

He rang the doorbell but no one came. He knocked on the door and called out Frank's name. Finally, he heard heavy footfalls and the sound of the deadbolt turning. Frank's ample face appeared in the open slice of doorway.

Roughly the size of a professional linebacker, with a vocabulary of well-versed expletives and a horseshoe-shaped mustache that pulled the corners of his mouth down in a perpetual scowl, Frank DeMarco cut a menacing figure. Jack knew better. This was the same man who, at the height of Norma's illness, had carried her from the sofa to her bedroom when she no longer had the strength to walk on her own.

"Hey, Jack. Haven't seen you in a while." Beneath his bathrobe, he wore a rumpled pair of boxer shorts and a T-shirt. His eyes were puffy with sleep.

"Sorry I woke you." Jack stole a glance at the tile floor of the foyer. No sign of the envelope.

"It was time for me to get up anyways." His mouth opened wide in a massive yawn. The gesture reminded Jack of a grizzly bear emerging from its den after a long hibernation.

Frank stepped back to let him into the apartment. A corner of the envelope came into view beneath the door. "C'mon in," he offered.

19

"That's okay." Jack bent down to pick up the envelope. "I dropped this through your mail slot by mistake earlier and I came by to get it."

A sudden jolt of white-hot pain shot through his knees, and he nearly fell forward.

"Whoa—take it easy there," Frank cautioned as he grasped Jack's elbow. "I'll get it." He picked up the envelope and saw his name scrawled across the front. His bushy eyebrows shot upward as he laughed. "Is there another Frank living in this building?"

Jack took the envelope from his hand. "Uh … no. I don't think so." He took a step backward into the hallway. "It was a mistake."

Frank eyed him carefully. "Everything okay, Jack?"

"I'm fine. Really." He pasted on a smile. "I'm just a little forgetful these days. Sorry for waking you. Talk to you later." He didn't hear Frank's door close until he was almost to the elevator.

When he got back to his apartment, Karen was standing in the living room with her purse draped over her shoulder.

"I apologize if I interrupted your plans this afternoon."
She handed him a business card with a phone number written on the back of it. "I booked a room in case I couldn't reach you right away. I'm at the Hilton downtown. You can call me day or night."

She left his wallet and the photograph on the coffee table. He showed her to the door. "I'm not the person your mother is looking for."

With one hand on the doorknob, Karen turned to face him. "You don't believe that," she said softly. "And neither do I."

Bright shafts of late afternoon sunlight inched their way across the far wall of Jack's living room as he sat on the sofa, his mind heavy with questions for which he had no answers. What a time for something like this to happen. The days and weeks spent thinking this whole thing out, the meticulous planning—all shot to pieces with a single phone call.

Or was it?

He went to the kitchen and removed the rope from the drawer. He felt the heavy weight of it in his hands. Not all was lost, he reminded himself. He could still go through with this. If he wanted to.

Jack was suddenly aware of a strong burning odor permeating the room. The coffee maker. He had brewed a small pot of coffee after Karen left and had forgotten to turn it off.

He removed the glass pot from the burner. A hardened toffee-brown residue stained the bottom. He filled it with cold water from the tap while he considered his options.

Frank should have left for work by now. He thought about dropping the envelope back through Frank's mail slot, but he dreaded the thought of making the trip to his apartment. His knees were throbbing, and the muscles of his lower back were knotted into tight fists.

Maybe he would call him, leave a message on his answering machine, asking him to come by in the morning after he got off work. Tell him he needed help moving a piece of furniture or something. Frank was good about things like that.

He looked over his shoulder at his apartment door and imagined Frank on the other side. He would ring the doorbell first, then knock. Finally, he would try the doorknob and let himself in. He wouldn't go far before he found what he was supposed to find.

Leaving the coffee pot to soak, Jack picked up the phone. He started to dial Frank's number, then hung up. He might still be home. From his kitchen window, he looked out onto the street. Frank's truck was gone. He dialed his number again, then hung up a second time.

No, not yet. Best to make sure the entire scenario was planned out first. He went to the living room and looked around.

Where to place the envelope? On the sofa? The coffee table? Better yet, maybe he should set it on the floor by the chair, to make sure Frank would see it. He placed the envelope in the chosen spot and stood back to survey the scene. No way would Frank miss it there. Satisfied everything was in order, he made the call to Frank and left his message.

Now the only question was when.

He took the rope from the drawer and laid it on the coffee table next to the photograph and wallet. Very clever of her to leave the items behind. She knew, as he had known, he would inevitably return to them.

21

He sat on the sofa and went through the contents of the wallet once more, allowing the memories from worn bits of paper and faded snapshots to wash over him. How strange to have the item in his possession after all these years. He never thought he'd see it again.

Outside, early dusk spread its soft gray wings over the city as rush hour traffic grew thick in the streets below. Along the sidewalks, streetlights sputtered as they awakened from their slumber to resume their nocturnal duties.

He should be getting on with this. But he made no effort to get up. Karen had seemed so earnest, so sincere. A thread of doubt wove its way through his troubled mind.

What if I'm wrong? What if I do have a daughter and granddaughter?

Karen was expecting to hear from him soon. Common sense told him if he went through with this now, she would come looking for him when her repeated phone calls went unreturned. Someone would tell her what had happened.

She might blame herself; she might conclude that her impromptu visit had pushed him over the edge, unable to deal with the guilt over the stirring revelations brought to light.

Jack tossed the wallet onto the coffee table. Ridiculous. Why should he care? He didn't even know this person.

He stared at the noose.

So get on with it already and sling the blasted thing over the beam!

Hours later, after the interior of his apartment had grown dark and a heavy cloak of stars were spread out across the night sky, Jack found his answer. But it wasn't the one he was looking for.

In the end, the what ifs finally won out.

He picked up the phone and called Karen, awakening her from a sound sleep, and told her he would go with her to North Carolina to meet Helen Price.

3

Karen arrived at Jack's apartment early the next morning and helped him carry his few items of luggage downstairs. "There's something I forgot to ask you," she said, as they rode the elevator to the lobby. "I never mentioned a time frame. We were hoping you could stay with us for at least a week."

Jack's initial reaction was to say no. He thought he'd be gone for a night or two at the most. But an entire week?

Then he reconsidered. He had no obligations to family or friends, no pets requiring his attention, no urgent business to take care of. Unless a standing appointment to commit suicide was an item of urgency. The rope would still be there when he got back.

"I'll play it by ear." He'd give himself an out if he so chose. "But I'll need to go back and get a few more things if I decide to stay that long."

When he returned, Karen was making room for his luggage in the trunk of her rental car. "We can use my car if you want," he suggested. "It's parked around back."

"I appreciate the offer." She took his overnight bag from him. "But I already leased this one for a month, so I might as well get my money's worth out of it."

As they pulled out into traffic, Jack spied Norma's silver Toyota Camry, parked in its designated spot behind the apartment complex. After she passed away, he had sold his car and kept hers. No sense in having two vehicles. Jack seldom drove anymore. He should probably sell it. But he couldn't bring himself to do it.

As they crossed over the Berkley Bridge and headed toward Chesapeake, the sun was starting its ascent into the eastern sky. Along the horizon to the right, the Elizabeth River was a flat gray thread the color of old nickels.

Despite the promise of warmer days to come, it was still cold at that hour of the morning, and they both had dressed accordingly. Jack had on corduroy trousers and a heavy jacket, and Karen wore jeans and a thick cable sweater.

Jack stole a glance in her direction as the car inched along through the morning commuter traffic. She looked so different today, with her casual attire and long dark hair spilling around her shoulders. Her demeanor was more at ease as well, not as stiff and formal as the day before, almost as if once she shed her tailored suits and sensible pumps, a different persona emerged.

Alone together, they found themselves as awkward as two strangers forced to share a taxi. The conversation lulled, and Karen turned on the radio, filling the silence. "Do you have a favorite station?"

"Not really." His musical tastes ran toward jazz and old swing tunes. Few radio stations catered to those genres anymore. Karen chose a local adult contemporary station, something palatable and easy to digest. She turned the volume down low, and the Backstreet Boys proclaimed they wanted it that way and Celine Dion crooned her heart would go on.

An hour later, they left Virginia behind and crossed over into North Carolina. As they neared Moyock, Karen's stomach rumbled. "Do you want to stop and get something to eat?"

He shrugged. "I'm not really hungry. But if you want to, that's fine."

A few miles further, they found a diner. Even in the off-season for tourists, the parking lot was full. Karen peered over the steering wheel at the large plate glass windows fronting the diner. "Does this look like a good place to you?"

Jack pointed to the row of vehicles parked beside them. They all bore Carolina license plates with the sky-blue silhouette of an airplane and the state motto, First in Flight. "Always trust the locals."

Inside, the décor was predominantly chrome and vinyl, with a strong emphasis on the latter. The place reminded Jack of similar establishments from the '50s. Antique aluminum signs, rusted and spotted with age, hung along the walls, displaying ads for Redman and Marlboro. Tucked in amongst these were black-and-white photographs of ponytailed girls in poodle skirts and young men with greased hair and James Dean sneers.

On the back wall next to the cash register, a line of red upholstered stools stood in front of a long Formica countertop. A tangle of forearms and elbows jostled for position as a cluster of fishermen sat in tight formation, talking amongst themselves as they drank coffee and mopped up puddles of egg yolk with their toast. Behind the counter, a pair of short order cooks in white aprons flipped hash browns and poured pancake batter onto a sizzling hot griddle.

After a short wait, Jack and Karen were seated in a front booth facing the parking lot. The menu offerings were sparse, listed on one side of a laminated placemat. No refills, except for coffee and tea. No doggie bags. No substitutes. The special for the day was a slice of homemade apple pie for $1.99, served with lunch only.

When their waitress arrived, she pulled her order pad from the pocket of her bright pink uniform dress and flipped to a clean page. "What can I get for you folks today?"

"What's good here?" Karen asked.

The woman arched a penciled-in eyebrow. "Everything's good here."

She chose blueberry pancakes. Jack surprised himself by not only ordering but also completing a full breakfast of poached eggs, bacon, toast, and a side order of home fries.

Well into his third cup of coffee, he asked Karen if she would like a refill on hers. She declined. A faint ringing sound came from her purse, and she pulled out her cell phone. When she glanced at the display screen she stood up. "I'll be right back."

Several minutes later, she returned to her seat. The waitress had already taken Jack's plate. Karen looked at the cold, soggy remains of her breakfast. She pushed her plate away. "That was my dad on the phone. He asked if we could delay coming out to the beach house this morning."

Jack took another sip of his coffee. "Is everything okay?"

"Mom got sick during the night. Probably a reaction to one of her new medicines. She didn't sleep well. She has her good days and bad days. Apparently, yesterday wasn't one of her good ones."

Jack wasn't sure how to broach his next question. "What exactly is your mother dying of?"

"She has lymphoma," she replied, without hesitation. "She's reversed back from the remission stage to the acute stage."

Jack wasn't sure what that meant.

"It's a relapse," she explained. "From three years ago when she was first diagnosed. Her doctors caught it early and they were able to treat it with chemotherapy and a bone marrow transplant." She brushed away crumbs from the checkered oilcloth. "They were hopeful after she passed the two-year mark it wouldn't come back. But it did."

Her face fell, and Jack could see she was trying hard not to cry. He sat back in his seat and stirred his coffee, feeling oddly out of place. In all of his years, he'd never quite learned how to react to a woman's tears.

Karen composed herself. "Now they say it's too far along, even with the new advances that have been made like other drugs and stem cell transplants." She stared out the window at the blur of passing traffic on the highway. "She's forty-nine years old."

Looking at her face in profile, Jack was once again struck by the realization this young woman might be his granddaughter.

Or not.

A jumble of emotions tumbled through his mind—doubt, confusion, regret. He lacked the energy or inclination to address any of them.

Karen cleared her throat and held out her coffee cup. "I think I've changed my mind about that refill, Mr. Dozier."

"Please. Call me Jack. 'Mr. Dozier' makes me feel old."

She smiled. "All right. Jack it is."

Silence fell between them again. From a jukebox in a far corner, the strains of an old Garth Brooks song rose above the din of clanging silverware and rattling plates.

"It's good they found the cancer as soon as they did." The words sounded trite and empty, but he felt he should say something.

"Actually, my mom practically diagnosed it herself. She's a physician. Family practice. She's a good doctor. And I'm not just saying that because she's my mother. She started out in lower Manhattan. Then about five years ago, my mom and dad decided they were tired of the hustle and bustle of the city, so she moved her

26

practice to upstate New York. She thought she'd be starting all over again from scratch, but a lot of her patients kept her as their doctor, even though it's over an hour's drive from the city."

Jack was impressed. "That's rare." He recalled the seemingly endless list of doctors Norma was farmed out to during her illness. "To find a physician you trust and feel comfortable with. It's not an easy thing these days."

Karen picked idly at the blueberries on her plate. "About three years ago, she started having really bad headaches and feeling tired all the time. She thought it was stress. She was putting in a lot of hours at work and not taking care of herself. She hired a nurse practitioner to help with the workload and tried some herbal remedies for the headaches and fatigue, but nothing seemed to help. She called an associate of hers and he did some blood work. That's when this whole nightmare started.

"She was officially diagnosed by an oncologist in New York. He sent her to Johns Hopkins in Baltimore. Then Duke. Then back to Hopkins again. She had two bone marrow transplants. The first one took, the second one didn't. They tried a few more rounds of chemo, but all they did was make her hair fall out."

"You finished with that, hon?" The waitress indicated Karen's plate.

"Yes. You can take it."

She scribbled on her pad. "Anything else I can get for you folks today?" They both declined. She left the tab on the table.

Karen briefly met Jack's gaze, then looked away. He watched as she rearranged the salt and pepper shakers and napkin dispenser along the edge of the table. "There's something I need to tell you about my father."

Jack set his coffee cup down. "Okay."

"My dad isn't exactly thrilled about you coming."

He waited for her to continue.

"My father means well. But he's having a hard time accepting the fact that Mom is dying. He's very protective of her right now. He doesn't want to see her get hurt."

"You mean, as in bringing me all the way down there and then finding out I'm not who she thinks I am?"

She nodded. "Something like that, yes."

"Well, I can certainly understand where he's coming from. Like I told you yesterday, I'm not at all convinced there's any real proof concerning my part in this."

"Then why are you here?" she asked quietly.

Jack studied the contents of his coffee cup. He had no idea how to answer the question. He decided to be honest with her. "I'm not entirely sure." They both dropped the subject.

Minutes later, they gathered their things to leave. "Do we need to turn around and go back?" Jack asked.

Karen shook her head. "We're still about two hours away from Hatteras. We'll take the scenic route. Mom should be ready for us by then." She reached across the table for the bill. "I've got this."

"No, no," he insisted. "I'll pay my half."

"Then I'll get the tip."

Jack grabbed his cane and pulled his jacket on. He looked down at the five-dollar bill and two ones Karen had tucked beneath the sugar dispenser. The tip was more than his entire meal had cost. He shook his head. "If you think she was worth that much, then be my guest."

A smile pulled at the corner of her mouth. She shrugged. "I guess I'm still in a New York state of mind."

Back inside the car, Jack said, "I have a question before we go any further. Your father—what kind of reaction should I expect from him?"

"What do you mean?"

"When you say he isn't exactly thrilled with my coming, I take it I shouldn't expect a hug and a big sloppy kiss."

Karen's lyrical laughter filled the small space. The sound was contagious. Jack found himself smiling back. "I'm sorry," she said. "It's just—well, that mental picture is so *not* my dad."

Her smile faded. "My father is not a cruel man. He loves my mom and our family very much. He doesn't know how to act in situations where he's not in control. And right now, I think he's angry and frustrated and grieving all at the same time because he knows there's nothing he can do to help her." She turned to face him. "Does that make any sense?"

Jack looked away.

More than you know, he thought.

More than you know.

4

Helen Price walked along a deserted stretch of rocky beach. It wasn't a place she recognized. Far away, she saw the lone figure of a man standing on the shore. His back was to her. She instantly recognized the downward slope of his broad shoulders and thick, stocky frame.

Daddy? Daddy, is that you?

She started toward him. Above her, purple-black clouds boiled. But there was no rain or thunder. The sand felt coarse and firm beneath her bare feet.

Helen was confused. She didn't seem to be making any headway. Digging her toes deeper into the sand, she lengthened her stride. The muscles in her calves began to burn. But still the man remained the same distance away from her.

She ran. The sky churned as a gust of wind whipped her hair and pulled the skirt of her white dress out behind her like a handkerchief. Her heart galloped in her chest. Finally, she caught up to him. He still had his back to her.

She stopped short, her breath coming in ragged gasps. She reached out her hand to him, but then she drew back. The broad shoulders were now slumped and narrow, the sturdy frame frail and gaunt. "Please," she begged. "Show me who you are."

Slowly, he turned around. Helen began to weep. The man had no face.

She awoke to the sound of ocean waves crashing onto the shore. Snuggled beneath the thick down comforter, her dream drifted upward into her conscious mind like tendrils of smoke curling from a chimney.

This was the third time she'd had the dream. Only the endings were different. The first time was right before she and Kenneth left New York for the beach house. In that dream, it was her adoptive father's face she saw, exactly as she remembered him, with his straw-blonde hair and smiling blue eyes. And in the dream, he lifted her in his arms and slowly spun her around in a circle in the sand.

In the second one, the man she saw was again her adoptive father, but his face was lined with age and sorrow, and his eyes, gray and dim like ashes doused by water, registered only confusion.

She didn't need a crystal ball to figure out what the third version meant.

Helen believed in the power of dreams. Ever since she was a teenager, she had kept a dream diary. Whenever she awoke from a particularly vivid one, she would grab pen and paper and scribble down everything she could recall while the images were still fresh in her mind. Later, she would come back to her notes and try to decipher the subconscious message being telegraphed to her while she slept. The process was of enormous help to her when her waking hours were troubled by problems and obstacles she didn't have answers for.

She turned over and looked at the alarm clock on the wicker table beside the bed. The time said midmorning, but she felt as though she had fallen asleep only minutes ago. Behind the drawn shades, bright sunshine pressed against the windows. Downstairs in the kitchen, she could hear Kenneth on the phone, no doubt talking to Dr. Laura Kirkson, her oncologist back in New York, giving her a full report on the bad night she'd had.

How he fussed over her these days. Nadine, their housekeeper, once told her Kenneth made the proverbial mother hen look like an unfit parent. Keeping an almost constant vigil over her, he duly noted the slightest change in her condition, writing down his observations in his careful hand. He would then report his findings to Dr. Kirkson.

Thank goodness Laura was the patient type. Helen smiled at her own pun. Not once had Laura complained about Kenneth's numerous phone calls over the past several weeks. She would listen to what he had to say and then explain to him in layman's terms what was happening as the disease progressed. Which, of course, Helen could have done just as easily. But somehow, her own clout as a physician didn't seem to hold much weight with her husband these days.

Her decision to forgo any further chemotherapy or treatment had not gone over well. They had argued in the car on their way home from the doctor's office.

"Even Laura agreed it would buy you more time," Kenneth said.

"She said no such thing," Helen corrected him. "She said the chemo *might* slow it down. There's a big difference."

"But there's still a chance the treatments could work."

Helen was adamant. "I'm not willing to take that chance."

"But … *why?*"

They stopped at a red light. She watched the color rise in her husband's cheeks as he stared straight ahead. His sure, steady hands gripped the steering wheel so tight his knuckles turned white.

She reached out and touched his cheek. "Kenneth," she said softly. "We both know this is the beginning of the end for me. I want quality of life now, not quantity. Can you understand that?"

He said nothing in return, only squeezed her hand once before letting go when the light turned green.

The subject wasn't brought up again.

Turning over onto her back, Helen stretched like a cat beneath the covers. Her joints ached a little and her stomach was still queasy, but she considered such discomforts to be minor. Thankfully, she had endured little pain so far.

She closed her eyes and listened to the lulling, rhythmic sounds of surf and wind. Ever since she and Kenneth had settled into the beach house two weeks ago, she felt a quickening in her spirit, something akin to rebirth. The minute she went out onto the back deck and caught sight of the foamy white breakers pounding the sand, she knew she had made the right decision to come here. She liked to tell people she felt closer to God whenever she looked out at the vast open sea because it put her in her place, reminding her where she fit into the scheme of things. To see and hear the ocean's power in its crashing waves, to sense the ageless rhythm in its sure tides, to smell the briny abundance of life within its depths—for Helen, to stand on a shoreline was both an exhilarating and humbling experience.

She wondered if Jack loved the ocean. There were so many questions she wanted to ask him.

When Karen had called to tell her she was bringing Jack with her to Hatteras, Helen had cried tears of joy. She had long ago committed to memory the lines and contours of his features from the photographs in his wallet. She tried to imagine what he looked like now. Was his smile still as bright? Were his eyes still as blue?

She had often wondered about the pretty, dark-haired woman in the snapshots. Helen assumed she was his wife. Was she still alive? Did they have children? Grandchildren?

But most of all, she wanted to know if Jack was happy.

The lure of slumber beckoned her, and her eyelids grew heavy. Maybe she would sleep a little while longer. Above her, the white blades of the ceiling fan circled lazily. Around and around they went in the same endless circuit.

Round and round and round …

It reminded her of the request she had for Jack. She wondered what his answer would be.

She drifted off to sleep. And in her dreams, a lyrical tune floated in the air around her as she stood in the midst of a revolving ring of pretty painted horses.

5

The first time Karen saw her mother without her hair was two months after her last chemo treatment. She was admitted to the hospital for dehydration and pneumonia. Karen had been out of town for almost a month working on a case. Her mother was sound asleep when she walked into the hospital room. She stopped short when she saw her nearly bald head nestled there on her pillow, like a newly-hatched baby bird, with its network of delicate blue veins and wispy tufts of hair. Karen had promptly fled the room.

She was adept at hiding her nerves, a trick she had learned early in her career whenever she presented a case in court. Most of the time, it worked. But sometimes, like today, when she found herself venturing into uncharted territory, the outward evidences of her inner tension were harder to keep at bay.

Karen drove Jack along a four-lane ribbon of highway in a rural area of Dare County, right outside Currituck. The passing landscape was mostly open fields and thick patches of woods, with an occasional farmhouse or antique shop set back from the road. Every few miles or so, the monotony was broken by large billboards, the gamut of ads running from Nags Head hammocks to upscale beach resorts. Near a distant tree line lay an abandoned cotton field. The uneven rows of spindly plants were still in full bloom from the previous summer, a sea of white puffs spilling forth from the dried brown pods onto the untilled ground. High above the fringed tops of the evergreens, a pair of white-tailed hawks hovered.

"Have you been to the Outer Banks before?" Karen asked.

"Many times," Jack replied. "But it's been many years since I last visited there."

"We love the Outer Banks. When we were little, we used to rent a cottage out on Silver Lake on Ocracoke Island. We vacationed there almost every summer."

"Do you have any brothers or sisters?"

"One brother, Scott. He's a sophomore at Iowa State. They're letting him take his exams early before the Thanksgiving break. He'll arrive later this week."

"Iowa State," Jack mused. "That's a rather unusual choice."

"He's there on a wrestling scholarship."

"And they're known for their wrestling program there?"

"One of the best in the country. How about you?" she asked. "Do you have any siblings?"

"I did. A younger brother, Charles. But he died of a heart attack several years ago."

"Where did you grow up?"

"In a backwoods area of Indiana." He tapped a finger on the window glass. "Looked a lot like this, actually. But I haven't been back in ages. Not since our mother passed away."

"What brought you to Virginia?"

"The Navy. Portsmouth was my first duty station. But Norma and I moved all over. We were stationed in Hawaii, Maine, California. When they transferred me back to Norfolk, we decided to stay."

"Hawaii sure sounds nice," she said.

"Yes," he agreed. "It was."

As they neared Kitty Hawk, the rural countryside transformed into an area of dense population, with small clapboard houses pressed close to the road and rows of mobile homes lined up along the highway like cracker boxes on a pantry shelf. A mile or so later, urban sprawl abruptly gave way to vast expanses of beach and sky. To their left, framed between feathery outcroppings of sea grass, were fleeting glimpses of sand and blue-green surf. On their right, a procession of massive sand dunes stood at attention for as far as the eye could see.

Karen rolled down her window and allowed the brisk scent of the ocean to flood the interior of the car. She inhaled deeply, holding the salt-tinged air inside her lungs until they burned. How she loved that smell. It reminded her of so many good memories from her childhood.

The ring of her cell phone dragged her back to the present. She cringed when she saw Kelli's name on the screen.

She answered the phone. "Hello?"

Kelli's voice was frantic. And loud. Karen had to hold the receiver away from her ear. She was sure Jack could hear the woman's incoherent ramblings from where he sat.

"Kelli, calm down. I can't understand a word you're saying."

After listening for a moment, Karen's posture stiffened, and she leaned forward in her seat. "You did *what*?" she exclaimed. "How could you forget to do this?"

She ignored the long-winded explanation. She placed the phone on her lap and counted to ten while Kelli's shrill voice rambled on into thin air. Picking up the phone again, she said evenly, "I'm going to hang up now," and cut her off in midsentence.

She dialed Paul's private office number. It was busy. She then tried his secretary.

"Uh … You're going a little fast," Jack cautioned.

Startled, Karen looked at the dash. The speedometer was pushing seventy-five. She mumbled an apology as she eased her foot off the gas pedal.

"Is everything okay?"

"Nothing I can't handle," she assured him.

Paul's secretary came on the line. "This is Karen. It's urgent."

She put her through immediately.

"I just received a call from Kelli," she told Paul. "She missed the deadline to respond to opposing counsel's request for admissions in the Robinson case."

Her boss made a sound like someone had punched him in the stomach. "You're joking, right?"

"Would I joke about something like this?" There was a long moment of silence, followed by a familiar creaking sound. Karen pictured him leaning back in his leather office chair to stare at the ceiling, something he often did whenever he was at a loss for words.

"Paul, listen to me," she said. "I don't care what connections this woman has or who she's sleeping with." She had heard rumors, but she chose not to elaborate. "That woman is the most incompetent intern I've ever seen. She couldn't find her way out of a wet paper sack."

"Now, Karen— "

"No, Paul," she interrupted. "I've dealt with this long enough. She made a mess of things over in corporate, so they dumped her on us. She's not dependable, her research is lousy, and half the time you can't even read her briefs. All everyone does is make excuses for her mistakes. *Serious* mistakes, I might add, that no other intern would ever be allowed to get away with. I'd like to know why."

There was more creaking on the line, followed by a shuffling of papers and a heavy sigh. "She's Councilman Davis' niece."

Karen felt the blood rush to her ears. "I see." She counted to ten again. Everything made sense now. She felt embarrassed, angry, humiliated. She thought about asking Paul when exactly he had planned on bringing her into the loop, but now wasn't the time or place. "We'll discuss this later, but for right now, I'm dumping this ball of wax back in your lap. It's yours to fix."

She ended the call and tossed the phone onto the dashboard. The car picked up speed once more. Jack looked from her to the road and then back again.

"What an idiot," she muttered, as she worried a hangnail on her index finger with her teeth. "Of all the stupid, brainless—"

She slowly inhaled and counted to ten again. She hated the Robinson case, a bitter child custody battle involving a prominent local politician that was promising to be one of the biggest headaches the firm had ever taken on. When she had requested an indefinite leave of absence to be with her mom, Paul had called her into his office.

"I really need you on this one," he said.

Karen was dumbfounded. "Paul, my mother is dying!"

"I'm not saying you can't take temporary leave." He loosened his tie and ran a hand through his unruly gray hair. "I'm just asking you to remain as lead counsel on this one case. It'll be months before this goes to court. Ron and Carolyn can run interference for you here at the office. Just stay in contact to keep up with what's going on, okay?"

Karen reluctantly agreed. Bad decision.

She pulled over to the side of the road and put the car in park. She leaned her head back against the headrest and closed her eyes. "I can't deal with all of this. Work is driving me crazy, my mother is dying, and now this thing with you …" She turned toward the window. The only sound was the whoosh of cars as they sped past on the highway.

Jack stared toward the outskirts of Kitty Hawk, just visible beyond the line of sand dunes. "I didn't ask to be brought into this," he said quietly.

Karen's shoulders fell. Digging through her purse for a Kleenex, she berated herself for the thoughtless remark. "You're right. I apologize." She turned the car back onto the main road. "Help me find a car wash."

"A car wash?" His eyes scanned the spotless interior of the rental car. "Well, I'm sure we can find a gas station—"

"No," she interrupted. "I want the kind where you do it yourself."

They had gone only a few miles into Kitty Hawk when they found what she was looking for. Marching over to a vending machine mounted against the far wall, she fished for cash in her jeans pocket and deposited the bills to activate the water system. Then she grabbed a spray nozzle with an attached brush and walked back to the car.

"You might want to roll that up." She indicated Jack's open car window. He had no sooner closed it when she blasted the glass with a jet of water.

Over the next thirty minutes, Karen scrubbed the rental car from bumper to bumper, including the tires and rims. By the time she got to the final rinse, her cheeks were flushed warm from her efforts. She then pulled up to the vacuum station and deposited more coins.

"You want some help?" Jack offered.

"No thanks, I'm good." She took off her jacket and tossed it into the back seat. Then she rolled up the sleeves of her sweater and vacuumed the car. She didn't stop until the allotted time had run out.

"There," she said, as the whine of the vacuum slowly died down. "I feel better now." Sliding back in behind the wheel, she noticed Jack eyeing her curiously.

"Would you mind explaining to me what that was about?" he asked. "The car wasn't dirty."

"I know. I just needed to blow off some steam."

Jack smiled. "That's what you do to blow off steam?"

She shrugged. "People deal with stress in different ways. I tried yoga once. It wasn't for me. And exercise bores me. So... I clean."

"Well," he said, "I suppose it's healthier than drinking or gambling. Plus, you get a clean car in the bargain."

"That's nothing," she quipped. "You should see my shower and toilet bowls the night before a big trial."

Jack noticed that the exertion of car-washing did seem to calm Karen down. They didn't stop again until they came to the tourist-friendly regions of Kill Devil Hills and Nags Head. At a Forbes Candy shop, Karen bought a bag of saltwater taffy. "For my husband, Michael," she said. "He loves this stuff."

Like the diner in Moyock, the parking lots of the strip malls and shopping outlets were filled to capacity. Only the first week of November, and the holiday rush was already in full swing.

Right outside Nags Head, a lone brick beacon stood atop a grassy knoll, commemorating the site where the Wright brothers first took to the skies in their flying machine. Behind the structure, hang gliders hovered in the brisk air above the dunes like brightly colored birds. A few miles later, they left the trappings of commercialism behind as they veered onto Highway 12 and headed toward Hatteras.

Jack felt the change immediately. Here was where the true heart of the Outer Banks began, with the Atlantic spread out like a blanket of cobalt on one side and endless stretches of marsh and wetlands on the other, ablaze in dappled colors of burnished copper and green.

He pointed out Bodie Island Lighthouse, situated on a finger-width of land jutting out into the marsh. "I took Norma there years ago, before it was closed to the public."

"What was it like inside?"

"Cold," he replied. "And cramped. Especially near the top."

Karen took another glance at it before directing her attention back to the road. "When I was a little girl, I used to imagine what it would be like to live in a lighthouse. I told my parents I was going to buy one someday. My bed would be on a platform at the top, so I could sleep next to the big light." She smiled. "Sounds kind of silly, doesn't it?"

"Not at all." Jack told her a story about a long-ago summer when the task of building the ultimate tree house had all but occupied his eleven-year-old mind. He had imagined the structure as a mighty fortress, an impenetrable stronghold against the make-believe villains he and his friends waged battle along the muddy shores of Tanner's Creek.

"It was lopsided and drafty," he told her. "And the roof leaked like a sieve when it rained." But it was theirs.

A month later, a fierce summer storm swelled Tanner's Creek to nearly twice its size, and when Jack and his buddies went to check on the tree house afterward, not a single board was left standing. Only the ladder rungs nailed to the trunk remained.

"It's a near miracle the thing didn't fall apart while we were in it," Jack mused, "but kids need to have dreams."

By the time they reached the mile-long bridge spanning the Oregon Inlet, the late morning sun had warmed the interior of the car, and Jack shed his heavy jacket. Along the sandbars, fishermen baited their hooks with live bait and cast their lines. Near the shoreline, a man stood in the shallow water in a pair of black rubber waders. With a flick of his wrist, he sent his shrimp net flying through the air, where it bloomed into a perfect circle before alighting upon the surface of the water. Alongside, his companion pulled a crab pot from the murky water.

The bridge was long and shaped like a camel's hump to accommodate the numerous tall ships and boats that passed beneath it. At the top of the incline, seagulls hung motionless in the brisk air, unable to make headway against the current, like puppets dangling on strings, with the master puppeteer hidden in the clouds.

Jack shifted uncomfortably in his seat. His knees and lower back were stiff from the long ride, and he needed to relieve his bladder. At Pea Island, Karen pulled into the visitor center and Jack got out to stretch his legs and use the restroom. Behind the main building, a large estuary was designated as a natural wildlife refuge, with nature trails and observation decks extending several hundred yards out into the heart of the marsh.

Karen bought drinks from a vending machine and handed Jack a can of ginger ale. "You want to take a walk? We have time."

Jack grabbed his cane from the car, and they started down the shorter of the two nature trails. The wild laurel and scrub brush were cut back severely along the asphalt path, but nature continued going about her business, despite man's interference. Over the years, the sturdy plants had formed a thick canopy, creating a shady tunnel lush with green foliage and the trill of songbirds.

Jack recognized the *teakettle teakettle teakettle* call of a Carolina wren. Looking around for the source, he found the small bird perched among the branches of a juniper. Nearby, a black-capped chickadee and two nuthatches warbled softly, while a common grackle belted out his rusty pump handle song. He pointed them out to Karen. "My Norma loved her birds."

At a small clearing, they took a side path leading to the mouth of the estuary. Cattails and cord grass were in abundance, as well as flocks of tundra swans and snow geese. Jack and Karen sat down on a park bench.

"You would think they would have flown south for the winter by now," Karen said, as the birds paddled in lazy circles in front of them at the water's edge in search of bread crumbs.

Jack shook his head. "This is south for tundras and snow geese. Come spring, they'll fly north toward the Great Lakes and Canada to nest."

Karen dropped some coins into a feeding dispenser and threw a handful of brown-green pellets into the water. The swans and geese wasted no time gobbling them up. When the pellets were gone, they craned their necks toward Karen and paddled closer, eager for more treats.

"Sorry, guys." She brushed off her hands. "That's it." The birds quickly lost interest and paddled away.

Karen came back to the park bench. "You sure know a lot about birds."

"My Norma was the expert. Anything I know I learned from her."

"How long ago did your wife pass away?"

Jack watched as a fiddler crab emerged from its muddy cavern along the bank. It scurried back inside when it noticed the presence of a blue heron wading in the water. "A little over eight months ago. She had ovarian cancer." He looked away, grief carving into his features.

"What did you love most about her?"

Jack was taken aback. After Norma's death, with the phone calls and the covered-dish suppers and the visits from well-meaning friends and acquaintances, no one had ever asked him that. "Well, I would say I loved her big heart the most. She was the most generous person I've ever known."

"She had a kind face," Karen said.

Jack didn't understand the comment at first. Then he remembered the snapshots from his old wallet. He pulled out a more current photo, taken a couple of years before Norma had died. Even in her late seventies, she was still a striking woman. "Wasn't she beautiful?"

Karen held the picture in her hand. "Yes. Yes, she was." She handed the picture back to him.

"My Norma loved all living things." He tucked the photograph away. "Plants, flowers, animals. She couldn't pass by a dog or cat without stopping to pet it. She was always taking in strays. She'd find homes for them. And she loved children with all her heart."

"But you didn't have any of your own."

"No, we didn't." He turned the conversation elsewhere. "Do you and your husband have any children?"

"Not yet. But we both want a family. Maybe in a few years." She smiled. "I have a little cousin, Brooklyn, who's six. She's quite full of herself. You'll meet her at the house. She and my uncle David arrived from New York yesterday."

"Is he your mother's brother or your father's?"

"My mom's. My dad is an only child. My mom also has an adopted sister, Lizzie, who's flying in later this week."

"Sounds like you're going to have a full house." He picked up a smooth black stone from the muddy bank and threw it sideways. It skipped three times across the flat surface of the water. "What has everyone been told about me?"

"My dad and David and Lizzie know the full story. And my grandmother. I think my husband has a pretty good idea what's going on. My mother told Nadine, our housekeeper, that you're an old friend. I don't think she's found the right opportunity yet to talk to my brother Scott."

"I'm curious about something." He hesitated. "I think you know where I stand concerning this whole thing. I think I've been honest with you about this."

"Yes, you have," she agreed.

"And you've made it clear where your father stands. But I'm not sure how you feel about it."

Karen tilted her head back as a flock of Canada geese flew toward the distant horizon in a perfect V formation. Across the still, tea-colored water of the estuary, a white egret called out to its mate.

"There's a certain curiosity, of course," she replied. "I think it's only natural. A part of me wants to get to know you and form some kind of relationship with you. But at the same time, if you were to ask me if I would have ever sought you out on my own, I would probably say no."

Jack nodded. "Fair enough."

"I don't mean to sound harsh." She touched his sleeve. "I'm a bit removed from this. The stakes aren't nearly as high for me as they are for my mom."

As they retraced their steps along the path to the parking lot, Jack pointed out the different varieties of birds flitting and chirping among the foliage, pleased to pass along something he and Norma had once shared.

By early afternoon, after passing through the sleepy residential section of Avon, the scenery turned to ocean and marsh once again. Around a bend, the Cape Hatteras Lighthouse came into view, its black and white candy-stripe bands standing out in sharp contrast against the fair blue sky.

Karen frowned. "I don't remember it being here."

"It probably wasn't," he replied. "They moved it a few years ago."

"Moved it? Why?"

"Beach erosion." He craned his head around to look behind him. "Its original location used to be back there, closer to the water. But they were afraid it would eventually topple into the ocean. So, they moved it."

"I remember now. I read about it in the paper. I imagine it was quite a task." Karen slowed to admire the century-old beacon. "It was worth it though, don't you think? To preserve a piece of history like that?"

"Not enough people care about preserving the past." He watched the lighthouse pass from view. "Especially young people." He looked over at her. "No offense."

"None taken."

"My father used to say you can't know where you're going in life if you don't know where you came from."

Karen considered the statement. "Maybe that's why my mother wanted you to come here. So that she can fill in the blanks concerning her own history."

Outside of Hatteras, sand and surf gave way to civilization once again, with gated communities skirted by golf courses and man-made lakes. Evidence of new construction was everywhere, with pricey condominiums and homes springing up between the dunes.

Karen veered onto a narrow side road that ran parallel to the shoreline. About a mile inland, they came to a wrought-iron gate. Beyond it were a dozen or so homes situated on spacious lots, with marsh and ocean views on every side. Karen took out a keycard from her purse and waved it past a sensor to open the gate. At the last residence, she pulled into the driveway.

The beach house was three stories tall with a crow's nest deck at the top and cozy dormers all around. Dressed in cedar shingles turned silver-gray from the salty air, the front of the house sported a massive peak in the center and a deep wraparound porch with white pickets.

"Your family owns this place?"

"Heavens, no." Karen reached for her coat and purse in the back seat. "It belongs to one of the corporate partners at my dad's bank. They only use it during the summer."

A man carrying a hanging basket of dark purple pansies stepped out onto the front porch. As he reached to place the basket on a hook, he looked toward the rental car parked in the driveway.

"That's my dad." Karen waved at him from inside the car, but he didn't return the greeting. His gaze settled briefly on Jack. Then he turned and went back inside.

A flush of red colored Karen's cheeks. She pasted on a smile. "Shall we go in?"

6

"Hello?" Karen called out from the foyer. "We're here."

Leaving the front door open, she slipped her shoes off and placed them alongside several other pairs lined up neatly on the porch. Jack did the same.

"You don't have to," she said.

"It's all right. I understand the custom."

Jack took in his surroundings as he followed her past a wide maple staircase and down two carpeted steps to a sunken living room. The place had an open, airy feel, with shell-white plaster walls and high ceilings. The furniture was sparse but inviting, with plush sofas and occasional chairs upholstered in subtle earth tones. In the center of the room, a low glass coffee table held an enormous weathered copper sculpture depicting a pair of sea turtles. The only décor on the walls was an abstract oil painting above the white brick fireplace. Beyond the living room he could see a formal dining room and a slice of sun-filled kitchen.

Karen called out again. "Dad? Michael?"

A door shut somewhere above them, and a jean-clad young man hurried down the stairs.

Karen smiled. "Hi, sweetie. Did you miss me?"

He gave her a lopsided grin. He was handsome in a boyish way, slight of build, with silver-rimmed glasses and a mass of dark, curly hair that framed his angular face in a pleasing wreath. He wrapped his arms around her and kissed her. "How was your trip?"

"Fine." She introduced him to Jack, and Michael greeted him with a firm handshake.

44

"Do we have any iced tea made?" Karen started toward the kitchen. "I've been so thirsty ever since my flight yesterday."

"I'll get it, honey." Michael blocked her way.

"But I—"

"I'm sure you must be tired."

Karen started to say something in reply, but he took her by the elbow and steered her back into the living room.

"Why don't the two of you sit down and relax."

Karen sat opposite Jack on one of the sofas, a bemused expression on her face. "What in the world has gotten into you?"

A man appeared in the dining room doorway. Powerfully built, with a shape reminiscent of a fire hydrant, he had a broad face, piercing gray eyes, and a salt-and-pepper brush-cut hair. He carried a small tray with a glass of water and an assortment of medicine vials.

Michael's eyes darted from Karen to Jack, then back to Karen. He eased out of the room and headed to the kitchen.

Karen went to the man and hugged him carefully so as not to upset the tray.

"Hello, sweetheart," he said, returning her hug with his free arm. "It's good to see you."

"You too, Daddy." She turned. "Dad, this is Jack Dozier."

He gave Jack only a cursory nod, then directed his attention back to his daughter. "If you'll excuse me, I need to administer your mother's medicines." He headed for the stairs.

Karen sat back down on the sofa and picked at a loose thread in the upholstery. "Sorry about that." From the kitchen came the sound of ice cubes clinking against glass.

"Not your fault," he replied, but his temper was beginning to simmer.

Karen started to say something, but was interrupted by the sound of the kitchen door slamming.

"Karen! Karen! Karen!" a shrill voice called.

Karen's face lit up. "Shhhh." She placed a finger to her lips and then ducked behind the other sofa.

A blur of red overalls and dark hair burst into the room. The child stopped in her tracks when she saw Jack.

Jack stared at the little girl, unsure of what to say or do. He looked over at the sofa, but Karen was hidden from view. He turned back to her and cleared his throat. "Hello there."

The child didn't answer.

"I'm Jack," he tried again. "What's your name?"

Thrusting her hands in the pockets of her overalls, she eyed Jack curiously for a moment longer, then looked around the room. "I'm Brooklyn. Did you see a lady come in here? Her name's Karen. My daddy said he saw her car while we were out on the beach." She started toward the windows to check for herself.

Jack couldn't help but join in on the game. "You say her name is Karen?"

Brooklyn stopped and blinked at him. "Uh-huh."

"Can you tell me what she looks like?"

Her impish face was a lesson in concentration. "Well… she's about this tall." She stretched her arm over her head as far as she could reach. "Maybe a little taller. And she has brown hair and wears red lipstick a lot."

Jack rubbed his chin. "Hmmm. No, I haven't seen anyone like that. The only person I saw was someone wearing a big orange wig and a clown suit with purple polka dots on it."

Brooklyn's eyes widened.

"As a matter of fact," he added, "I think he went into the kitchen."

She whirled around, almost taking the bait. Then she narrowed her eyes at him and said, "You made that up, didn't you?"

Karen finally let her off the hook. She poked her head out from behind the sofa and said, "Boo!"

Brooklyn stood with her fists balled on her hips, her bottom lip turned down in a fleshy pout. "You tricked me." She pointed a finger at Jack. "You, too."

Karen scooped the child into her arms. "I'm sorry, sweetie. Don't be mad at Mr. Dozier here. I was the one who put him up to it." She brushed the tip of Brooklyn's nose with her finger. "Did you miss me?"

Brooklyn wrapped her arms around Karen's neck in a fierce hug, the hurt feelings already forgotten. "I missed you a whole big bunch!"

"I missed you too, sweetie."

"Did you bring me any presents?"

Karen laughed. "So many the plane almost couldn't take off!"

"Can I see them?"

"Soon. But first, I want you to meet someone."

She set her back down and introduced her to Jack. The child held out a tiny hand to him, and Jack noticed her thumbtack-sized nails were painted a sheer blush of pink. "Nice to meet you, Mr. Dosy. I mean … Mr. Doosey." She frowned and looked up at Karen. "How do you say his name?"

Jack smiled. "Tell you what. You can call me Mr. Jack."

She took Karen's hand as they went into the kitchen to join Michael. Jack stopped inside the doorway and looked around. "My Norma would have loved this kitchen."

The room was bright and spacious, with white glass-fronted cabinets, a spotless cooktop island, and maple plank floors. In the breakfast nook, late afternoon sunlight spilled in through a set of palladium windows topped with stained-glass transoms.

"I'll be right back." Karen took her tea and headed for the stairs. Brooklyn tagged along behind her.

Michael handed Jack a glass. "Why don't we go out onto the deck? It has a great view."

He led the way through an enclosed sunroom to a set of double French doors that opened onto the deck. The first thing Jack noticed was the sound of a gentle breeze strumming its invisible fingers against a pewter wind chime. Upon closer inspection, Jack saw the body of the wind chime was crafted in the shape of a carousel, with a circle of galloping horses revolving around it.

Sipping his tea, he leaned over the deck railing and looked out at a seemingly endless blue-green patch of ocean. Michael was right. The view was indeed spectacular. Above, a widow's walk ran the entire length of the third floor, no doubt providing an even more spectacular view.

To the left of the house, a spindly picket fence, weathered and worn to a dull white, followed the natural curve of the sand dunes to the water's edge. To the right were fields of cord grass and sea oats, their heavy plumed heads leaning forward in the wind like baby birds at the edge of a nest. Far out to sea, a large cargo ship inched its way across the distant horizon.

"Coming here was Helen's idea," Michael said. "About a month ago, she got us together and told us this was where she wanted to go. Kenneth knew someone affiliated with the bank who owned this place. When he found out about Helen's situation, he told Kenneth we could stay as long as we wanted at no charge. We only have to pay for the utilities."

Behind the sea of cord grass, a man stood alone with what appeared to be an easel in front of him. Michael followed Jack's gaze. "That's Helen's brother, David," he explained. "The little girl you met is his daughter."

"Your wife told me they would be here." He squinted his eyes. "Is he painting?"

"Probably. Or sketching. David's an artist. He and his wife Janice have a gallery in New York City."

Jack's knees beginning to throb again, he eased himself into a deck chair. "What do you do back in New York?"

"I'm a CPA," he replied.

He went on to say something else, but Jack didn't hear him. He wondered where Karen was. Was she with Helen now? What was she telling her? His thoughts kept returning to the staircase in the foyer. What if she was on the third floor? He couldn't possibly climb that many stairs.

"Hey!" a voice called out from inside the house. "Isn't anyone gonna help me?"

Michael grinned. "That's Nadine. You're going to love her. Everyone does. Nadine is ... well, I'll let you decide for yourself."

In the kitchen, a dozen grocery bags were lined up along the island. From the open door leading to the garage, Jack heard what sounded like dogs barking.

"I'm coming, I'm coming!" Nadine exclaimed. The barking stopped. She lumbered up the steps, loaded down with more groceries. She eyed Jack and Michael. "Well, don't just stand there like two bumps on a log. Make yourself useful." She handed each of them a bag and headed back to the garage.

Michael caught Jack's eye and grinned. "See what I mean? You stay here. I'll help bring in the rest of the stuff." The two of them made several more trips, with Nadine talking nonstop the entire time.

Jack had never seen so much food for one household. "How many people are going to be here?"

"Ten," Nadine replied. "And don't think I'm looking forward to cooking for that many people, either."

"Don't let her fool you," Michael said. "She's in her element right now."

When the last of the groceries were brought in, Nadine marched over to Jack and gave him a hearty handshake. She appeared to be somewhere in her mid-to-late forties, with shoulder-length red hair and sparkling blue eyes set like raisins in the rounded dough of her plump face.

"I'm Nadine Hines, the Price's housekeeper. Although Lord knows I'm so much more than that. Right, Michael?"

He smiled as he put away cartons of milk and fresh produce in the refrigerator. "Oh, yes. Nadine here does it all. Housekeeper, chef, amateur gardener—"

"Amateur?" She sniffed. "Need I remind you of those prize dahlias I grew last year?"

Michael held up his hands in mock surrender. "I stand corrected."

She looked out through the bay windows at the barren deck. "What this place needs is more flowers. Those hanging baskets we found on the way down here just aren't going to cut it. I'll find a nursery tomorrow and get some pansies for the window boxes and some bulbs for inside the house and—" She whirled around. "Oh! I forgot my babies!" She hurried back out to the garage.

"You're not allergic to dogs are you, Jack?" Michael asked.

Before Jack could reply, what sounded like a minor earthquake pounded up the garage steps. A pair of miniature dachshunds scrambled into the room, nipping at each other's heels as they raced around the island. Each dog wore a cloth bandana around its neck, one a floral print with lace trim, the other a pattern of pint-size Harley Davidson motorcycles.

Nadine got down on her hands and knees. "These here are my babies." The dogs darted happily around her. "This one is Ringo." She pointed to the one with the motorcycle bandana. "And the other one is Star. They're brother and sister."

There was silence in the room while Jack made the connection. "You named your dogs after one of the Beatles?"

"Ringo was my favorite," she replied.

Michael was putting away packages of meat in the freezer. "When baseball season starts, she dresses those dogs up in baseball jerseys."

"*Yankees* jerseys," she emphasized.

"Nadine is a diehard Yankees fan," Michael explained.

"Number forty-six and number two," she added.

Jack was confused. "I beg your pardon?"

"Andy Pettitte and Derek Jeter, of course," she replied. "My two favorite players in all of baseball. Tino was a favorite too, before he went with the Cardinals. But I gotta be true to my Yanks."

"I see," Jack replied. He tried to imagine the two dogs in Yankee pinstripes. Were there sleeves for just the front paws, or were the jerseys custom-made for all four legs? He thought of asking but decided the question would probably sound ridiculous.

Nadine threw a rag toy across the kitchen floor and the dogs raced after it. "Michael thinks I'm crazy, but I don't care." She eyed Jack carefully, like a jeweler studying a gem to determine its worth. "Do you like dogs, Jack?"

Ringo came over to him and sniffed tentatively at his shoes. Jack bent down and scratched his ears. "I've always liked dogs."

"Good. I don't trust people who don't like dogs." She picked up Star and pressed the canine's face to her cheek. "That *mean* old Kenneth didn't *want* you guys here, *did* he?" she cooed, in a singsong voice clearly meant only for them. Ringo scampered over and begged to be picked up.

"Yes, he *did*! But Miss Helen said you could come, didn't she? And we all know who the *real* boss is around here, don't we?"

She scooted the dogs off to their kennel in the laundry room and wagged a finger in Michael's direction. "You're not to repeat anything I just said."

He held up the first three fingers of his right hand. "Scout's honor."

Nadine snorted. "You were never a Boy Scout."

Jack glanced in the direction of the stairs. Still no Karen. He was putting away the last of the groceries in the pantry when Brooklyn ran in.

"Karen says to come upstairs." She took Jack's hand and led the way. "I'll show you where it is. But we have to be quiet because Nana is taking a nap."

Karen met them at the bottom of the staircase.

Jack reached out and grasped the rounded newel post but didn't go any further. "I'm going to need my cane."

"Oh. Of course. I'll get it for you." She must have sensed his unease at having an audience. "Brooklyn, honey … why don't you go on upstairs and we'll meet you in Aunt Helen's room, okay?" The child let go of Jack's hand and ran up the stairs.

50

After Karen left to fetch his cane, Jack tried out the first few steps. Not too bad. He measured the distance. Ten steps to the first landing, then another ten to the second floor. He saw a third stairwell, but he hoped he wouldn't have to climb that one. He went a few more steps. By the time Karen came back, he was halfway up the first flight.

She handed him his cane. "My mom can come down here."

Jack shook his head. "I'm okay. Just some arthritis in my knees."

"Second floor, last door on the right at the end of the hall," she said. "I'll meet you there."

7

Helen studied her appearance in the bathroom mirror as she ran a brush through her thick auburn hair. She turned her head from side to side. It wasn't her natural hair, of course. The chemo had seen to that. The style was much shorter than how she usually wore it, but the wigmaker had done an excellent job at creating two hairpieces that looked nearly as real as her old hair. An added bonus was a bit of wave she didn't have before.

There were a few downsides to fake hair. There was the cost, but Kenneth insisted she have only the best. And there was the hassle of sending them out every few months for cleaning and styling. The worst part, though, was the itchy scalp, especially in the summer. At times it became unbearable, and she would yank her wig off in exasperation and sprinkle her head with baby powder and resort to a scarf.

She leaned in closer to the mirror. The dark circles beneath her eyes were carefully concealed with makeup. A bit of blush added some color to her cheeks. She removed a tube of lipstick from her makeup bag and applied a generous layer of dark rose to her lips.

Beside her, Brooklyn sat atop the vanity next to the sink, her watchful eyes taking in everything. "Why do you wear lipstick?"

Helen blotted her mouth with a tissue. "Because it makes me feel pretty."

"Can I wear some, too?"

Her knee-jerk reaction was to say no, that she was far too young; the same words her own mother had said to her when she was

52

Brooklyn's age and had asked the same thing. Then she reconsidered. What harm would it do?

"I tell you what." She searched through her makeup bag for the lightest shade she could find. "We'll put just a little bit on, okay?" She hoped David wouldn't be too upset.

Brooklyn sat perfectly still as Helen applied a tiny touch of pink to her lips. She handed her a mirror so that she could see the end result.

"But you can hardly see it," she protested. "Yours looks a lot darker."

"That's because I'm an old lady compared to you. When you get to be my age, you can wear as much as you want, okay? Now help me put all this stuff away."

As they tucked away various cosmetics and compacts into the medicine cabinet and vanity drawers, Brooklyn asked, "Who's Mr. Jack?"

Helen's brow furrowed. "Who?"

"Mr. Jack. The man downstairs. He told me I could call him that."

"Oh. Well, he's a friend of mine."

"Then how come I've never seen him before?"

"Well ... because this is the first time he's come to visit me."

Brooklyn leaned forward and whispered, "He's kinda old. Like Nana. But he seems nice. And he's funny." She told her about the joke Jack and Karen had played on her earlier. Helen took it as a good sign.

Karen's face appeared in the doorway. "You ready?"

"Is he on his way up?"

She nodded and turned to Brooklyn. "Sweetie, I need to talk to Aunt Helen in private for a minute, okay?"

"You mean 'big people' talk?"

"Yep. I'm afraid so."

"I hate 'big people' talk. That always means I have to leave." She jammed her hands in her pockets and shuffled out of the room.

"Is that new?" Karen gestured to Helen's powder blue jogging suit. Embroidered across the front of her sweatshirt was a line of prancing white carousel horses, adorned in pink and blue flowing ribbons.

"Your father and I bought it in town the other day. It's a little big, but it was the last one they had, and you know I had to have it." She took a deep breath and smoothed her hair once more. Her heart pounded inside her chest.

"You look fine, Mom. Don't worry. You'll charm him just like you do everyone else." She smiled and left the room.

Helen wished she could feel as confident. She felt raw, vulnerable; as if the most intimate parts of her being were about to be exposed for all the world to see.

It's not too late! Just tell him this was all a big mistake and have Karen drive him back home.

But she knew she couldn't do that.

"He made the decision to come here," she told her reflection. "That has to say something."

Out of the corner of her eye, she spied Kenneth in the master bedroom. His hair was shot through with a little more gray than a few years ago, and the sharp planes of his face had softened a bit, but he was still a ruggedly handsome man. Karen was saying something to him about dinner plans as he filled Helen's pillbox with her daily doses of medication. Helen knew the task was merely a charade to keep him in the room. She started to say something along the lines of being fully capable of handling this by herself, but then she thought better of it. While her husband didn't always go about things the right way, she knew he had her best interests in mind.

She quietly closed the bathroom door and slid open a bottom drawer of the vanity. From beneath a bundle of head scarves, she removed a prescription bottle and shook out two Xanax tablets. Kenneth didn't know about them. She didn't need him worrying about her any more than he already did. The pills helped a lot, especially over the last several months as her disease had progressed.

Swallowing the tablets with a glass of water from the tap, she checked her hair and makeup one last time. Then she went over to a wicker sofa in front of the bedroom's bay windows and sat down to wait for Jack.

Jack's knees were popping painfully by the time he got to the first landing. He stopped to rest for a moment. In the open gallery above him, Brooklyn flew past the stairs, ran into another bedroom, and

54

closed the door behind her. The muted sounds of a television floated up to him from the first floor. The rest of the house was quiet.

He turned back and looked down the stairs. *This is ridiculous. How in the world did I let myself get talked into this?*

He contemplated leaving. He figured he could walk up the main road until he reached a gas station or convenience store with a pay phone. He wondered how much it would cost to have a cab take him back to Norfolk. He tallied up the mileage in his mind. Way too much for a cab. Maybe he'd rent a car and drive himself home.

He had almost talked himself into leaving when he felt the weight of his old wallet in the back pocket of his trousers. He hesitated. Then he sighed and turned back toward the second flight of stairs and began to climb.

This won't take long. Everyone will see what a huge mistake this is and then I'll excuse myself and go back home.

When he reached the second floor, he followed Karen's directions and went to the end of the hallway. Sheer lace curtains covered the glass of the double French doors, and he couldn't see inside the room. Determined now to get this over with as quickly as possible, he opened the door and went inside.

He stopped short when he saw Karen's mother sitting in front of a bay window across the room. Kenneth turned to look at him briefly. Then he went back to filling Helen's pillbox. The silence inside the room was stifling. Jack shifted his cane from one hand to the other. Finally, Karen spoke up.

"Dad, why don't we go downstairs and let Mom and Jack talk."

"I'll be done in a minute," he replied.

Helen pushed herself up from the sofa. "Won't you come sit down?"

Her dark, gentle eyes followed him as he came over to where she was. He stood awkwardly in front of her in his stocking feet, his gaze skimming over the delicate features of her face. Her hair was shorter and lighter in color than it was in Karen's picture. And her face was thinner. But there was no mistaking the striking similarities. Jack felt his stomach clench and his knees weaken as the cocoon of doubt he had wrapped himself in began to slowly unwind.

She extended her hand. "It's nice to finally meet you."

Jack felt the weight of Kenneth's stare as he took her hand in his. Her skin was cool, and the bones of her fingers felt tiny and light, like a bird's. She indicated a wicker chair across from her. Jack perched himself on the edge of the seat cushion, his cane between his knees.

Helen stared at him for a long, uncomfortable moment. "You look just like your pictures." She smiled. "Well … not exactly. But you know what I mean."

Kenneth came over and placed the medicine tray on the wicker table between them. On the tray were some cotton balls, a bottle of rubbing alcohol, and a syringe filled with an amber-colored fluid.

Helen appeared to be caught off guard by the intrusion. "Have you met my husband?"

"We've met," Kenneth replied curtly. He moistened a cotton ball with alcohol and uncapped the syringe.

Helen looked from her husband to Jack and then back again. Leaning forward, she said, almost in a whisper, "Kenneth, we talked about this."

"Honey, you need to build up your red blood cells. Your last blood counts were extremely low."

Helen shook her head. "Those injections are what made me so sick last night."

As if his wife hadn't said a word to him, Kenneth pushed up her sleeve and swabbed a spot on her upper arm with the cotton ball. "Honey, we don't know that for sure. You've only had three doses." He brought the needle toward her.

"Kenneth," she said, calmly but firmly. "I said no."

Helen's admonition affected her husband like a slap. He released her arm and laid the syringe on the tray. A rush of crimson colored his neck and lower jaw. Despite the man's earlier rudeness, Jack felt sorry for him.

Helen leaned forward again and said softly, "We'll talk about this later, okay?"

Staring down at the tray, Kenneth gave her a barely perceptible nod. Then he turned and quickly walked out of the room.

In the silence following his departure, Jack shifted uncomfortably in his chair. Helen seemed unnerved by the scene.

She gave a smile that looked forced. "How was your trip down here?"

"Very nice. I heard we'll be getting some warmer weather soon." He hated the triteness of his words, but he didn't know what else to say. Looking everywhere but at Helen, his eyes darted around the room, seeing nothing. Beyond the bay windows, distant ocean waves curled in on themselves, then flattened out to crash against the shore. The silence between them lengthened.

He cleared his throat. "I understand you have a medical practice in New York."

"Not for long, I'm afraid." Her vocal tone was wistful. "I sold my practice. We should close on the deal by the end of next week."

"I'm sure it was a difficult decision."

Helen shrugged, but the regret that shone in her eyes told a different story. "The doctor taking over for me is a good man. He's hiring another nurse practitioner, and the rest of the staff get to keep their jobs."

"That's good," he replied.

More silence.

"So … you live in the Norfolk area?" Helen asked.

"After I retired, my wife and I decided to stay there." He met her gaze. "But of course, you already knew that, didn't you?"

One corner of Helen's mouth curved upward in a smile. "You're obviously an astute man, Mr. Dozier. Why don't we cut to the chase, shall we?"

Jack nodded. "All right."

Helen settled back into her seat and laced her fingers together loosely in her lap. "You must have a million and one questions for me."

Jack was taken aback. He thought it would be the other way around, with him being the one to be peppered with questions. He shook his head. "No, I—" Then it dawned on him. He *did* want some answers to a few things. "How did you track me down?"

"Department of Naval Affairs," she replied. "I admit we used a few ruses to obtain information, but for the most part, they were most accommodating in helping us locate you."

A derisive sound escaped his throat. "I see."

"I'm sure you must feel like your privacy was invaded," she offered. "But let me assure you it wasn't my intention to do so. The first time I went looking for you I was very young. Fresh out of college, actually. I was about to start medical school, and I was doing some soul-searching in my life, trying to figure some things out."

"And what did you find out about me?"

"That you were stationed in California. That was around 1975 or so."

Jack did some quick calculations in his head. He was serving his second of two tours on the west coast during that time.

"I thought about trying to contact you," she said. "But I never did. At least not then."

"Was there a time when you did?"

"Around three years ago when I was first diagnosed with cancer." She turned her face toward the sun-filled window. In the harsh, unforgiving light, the pallor of her complexion was visible beneath her makeup.

"Coming face to face with your own mortality makes you rethink a lot of things in your life," she said. "I decided there were a few things left undone I wanted to fix. One of those was finding my biological father."

Turning from the window, she tucked one of her legs beneath her. Jack noticed how small her feet were, clad in a pair of pink wool socks.

"I went so far as to get an address and phone number," she continued. "I can't tell you how many times I picked up the phone to call you. But in the end, I decided not to go through with it."

"Was there a reason why you didn't?"

"I'm not entirely sure." She looked down at a spot of sunlight warming an area of carpet next to her chair. "Fear of rejection, I suppose. And I didn't want to cause you or your family any embarrassment." She looked at him. "I'm sorry about your wife. Karen told me."

A wave of unexpected pain washed over him. He pushed it away. "Your daughter told me you have a favor to ask of me."

The statement hung suspended in the air for a long moment. "All in good time," Helen replied. "I promise."

Nothing further was said, and Jack decided not to pursue it. He stood up and pulled his old wallet from his back pocket and laid it on the table. He eased back into his chair.

"Tell me more about how this was found."

"What do you want to know?"

"When is your birthday?"

"March 10, 1953. That's when I was found."

Jack did the subtraction. The timing was right. He had served two tours in South Korea, one at the beginning of the Korean War in 1950, and the other in the summer of 1952.

"Karen told me the wallet was found sewn into the lining of your diaper."

"Yes, that's the story I was told."

"By your adoptive parents?"

"Actually, it was my mother who told me. My adoptive father passed away when I was seven."

Jack took a moment to absorb that last bit of information. Now he understood a little better her reasons for pursuing this particular avenue concerning her past.

As if reading his mind, Helen went over to a bureau and pulled out a framed picture from a drawer. The photograph was of a thick young man, blonde and deeply tanned, standing on a fishing dock with the Manhattan skyline spread out behind him. Next to him was a petite, dark-haired woman, her eyes and facial features obscured by dark sunglasses and a floppy hat. The man had one arm curled around the woman's shoulders. The other cradled a small child to his side. All three were smiling for the camera.

"That's me." She pointed to the little girl. "And that's my mother, Kim Sung."

Jack looked closer at the photograph. "Your father married a Korean woman?"

"My father was a missionary in South Korea. They met there." She pointed to the man in the picture. "That's my dad, John Gable."

He handed the photo back to her. "Tell me about him."

Settling back into her seat, Helen reminisced about the only father she'd ever known. "He was a very good man," she said. "And a wonderful father."

After coming to America, her young life revolved around the comings and goings of her dad on the New Jersey docks, where he worked as a commercial fisherman. Every Monday at dawn, before they awoke, he left for the open sea. Helen counted the days until dusk on Thursday when they took the ferry to the Jersey shore to wait for John's fishing boat to dock. When he came down the gangplank, she and her siblings would race across the pier to greet him. She could still feel the prickle of his whiskers against her cheek and how his clothes always smelled of the ocean, no matter how many times her mother washed them.

"I felt so lost when my dad died," she said quietly. "I became a rather sullen child for a while. Introverted. I think my mother sensed my need for a father figure and wanted to do something to fill that void somehow. When I was eleven, she showed me your wallet. I knew I was adopted, but I wasn't told the full story behind it." She paused and looked away. "I don't know if—I mean—I understand if you don't want to hear this."

"Go on," Jack urged. "I'd like to hear it."

Helen and her family were living in a cramped, stuffy apartment a few blocks from the South Street fish markets where her mother worked. Her dad had been gone for over four years. One evening, her mother came into the room Helen shared with Lizzie and sat down beside her on the bed.

"*Ch'onsa Kom,*" she began, using a pet name which meant angel bear. "Remember long time ago how we tell you and your sister and brother how God's angels bring you to us?"

Helen nodded. "You said our first parents—the ones who made us—couldn't take care of us, so God picked you and Daddy to be our new parents."

"Is right. But you are older now, almost young woman. Is time you were told whole story of how you came to be with us."

"What do you mean, Omma?"

She pulled a wallet from the pocket of her apron and laid it on Helen's lap. It was similar to the type of wallet her dad used to carry in his back pocket. She picked it up and went through the contents. There was a driver's license for the state of California, and a military ID card that read *United States Navy.* The photos on both cards were of the same dark-haired man. Jack Dozier. Then she came to several photographs, tucked away behind plastic. Most of the pictures were of a pretty young woman with a bright smile. In others, the dark-haired man and the pretty woman were posed together. She felt her young heart pick up its pace. "Who are these people?"

60

"I not know who woman is. I am thinking this man's *anae*. His wife?"

Helen stared at the man's image. "But … this man. He's—he's my father, isn't he? The first one."

Her mother stroked a hand down the length of Helen's glossy, dark hair. "We believe it to be, *Ch'onsa Kom*. You know John your father come to Korea to start God's church. He very young man then. I not meet him yet. He say one day he open door and find you in basket on the *hyeongwan*."

Helen's head jerked up. "The what?"

Her mother mumbled something in Korean. Her brow furrowed as she searched for the right word. "Like outside this building here. Like—how do you say—doorstep?"

Helen stared at her, horrified. She thought of a kitten she and Lizzie had found once inside a box in a muddy culvert behind their school. The poor thing was rail-thin and covered in filth.

"I was left in a basket on a *doorstep*? Why? Who left me there?"

Her mother shook her head. "John tell me he do not know."

"How old was I?"

"You very small. You were new baby."

Helen's mind was tumbling. Tears filled her eyes. "I don't understand, Omma." She pointed at the photo of the dark-haired man. "How do you know this man is my father?"

"Because when John find you, this with you in the *baguni*. The basket." She sighed and took Helen's hand. "It happen many times, during war. Many soldiers come here to fight. They make babies with Korean women and go back home."

Helen picked up the photograph. "But… what about this woman in the picture? How do you know she wasn't the one who left me there? Maybe *she's* my real mother!"

Her mother gently ran her fingers over Helen's forearm. "Look at color of your skin. Shape of your eyes. You have Korean blood in you, *Ch'onsa Kom*." She indicated the photo. "This woman does not."

Helen began to cry in earnest. She couldn't get the image of the abandoned kitten out of her mind. "But… whoever she is… why did my real mother give me away? Why didn't she want me, Omma? Why?"

Her mother held her and stroked her hair until her tears subsided. When she stood up, her face was pinched and wan. She shook her head. "I not say these things right," she said quietly, smoothing her hands over her apron. "I see this has upset you. I thought you old enough to know truth. I am sorry, *Ch'onsa Kom*." She quickly left the room and closed the door behind her.

They never talked about it again.

"At first, I didn't know what to think," Helen told Jack. "I had resolved myself to the fact the only father figure in my life was gone. But then to be hit with this, to be told my real father was alive somewhere …"

Jack started to offer up a weak line of protest, that there wasn't any actual proof he was her father. But when he saw the look on Helen's face, he stopped short.

"I carried that wallet with me everywhere. I would think up stories of where you lived and what you were like. I imagined what I would say to you if we ever met." She blinked away tears. "Do you have any idea what it's like to go your whole life and never come into contact with another person who shares your blood?"

Jack tried to imagine the sense of isolation and loneliness she must have felt growing up, even in the midst of a loving family. His own childhood was spent surrounded by a barrage of cousins and nephews and other relatives he had long lost touch with. He thought of his parents and younger brother, dead and gone. Although he was alone in a physical sense now, those blood ties from his past were still there, permanent and unwavering. Helen had never known that.

"No, I can't say that I do," he replied softly.

"When I was little," she continued, "I always wondered why my parents hadn't wanted me. Why they had given me away. I would see couples walking in a crowd, and I'd fantasize they were my real mother and father. Then, after I was told about you, I started to notice every tall, dark-haired man around me. Each one I saw, I wondered if he was you." Helen grabbed a tissue from a box on the table and held it in her hand.

Jack could see she was fighting back tears. He cleared his throat. "What about your biological mother?"

"It was a dead end," she said, shaking her head. "We tried, but we weren't able to find out anything. I was hoping maybe you could fill in some of those blanks for me."

Jack didn't reply.

"Karen tells me you weren't … involved with the woman who gave me up for adoption."

Placing his cane beside him, Jack leaned forward in his chair and laced his fingers together. "No, I wasn't," he replied.

"Will you tell me what happened?"

Jack hung his head and closed his eyes. He had known it would eventually come to this. He tried to recall that long-ago night, the young girl's face.

Finally, he said, "I have no idea who your mother is. But I'll tell you what happened when I was in Korea."

8

Early summer. 1950. South Korea.

Thirteen-year-old Song Min lay on her grass mat, feigning sleep. In the next room, her parents spoke in hushed tones. Her father used words and phrases she had never heard before.

Invasion… Red Army … Prisoners of war.

She wondered what it all meant. Perhaps in the morning, her sister, Song Joo Hee, could explain. She was two years older.

Earlier that evening, the elders had summoned the men of the village to a meeting. From Seoul, accounts of violence and political unrest in North Korea had trickled down to their tiny coastal village of Suwon. The northern region of their homeland had long been an area of upheaval and turmoil. Rumors of war were nothing new. But Min could tell by the tone of her father's voice that these latest reports were disturbing.

The next day, her father gave them small field whistles made of bamboo to put in the pockets of their *hanboks*. Usually only the men routinely carried whistles with them when working outdoors, to warn others of wild animals or other danger. Now everyone who lived within the village walls, from the youngest *orini* to the oldest *orun*, would have one.

"You are not to leave the house alone, even while doing chores or when you go to the well to draw water," her father said. "Keep the whistles with you at all times. If you see anyone you don't recognize, blow the whistle several times and come directly home."

He didn't say why, and they didn't ask. It was not honorable to question an elder's judgment.

A week later, Min stood on the back stoop of their thatched-roof home and took a moment to breathe in the fragrant aroma of the lotus flowers that grew in tangled vines along the ground in her mother's garden. The scent was strongest in the early morning, before the heat of the day caused the delicate pink blooms to seek refuge beneath the large heart-shaped leaves. Far away to the east, masses of wild azaleas carpeted the foothills of the T'aebaek Mountains in vibrant hues of lilac and red.

In the field next to their home, Mother and Joo Hee were working. Floppy mesh hats and long cotton sleeves shielded their faces and arms from the blazing sun as they arranged fresh-cut peppers and grasses along the ground.

Today was drying day. Tomorrow, they would work in the rice paddies alongside her father and grandfather, slogging through the watery rows of tender green sprouts. In late summer, they would gather the long russet-colored blades by hand, then hang the tied bundles across raised trellises to dry. It was backbreaking work. Her father and grandfather said that to honor the land and to make a living by the sweat of one's brow was a noble thing.

She slipped her bare feet into a pair of straw thong sandals and crossed the hard-packed ground to a small wooden building that housed the family shrine. Inside the cramped structure, she knelt and lit candles and burned incense as she prayed for her family's safety.

When she was finished, Min blew out the candles but left the incense burning, filling her nose with the subtle scent of sandalwood. She felt for the whistle in her pocket. Then she went to join her sister and Mother in the fields.

The shrill cries of a dozen field whistles, like the screeching of fruit bats crazed by the summer heat, resounded in the air. Something was very wrong.

Min stood with her mother and Joo Hee outside the entrance to their family's hut. The sisters clung to one another as they watched their father's wagon come tearing around the bend that led to the barley fields. The pair of old work horses were straining at their harnesses, running at a full gallop. Her father was goading them with a whip, something Min rarely saw him do.

He brought the wagon to an abrupt halt in the village square. The backs and bellowing sides of the horses were lathered in sweat and foam. Her father ran down the lane, then cut through the large vegetable garden in front of their home. His thin leather sandals made wet, sucking sounds in the sodden earth, and spatters of mud covered the legs of his *paji*. By the time he reached them, he was panting for breath.

"The village is under attack!" he exclaimed. His face was slick with fear. He asked where Min's grandfather was.

Her mother's face went slack. She turned her head toward the distant hills. A thick cloud of smoke billowed from the direction of the barley fields.

"I will find him," her father said. "All of you! Get down to the root cellar!"

He flung open the small wooden door to the cellar, and the sisters descended the short flight of mud-packed stairs. Then they turned their tear-streaked faces toward their mother and waited for her to join them. Outside, the *tat-tat-tat-tat-tat* of distant gunfire could be heard. The girls cried harder. Their mother looked over her shoulder and uttered a shrill cry. Then she hurried down, leaving the door slightly ajar to admit a faint trickling of light into the cool, darkened space.

She stood in front of them. Her eyes were wide with panic but her voice was calm. She pointed to an empty vegetable bin standing in the murky shadows behind them.

"Get in," she ordered.

Confused and frightened, they climbed inside the bin, first Min, then Joo Hee. There was barely enough room for the two of them as they huddled together on the filthy wooden floor of the container. Min craned her neck over the rim of the bin and watched as her mother carted over two more bins that were filled to the brim with seasonal produce. The girls cried out when a shower of lettuces and cabbages rained down on them, along with gourds and melons and other fruits and vegetables.

Min felt as though she were being buried alive. She couldn't move her arms or legs and it was hard to breathe. Then their mother placed a large burlap sack over their heads.

"Do not make a sound," she whispered. "Stay here until I come back for you."

"Don't leave us!" Joo Hee cried. Her words were cut short by heavy footfalls and shouting right outside the cellar door.

Min felt her mother's tiny hand, light as an eggshell, on her head. Through the woven mesh of the burlap bag, her dread-filled features were transformed into something eerie in the shadowy light as she watched her lips move in silent prayer. Then she quickly crossed over to the other side of the root cellar at the foot of the steps and started filling the lap of her apron with radishes and green onions, as though she had made this routine trip to the root cellar, alone, to gather vegetables.

Everything happened so fast then.

The bark of a man's voice from the top of the steps …

Their mother whirling around to look up at the source …

Her small mouth opening in a silent scream …

The ear-splitting sound of rapid gunfire …

Her body crumpling to the ground …

Then silence.

A North Korean soldier slowly descended the steps into the bowels of the root cellar. He was young, probably not much older than Joo Hee. He wore a dark green uniform and black lace-up boots caked with mud. Holding his weapon in front of him, he gave only a cursory glance around the space. Then he was gone.

Too terrified to speak or move, Min and Joo Hee huddled together inside the bin as the only home they had ever known was torched above them. The grievous sounds of the dying and the pungent stench of burning flesh, both human and animal, would stay with Min forever.

How long they remained inside the cellar, Min could not tell. When they finally emerged under the welcome cover of darkness, muscle cramps racked their legs and they could barely walk. Dazed, they stumbled around in circles amid the smoking remains of their village, calling out for their father and grandfather until their voices were raw.

Soon, others came out from their hiding places and began their own frantic search for family and loved ones. There were only a handful of survivors. Most were women and children.

By the next day, news came that North Korea had officially declared war against the South. Their village was one of the first to be attacked. Dozens of defenseless villagers were slaughtered in cold blood. Everything of value—homes, livestock, harvests—was taken or destroyed. Even their small Buddhist temple, tucked away in an obscure area atop a hill, was ransacked and burned.

As the day wore on, other reports began to circulate. One woman told of seeing several village men, barefoot and stripped to the waist, being led away in shackles and chains and herded into the cargo hold of a military truck. Min feared her father and grandfather were among them. With their mother now dead, there was no one else for her and Joo Hee to turn to. A kindly village elder offered to take care of the girls until he could find a more suitable place for them.

Later that day, they laid their mother's bullet-ridden body to rest. They chose an area of soft ground behind the charred remains of what used to be their home, beneath the shade of a flowering Japanese alder tree. Min and Joo Hee had often seen her go there in the evening to mediate. They knew it was a special place for her.

Traditionally, a body would be cremated and the ashes taken to a high place and scattered to the four corners of the wind, where they would later settle upon the rivers and hillsides. But they had neither the time nor the resources to send their mother's spirit into the next life in the proper manner. The North Korean Army could attack again at any time. They needed to move on.

Someone had dressed their mother in a white silk *hanbok* with a purple sash draped across the midriff. The garment was not hers. The thick smell of smoke clung to the material. She had no casket. The village *shaman* presided over the brief ceremony. His vocal tone was without inflection, but his eyes were full of grief and sorrow. Then he moved on to the next grouping, where others lay waiting.

The girls stood beside the freshly dug grave as their mother's body was placed onto a piece of broadcloth sprinkled with ashes and lowered into the ground.

This isn't happening, Min kept telling herself. Closing her eyes, she bit down on her tongue until the coppery taste of blood filled her mouth.

She opened her eyes.

Not a dream. Her mother was still dead. Her sister was still standing next to her, trembling and crying. Min felt numb. No sorrow, no grief, no anger. She wondered why she couldn't cry.

Someone placed a hand on her shoulder and led her away from her mother's grave. A small bundle was thrust into her arms. Inside the sack were the few items of clothing they had managed to salvage from their home.

The village elder told them it was time to depart. On his back, he carried a large stone pot of *kimchi*. Joo Hee carried several flasks of water and a cloth pouch filled with Chinese apples and dried apricots. It was the only thing they had to eat or drink for the journey.

They started down a dirt road, heading north. Song Min glanced back over her shoulder, only once, then set her eyes straight ahead. Her last memory of their village was of the Japanese alder tree, its branches caught in a brisk wind as tears of ivory white petals rained down onto the mounded earth of her mother's grave.

Three days later, they arrived in the village of Anyang, hungry and exhausted, with little more than the shoes on their feet and the clothes on their backs. They were soaked to the bone. The monsoon season had begun, and a steady downpour had followed them for the last ten miles.

Either by divine provision or as a result of poor strategic planning on the part of the North Korean Army, this particular village was untouched. The majority of the villagers had taken what they could and fled after hearing the news of the attacks. But some had staunchly refused to leave, choosing instead to fight for what was rightfully theirs.

Those who remained were most gracious. At two separate dwellings, food and drink were offered. At one home, the old woman living there took one look at Min and Joo Hee's disheveled appearance and promptly ushered them into a back room cordoned off by curtains, where she drew a bath for them in a large wooden laundry tub. The girls stripped off their filthy clothes and climbed in together.

Min hadn't spoken a word since leaving the village. This was unusual for her. She was a talkative girl, with a sunny disposition, unlike Joo Hee, who had inherited their mother's more soft-spoken nature and economy with words.

As Joo Hee soaped Min's tangled hair, she stammered something about how everything would turn out all right. But her words stuck in her throat.

After their bath, the girls pulled on clean cotton *hanboks* the old woman had left for them, and Joo Hee brushed out Min's hair as they sat in front of an open window. She hummed a folk tune their mother had taught them when they were very young. Min's body tensed. Her slender shoulders began to shake. Finally, she let go and broke into sobs.

Joo Hee held her close as a gentle breeze rustled the fan-shaped fronds of a ginkgo tree outside the window. No words were said. Min's sobs subsided. The old woman's face appeared around the corner of the front curtain. It was time to move on.

Before they left the woman's home with the village elder, she gave each of the girls a bundle filled with dry clothing and a bar of milled soap. She then directed the elder to the other side of the village. A church was there, she told him. Not Buddhist, but from America. She had seen many children at this place. Maybe they would allow the girls to stay there.

As they neared the grouping of low-slung buildings, a man came out to greet them. He was short and stocky in build, with ginger-red hair and ruddy cheeks. He beckoned them inside with a thick, lilting accent.

The elder could not speak English, but the priest knew some Korean, and he was able to grasp the gist of what the elder was trying to tell him. The priest removed his silver-rimmed glasses and wiped the lenses with a handkerchief.

"Aye," he remarked sadly, gazing out the window. "'Tis the third one this week."

He agreed to provide sanctuary for the girls. His parish ran a small orphanage, a *kajong* for children, he explained. He assured him they would be properly taken care of. The elder nodded and bowed his head. The priest returned the gesture. Then, without another word, the man who had brought them so far went on his way.

Min was confused and afraid. She couldn't understand the words of the priest as he led them to a small chapel. Min stared at his strange clothes and pale face. She had never seen someone with skin so white.

From a distance, the squat stucco building looked presentable, with a coat of bright yellow paint and a thatched roof. Along the northern wall, a tangle of bougainvillea vines, heavy with brilliant purple blooms, had taken hold and twined their way to the roof. But as they came closer, it was evident the roof was beginning to sag and the stucco was crumbling in several places.

The priest opened a heavy wooden door and ushered them inside. The room smelled of old linen and dust. A single window, coated in a thick layer of dirt and grime, emitted only a faint trickling of light. At the front of the room was a platform with altars and a large wooden cross. To the side was a table covered in cloth with a large silver bowl in the middle. They watched as the priest dipped his hand into a basin of water next to the doorway. He then made several quick gestures across his chest and beckoned the girls to follow him. Min held fast to Joo Hee's hand.

After passing through a long hallway with closed wooden doors on either side, they came to a large room filled with noise and people. Along the walls, portable cribs were stacked one on top of the other, almost to the ceiling. From inside the pens, tiny faces appeared, their small hands gripping the bars. Most were crying. The others stared out through the slats with sunken eyes and blank stares.

Several women dressed all in white scurried around the room, tending to the infants and toddlers. A strong scent of ammonia filled the air, with an underlying odor of sour diapers and sweat. In a far corner, two older children, a boy and a girl, lay sleeping on a cot. The little girl was sucking her thumb. Min wondered how they could sleep with the commotion.

The priest said something to one of the nuns, who was trying to coax a crying baby with a bottle. Amidst a swathing of blanket, a tiny face emerged, mouth open wide in a deafening wail. The infant's purple-red face reminded Min of the little round crabapples her mother used to buy at the village market.

The nun looked over in their direction. Then she handed the infant over to another woman. Her rubber-soled shoes squeaked on the tile floor as she approached. Min shrank away. The priest spoke to the nun in soft tones. Then he left, closing the door behind him.

71

The woman's smile was kind but her eyes were tired. She took them to another room in the back, where she told them to bathe. Joo Hee tried to explain they had already taken a bath that day, but the nun pressed a bottle of disinfectant into her hand and made scrubbing motions with her hands. She turned on a shower spout, and the girls undressed and stood under the tepid water and did as they were instructed. When they were done, they found their clothes replaced with threadbare cotton pants and blouses. They were given rubber shower shoes to wear on their feet.

By this time, the supper hour had arrived. They were led back to the same room where they were first taken. A table and chairs were set up in the middle of the room for the older children. The boy and girl who were sleeping earlier, along with three other preschool-aged Korean girls, stared at them in wide-eyed curiosity.

Bowls of *kimchi* mixed with a little rice were placed in front of them. Min tasted hers. Hardly any spices were used to season the dish, and the cabbage was sour and rubbery. She spit it out into her bowl. One of the nuns rushed over to the table, scolding her. Her bowl was taken away. Nothing else was brought to her. Joo Hee forced down a few bites.

After dinner, it was time for bed. It was still light outside, about an hour before dusk. Two cots were set up for the girls in a far corner of the room. They weren't given any nightclothes, only some scratchy wool blankets and a couple of pillows encased in plastic.

As soon as the door was shut and locked behind them, Min got up from her cot and crawled in beside Joo Hee. Throughout the night, the crying never ceased. Neither one slept. Staring out the window across the room, Min watched as the charcoal black night slowly gave way to another day.

Kajong.
I want to go home.

9

Over the next several months, Min and Joo Hee stayed at the orphanage, where there was never a lack of work to be done. Along with a list of daily chores, they also took care of the smaller children and helped with the cooking.

Within a month, both the chapel and the outlying buildings were packed to overflowing with new arrivals. Most were women and children made homeless by the war. With each new arrival, Min saw the desperation and fear reflected in their eyes, as familiar to her as the beating of her own heart, reminding her once again of all she had lost.

She and Joo Hee never spoke of what happened the day the Red Army came to their village. There wasn't a need. Having seen the unthinkable carried out right before their eyes, they were bound in a way that surpassed words and understanding.

Only when they were together did Min feel safe, as if she feared her sister would be taken away, never to return. During the daytime hours, they worked side by side at their tasks. At night, Min went to Joo Hee's cot and slipped beneath the covers.

The nuns took care of their physical needs. They were given three meals a day and a roof over their heads. A few tried to communicate with them as best they could. But there were simply too many children to care for and not enough workers. For the most part, the girls were left to themselves.

But there was one nun who took a special interest in them. She told them her name was Rose. The other nuns called her Sister Rosa. She appeared to be only a few years older than Joo Hee. Her hair was dark and long, nearly to her waist, and her skin was the color of burnished copper, which stood out in stark contrast to the white of her habit. She was from Portugal and had joined the commune when she was sixteen. Min did not know where Portugal was. Rose had been at the mission for six months.

From the first day, she talked to the girls in broken Korean. She showed them how to do certain chores and taught them English names for things. In return, Min and Joo Hee taught her folk songs and told her stories about their ancestors.

Every morning after breakfast, Father Cavanaugh held mass in the chapel. Rose always sat beside them. Min marveled at the priest's flowing robes and words, and his soothing voice held a certain comfort for her. She watched what the others did and copied their actions.

After mass, Father Cavanaugh would stand outside the chapel door, and the children would flock around him as he dispensed candy and small treasures from the seemingly endless pockets of his robes. Once, he gave Song Min a seashell he had picked up from the beach. She held the item tightly in her hand and stared at his freckled cheeks and bright red hair, turned a fiery orange in the midmorning sun.

He reached down and touched her cheek. "Always remember you are God's child."

Twice a week, Sister Anne, one of the older nuns, taught English and math lessons. The class met in a cramped, windowless room next to the chapel with a water-stained ceiling and a few wooden desks. Most of the children sat on the floor.

In the summer, when the heat became unbearable, Sister Anne took them outside. They sat cross-legged on the grass in a tight circle beneath the shade of an ancient katsura tree. She held up cards depicting the alphabet, and the children would work simple addition and subtraction problems. Sometimes she would read to them, mostly English storybooks, but occasionally she chose Korean ones.

When the heat was too much even in the shade, she closed her lesson books and leaned forward, her elbows resting on her knees, her lined face peering out from the white oval of her headdress. In a muted voice as soothing as a lulling tide, she encouraged the children to talk about things, and she tried to address their concerns.

The younger ones didn't talk much, still in shock over the atrocities they had seen. But after a while, some of the older ones described in halting phrases how they came to be orphaned and left homeless. These stories were immensely disturbing to Min. She rested her chin on her knees and studied the clouds peeking through the dense foliage of blue-green leaves above her, taking solace in their floating, ever-changing shapes.

One day, Sister Anne spoke to them about *yongso*, or forgiveness. *Yongso*, she explained, was the key to peace and happiness. With God's help, they could find pardon in their hearts for those who had caused them so much pain.

Min was outraged. How could she say such things? What did these *whited stupas* know about her life? Min would never forgive the North Korean soldiers who had so callously taken her beloved *omma* and *aboji* and *haraboji* from her.

From that day on, Min refused to attend Sister Anne's classes. She wanted nothing to do with a God who demanded such impossible tasks of the heart.

At night, after everyone else had gone to sleep, Min would kneel beside her cot and place a small hand-carved Buddha on her mattress. Min had discovered the icon tucked inside the bundle of clothing the old village woman had given to her and Joo Hee. Every night, she prayed to the Buddha of Mercy and Compassion for the return of her father and grandfather so that she and her sister could leave this strange place.

One night, as she was praying, one of the nuns came up behind her, startling her. The woman uttered harsh words as she wagged an angry finger at Min's face. Then she snatched up the figurine and left the room.

Two days later, as the girls were making their beds, Min found the Buddha tucked under her pillow. Clutching the figure to her chest, her eyes darted around the room. No one paid any attention to her. Then her gaze fell on Rose. She was tending to an infant, one of the new arrivals. Their eyes met, and Rose offered her a knowing smile. Min bowed her head in Rose's direction. She hid the statue in the folds of her clothing and never let it out of her sight again.

The weeks slowly blended into months as the changing seasons passed in a blur. After a while, Min stopped thinking about leaving the orphanage. Some of the babies and younger children were adopted and sent to live with white people in America. But no one wanted teenage girls. She resigned herself to the fact that this was now her home.

Two years after Min and Joo Hee arrived at the mission, Rose came to them with tears in her eyes. "The mission will be shut down. Our sister churches in other countries have stopped sending funds. There is no money left to run the mission. Father Cavanaugh and the nuns are leaving by boat next week to go to the United States."

A few days later, a group of people dressed in western-style suits and hats came to the mission from Seoul and took the younger children into custody. Father Cavanaugh stood next to Min and Joo Hee, nervously fumbling with his rosary beads. "What will become of these two girls?" he asked one of the workers.

The man looked at Min and Joo Hee. He had hard eyes and a thin slash of a mouth. He snuffed out his cigarette with the heel of his shoe, then he turned to face the priest. "They too old now," he told him in broken English. "Besides, they be girls. Would be better if they were boys." Then he turned on his heel and walked away.

It was a sorrowful time as Rose hugged the girls and told them goodbye. She gave them silver crosses on chains to wear around their necks. Min and Joo Hee gave her a small stone amulet to keep for good luck.

Rose tucked it away in the pocket of her habit. "God be with you," she told them.

"And also with you," they said in unison.

Then Rose climbed into the back of a wagon and was driven away. The priest was the last to leave the village. Before he left, he directed the girls to a province twenty miles away to the west which was much larger and held a better promise of finding work, especially for Joo Hee, who was almost eighteen. From his own pocket, he gave them what money he had to help them on their way.

The money soon ran out. Steady work could not be found. The two sisters became nomads in their own homeland, moving from village to village, taking whatever work they could, which was mostly field labor jobs that paid little.

During the warmer months, they slept on the ground beneath the stars or with other laborers in a farmer's stable. But when the weather turned cold and harvest time was over, they were forced to head into the larger towns and seek refuge in the streets. Many times, Min and Joo Hee lived on nothing but a small bowl of cold gruel or rice as their daily meal.

Their bodies paid the price for the harsh life they led, their thin frames dwarfed by the baggy, threadbare clothes they wore. Their skin turned sallow. And their long dark hair, which at one time was thick and glossy with health, was now ragged and dull.

In the spring of 1952, the girls found themselves in the seaport town of Inch'ŏn, and their eyes were opened to a whole new way of life. This place was *busy*, bustling with people and prospects, energized by a healthier economy from the endless parade of ships, both foreign and domestic, coming and going from the harbor.

But after a week of living on the streets, unable to find work even as washwomen and down to a few meager *won* in their pockets, Joo Hee took Min over to the docks, where she watched an older Korean woman standing alone at dusk outside the entrance to a *sake* bar. Thick through the waist and hips but with a small bust and spindly legs, the woman wore a form-fitting blue silk dress and matching pumps. Her demeanor was cautious as she scanned the passing faces.

"I know what she is," Joo Hee said. "I have seen her before."

Min wondered what her sister meant. But Joo Hee didn't explain.

A white man approached the woman, an American dressed in uniform. She said something to him, and the man produced some bills from his pocket. The woman gestured toward the front door of the bar and the man went inside.

Taking Min by the hand, Joo Hee walked over to her. "My sister and I need a place to stay, and we need work."

The woman's jaded eyes studied their faces and forms carefully, as if she were looking past their haggard appearance to ascertain whether or not they held any desirable attributes.

"Come with me," she told them.

By that evening, the girls had settled into a cramped two-room apartment not far from the piers, located above a rundown shoe repair shop. They shared the space with five other girls, all of whom were under the older woman's employ. For a portion of their earnings, she provided a room and one meal a day.

Later, while Min took the first real bath she'd had in weeks, Joo Hee and her new employer left the apartment together. Min barely recognized her sister as she passed by in the hallway. She was wearing makeup on her face, and she was dressed in stylish clothes Min had never seen before. She returned at dawn with a fistful of American dollars and bloodshot eyes. Whether the redness was from crying or lack of sleep, Min didn't know.

It wasn't long before Min was forced to do the same. Only her first experience was bad. From then on, she tried to block everything out while it was happening and go someplace else in her mind. For the most part, she could. But not always.

Min no longer prayed for the return of her father and grandfather. She did not wish for them to see what she and Joo Hee had become. To dishonor them in this way was unthinkable. But hard as she tried, she could not hide her shame from her mother. Min believed she was still with her, watching over them from somewhere in the heavens. She used to feel her presence beside her, could hear the echo of her lulling voice in her head. She now believed her *omma* was hiding her face from her.

The mere thought of it broke Min's heart.

10

May 1952. City of Inch'ŏn. South Korea.

While truce talks dragged on, Jack Dozier's ship, a U.S. Navy frigate, was part of a small international fleet assigned to guard the shores of South Korea. The modest blockade patrolled the Tsushima Strait to prevent smuggling of weapons.

In the latter part of May, the crew was given a seventy-two-hour liberty. Leaving the coral-filled waters of the Yellow Sea, the vessel made its way to the western shore and dropped anchor at Inch'ŏn.

Jack plodded to his bunk after a twelve-hour shift inside the sweltering gun hold.

Some of his shipmates were dressed in clean uniforms. "Hey, Jack, we're going into Seoul for some sightseeing," one of them said.

A few others laughed and joked about just what sort of sights they wanted to see.

"You wanna go?"

"Nah. I'm exhausted." Jack flopped onto his rack. Seoul was thirty miles inland. Too long a haul. His shipmates left in a raucous clamor.

A few hours later, after showering and grabbing a bite to eat on the mess deck, Jack felt revived. Suddenly, the prospect of spending the evening alone on the nearly deserted frigate wasn't appealing. Besides, he had cashed part of his paycheck earlier that day and had money to spend. Catching up to a few of his shipmates, he went with them to a nearby bar.

Owned and operated by the U.S. Embassy, the place was shaped like a shoebox and dimly lit. The only air flow came from the front and back doors, which were propped open with concrete blocks. The front wall was taken up by a mirrored bar, with an impressive selection of spirits displayed on the shelves. Several poker games were in progress at rickety wooden tables scattered around the room. A lone pool table stood in the back.

Before long, the place was filled to capacity with eager, rowdy young males, the majority of whom had clearly come to the bar with two goals in mind. The first was to get as drunk as humanly possible. The second had to do with the young Korean girls and women lined up along the wall at the back of the room. Dressed provocatively in mail-order American fashions, they beckoned to potential customers in broken English, trading their favors for *won* amongst the sailors and servicemen.

Two women approached Jack at the bar. Both wore identical painted-on smiles and heavily applied makeup. They reminded Jack of the hollowed-out dolls in the windows of the five-and-dime store back home. False and plastic, with unseeing eyes forever focused on nothing, as if they knew once their usefulness was spent they would quickly be discarded for newer, more expensive toys.

Jack had no interest in them. He turned them away before either one could say anything. The women's smiles faltered, only for a moment. Then their eyes moved on in unison in search of the next likely prospect as they sauntered away into the crowd.

Taking his drink with him, Jack went over to one of the tables to play poker. Winning nearly as many hands as he lost, he had almost broken even a few hours later when he realized he was drunk. Judging from the glassy-eyed stares of those around him, so was everyone else at the table.

He couldn't recall how many shot glasses were placed in front of him over the course of the evening. But it was more than a few. When he looked down and saw two sets of cards in his hand instead of one, he knew it was time to call it quits.

At the back of the bar, a woman in a snug blue dress nudged a young Korean girl forward in the direction of Jack's table. The girl hesitated at first, looking back at the woman. She nodded, urging her on. As she came near to Jack's table, his alcohol-sodden senses took in her youthful face and long hair shining blue-black beneath the bare light bulb hanging from the ceiling.

Her eyes averted, she murmured something he couldn't make out.

"What?" he slurred, unsteady on his feet as he leaned toward her.

She looked up at him then, and something in her eyes held him. He couldn't discern what it was at first. Then it came to him. Despite her obvious youth, this girl had the world-weary eyes of a much older woman, one who had seen and experienced far too much too soon.

Abruptly, the girl's face began to shimmer. Her voice floated around him, as if it were coming from somewhere else. She took him by the hand and Jack followed as she led him across the room and out the back door.

Afterwards, as the American sailor lay passed out on the bed, Min groped around in the dark in search of her clothes. She dressed quickly. Then she stood in front of the room's only window and stared out at the starless night. She cracked the window to let in some fresh air. A whiff of gingerroot and stale cooking oil blended with the briny smell of the nearby docks to form an unpleasant cocktail of odors. A few streets over, muffled shouting and the sound of breaking glass broke the silence of the pre-dawn stillness.

It had been a long time since Min lined up with the other girls along the wall of the bar. But she didn't have a choice. She had lost her laundering job, and Joo Hee couldn't support the two of them by herself. At least this man had been kind to her, even gentle. Not like the others.

Closing her eyes, she tried to recall the gentle features of her mother's face and the soothing notes of her father's zither as he played. In her mind's eye, she saw him sitting on the floor of their hut next to the open *ondol* where they cooked their meals, his fingers dancing across the taut strings of the instrument.

She wiped away tears. As time passed, she found it more and more difficult to conjure up those memories that at one time were as familiar to her as her own reflection. She wondered if the same was happening to Joo Hee.

Making her way back to the bedside, she found the man's pants and shirt on the floor and quickly went through the pockets in search of a billfold or anything else of value. She found only a few crumpled bills and some change. She looked over at his hands. No watch on his wrist. No rings except for a thin gold wedding band she didn't dare try to remove while he was sleeping. Cursing the fates under her breath, she took the meager find and turned to leave.

As she walked across the darkened room she stumbled upon the wallet. It had fallen out of the man's pocket. She picked it up, looking over her shoulder at his sleeping form. Her first impulse was to get out and go through the contents later. But a sense of curiosity about this man compelled her, and she crept into the cubbyhole lavatory and turned on the light. Opening the wallet, she found his military ID.

Jack Thomas Dozier. United States Navy.

She tried to sound out the name in her mind. Her English skills being limited, she doubted she got it right.

Next to his name and title was a picture. Inside the bar, the lighting was poor, and she hadn't gotten a good look at his face. She studied the image staring back at her. He looked like any other white man she had encountered in her short lifetime, with the exception of his eyes. This man's eyes were kind.

Digging around further, she found another plastic card with his picture. It reminded her of the placards the bus drivers in Seoul wore on tethers around their necks. Min doubted Jack was a bus driver. It was probably a permit of some kind for driving an automobile.

She marveled at the thought of being able to travel from one place to the next, free to go about as you pleased. Rose at the orphanage had once told her that in America, you could go across state borders or even travel to other countries without fear of penalty or imprisonment. Min wasn't sure she believed her.

She leafed through some photographs, tucked away behind squares of clear plastic. Most of the pictures were of a young woman with sparkling blue eyes and a lilting smile. Min thought she was very pretty. Korean women all had similar eyes and hair, but American women, in her mind, had the luxury of being able to alter their appearance in any way they chose.

In the main section of the billfold she found a thick wad of currency, held together by a silver money clip. Min stared at the cash in disbelief. She had never seen this much money before in her life. And it was American money! Foreign currency went much further than the humble Korean *won*. Especially American one-color money.

A scenario formed in her mind as she thumbed through the bills. She had no idea how much was there, but she felt certain it was a lot.

With this kind of money, along with the meager savings they had stashed away, maybe she and Joo Hee could leave this wretched city and go elsewhere. No more crowded, smoke-filled bars. No more bowls of cold gruel. No more unwanted intimacies with piggish American men and their incessant appetites. Someplace quiet and remote, where the air was clean and the roar of tiger tanks didn't rumble through the streets at all hours of the day and night.

After gathering the few items of clothing she had left behind, she tip-toed to the door. She looked back at the darkened silhouette asleep on the mattress. A twinge of guilt pricked her conscience. It would be easier to steal from him had he been harsh or cruel.

Nevertheless, Min knew that if she and Joo Hee were to ever break away from the dismal existence they were now living, she had to seize this opportunity now and not look back.

Pocketing the wallet, she closed the door behind her and engaged the lock to ensure no one would disturb him. He would be safe there until morning.

Jack woke up alone in a dingy, single-room apartment above the bar, sprawled across a filthy mattress, his head throbbing and his wallet missing. The room smelled of sweat and hurried sex. Finding his clothes in a tangled ball on the floor, he stood and attempted to pull on his pants. He managed to get his left leg in before he lost his balance and fell back onto the bed.

The place was a dive. It wasn't even a real bed he was sitting on. Just a discarded, sagging mattress in the middle of the floor.

The room swam around him, and Jack fought back a wave of nausea. He leaned forward and held his aching head in his hands. As he sat there, bits and pieces of the night before started coming back to him.

Making his way up a rickety flight of stairs. A darkened room. The soft echo of a female voice beside him ... then beneath him. He remembered hearing the muffled sound of crying right before he passed out. Or maybe he had only imagined that part.

He immediately thought of Norma.

What have I done?

He hurriedly gathered his things and made his way back to the dock. Later, he went to the Master at Arms aboard ship and reported his wallet and military ID lost. He didn't want to report it as stolen for fear of an investigation. As far as he knew, no one else was aware of his indiscretion. Jack wanted to keep it that way.

He phoned Norma the next day before his ship headed back out to sea. In the ten minutes he was on the phone with her, as he tried to make himself heard above the hiss and crackle of static over the line, he told her three times that he loved her.

She laughed. "What has gotten into you?"

"I just miss you."

"Then maybe you should go away more often," she teased.

A month later, he was back home.

He never told Norma.

11

Late winter. 1953. Village of Yosu on the southernmost coast of South Korea.

Song Min had been in labor most of the long day. Sweat streamed down her face, despite the cold March air rattling the frosted panes of glass in the windows.

She held Joo Hee's hand and focused hard on the scattering of flakes swirling around in the night air. Earlier that day, a light dusting of snow had started to fall. Now it coated the frozen ground and surrounding hills of the remote village in a thin layer of white, eerily luminous beneath a full moon.

A plain-faced peasant woman, bundled in cumbersome layers of clothing and carrying a stack of kindling in her arms, shuffled into the room from outside. A gust of wind blew the door back onto its hinges. Another woman hurried to shut it behind her.

The pile of kindling landed on the floor with a clatter, and the peasant woman began stoking the fire in the small wood stove against the far wall. When she was finished, she settled her sturdy frame into a chair and stared at the floor, her mitten-clad hands clasped in her lap.

Min let out a guttural cry of agony as the muscles of her swollen belly tightened once again into a hard ball.

Finally, the pain subsided, and she fell back against the sweat-soaked sheets. Her young heart galloped in her chest as her breath came in ragged gasps. She knew the reprieve was only fleeting. The next contraction would come in a matter of minutes.

85

When Min's labor reached the eighteen-hour mark and her water still hadn't broken, the midwife—a tall, large-boned white woman with graying hair pulled back in a tight bun to reveal a pale, angular face—brought in a rolled-up cloth bundle. From it she took what looked like a long knitting needle with a curved hook at one end.

Almost as soon as the instrument was inserted, a gush of warm fluid soaked the sheets and towels beneath Min. She looked over at her sister with wide eyes.

"Everything is okay," the midwife said. "Your labor should be easier now." Min didn't understand what she said, but she saw the concern on the woman's face when she spied streaks of bright red mixed in with the clear fluid.

Min's labor continued two more hours.

Her eyes burned from crying and fatigue. Why had the gods allowed this kind of suffering to be bestowed upon her? Min cursed the fates and the day the American sailor had crossed her path. As soon as she and Joo Hee realized she was with child, Min had fallen to her knees beside her bed mat in their thatched hut, begging for this unwelcome product of that single night to be purged from her body. But with each passing month, her stomach only got bigger and bigger.

Min refused to pray anymore. She no longer believed anyone was listening.

The next contraction came on quickly, engulfing her entire mind and body in a white-hot vice of pain. She reached for her sister's hand.

"*Onni*!" she cried.

Joo Hee rushed to her side. She grasped her sister's hand tightly as she wiped her brow with a cool, damp cloth.

Taking deep breaths in and out, Min tried to focus on the flickering flame of a beeswax candle sitting on the wooden table beside her. The contraction lasted for a full minute. She loosened her grip on her sister's hand.

The midwife appeared at the foot of the bed. She lifted back the sheets, and Min felt fingers probing inside her. The woman frowned and withdrew her gloved hand.

"The baby is taking too long," she tried to explain in halting Korean. "It's a big baby." She shook her head. "I am not sure it can be born here this way."

"What do you mean?" Joo Hee asked.

"The labor is not progressing well. A doctor is needed to complete the delivery."

The advice sounded rational, but the small rural clinic was at least thirty miles from the nearest hospital, and they had no speedy means of getting there.

Min had no choice. She would have to deliver the baby here.

Exhausted and afraid, she burst into tears as she reached out once again for her sister's hand. The midwife's face softened. She patted Min's knee. "I will do what I can to get the baby here." Then she left the room to give instructions to the two other women standing outside the doorway.

Joo Hee held Min in her arms and rocked her gently as she cried. "This will be over soon," she told her. "This will be over and the baby will be gone."

Min's tears finally subsided, and she drifted off. Fatigue left her defenseless. But she did not sleep for long.

Min opened her eyes wide and sat up. A piercing wail escaped her throat as the next contraction racked her body. Joo Hee held her hand and talked her through it. Min begged for something—anything—to take away the pain.

The midwife injected some medicine through the plastic tubing that snaked from Min's arm to a glass bottle hanging next to the bed on a metal pole. "I can't give you too much," she explained. "I need you to push later."

As Min closed her eyes once again, Joo Hee sat on the edge of the narrow bed and leaned in close. She started humming softly in her ear—the same tune she had hummed in the peasant woman's hut as she combed out Min's wet hair the day they had first arrived in Anyang.

Hot tears burned behind her eyelids. How long ago that now seemed. More than anything else, she wished her *omma* was here with her now.

From somewhere far away, Min heard her mother's lulling voice singing to her. A smile lifted the corners of her mouth. She sounded so beautiful.

Then a more insistent voice cut in, one she couldn't quite place. Someone was calling her name, over and over again. Slowly, she opened her eyes. Her mouth was dry and her tongue felt thick. The midwife was shaking her shoulder, telling her to wake up. Joo Hee stood behind her.

"Time to push," the woman said.

Min tried to prop herself up against the pillows, but she couldn't. Her head felt too heavy for her body, like the weight of a drooping flower atop a delicate stem.

At the foot of the bed, the midwife placed Min's bare feet into two metal brackets. Her sister's face suddenly appeared next to her. "Almost finished." She squeezed Min's hand.

Min nodded. She tried once more to pull herself up in the bed. This time she was able to do so. She moistened her parched lips with her tongue. "Thirsty," she croaked. Her vocal cords felt raw.

The midwife nodded consent, and one of the women offered her a small tin cup. Min couldn't recall when a drink of water had tasted so good.

The sudden bolt of pain shooting through her abdomen took Min's breath away. The cup dropped to the floor with a clatter. Pressing her head back into her pillow, she clamped her teeth together to stop the anguished cry threatening to escape her throat.

It was no use. She opened her mouth wide and screamed.

Several people were in the room now. An air of urgency permeated the cramped space as they scurried about, fetching stacks of towels and other supplies at the midwife's direction. Two Korean women Min had never seen before came to the head of the bed, one on either side. They helped her sit up straight, offering her words of encouragement and instructions on what to do. Min could barely hear the sound of their voices through the thick veil of pain.

Leaning forward on her low wooden stool at the foot of the bed, the midwife's expression was bleak. She looked up at Min. "We must get the baby out now."

Min clenched Joo Hee's hand and pushed with every ounce of strength she had left. Finally, the midwife told her to stop. The pain was even worse now. With the next contraction less than a minute later, she was instructed to start pushing again. Min's eye caught the flash of a needle. A quick glint of steel. A bloody towel.

She looked over at Joo Hee. She was crying. The room began to spin. She couldn't seem to catch her breath. The midwife was shouting at her now.

"Push!" she exclaimed. "Push hard!"

Min did as she was told, drawing from some unknown reserve deep within her. With a final agonized scream, Min felt a sudden forward rush between her legs, like the breaking of a dam, as if her entire insides were flowing from her body.

She fell back against the mattress, bathed in sweat. It was over. She felt Joo Hee's arms wrap around her, felt her hot tears on her neck. The shrill sound of her baby's first cries filled the air.

Min closed her eyes. She felt strange, disconnected from her body somehow. As if she had turned into a wisp of smoke floating upward toward the low ceiling.

The midwife called for more towels as she filled a syringe with clear fluid. Joo Hee's face was a mask of concern. Neither one understood the words the midwife was saying.

A blood pressure cuff was wrapped around Min's arm. She felt it tighten once, twice, three times. Clearly, the midwife was not pleased with the results. Min saw her throw yet another towel, saturated with blood, onto the floor and reach for another.

To her surprise, she felt no pain now. A sense of calm enveloped her, like a warm bath. The feeling was unlike anything she had ever experienced before. She watched as one of the women wrapped her squirming daughter in a blanket and laid her on a nearby table. She could see the top of the baby's head, covered in dark silky hair. One tiny foot freed itself from the bunting cloth and kicked at the air.

My baby.

Min's body responded to her newborn's cries. Milk trickled from her engorged breasts and stained the front of her cotton gown. The urge to nurse was strong. She turned to her sister.

"*Onni,*" she said, her voice barely more than a whisper.

Joo Hee leaned forward to hear her.

"The baby... I do not want to do as we talked about."

Her brow furrowed. "But... we agreed. We were going to take it—"

Min reached over and grasped her sister's hand. "Promise me, *Onni.* Promise me this baby will go to America."

"But... *why?*"

89

Min looked out the window at the cold, harsh terrain. Across the way, she saw an old man leading a donkey laden with firewood through the snow. She remembered the cruel words the man had said to her earlier that day as she leaned against the clinic door holding her belly, waiting for the midwife to open the door.

"It does not belong here," she whispered. She turned to her sister. "Now promise me."

Tears spilled from Joo Hee's eyes and ran down her cheeks. "I promise," she said.

The light in the room began to dim, like the nub of a candle flickering out. The voices surrounding her seemed far away. Min looked over at her daughter again. Her mouth was moving, but she couldn't hear her cries. She found it hard to keep her eyes open.

Something is very wrong.

12

Kenneth Price stood alone on the third-floor landing, his hands clasped behind him as he looked out the window. Brooklyn and David were walking along the surf. She bent down and added another seashell to the collection in her bucket. Out on the deck, Michael was reading the paper with his feet propped on the railing.

Kenneth turned away and absently straightened a framed print on the wall. Every few minutes or so, he peered down the flight of stairs leading to the second floor. The door to the master bedroom was still closed.

What in the world could they be talking about for so long?

From the kitchen, he heard muted voices and the clanging of pots and pans. The pungent aroma of green onions and braised beef drifted up to him.

Shoving his hands into the pockets of his khakis, he began to pace. He craned his neck toward the stairwell once more. What hurtful things might that man be saying to his wife? *Sorry, lady. I don't care what kind of proof you say you have. I'm not your father. So long.*

Kenneth quickly dismissed the thought. He would have left by now if he had told her something like that. And besides, why would this man go through the trouble of making the trip down here when he could have written Helen off with a simple phone call? Or not even acknowledged her at all.

So… what was Jack Dozier's ulterior motive then? He had to have one. People usually did.

Maybe the old man was after money. He could imagine him schmoozing Helen even now.

Yes, I'm your daddy, sweetheart! I'm so glad we finally found one another. By the way ... I sure could use a little extra cash right now, the economy being what it is these days. After all, we're family, right?

Helen was so vulnerable right now, wanting so much to believe. She would probably give him whatever he asked.

Kenneth seethed inwardly. It wasn't the money. That wasn't the point. The bottom line was that he didn't trust this man. They knew nothing about him—the kind of person he was, what kind of life he led, the things he deemed important.

Jack Dozier obviously had no scruples. What kind of man woos a young woman to his bed, gets her pregnant, then leaves her behind in some war-torn country to survive on her own? He had no tolerance for those who failed to acknowledge their responsibilities.

He glanced at his watch again. They'd been in there for over an hour. He pondered the money angle once more, but with less conviction. As much as he hated to admit it, he knew the theory didn't hold much water. Kenneth had done his own research on Jack Thomas Dozier.

Earlier, he had taken note of Jack's Rolex watch and L. L. Bean clothing. Not top-of-the-line, but still pricey. Through his bank, he learned Jack's condo in Norfolk was mortgage-free and his credit rating was excellent. His car, a Toyota Camry, was also paid for. His only credit card, a Visa Platinum, showed an outstanding balance of less than two hundred dollars. The combined amount in his savings and checking accounts was in the six-digit range.

Not rich, but neither was Jack Dozier in any real need of money. There had to be another angle, one he hadn't thought of yet.

He stopped pacing. The door to the bedroom remained closed. Frustrated, he yanked his hand from his pocket to look at his watch again. A sudden shower of coins rained down the stairs, bouncing noisily off the maple treads to the next landing. In the closed confines of the stairwell, the sound was like bullets being discharged from a gun.

Kenneth froze. He expected the door to open any minute, a quizzical expression on his wife's face as she took in the silver and copper coins scattered across the stairs. Then her gaze would travel upward to the third-floor stairwell and find him there. The thought was too humiliating to ponder.

A minute passed, then another. Kenneth realized he was holding his breath. He quietly went down the stairs, pocketing the wayward coins as he went. When he got to the second-floor landing, he listened for a moment. He heard muffled voices, a snippet of Helen's laughter. He wondered what she could possibly find amusing.

He thought about pressing an ear to the door, but he wouldn't do that. It was one thing to pull up a stranger's financial records and credit scores. But to invade his wife's privacy was another matter.

He turned and headed down the stairs.

"Where is red pepper?" Karen's grandmother sorted through the bottles of spices and condiments in the kitchen cupboard. "Need more for *kimchi*."

Karen was at the island, chopping vegetables. "Nadine put it on her grocery list. It should be in there."

She finally found what she was looking for. "Nadine not here?" She added a healthy pinch of the fine red powder to the contents simmering in a crock-pot.

"She went to visit her sister in Raleigh. She'll be back tomorrow."

Nana joined her at the island and began slicing carrots. "She take the dogs with her?"

Karen nodded.

"Brooklyn not going to like that. You watch. She going to ask David now for a dog when they get home." She shook her head. "Can you believe those dogs be in bed with her this morning?"

Karen smiled. "I heard about that."

Nana resumed her chopping. "Dogs not belong in person's bed. Never heard of such thing until I come to this country. Okay to have as pet. But not sleep in your bed."

Karen's mouth twitched. The rule probably applied to cats as well. It was probably best not to tell her about Oreo, her outrageously spoiled black and white tabby who had a propensity for snuggling in the crook of her knees while she slept.

"Your Uncle David, he try to sleep with a lizard beneath his pillow once."

A burst of laughter escaped Karen. "A *lizard*?"

93

"No, not lizard. What the word for it? The wet kind that live in water."

"A salamander?"

"He find it by the pond. He think I wouldn't let him keep it." She shook her head. "I about jump out of my skin when I find it the next morning." She started on the celery. "They still talk upstairs?"

Karen nodded again. Nothing more was said, and they continued their work in silence.

A few minutes later, Jack and Mom appeared in the kitchen. Her mother lifted her nose and breathed deeply. "Something sure smells good." She held out her hand. "Omma, I'd like you to meet Mr. Jack Dozier. Jack, this is my mother, Kim Sung Gable."

She studied him for a moment, her sable brown eyes unblinking. Then she slowly bowed her head to him in greeting. He awkwardly returned the gesture.

"Is a pleasure to meet your acquaintance." Then she gestured for Jack to follow her. "Come, I show you how we make authentic Korean meal."

While Jack was busy with Nana, Mom joined Karen at the sink. "Where's your father?" She kept her voice low as she washed her hands.

"I think he's in the study." Karen glanced over in Jack's direction. His back was to them. "Well? How did things go?" she whispered.

"Very well, I think. I'll tell you later."

Kim Sung removed the lid from a large pot on the stove and stirred the contents with a spoon. The aroma was mouthwatering, with hints of braised beef and garlic and a spice Jack couldn't place. "This we call *galbi-gui*."

"They're beef short ribs," Helen explained.

"We soak overnight in marinade made of green onions and spices and sesame oil. Marinade very important. Then we grill."

"They smell delicious," Jack replied.

Kim Sung nodded. "They are." She took him over to the counter. "You have *kimchi* while in Korea?"

"Once." He hesitated to tell her the dish was awful.

"You have prepared by local villager or in restaurant?"

94

"In a restaurant. By the docks in Inch'ŏn."

"You not have real *kimchi* then," she scoffed. "Try this." She pierced some cabbage pieces with a fork and handed it to him.

The cabbage was tender, mixed with a little rice and cooked pork, flavored with red pepper and garlic. The morsel melted in his mouth. "Delicious."

"Secret is in fermenting."

"Fermenting?"

"In Korea, we have *kimchi* family recipe we hand down for many generations. We place *kimchi* in stone pots and bury in ground. When it is done, we have meal for many days. Here, we cook slow for full day in crack-pot." Jack suppressed a smile at her misuse of the word.

"You mean crock-pot, Omma?" Helen said.

Kim Sung waved a dismissive hand in the air. "No matter. My English good enough." She turned to Jack. "When we come here from Korea, I already adult. Only learn English when husband teach me before we get married. English a hard language to learn. Korean vocabulary much simpler. Americans take too many words to get to point."

"You're probably right about that."

She added more spices to the pot and turned up the temperature dial. "Please not misunderstand. English good language to know. Is language of the world, no? But hard to learn once you have Korean words stuck in your head. But my children, I make sure they learn both. They have teachers to help them with English I do not know. And at home, they speak both Korean and American language. Is good for them."

Michael stuck his head inside the doorway. "Need any help?"

Kim Sung put both him and Jack to work. She handed Michael a ceramic bowl filled with salad greens. "You can finish this. And we need dressing. Not the bottle kind." She gave him a recipe card. "Oil and vinegar are in pantry. I make the *bokgeumbap*." She then went over to the stove and started a large pot of water boiling.

When David and Brooklyn returned from their walk on the beach, Helen introduced Jack to David, who shook his hand instead of bowing. He was a slight man, with a relaxed, open face and straight black hair that fell like a drape across his forehead. Like Helen, his facial features and coloring gave away his Korean-American heritage.

Within minutes, he too had fallen under Kim Sung's direction in preparing dinner.

Jack leaned back against the counter and listened to the snippets of conversation flowing around him. Brooklyn talked nonstop to Helen about the treasures she had found on the beach, while the adults huddled around the island, discussing the food and other mundane topics.

Jack was perplexed. The scene was so *normal*. No grim faces, no tears, no talk of Helen's declining health and impending death. It wasn't anything like he expected. Some of the tension drained from his shoulders and back.

Helen came over to him. "Well, I see my mother has everything under control."

Jack glanced over her shoulder at Kim Sung, who was showing Michael the proper way to arrange the after-dinner fruit and tea platter.

"She does have a way of taking control of things, doesn't she?"

Helen followed his gaze and smiled. "That's my Omma." Facing him again, she said, "If you don't mind, I think I'll go track down my husband, see where he's been hiding for the past couple of hours. Dinner should be ready in about an hour." She touched his arm lightly. "Will you be okay here?"

Jack was embarrassed by her concern. "I'm sure I'll be all right."

Helen must have realized how she came across because she added, "I didn't mean anything by—I just didn't want you to think me rude, that's all."

"Of course I don't."

Brooklyn soon found another recipient for her seaside tale in Jack. She repeated her story to him as they set the table in the formal dining room.

"Daddy found a huge shell." Her eyes were wide with wonder. "It's orange and pointy all over and it's bigger than his whole hand!"

Jack folded a linen napkin at each setting. "Sounds like a conch shell to me."

"What's that?"

"Kind of like a snail shell. An animal used to live inside it."

"Yuck." Her eyes grew wide once again. "You don't think it's still *in* there, do you?"

"No, you would have seen the foot sticking out from the bottom of the shell."

"You mean snails have *feet*?"

Jack smiled. "Not really. They just call it a foot. It's so they can move across the ocean floor." Brooklyn still appeared stymied by this new revelation. "You'll have to show me all the shells you collected."

Her face brightened. "Do you really want to see them?"

"Sure." Jack handed the dinner plates to her, one at a time, as he followed her around the table. "How about after dinner?"

She set the last plate down with a flourish. "Can we have dessert first?"

13

Kenneth emerged from the den right before dinner was served. He gave a fleeting glance in Jack's direction as he sat at the head of the table. Jack didn't acknowledge him.

Brooklyn pulled out a chair. "Here, Mr. Jack. You can sit next to me."

He gave a mock bow. "I would be honored, my lady." Brooklyn clamped a hand over her mouth and giggled.

The conversation was light as everyone waited for Kim Sung to take her place at the table. Jack was overwhelmed by the amount of food. He counted close to a dozen bowls and platters of various dishes. Then he looked down at his napkin folded next to his plate. There was no fork or knife, only a set of wooden chopsticks and a soup spoon. Out of the corner of his eye, he saw Kenneth watching him with an amused expression.

After Kim Sung was seated, Helen said to Kenneth, "Honey, why don't you— "

"I was thinking," he interrupted, "since Mr. Dozier is our guest, I thought I would ask him to say the blessing for us."

Helen's gaze darted back and forth between her husband and Jack. She leaned toward Kenneth and said quietly, "Honey, maybe Jack doesn't feel comfortable—"

Kenneth held up a hand with a smile that didn't quite reach his eyes. "It's just saying grace." He took a sip of his tea, clearly savoring the awkward silence that had descended upon the room. "Is that all right with you, Jack?"

Jack surveyed the blank faces surrounding him. He knew full well what this man's intentions were. He contemplated getting up from the table, but then Brooklyn's shrill voice cut through the silence.

"We forgot to hold hands!" She took her father's hand, then Jack's. Everyone woodenly followed her lead. "Now we're ready, Mr. Jack."

Bowing his head, he racked his brain to come up with a suitable prayer for grace. Then he remembered a farmer's prayer his grandmother had taught him as a child. A simple incantation, giving thanks for friends and family and for the bounty of the earth.

When the prayer was finished, Karen said, "That was lovely, Jack." Helen smiled at him. He noticed the gleam in Kenneth's eye had dampened a bit. Jack considered the episode a minor victory.

David stood and addressed his mother. "What would you like to have first, Omma?" Jack noticed no one else had served themselves yet.

Kim Sung's eyes scanned the table. They settled on a large silver tureen. "*Guk,* please." He ladled out a bowl of thick, hot liquid and placed it in front of her.

Jack wasn't sure where to start. The aromas were enticing, but he wasn't familiar with any of the dishes.

Kim Sung must have noticed his hesitation. "Try the soup. We call it *guk.* Is very good."

Helen poured him a bowl and passed it to him.

"What kind is it?" The color and texture were unlike anything he'd ever seen.

"Seaweed soup," she replied. "With leeks and onions."

"It sounds gross," Brooklyn chimed in, "but it's really good. I cried the first time Nana made me try it. But then I liked it."

Jack smiled. He tasted a spoonful.

"You like?" Kim Sung asked.

He nodded his approval. "Very good."

She then explained the other dishes to him, and Jack took samplings from several bowls. Soon, his plate was filled with beef short ribs, *kimchi*, fried rice, *sinseollo*, steamed vegetables, and green salad with sesame oil dressing. He watched as the others took chopsticks in hand and began to eat. He finished his soup, then used his spoon to sample his fried rice.

Kim Sung turned to Kenneth. "*Sawi*, give our guest a dinner fork, please."

Kenneth hesitated for a moment. Then he went into the kitchen and did as his mother-in-law had asked. Jack made sure Kenneth saw him wipe the fork off with his napkin before using it.

Michael asked him about the Tidewater area of Virginia, and Kim Sung inquired about his time in the Navy. Kenneth concentrated on his food. No one asked any questions about a wife or children. Jack wondered if Karen had filled everyone in beforehand.

"Have you ever shot anyone?" Brooklyn asked.

David gave her a stern look. "Brooklyn."

Jack smiled. "No, I'm happy to say I never shot anyone. The ones who carry the guns are the Army and Marines. The Navy mostly stays in the water."

"Oh," she replied, sounding disappointed.

"Your father ... was he Navy, too?" Kim Sung asked.

"No. My grandfather was. My father served in the Army. He fought against the Germans in World War I. He was injured right before the war ended and was sent home lame."

She was solemn as she stirred her soup. "Very bad this war. And the one after that."

Kenneth's voice abruptly cut in from the other end of the table. "All war is bad."

"Sometimes it's necessary," Jack said.

Kenneth's gray eyes narrowed as he sat back in his chair. "Not when it involves sending our boys and men over to a foreign country to fight for a cause that doesn't concern us."

"Is there a particular war you're referring to?"

Kenneth shrugged. "Vietnam. Korea. I can see the Revolutionary War. Maybe the Civil War, although that particular conflict was about slavery and not about any physical threat to our country. But Vietnam and the Korean War? What business did we have being over there?"

"Fighting communism," Jack replied.

Kenneth sneered. "Spoken like a true military man. I don't believe any of it. Our military and the general public were force-fed a bunch of lies. Vietnam was about commerce and the exportation of tin, not communism." He pointed his chopsticks in Jack's direction. "The bottom line was money. That's what Vietnam was about."

"I see," he mused. "And what about the Korean War?"

"Communism may have played a small part. But the truth is that Truman was a pig-headed man who rarely took the advice of others, including those in his own cabinet. After the Chambers scandal, he needed something to put him back into the public's good graces." He shook his head. "Nothing like rallying millions of Americans around a war effort to win the nation's approval. Truman had no business conducting war efforts. He should have left those decisions to MacArthur."

Jack sensed this man was used to having the last word. He wasn't about to give him the satisfaction. "It's obvious you know nothing about either the Korean War or Truman," he said quietly. He did some quick calculations in his head. "In fact, I would say you adopted your views from someone else. You couldn't have been more than a toddler when the Korean War broke out."

Kenneth started to say something in reply, but Jack cut him off. "My father served under Truman during World War I in France. He was a captain in the U.S. Army at the time. He was put in charge of Battery D, my father's regiment. The only reason my father and his unit even made it home alive from that hellhole was because of Captain Truman's superb leadership."

Kenneth pushed his food around on his plate. He wouldn't look at Jack.

"And don't give MacArthur too much credit," Jack added. "Once Truman realized his error in trying to reunify Korea by force and pulled our troops back behind the Thirty-Eighth Parallel, it was MacArthur who got himself into hot water by publicly denouncing the president's decision—which I happened to agree with, by the way."

Kenneth leveled his gaze at him. "You're a Republican, aren't you, Jack?"

Jack was thrown off balance by the question. He looked around him. With the exception of Brooklyn, everyone had stopped eating.

"I usually vote Republican, yes," he replied.

"I figured as much."

"Why do you say that?"

"I can smell a Republican from a mile away," he said, as if the particular voting preference were some kind of dreaded disease.

"And I recognize a draft dodger when I see one," Jack tossed back.

Kenneth's tea glass stopped in midair. He looked as though he would rather toss out the drink and eat the glass.

"Where exactly did you run to?" Jack asked, goading him further. "Canada? Some neutral province over in Switzerland, maybe?"

Kenneth set his glass on the table. "The political stand I took over Vietnam is none of your business."

Jack returned his baleful stare. "And neither is my political leaning any of yours."

Helen spoke up. "Can we talk about something else, please?"

Kenneth continued as if he hadn't heard a word his wife said. "Do you believe in the draft, Jack?"

He nodded. "Yes, I do. I believe as a citizen of this country, if you're needed in time of war, you should go."

"Even if you don't believe in the cause behind it?"

"All war has political and financial overtones. But the bottom line in any war the United States has ever waged is national security, whether it's fighting the spread of communism or retaliation against terrorism. If you live in this country, you should be willing to defend it."

"How quaintly put," he scoffed. "You live in this country, therefore you're supposed to put your trust in the powers that be and just go off blindly into whatever conflict they deem necessary to involve themselves in?"

Jack nodded. "In a nutshell, yes."

He shook his head. "That's pathetic."

"Kenneth… please," Helen said.

Jack felt his anger rise. "Maybe so. But it's because of so-called pathetic men like me you still have freedom in this country today."

"Oh, *please*! Save me the Jack Nicholson rhetoric, okay? I saw the movie."

Brooklyn's head shot up at the sound of Kenneth's outburst. "Are you two arguing?"

"Your uncle is, yes." Jack reached for his tea.

"Don't try and throw this all back on me!" Kenneth fumed.

Well, you started it. The childish retort almost rolled off his tongue, but he caught himself in time. He picked up his fork and resumed eating his dinner, determined not to let this man get the best of him.

102

Helen made another attempt at steering the conversation elsewhere, but Kenneth continued his tirade. "I protested the Vietnam War because I didn't believe in it. A lot of us didn't. And we exercised our right to speak out against what we considered to be a waste of American lives. I was raised to question things, make my own choices. A man like you probably can't understand that."

"I'm no puppet," Jack replied. "But when my country needed me, I went. There's no shame in that."

"And there's no shame in my generation telling Uncle Sam we wanted no part in walking the Ho Chi Minh Trail just because a bunch of gooks and commies decided to declare war!"

Helen's fork dropped onto her plate with a clatter. "Kenneth!" she exclaimed, her eyes wide. Kim Sung stared at her plate. David was silent.

Kenneth's face fell. "I didn't mean—I meant the Vietnamese, not—"

"Daddy?" Brooklyn asked. "What are gooks?"

The color drained from Kenneth's face. He started to say something, but Kim Sung cut in.

"*Sawi.*" Not looking up from her plate, she spoke rapidly to him in Korean. Jack couldn't understand what she was saying, but her words hit their intended mark. Kenneth's cheeks turned crimson, and he hung his head.

Brooklyn asked the question again, and David told her he would talk to her about it later.

"But Daddy—"

"Not now, Brooklyn. You may go outside and play on the deck if you're finished with your dinner."

She pushed back her chair. "Don't forget about the shells," she whispered to Jack.

Karen stood and took the child's hand. "I'll go with you."

Dinner was finished in a shroud of silence. Helen dabbed the corners of her eyes with her napkin and only picked at her food.

Kenneth finally gave up. "To my wife, and to my brother and mother-in-law, I am truly sorry for offending you. It was not my intention." He excused himself, but not before leveling a fierce glare at Jack, as if he were the sole cause of this whole debacle.

In some ways, Jack felt the man was justified in his assessment. He shouldn't have allowed the episode to escalate like it had. "I apologize as well," he said, after Kenneth had left. "We shouldn't have argued at the dinner table."

"You didn't do anything wrong." Helen let out a breath. "Kenneth is very… passionate in his views, especially where politics are concerned. Sometimes he gets a little carried away. But he has his reasons for feeling the way he does."

She didn't say anything more, and Jack felt it best to leave it at that.

Helen forced a smile. "Who wants dessert?"

Coffee and dessert were served outside on the deck, and the conversation was steered far away from anything even remotely controversial. Kenneth didn't join them. Michael and Karen did most of the talking, and Brooklyn's animated chatter helped lighten the mood. David and Kim Sung listened but didn't say much.

Jack insisted on helping with the cleanup, so he and Michael loaded plates and bowls into the dishwasher while Brooklyn helped Karen and Helen wash the remaining dishes in the sink. David and Kim Sung excused themselves to their rooms.

When they were finished, Brooklyn took Jack outside onto the deck where her collection of shells sat soaking in a bucket of bleach water.

"Nana says I have to get the stink out before I can bring them into the house." She plucked a clamshell from the pile and brought it to her nose. She quickly drew it back. "Still smelly."

She then proceeded to show him the treasures she had found on the beach that day. One by one, she lined them up along the deck, telling him what kind of shell it was and where she had found it. Jack nodded and made the occasional comment, but his thoughts were elsewhere. How soon could he make his exit from this place? Tomorrow? The day after that? He decided he would give it two days at the most.

When they went back into the house, Helen met them in the kitchen. "I'll show you to your room." He bid Brooklyn goodnight and she scampered off.

As they neared the stairs, they caught up with Michael. He was carrying a suitcase in each hand, and a plastic container of toiletries was tucked under one arm as he bounded up the staircase to the second floor. Helen led Jack down a hallway to a back bedroom.

Karen emerged, her arms loaded down with clothes. "Michael will bring your luggage down in a minute." Helen busied herself with bureau drawers, stacking clothing into a laundry basket. The closet door stood open, empty except for a few pairs of shoes and another small suitcase.

It finally dawned on him that Karen must have told Helen his problem with the stairs. Now Karen and Michael were switching to another room so that he could stay on the first floor. "This really isn't necessary." First the argument with Kenneth. Now this. He stifled a sigh as he hung his cane on the back of the door.

"It's no bother," Helen assured him. "The guest room upstairs is bigger."

Michael returned with Jack's suitcase and overnight bag.

"Sorry for all the trouble," Jack offered.

"No problem." Michael took the laundry basket of clothes from Helen and ducked his head inside the bathroom to ensure he'd gotten everything. "That's all of it. See you in the morning."

Helen stood in the doorway. "Pleasant dreams," she told him.

Jack sat down heavily on the edge of the bed. The room was spacious and well-appointed, with a separate full bath, a sitting area, and French doors leading to a side deck overlooking the marsh. An antique bureau and armoire took up opposing walls. Beneath the turned-down duvet on his bed, he caught a glimpse of crisp white sheets and scalloped lace.

This could very well end up being my worst nightmare. But at least it's tastefully decorated.

A wave of fatigue swept over him, seeping into the very core of his being, clouding his thoughts. He pondered the extraordinary circumstances which had brought him to this beach house at this particular moment in time, a chain of events that began falling into place nearly fifty years ago, the moment he walked into that crowded Inch'ŏn bar.

Threads of doubt once again weaved their way through his mind. No one could prove he was Helen's father, not without a DNA test. Despite Karen's assurances about not having to provide a blood sample, he wondered what his response would be if he were asked to do so. Did he really want to know? The question plagued him, gnawing at the periphery of his weary mind.

Ten minutes. If I had tightened the noose around my neck just ten minutes earlier, I wouldn't be sitting here now.

Despite his eagerness to slip beneath the covers and go to sleep, Jack forced himself to ponder that last point a moment longer. He considered himself a rational man. He wasn't superstitious, nor did he believe in things such as horoscopes or tellers of fortune. But there was no denying that his being here defied logic.

I'm here for a reason. I have to be.

Outside his door in the hallway, a grandfather clock ticked off the minutes and hours. The only other sound was the cool breath of night whispering softly through the crack in the open window. He walked over and looked out through the glass. A half-moon the color of bone shone brightly against a backdrop of black sky. There were few stars. The ocean was calm.

He pressed his forehead against the window and closed his eyes. He saw Norma standing at the edge of a pier in a floral print dress, shielding her eyes from the sun's glare with a white-gloved hand as Jack's ship pulled in alongside the dock. Aboard deck, Jack stood back from the others and allowed himself to become lost in the crowd. He watched as Norma surveyed the clusters of men gathered along the railing, waving and blowing kisses to their families and loved ones below. Her facial expression started out eager, expectant. But after a few minutes of fruitless searching, her smile slowly transformed into a thin line of worry, and Jack could almost read her mind. Was he below deck? Had she missed him?

Then, at exactly the right moment, he stepped out from among the throng and leaned over the railing to capture her attention. Their eyes met, and she gave him her most dazzling smile, the one which never ceased to make his heart swell.

Jack opened his eyes.

That particular scene had taken place in late summer, 1953, after his last tour of Korea was completed. After a young Korean girl had approached his table in a smoke-filled bar.

Back then, he was determined to forget about her. But he remembered her now.

"I didn't know," he whispered. "I didn't know."

106

14

Jack usually didn't sleep well in any bed other than his own. But to his surprise, he fell into a deep sleep almost as soon as his head hit the pillow. He awoke early, before six, and after showering and shaving, he left his room in search of a cup of coffee.

The house was quiet. He thought he was the only one awake at this hour. But when he went into the kitchen, he heard a shuffling noise over by the breakfast nook. He turned to find David standing there, paint palette in hand, a wooden easel in front of him. He whirled around at the sound of Jack's approach.

"Sorry," Jack said. "I didn't know anyone was down here."

"This is late for me," David replied. "I rarely sleep more than four or five hours a night." He dipped his paintbrush into a splotch of color and returned to his work.

Jack looked around the kitchen. "Uh... do you know if there's any coffee around here?" He would even settle for instant.

"Try the freezer."

Jack opened the door and found an open package of Folgers. Within minutes, the rich aroma of roasted coffee beans permeated the room.

"Would you like some?" He poured himself a cup.

"No, thank you. Caffeine makes me edgy," David replied.

Taking his mug with him, Jack went over to where David was working. He had chosen a corner of the room where the early morning light came in through the bay windows. On the canvas, a solitary golden yellow pear sat upright in a wooden bowl. Jack watched as he wielded a thin liner brush and applied the final strokes to a single olive-green leaf on pear's stem.

David lifted his paintbrush from the canvas and looked over in Jack's direction.

"Am I distracting you?" Jack asked.

"No." He pointed the blunt end of his brush at a spot somewhere behind Jack's shoulder. "You're standing in front of my model."

Jack took a step back and compared the fruit sitting on the table and the image David had created. He could hardly tell the two apart. "Have you been an artist for a long time?"

David nodded. "Since I was a child."

"Well, you're very good."

He pressed his lips together in acknowledgement, then continued working with a quiet intensity. Had it been anyone else, Jack would have thought the person rude or arrogant. But he sensed he was a soft-spoken man by nature, one who chose both his words and his actions carefully.

"Michael tells me you and your wife have an art gallery in New York."

"Yes, we do." He didn't take his eyes off the canvas. He switched brushes and added more highlight to one side of the pear. "It took us a few years to get established. But now we have a stable of regular artists that we feature." Like Helen, his speech was clear and concise, with only a trace of his native accent.

"Do you live in Brooklyn?"

He shook his head. "East Manhattan."

"I thought maybe you named Brooklyn after where you lived in New York."

David smiled. The gesture made his boyish face appear even younger. "There's a story behind that, actually." He rinsed his brush in a cup of water. "When my wife, Janice, went into labor, she didn't make it to the hospital in time. She gave birth in the back of the ambulance while we were stuck in traffic on the Brooklyn Bridge."

"Is she your only one?"

"Yes."

"Well, she's a charming child. And quite intelligent. You and your wife must be very proud of her."

Making eye contact with Jack for the first time since he had come into the room, he nodded once. "Thank you."

Jack watched him work for a couple of minutes longer. Then he poured himself another cup of coffee and went out onto the deck. The promised warm front was making its presence known as an easterly breeze pushed lazy clouds across the sky. A handful of black-capped gulls swooped and chattered. Foamy white breakers lapped the shoreline.

Taking the steps down to the beach, Jack found his knees somewhat cooperative, and he walked out to where the sand was moist and firm. He was tempted to take off his shoes and socks. But the nip of the wind through the sleeves of his shirt told him it wasn't quite warm enough for that.

To the right of the beach house and across the main highway were the vast wetlands of the Outer Banks. He walked across the road to the marshy shoreline, the beach house looming behind him.

Endless acres of scrub and cypress trees, their knobby, moss-encrusted knees visible above the water, mingled with the inlets and passageways of the marsh in an ageless dance of harmony and accord. Beneath the murky water, oyster shells lay half-embedded in the muddy bottom of the estuary like the crooked teeth of a giant ogre. A few yards from the shore, a white heron stood at attention on stilted legs, half-obscured behind a clump of golden swamp grass, its graceful neck curving in on itself in a perfect letter *S*. The bird slowly turned its head in Jack's direction, its baleful gray eyes seeming to stare right through him. Then suddenly, it took to the sky, its massive wings beating the air with a rhythmic *thwump thwump*, like a bellows stoking a flame in a fireplace.

Norma would have loved it here.

He set his coffee cup on the ground and shoved his hands into his pants pockets and closed his eyes. Across the marsh, the cheeping of frogs was drowned out by the droning buzz of the few remaining cicadas and dragonflies.

Only in the past twenty years or so had Jack learned to truly relax. His early years were spent on the family farm in rural Indiana, working twelve-hour days in the fields alongside his father and the farm hands.

His father had loved the land. Jack didn't. The day after his eighteenth birthday, in an attempt to get as far away as he could from what he considered a barren existence, he joined the United States Navy.

But some things can never be entirely left behind. The strong work ethic and sense of responsibility honed on the farm served him well in the military. But his narrow outlook made it difficult to shed that persona once he walked off the pier.

Norma tried. She encouraged Jack to find a hobby, to bring out his creative side. She lured him with leisurely picnics in the park, long Sunday drives, and hours tending their garden. Gradually, he learned to let go. By the time retirement age came around, he was ready for it. Cooking classes, gardening, travel—they did it all. And he was a better man for it.

When Jack returned to the beach house, he found Kenneth busy at the stove. Clad in a chef's apron dotted with lobsters and blue shell crabs, he was pouring pancake batter onto a griddle. David was at the sink, rinsing out his paintbrushes. Brooklyn was perched on the countertop beside the stove, spouting instructions to her uncle. "They have to be just the right size."

Kenneth dropped a dollop of batter onto the Teflon surface. The mixture slowly spread out into a circle roughly the size of a small salad plate.

"No, no, no," she insisted. "That's too big."

"I think you're right. Someone else can have that one." He moved the bowl over to another spot on the griddle. "Let's try again."

The next pancake turned out too small, at least according to Brooklyn. "We'll let Aunt Helen have that one," he said.

He finally got it right on the third try. "That one's just right!" she exclaimed.

Jack felt as though he were caught up in a modern-day version of a classic children's story. He suspected this particular heroine would not be intimidated in the least by something as trivial as a trio of burly brown bears.

"Good morning, Mr. Jack," she said. "Uncle Kenneth is making me silver dollar pancakes. Do you know what those are?"

"I sure do." Jack went over to the coffee pot and poured himself a fresh cup. "I used to get them with whipped cream and peach slices at a place called IHOP. Is that where you had yours?"

"Mine came with chocolate chips sprinkled on top," she said. "It was at a pancake place Aunt Helen took me to in Kill the Devil Hills."

Kenneth and Jack smiled. Neither of them had acknowledged the other. Jack was content with the situation.

"Where's Aunt Helen?" Brooklyn asked.

Kenneth frowned. "She's not feeling well, sweetie. She's sleeping in this morning."

"Is she all right?" Jack asked.

Kenneth placed another pint-sized flapjack onto a serving platter. "She didn't sleep well," he replied curtly.

Jack went over to the breakfast nook. As David poured orange juice into glasses, Brooklyn hopped down from the counter and joined them. "Nadine sure is going to miss a good breakfast. Is she coming back today?"

"She's supposed to," David said.

"Is she bringing Star and Ringo back, too?"

"I'm sure she is."

Brooklyn didn't say anything more at first, but Jack could see the wheels turning inside her head. She followed her father into the formal dining room, where three more place settings were laid out to accommodate everyone.

"They're nice dogs, don't you think, Daddy?"

"Yes, they are indeed nice dogs."

"I was thinking..." she said.

Jack knew where the conversation was going.

"Nadine says she might let Star have puppies next spring." She toyed with one of the forks. "They're not very big, and they don't eat a whole lot. Maybe we could keep one."

"You know how your mother feels about dogs." His vocal tone held little conviction.

"She doesn't like *big* dogs, Daddy. Dachshunds are little." She pronounced the word like *Datsun*. She looked up at her father expectantly. "*Pleeeeeaase?*"

"Hmm... I have a feeling your mother and I would end up taking care of it."

"Oh *no*, Daddy!" she exclaimed. "I'd take care of him. I promise! I'd feed him every day and give him water and take him for walks and—"

111

"Let's wait and see, okay?"

Jack suppressed a smile as Brooklyn trotted off, her mission accomplished. He caught a glimpse of her as she skipped down the back hallway, humming to herself.

"We have a loft apartment in the middle of New York City." David shook his head. "Not very convenient for a dog."

But Jack had the distinct impression the decision was already a done deal.

Breakfast was a casual affair, with everyone coming downstairs at their leisure and helping themselves to the plates of food laid out on the kitchen island. Michael and Kenneth did the majority of the cooking, while Karen laid out store-bought muffins.

"What is it about men and breakfast?" She watched her husband deftly turn slices of bacon in a skillet.

"What do you mean?" Jack asked.

"Breakfast food. It's the only type of cooking men seem capable of doing. Why is that?"

"You forgot outdoor grilling."

"Oh, yes. How could I forget that?"

"It's a gene thing, I think," he quipped. "We're born with it. That one and the I'm-too-smart-to-stop-and-ask-for-directions gene."

She laughed. "You have a great sense of humor, Jack."

"You have to these days."

"Can I ask you a question?"

"Sure."

"The way you interact with Brooklyn. You're obviously very good with children. And yet…"

"You mean, where did I learn that since Norma and I never had any?" Jack opened a bag of bagels and placed them in a basket. "Growing up, I always had younger nieces and cousins and nephews hanging around. And you can't be married to someone who taught grade school for thirty years without some of it rubbing off on you."

Kim Sung came down a few minutes later, dressed in a floor-length silk dressing robe, her hair pulled back and wound into a tight knot at the nape of her neck. Helen wasn't with her. She and Jack filled their plates at the island. "Would you join me in the dining room?"

"Of course." He was glad for an excuse not to sit at the breakfast nook table, where Kenneth sat absorbed in his coffee and morning paper.

Kim Sung gave Jack a knowing smile and carried her plate to the dining room.

David appeared in the doorway with a teakettle. "Tea, Omma?"

"Yes. Thank you." She sat with perfect posture as her son poured, her small hands clasped in her lap. "Have you ever tried green tea, Jack?"

He shook his head, and Kim Sung indicated for David to serve him a cup as well. He stood with kettle in hand as Jack sampled it. At first, he detected little taste. Then a hint of something sweet washed over his taste buds. "What flavor is that?"

"The base is green tea. Korean blend. Very different from black tea. Then I add cranberry and almond for flavor."

David returned the kettle to the stove before he went to fill his plate at the island.

"Your son is quite attentive to you," Jack said.

"David is very good son." She poured maple syrup over her pancakes. "In Korea, is custom for the young to show respect for elders. Is important aspect of our culture."

"I think our youth here in America could benefit from more of that."

"Yes. All three of my children went through… what do you call… phases. They try to get away with things. Especially my youngest, Elizabeth. It did not last long."

Jack remembered what Helen had told him about her father's early death. "That must have been hard for you. Raising three children by yourself."

Kim Sung moved her eggs around on her plate. In the faint morning light filtering through the dining room window, her complexion was the color and texture of old parchment.

"Yes. It was," she said softly. "But when you have children—when you watch their faces while they are sleeping, knowing they depend on you—somehow you find a way to put aside sorrow and continue." She sighed. "I have learned over many years you cannot control the seas. But you can control sails of your boat."

113

Jack sensed she was referring to more than the passing of her late husband. She grew quiet then, and both found themselves oddly comfortable in each other's silence. As they were finishing the last of their tea, Jack spoke up. "I would like to hear about how you and your husband met. Helen tells me it's an interesting story."

A glimmer shone in Kim Sung's dark eyes. "I would be honored," she said softly. She pushed her chair back from the table. "I go check on my daughter now. We will talk another time." The sound of rustling silk followed after her.

Jack collected their plates and cups and was headed toward the kitchen when Kenneth strode into the room. He didn't bother with any pleasantries.

"We need to talk." He looked at his watch. "My study. Be there in ten minutes."

15

Jack waited only a few minutes, then went off in search of the den. By the time he reached the open door, his irritation was at full boil.

Kenneth sat behind a massive mahogany desk, his newspaper folded into quarters on the leather-trimmed blotter. He was working the crossword puzzle. Jack took note of the writing instrument in his hand.

"Someone once told me that people who use a pen to do crossword puzzles are either extremely arrogant or too smart for their own good. Which one are you?"

Kenneth let the question hang in the air.

Jack shut the French doors behind him and strode over to the desk. "How dare you speak to me like some kind of hired servant! You've treated me with disdain from the minute we pulled into the driveway yesterday. I want to know why."

Kenneth placed his Mont Blanc pen into a holder on the desk and slipped the newspaper into a drawer. He still hadn't made eye contact. He stood and walked over to an antique sideboard on the other side of the room. "My wife has informed me I behaved rather badly at the dinner table last night." He poured himself a glass of water from a pitcher. He didn't offer any to Jack. "Actually, I believe the exact phrase she used was 'horse's ass.'"

Jack pursed his lips and nodded. "That about sums it up."

Kenneth set down his water glass and went back to his seat. He extracted a cigar from a small humidor on the desk, then leaned back in his chair and rolled the cigar between his palms. He fixed Jack with a steady gaze. "Why don't you sit?"

"I'd rather stand."

He shrugged. "Suit yourself."

He rummaged through the drawers. Jack noted the items atop the desk. The man had certainly made himself at home. Kenneth's personalized stationary lay stacked in a letter holder, next to several framed pictures. He recognized Karen and Helen in a few of them. In the last one, a beaming Kenneth stood next to a dark-haired young man, his arm around his shoulder as the youth hoisted a huge trophy over his head.

More desk drawers opened and closed, with Kenneth muttering under his breath. Jack spied a sterling silver lighter, hidden from Kenneth's view behind one of the photographs. He didn't bother to tell him.

In the last drawer, Kenneth found a pack of matches. He took his time, stoking the flame until the end of the cigar was a red-gold ember. "At Helen's request, I've brought you here to apologize."

Jack knew it couldn't be this easy. "It's only lip service. You don't mean it."

"Doesn't matter. I'll just tell Helen you refused to accept my apology."

"And you could do that with a clear conscience?"

Kenneth blew a plume of blue smoke in Jack's direction. "Absolutely."

Jack shook his head. It was pointless to argue with him. "You still haven't answered my question."

"And what was that?"

Jack placed his palms on the edge of the desk. "You know perfectly well what my question was. And I want it answered."

Kenneth leaned back in his chair, the soft worn leather creaking beneath his weight. "I'm sure you're familiar with the term *opportunist*, aren't you, Jack?"

Jack was dumbfounded. "How can you possibly think—"

"I'm an intelligent man. I've seen every scam there is to pull, believe me." He removed the cigar from his mouth and sat forward, crossing his arms on the blotter. "I will not allow anyone to harm my family. Period. Is that understood?"

116

Jack didn't know whether to laugh in his face or punch him in the nose. He stood back from the desk and stuffed his hands into his pockets. "What in the world could I possibly want from you?" Then it hit him. "It's money, isn't it? You think I'm here to milk you for money."

Kenneth only stared at him.

Jack croaked out a laugh. "For a man so intelligent, you seem to have forgotten one small detail. I didn't ask to be brought here, remember? Your wife asked me."

"A mere technicality." Kenneth let out a final puff from the cigar and stubbed it out. "Why don't I make this easier for both of us. How much will it take to send you on your way this very hour?"

Jack was so astounded he could neither speak nor move.

Kenneth waited him out.

Finally, he took a seat in one of the plush leather chairs. The dark mahogany desk stretched out between them in what seemed like a mile-long expanse as Jack avoided Kenneth's eyes. The smell of Aramis cologne and cigar smoke hung heavy in the air.

Jack cleared his throat. "How much are you willing to pay?"

Kenneth's mouth formed into a smug grin. He removed an accounting ledger from a desk drawer and opened it to a blank page. Jack watched as he wrote out his name on the first line of the check. "How does ten thousand sound?" He waited, pen poised over the amount box.

"A man willing to pay that much can surely pay more," Jack replied evenly.

Kenneth put his pen down and laced his fingers. "Maybe. But then again, maybe not."

"Small price to pay for one's peace of mind, wouldn't you say?"

Kenneth took a moment. "Very well. Twelve thousand and no more." He signed the check with a flourish, then stood and placed it on the edge of the desk.

Jack stared at it.

"I expect you to honor our agreement. Pack your things and leave now. No goodbyes. No explanations." Kenneth picked up the phone. "I'll call you a cab to take you back to Norfolk."

Swiftly, Jack rose from his chair and snatched the receiver from him. He dropped it back into its cradle. Then he grabbed the check and held it in front of Kenneth's face, his cheeks flushed with anger. "You think you can buy everyone, don't you?"

Jack tore the check into small pieces. Kenneth watched as the bits of paper fell to the surface of the desk like confetti.

"I'm not for sale." Jack lowered his voice. "Do you think you're the only man ever to lose the woman you love?"

Taking a step back, Kenneth blinked. Finally, a reaction.

"I—I don't know what—"

"I've been where you are," Jack said. "I know what you're feeling."

For a moment, Kenneth's features went slack, and he looked away. Then his mouth formed a tight line and Jack saw something close in his eyes, like a shutter across a window.

"Don't ever presume to think you know how I feel." Kenneth swept the torn bits of paper into a wastebasket. "I'll see you out."

He quickly crossed the room and opened the French doors wide. Jack had no choice but to leave. As he passed by him in the doorway, Kenneth said, "For my wife's sake, I will not interfere with her wishes. But don't expect me to embrace you being here. Because I won't."

16

By early afternoon, Helen felt well enough to come downstairs. Kenneth had saved her a plate from breakfast, but she opted instead for dry toast and herbal tea. Outside, Michael helped Nadine bring her things in from her car while Karen and Brooklyn played with the dogs out on the beach. Jack sat in a wooden deck chair and watched.

"I would tell you good morning," she said, "but I think I'm a little too late for that."

"Feeling better?"

"Like new." She settled into a chair next to him. "I just needed a good night's sleep."

Despite the warmer temperature and the turtleneck shirt beneath her thick wool sweater, she still felt chilled. She knew she was overdressed, with Jack in a long-sleeved shirt and Brooklyn wearing only a light jacket, but she couldn't seem to get warm enough. She shivered.

"Are you cold?" He got up from his chair and brought back an afghan from the sunroom.

A lump formed in Helen's throat as he spread the blanket across her lap and legs. "Much better. Thank you. Did my husband talk with you this morning?"

"We spoke, yes."

"Then everything's okay between the two of you?"

Jack hesitated a moment. "Of course."

"Good." She knew the statement wasn't true. She looked over at the marsh with its breezy reeds of pampas grass and stalks of brown velvet cattails going to seed. "Sometimes my husband comes across the wrong way. But he really is a good man."

"I'm sure he is."

They sat in silence, listening to the crash of the pounding surf and the yipping of the dogs as they chased after Brooklyn. Overhead, stippled clouds, like splotches of white from a paintbrush, hung low in the midday sky.

"Where did everyone else go?" Jack asked.

"My mother went into town to run some errands. Kenneth and David went to the airport to pick up my sister." She smiled. "You'll like Lizzie. I guarantee it."

"Where is she traveling from?"

"Arizona. Not far from Sedona. She and her husband Dan have lived there for about five years now. He's a minister."

"Oh." Jack shifted in his seat. "That sounds... interesting."

"Does his being a minister make you feel uncomfortable?"

He shook his head. "No. It's just—well, the clergy I knew as a child didn't exactly leave a favorable impression with me. When I was growing up, the only minister I knew was Preacher Tucker. He was the most disgruntled man I've ever seen. And his wife—whenever us kids tried to cut through the parsonage yard to get to the swimming hole, she would come out onto the back porch with her broom and shoo us away like we were cats or something."

"They certainly sound like a jolly pair," Helen mused.

"Life of the party," he replied dryly. "I can see them now, tossing back a few and joining in on a rousing hand of strip poker."

Helen tilted her head back and laughed.

"No, wait. That would never happen," he said.

"You mean the strip poker part?"

"No, the playing cards part. Pastor Tucker preached against those."

"He preached against *card games*? For heaven's sake, why?"

He shrugged. "Something about playing cards going hand in hand with gambling and drinking and mingling with the wrong kind of people. Guilt by association."

She shook her head. "Well, let me reassure you Dan isn't anything like that. And Liz isn't like any kind of minister's wife you've ever met."

"What do you mean?"

Helen smiled. "You'll see."

She got up from her chair. "Would you like to go for a walk? It's such a gorgeous day."

"Do we have time? When is your sister arriving?"

"She won't be here until this evening."

He nodded. "A walk sounds good."

Jack waited while Helen went inside to grab a windbreaker. She called out to Karen, who waved in reply. They walked toward the shoreline, following a twin trail of tiny, forked footprints pockmarking the sand at measured intervals to the water.

"A piper," Helen remarked.

At the water's edge, a flock of seagulls feasted on the carcass of a large puppy drum. The fish's copper-colored scales reminded Jack of new pennies. He studied the remains with admiration. The fish was a prize catch for any fisherman.

"An old buddy of mine in the Navy used to do a lot of saltwater fishing." They turned away from the sight. "I tried it a few times. Never quite caught on to it. I prefer freshwater fishing myself."

"My father worked as a commercial fisherman when we immigrated to New York. He first learned the trade in Korea. He did it as a side job to bring in extra money."

"I take it mission work doesn't bring in much revenue?"

"We learned to make do."

"Does Kenneth fish?" He didn't care about the answer but was trying to make pleasant conversation.

The distant moan of a foghorn blared out across the cresting waves. "He likes deep-sea fishing. He takes five or six weekend trips a year."

"Does he catch anything?"

"He's quite good, actually. He caught a marlin once. About two years ago, down in the Keys."

"Do you fish?"

"Not really. At least not saltwater fishing. But I've caught a few perch and crappie in my day."

"Where at?"

"Here in Carolina. Kenneth has family over in Moyock, so we've been coming here for years. But it was my father who originally taught me how to fish. I must have been around four or five. All three of us, me and David and Lizzie, would drop our strings over the side of the boat and wait for the fish to come by. We didn't even have bait on our hooks. But we were fishing, just like Daddy."

A sudden gust of wind blew Helen's hair across her face, and she tucked the wayward strands behind her ear. "What about you?" She skirted a mass of tangled sea purses that had washed ashore. "Did you do much fishing when you were a kid?"

"Oh, yes. My grandfather taught me." He recalled those long summer days during his youth, before the cotton came in, when he and his brother would take their poles and a coffee can full of bread dough balls over to the pond—lazy hours spent lounging on the grass at water's edge, barefoot and sunburned, their poles upright in the mud as they waited for a nibble.

"I used to fish a lot with my brother Charles when we were young. Catfish mostly. But once in a while we'd snag us a bream or a perch." He shook his head. "I haven't thought about Charles in a long time."

"Were you close growing up?"

"He was three years younger than me, and sometimes he was a pest following me around everywhere. But we were close."

"What happened?"

"People change. Charles and I had very different ideas about what we wanted out of life." He asked about Helen's relationships with her siblings.

"We're only about a year or so apart. Our parents adopted all three of us within the first two years after they were married. Liz is the oldest. I'm the middle child. And David is the baby."

"Your parents never had any children of their own?"

"Omma says they tried. But she pretty much had her hands full with raising the three of us. And then... well, after my father died..."

"You seem very close to your sister and brother," he said.

"We are," she replied. "Lizzie and I were like two peas in a pod from the beginning. But David and I have become closer as we've gotten older. We didn't share a lot of interests growing up. David is very quiet, more serious-minded, even when he was a child. But don't let his reserved demeanor fool you," she added. "That man is *always* thinking."

122

"My brother Charles was the same way. He was constantly thinking up stories and songs, writing music in his head. He definitely had an artistic streak to him."

"Really? That's interesting. Was he a musician?"

Jack nodded. "He could play just about anything—guitar, banjo, harmonica. But his real love was the piano. He taught himself to play by ear on an old upright my mother inherited. Beethoven, Tchaikovsky, Chopin—he could play them all."

"Sounds like he was quite talented. Did he pursue a career in music?"

Jack stood still for a moment as the tide pulsed across the sand at his feet. "No, he didn't." He continued walking.

When they came to a small tidal pool about a half-mile from the beach house, Helen suggested they sit down.

"Are you all right?" he asked.

"I get tired easily, that's all," she replied, catching her breath.

She chose a large outcropping encrusted with barnacles, next to the rim of the pool. Jack sat across from her. Torn bits of green seaweed clung to the surfaces of the rocks, as transparent and fragile as wet crepe paper. The remains of an ancient fishing pier jutted out from the shore, the bulk of which had washed away over the years, leaving only the creosoted support beams and pylons behind. Gray pelicans and sea gulls used them as resting spots, standing sentry on yellow webbed feet, their downy feathers ruffling in the stiff breeze.

Helen planted her feet on a nearby rock and adjusted the sleeves of her windbreaker. Jack noticed several dark blotches encircling her wrists and forearms.

"Those bruises," he asked. "Are those from your cancer?"

Helen followed his gaze. "It's a side effect of the disease."

"If you don't mind my asking, what type of cancer do you have?"

"I have acute myelogenous leukemia. It's incurable." She said the words matter-of-factly.

"You say that as if you've talked about it a few times."

"I've been very open with my family and friends about all of this. But please don't think I'm stoic. I've had my days of crying spells and shouting at the heavens and throwing things around the room, believe me."

"And now?"

She sighed. "I've come to the point where I realize there's nothing I can do to change this. It doesn't mean I've given up. It just means I faced reality and decided I want to live out whatever time I have left on my own terms." The tone of her voice was expectant as she turned to face him. "Does that make any sense?"

Jack watched the play of emotions as they danced across her face. He thought of the length of rope in his kitchen drawer back home. He was glad he didn't have to lie to her.

"I understand what you're saying."

They sat in silence for a moment and then Jack asked, "What exactly is leukemia?"

Helen leaned forward and wrapped her arms around her knees. "It's a form of cancer. Most people, when they think of cancer, think of tumors. Which is usually true. But cancer is actually an overabundance of the wrong kind of cells. With leukemia, it's the blood cells."

"So, with this disease, your blood produces cancer cells?"

"Not quite. My bone marrow is abnormal—producing immature cells, mostly red blood cells, which carry oxygen, and white blood cells, which fight infection. My platelets are also low, which means I have a tendency to bleed and bruise easily. My clotting factors aren't working right."

Jack picked up a handful of pebbles. "Karen tells me there aren't any treatment options left."

"That's why I'm here." She shrugged. "We gave it our best shot. We tried everything out there. And I went into remission for about a year. But this particular type of leukemia has a very low survival rate. We weren't surprised when it returned."

"Your family seems very supportive."

Sudden tears sprung to Helen's eyes. She blinked them away. "Yes, they are. They're wonderful."

Beneath the shallow water of the tidal pool, a school of minnows darted back and forth. "Did you have anyone with you while your wife was sick?" she asked.

"Norma had several close friends who helped out," he replied. "Especially toward the end. They would bring over meals and sit with her. Talk with her. That sort of thing. Us men aren't very good at that kind of stuff."

Helen smiled. "No, you're not."

"But at least I can admit it. Isn't that the first step?"

She nodded. "That's what they say."

"I can't speak for all of us." He plunked the pebbles one by one into the pool. "And you probably already know this. But men tend to be more action-oriented. We much prefer to solve problems rather than talk about them. Which doesn't sit well when there's nothing we can do to help."

He turned his head to look out over the ocean, and Helen reached out to touch his hand. "But you *were* helping. Simply by being there."

Jack acknowledged her words with a nod. "I realize that now."

He recalled the scene in Kenneth's study earlier. The man's anger, his hostility, his overprotectiveness toward his dying wife—it was just a cover for his helplessness. *He's treading water. Feeling like he's about to go under for the third time.* The two of them were more alike than he cared to admit.

He was brought out of his reverie by the sound of Helen's voice. She was looking at him expectantly.

"Sorry. My mind was elsewhere. What did you say?"

"I asked if you wouldn't mind telling me more about your childhood."

Jack scoffed. "It's quite boring, I can assure you."

"I want to know everything about you." She sat cross-legged on her rock, waiting.

"Well… what do you want me to tell you about?"

Helen thought for a moment. "What is your earliest memory of your mother and father?"

Jack's mind drew a blank at first. Then, with sudden clarity, he saw his father as he rounded the corner of their old barn in Indiana, mopping his forehead and wiping grease from his hands. Jack was playing outside on the front porch while his mother, six months pregnant with Charles, sat in her rocking chair, shelling peas into a bowl.

When his father reached the porch steps, Jack toddled over to him, and his dad bent down and swooped him up into the air. The gesture never failed to bring a whoop of laughter from young Jack, and he could still recall the plummeting feel of his stomach when, for that brief moment, he found himself suspended in the air with nothing between him and the earth to break his fall. Then his father

125

would catch him around his ribs with his firm, calloused hands and he'd ask if he wanted to do it again. Jack's answer was always yes.

As he had aged, his short-term memory had faded a bit, but his long-term memory had grown sharper. He might not be able to recall what he had ordered for breakfast at Doumar's last Tuesday, but he could still remember in vivid detail the way his mother had looked in her good dress and Sunday hat, holding his hand as he sat next to her in church, feeling stiff and uncomfortable in his short pants and pressed white shirt.

"Funny how memories sneak up on you like that," he said.

17

Perched on his rock by the tidal pool, Jack poured out story after story about his childhood on the farm. Helen sat beside him, mesmerized by all that he told her. Every time he tried to stop, she would urge him to continue, eager for more knowledge about him.

At eighteen, he'd joined the United States Navy to escape his small town, even though Jack knew his father had hopes of passing the farm on to him. He suffered a devastating stroke while Jack was stationed in Hawaii. That left Charles with the responsibility of running the farm.

"At the time, he was in his sophomore year at a small junior college in northern Michigan, on scholarship, with a major in music and a minor in teaching."

Jack grew silent once again. Bright sunshine reflected off his silver-white hair, and when he tilted his head back to watch a tern as it flew by, Helen spotted a place on his throat he had missed while shaving. For some reason, the sight of the sparse silver bristles poking out from the folds of his skin saddened her.

"What became of your brother?" she asked. "Was he able to go back and pursue his music?"

Overhead, the sky was transformed into a pearly shade of gray as the sun took momentary refuge behind the clouds. The sparkle of a million diamonds suddenly winked out across the surface of the ocean. A belted kingfisher broke the stillness with his dry rattle call.

Jack cleared his throat. "We—they—couldn't get out from under the farm for another five years. Charles taught piano lessons in town for extra money. Norma and I sent home as much as we could to help out. When Dad passed away, the insurance money allowed my mother to let the land go at a loss. By then, Charles had married and started a family. After Mother sold the house and moved into town, there was just enough money left over for him to go back and get his teaching degree. He taught history and music for twenty years."

"Where at?"

"Our old high school in Indiana. Right back where he started."

Jack plunked another stone into the water.

"Not exactly what your brother had in mind, was it?"

Jack shook his head. "No. Not at all."

"And you blamed yourself."

"For a long time, yes."

"And now?"

Jack didn't answer. Instead, he slapped his palms on his thighs and said, "Enough about me. Let's hear about you."

Helen took her cue. "What do you want to know?"

"Tell me about how *you* grew up," he replied.

She told him that until she was six, her family lived on Cheju Island, off the Southern Coast of Korea. It was a place of endless wonder for Helen and her siblings.

"That's where I fell in love with the sea," she said. "We lived very close to the beach, so it was the first sound I heard when I woke up each morning and the lullaby that sang me to sleep at night."

At dawn, her father would leave their modest home to set out lobster traps and cast his fishing nets in the shallow waters of the island's barrier reefs. He returned in the late afternoon with Helen scampering beside him. While her father pulled in his nets, she would scour the shoreline for seashells and other treasures the ocean's depths had offered up.

The sand was powder-white, almost like talc, and wild ponies grazed and frolicked on the high rocky bluffs formed from underwater volcanic eruptions. Legend held that the ponies, once a prized possession of an island demigod, were set free from the skies hundreds of years ago by an evil spirit, cursed to roam the rocky cliffs for eternity, searching in vain for a way back to their heavenly homeland.

"At least, that's what the local villagers believed," Helen said. "But Daddy told us they originally came over from Japan about a century ago when a cargo hold full of ponies and horses were lost overboard and the survivors swam to shore."

Wintertime was devoted mostly to school and mission activities. "My father was disciplined but loving, with a heart to serve others. No one in need was ever turned away, regardless of religious affiliation—or lack of one. He believed in healing the outer wounds of the body and mind first and focusing on the soul later." Her mother, a converted Buddhist from her youth, stood by her husband in similar belief. "My father used to tell us you have to add feet to your faith. He said faith didn't do a person any good if you didn't act on that faith by helping others."

In the late spring, when varieties of sea life came to spawn in the coral-filled waters, her father would dive for octopus and sea cucumbers. Both brought a hefty price at market. He also harvested red sea urchins when he could find them. The cream-colored flesh was used for meat, and the roe were harvested and sold as *uri* to Japanese fishermen.

Her mother sat in the helm of their small fishing boat, peeling the cukes into long strips and laying them in the sun to dry. She refused to take part in the slaying of the octopi, which entailed biting the slimy creature hard between the eyes, a process which made Helen's stomach turn. But once the animal was dead, she quickly went to work, cutting the head from the tentacles and placing the thick pieces of pink flesh on blocks of dry ice.

The children were kept busy mending fishnets or doing other chores. If a child was old enough to run and play, they were old enough to work, both on land and at sea. Helen sat cross-legged on the deck alongside her brother and sister, their small hands extracting shrimp and fish ensnared in the nets. It was hard work for a child, but they didn't know it.

She described in detail the lush landscape of the island, with its cascading waterfalls and rolling hills covered in pink and red azaleas and waving eulalia grass, which tinged the fields with a silver flush in the fall and fed the herds of wild roe deer during the winter. Further inland were the foothills and mountains, surrounded by groves of Mongolian oak and dense forests of evergreens.

"Several times a year, we'd make the trek to Mount Hallersan, in the middle of the island. We'd start out before sunrise. By afternoon, we reached the trails that wound through the thick stands of woods to the foot of the mountain."

Beneath the towering canopy of fir trees, the temperature was much cooler and only a meager light illuminated the needle-strewn ground, which served as fertile conditions for tangles of morning glory vines and wild mushrooms. Gathering leeks and mushrooms in the apron of her *hanbok* as she went along, Helen became dizzy from leaning her head back as she walked, searching in vain for a patch of sky.

When they reached the summit, they would sit down to a picnic lunch of dried meats, fruit, and green tea. "My father never knew a stranger. He would talk to the tourists and point out things about the island."

"This Mount Hallersan," Jack interrupted. "I think I went there once while on liberty. You had to take a ferry from the mainland, right?"

Helen was excited by the prospect Jack might have visited her birthplace. "Yes," she replied. "Back then, they had ferry rides that went from Inch'ŏn to the island. But are you sure it was Cheju Island you went to? There are lots of barrier islands surrounding South Korea."

Jack told her he was pretty sure. "We hiked up to the peak with a group of other people. Took a good hour or so if I remember correctly. You could see the whole island from up there. I remember there were these huge rock formations below in the water. Really beautiful. And there was one in particular that was shaped like an old man's head and face."

"Yes!" she exclaimed, feeling almost giddy in her excitement. "He's like a legend on the island. My father used to call him 'Old Man River' but the locals called him '*Nulgan Sonbae,*' which means ancient elder in Korean."

Jack tried to repeat the words. Helen burst into laughter.

"Did I say it wrong?"

She nodded. "Um… yes. What you said was 'winged man with a top knot.'"

Jack smiled. "I think I like your father's translation better."

On their way back down the mountain, Helen and her siblings would go exploring. Omma inevitably found some new discovery to show her children. A great hawk—or *mae*—feeding her young in their nest, an unusual variety of wildflower, or the sour-sweet taste of a kumquat plucked from a bush.

Her father helped nurture Helen's love of the ocean, but it was her mother who instilled in her children the beauty and awe of nature and their birthplace. And yet, while Korea was Helen's homeland, she no longer considered it her home. Unlike her mother, who'd never quite grown accustomed to the glass and concrete of New York City. Helen knew that, even now, her mother still yearned for those distant shores of her youth and often heard the echoes and sounds of her native land in her dreams.

"I don't think my mother wanted to leave Korea."

"Then why did you?"

"Our father felt there were better opportunities for us in America. Better education, that sort of thing. Korea is a very different place now from when we were growing up. Back then, most schools only went up to seventh or eighth grade, and girls weren't encouraged to attend classes past grade school."

"Why do you think that was?"

She shrugged. "Cultural belief, I suppose. It was considered unacceptable, or *kumgi*, for a woman to know more than a man. Once girls had mastered the basics of language and remedial math, they were expected to help out at home and wait for an acceptable suitor to come along."

"You certainly went against the grain, becoming a doctor."

"Oh, I had my obstacles here as well, believe me. They weren't exactly embracing female med students in the '70s. Plus, it was a bad time then, what with the Vietnam War and the hippie movement."

"With everything going on back then, it must have been difficult to keep yourself focused."

"Not really," she said. "I was too busy to get involved with any of the social reforms. And I never understood the hippie thing, that whole drug culture scene. Neither did Kenneth."

"You knew him in college?"

"That's where we met. I was in my sophomore year and he was a senior at UNC."

"Is that where you graduated from?"

"I went there for pre-med. I was granted a scholarship for my first four years of college. I finished out my medical training at Cornell. It was one of the few universities back then that encouraged women to enroll in their medical program. Kenneth got his business degree and we got married shortly after he graduated. He followed me to New York and supported us while I finished my residency. Karen came along in my final year of medical school. She was… a surprise."

"That does have a tendency to happen."

Helen smiled. "Yes, it does. The pregnancy kind of threw a monkey wrench into our plans. But we were both ecstatic. Kenneth fell in love with her the minute they placed her in his arms. I took a year off to stay home with her, then went back to finish out my residency. Scott didn't come along until six years later, after I had started my practice."

The sun emerged from its veil of cloud cover, and Helen closed her eyes and basked in its warming glow. "There's something I think you should know about Kenneth."

Jack waited for her to continue.

"Kenneth's grandfather was killed in an air strike over Japan in World War II. He was a pilot in the Army Air Corps. Had volunteered to go. Kenneth wasn't even born yet when he died, but his father took his death extremely hard."

"Hence the anti-war and Truman rhetoric pounded into your husband's head growing up."

"Exactly. But that's not all. Kenneth's best friend was drafted into the Army in '69. Believe it or not, Kenneth applied to the armed forces but was rejected because of a congenital hearing defect."

Jack arched his eyebrows.

"Davy was sent over to Cambodia in the early part of 1970. He didn't last a month. They sent him home in a body bag. At least, the parts of him that could be found. He was only twenty years old." She studied the toes of her shoes for a moment. "Something died inside Kenneth that day, alongside Davy. They'd known each other since they were kids. He was like a brother to him."

"Early 1970. Wasn't that right before the Kent State incident?"

Helen nodded. "It was the last straw for Kenneth. He jumped right in with the rest of the protesters. He did the marches, the rallies, everything. He was so full of anger and grief. He used the war as a scapegoat to vent his frustrations. It took him a long time to get over it."

"Now I know why he was so angry at me about my comment concerning him being a draft dodger." He shook his head. "I shouldn't have said that."

"How could you have known?"

The late afternoon sun's glare waned, tinting the sky a yellow hue reminiscent of tea-dyed lace and old book pages. Terns and gulls cried mournful refrains as they floated along the ocean breezes, wings outstretched.

Helen looked at her watch. "I can't believe we've been out here for over two hours."

Jack stood, wincing at the pain in his left knee. "I suppose we should be heading back."

"Karen tells me you have arthritis," she said.

"A little." They started walking back toward the beach house. Both knees were now throbbing in full chorus.

"Which of your joints are most affected?"

"Both of my knees, my lower back. Sometimes my hips and hands."

"Sounds like a lot more than just a little. Have you seen a doctor about it?"

"I've dealt with it for years now. They say there's not much that can be done about it except alleviate the symptoms."

"If you like, I could take a look at your medication history and see if there's anything else I could recommend."

Jack thought about the offer for a moment. "I suppose that would be all right."

Helen stopped walking and stood in front of him. "Let me see your hands."

He held them out to her, palms down. She studied the left one first, then the other, gently bending his finger joints forward and back. Then she examined his nail beds and cuticles. "No sign of rheumatoid arthritis. What you have is clearly osteo in nature. The best thing to do is try to rebuild what's been lost and alleviate the inflammation."

She let go of his hands. "Stick out your tongue."

"What?"

"Your tongue. Let me look at your tongue."

Jack reluctantly did as she asked. After what seemed like an unbearably long time, she stepped back.

"You have high blood pressure, no?"

"A little. But... how did you know that?"

"And I would say you're also a little anemic."

After his last physical, his doctor recommended iron pills for precisely what Helen had just diagnosed, along with something for his blood pressure. Both prescriptions were still tucked away in his wallet.

He laughed. "You can tell that by looking at a person's tongue?"

"You'd be surprised." They started walking again. "A good iron supplement should be sufficient for the anemia. And there's an herbal tea blend I can prescribe for the arthritis. Very good for the joints. Drink two cups a day and you should start to feel a difference in a couple of weeks."

Jack didn't reply.

She smiled. "Let me guess. You don't like to take pills."

"It's not that. Well... that's partly true," he admitted. "You hear so much these days about the dangers of medications, even supplements and herbs."

"They can be dangerous only if you don't know what you're doing. I can assure you, the tea is perfectly safe. I prescribe it for my own mother."

That was good enough for him. "All right. I'll give it a try."

18

As the beach house came into sight, the array of sparkling diamonds scattered across the ocean's surface were transformed into red rubies by the sun's rosy glow as it began its slow descent toward the horizon.

"How did your adoptive father die?" Jack asked.

The question came out of nowhere, and Helen wasn't prepared for it. Even after all these years, talking about her father's death was still difficult.

"He was killed in a boating accident off Long Island Sound. One of the cranes that haul in the fishing nets broke loose from its foundation while they were pulling in a large catch. One man was paralyzed from the waist down and another suffered severe head injuries. My father died instantly. At least that's the story according to the Port Authority. I don't think we'll ever know exactly what happened out there that day." She shook her head. "That's the best scenario the police were able to put together."

"There was an investigation?"

"Not at first. The owners of the fishery who ran the boats tried to keep things quiet about it. They told Omma our father's death was his own fault. That he shouldn't have been standing where he was when the crane collapsed. Something about not following protocol." She waved a dismissive hand in the air. "We knew it wasn't true. My father was a seasoned fisherman. He wouldn't have done what they said he did."

"So, what happened?"

"I think my mother had her suspicions, but she didn't say anything. That was simply her way. My father was supposed to have life insurance when he switched jobs, but the company came back and said he wasn't with them long enough. So, we received virtually no money—just a few weeks of severance pay. We moved into a much smaller apartment, and Omma worked two jobs to keep a roof over our heads. Mostly in the fish market. But also as a waitress at a coffee shop near where we lived."

The work at the cannery was by far the most grueling. Working twelve-hour shifts in a stench-ridden, airless warehouse by the docks, laborers didn't have the luxury of paid vacations or sick leave or even hourly pay. Rather, they were paid piecework wages, which meant efficiency and speed were a necessity. And in that department, her mother excelled. Her small hands worked swiftly, brandishing the various knives and utensils of her trade, deftly filleting the tuna and flounder heaped in piles along the cutting tables. Slop buckets overflowed with fish heads and entrails.

When she returned home at the end of her workday, she soaked her hands in hot water and Epsom salts to ease her weary joints and scrub away the briny smell of fish. But the miasma lingered about her person, as if it had seeped into her very pores.

Helen dreaded that smell. She much preferred the odors that clung to Omma's clothes after working at the coffee shop, the aromas of coffee and cinnamon rolls somehow managing to lighten her mother's mood. But that job didn't pay as well as the cannery, so she only worked there one or two shifts a week.

Sometimes, when her mother was scheduled to work the evening shift and couldn't find a sitter, she would take the children with her. At the coffee shop, the owner let them sleep on a cot in a back room. After her shift was over, Omma would awaken them, and they would trudge home, half-asleep, along the darkened streets.

It wasn't as easy at the cannery. For safety reasons, children weren't supposed to be allowed in the warehouse. But the shift manager routinely turned a blind eye because she was one of his best workers. Always on time. Never complained. Nevertheless, he paid her a nickel less per fish than the other workers.

"We were very young. But we knew how hard Omma worked. It wasn't unusual for her to put in sixty- and seventy-hour work weeks. Without a cent of overtime, I might add. It used to make me so sad to see her so tired. But fortunately, all of that ended a few years after our father passed away."

She explained how one of the wives of the injured fisherman came to their home unexpectedly one day, six months after the accident. They started comparing notes of what they were told by the company. The accounts didn't line up.

"In what way?"

"Too many discrepancies. A bunch of little things that added up to a whole lot. They hired an attorney to look into it. His private investigator interviewed some of the men who were on board when the accident occurred. Most of them refused to talk, which was a red flag, but those who chose to speak had plenty to say."

Helen's mouth was set in a thin, angry line. "The boat was in violation of several codes. And the crane that collapsed had failed an inspection two months prior and hadn't been repaired. My father died and two other men were seriously injured because the fishery didn't want to shell out the money to replace a few rusted-out couplings on a faulty mooring."

"I take it your mother and the other woman sued the company."

"Most definitely," she replied. "And they won. Eventually. It took almost two years for them to settle. Omma was granted the most damages, including the life insurance payout the company had originally withheld from her. Turns out Dad was eligible for compensation after all."

"So senseless." Jack shook his head. "I'm sorry your family went through all of that."

"We learned to appreciate things more and to depend on one another. It made us stronger."

"So, did your mother leave the cannery?"

"Absolutely. The day the check came in, she left for good. Called in sick for the first time since she'd been hired and told them she wouldn't be back. To this day, she refuses to fillet her own fish. She buys them dressed from the market."

Jack laughed out loud. "Good for her."

"You want to know what she did with the money?"

"Took an around-the-world cruise for four and bought out the owners of the cannery?"

Helen smiled. "She bought her first house in the suburbs and went to work at a bakery to learn the trade. After about a year, she opened her own coffee shop. The rest of the money she stashed away for our college funds. She promised us that somehow, we'd all go to college."

"How in the world did she manage that?"

"That's another story." She hooked her arm through Jack's and they continued on.

As they neared the house, Jack pondered everything Helen had told him—the sacrifices one makes in life for those we love, whether it be a parent, a child, a spouse, or a friend. And how, to the one who gives of himself for the sake and well-being of another, it never seems a difficult task. Although there were some lean times growing up, Jack had never faced the kind of hardships Helen's family had endured. Kim Sung's steadfastness and persistence to make a better life for her children, despite the odds, left him with a newfound sense of admiration for her.

"Your mother is a pretty remarkable woman."

She smiled. "I think so, too."

"And from what you've told me, I think I would have enjoyed fishing with your father."

They were nearing the back deck of the beach house. Karen and Brooklyn and the dogs were nowhere to be seen. Helen said, "What you talked about earlier… about how you were trying to figure out what to do with your life when you were younger? I think my son, Scott, is going through something similar. I don't think he's happy where he's at."

"At college, you mean?"

"No. His life in general. I know something is bothering him. I have an idea what it is, but I can't seem to get him to open up to me about it."

"Ahh… a mother's intuition." He smiled. His mother had read him the same way, before he left home to join the Navy. "The CIA could learn a thing or two from moms. Have you told him you think you know what it is that's bothering him?"

She shook her head. "No way. That would only alienate him further. I've learned over the years the way to go about approaching my son is the exact opposite of how I talk to my daughter. Karen tends to spill everything at the drop of a hat. But Scott has to come to you when he's ready and not before." Her face brightened. "I'm sure it will all work out in the end." She stopped on the bottom step of the deck. "I'd like to take a walk on the beach every day while I'm still able. I'd love for you to join me."

Jack found himself warming to the idea. "As long as these old legs hold out."

She grasped his hand. "I'm so glad you decided to come here." Her eyes and her touch said much more than words ever could.

Jack finally broached the question he'd waited all afternoon to ask. "You said you have a favor to ask of me."

Helen looked over her shoulder at the pewter wind chime hanging on the deck. As if the object knew it was being observed, the chimes began to tinkle and sway, the last of the day's sunlight bouncing off silver-gray horses prancing on air.

"Do you like carousels, Jack?"

"Carousels?"

"You know… merry-go-rounds?"

He didn't understand the significance of the question. "I've never thought about it before. But… sure. I like them. Why?"

"Good," she replied.

Before Jack could ask any further questions, Helen walked across the deck and went inside.

19

Elizabeth Blakely tossed her crumpled cocktail napkin into the trash bin offered by the perky, petite flight attendant. Throughout the flight, Liz had watched the young stewardess flit about the cabin, like a hummingbird darting from flower to flower, doling out mindless chatter and packets of peanuts with an air of false cheer that was downright irritating.

She's gotta be new. No one can keep up that kind of pace for long.

"Is there anything else I can get for you, ma'am?" the singsong voice asked.

Liz took in the woman's perfectly coiffed hair, her perfect posture, her perfect white teeth. *You'd never catch this one with gravy stains on her blouse.*

"A steak and baked potato would be nice," she replied, deadpan.

The woman's smile faltered a bit. "Excuse me?"

Liz patted her arm. "It's a joke, sweetie." She leaned forward. "Lighten up," she whispered. "You're trying too hard."

The flight attendant moved on. Liz could tell she had offended her. But it certainly wasn't her intent. She shrugged it off. Sometimes pearls of wisdom fall on deaf ears.

Shifting her attention to the cabin window beside her, she watched as the thick cloak of clouds thinned to wispy shreds and tatters, allowing the lush Virginia landscape to peek through. So different from Arizona, which consisted mostly of terra-cotta hills and thirsty, rugged terrain. Looking down at the snow-capped mountains and endless acres of pine forest carpet, she was reminded of those long-ago years of her childhood, exploring Cheju Island with her siblings. How good it would be to see Helen and David again. A reunion was well overdue. She only wished it were under better circumstances.

Knowing the seat belt sign would be turned on soon, she made her way down the aisle to the bathroom. The cramped space was so small, she couldn't even bend over to pull up her pantyhose.

"This is ridiculous," she muttered, tugging at the waistband of her stockings while her knees drummed an out-of-sync beat against the lavatory door. Liz could only imagine what the person in the last row thought she was doing. Breathless, she finished the arduous task and washed her hands in the tiny metal basin.

Flying was such a hassle these days. You can't stretch out your legs. No room in the lavatory.

In other words, if you're not a size four, you end up feeling like a turtle forced into its shell by the time you reach your destination.

Which Liz most assuredly was not. She hadn't seen that particular dress size since her teens. Not that she considered herself fat. Liz preferred the phrase "full-figured." Her husband, Dan, liked to say she was nicely rounded in all the right places. Which was fine with her. Liz was a woman who knew who she was. But more importantly, she knew what she wasn't.

As she settled back into her seat, the pilot's tin can voice informed the passengers he would begin their final descent shortly. They would land in approximately half an hour, only ten minutes behind schedule.

Across from her, a twenty-something man dressed in a charcoal gray suit and tasseled loafers, checked his watch. He tapped his foot impatiently. Both hands gripped the handle of a black leather briefcase propped on his lap. His lips formed into a tight line of dissatisfaction as he mumbled something under his breath.

Liz couldn't imagine living the kind of life that didn't allow for ten extra minutes in your day. What if you suddenly felt the urge to take a brisk walk around the block? Or have a bowl of ice cream out on your back porch? Or play fetch with your dog? Or, better yet, sit quietly and do nothing? Liz firmly believed one should routinely make time in one's schedule to do nothing. It was good for the soul.

The harried traveler squirmed in his seat. *Helen used to be like that.* So preoccupied… so *busy*. As if she were afraid she would miss out on something if she slowed down. Her being diagnosed with cancer

141

changed that. Nowadays she seemed to be enjoying herself more, savoring life's fleeting treasures, taking time to breathe.

Which was the exact opposite of Kenneth. Predictable was a good word to describe him. Tedious was another. In short, Kenneth Maurice Price was about as flexible as a chastity belt.

Liz supposed those particular qualities had their merits at times. At least you knew what to expect. And to be fair, he was a thoughtful and attentive husband to Helen—except for his wife's recent wish of bringing Jack to Hatteras.

Kenneth had been against the whole thing from the beginning. Liz could understand his wanting to protect Helen, but couldn't he see how much this meant to her? She pondered on that as the plane circled the airport. Maybe he really *didn't* see. Yes, he had raised two children with Helen and had shared the same bed with her for nearly thirty years. But with sisters, whether the relation is by blood or by barter, there exists a unique bond where secrets and disclosures, like rare and precious gemstones, are forever held close to their hearts for safekeeping, and not another soul is ever made privy to them.

Liz was aware of her sister's lifelong wish of finding her biological father. It was a frequent topic of discussion between them and a deep source of emotional anguish for Helen. Was he still alive? Should she look for him? Does he even know she exists?

She was especially earnest in her search during her college years. Liz encouraged her to pursue what she felt she needed to do. But Helen had stopped short of contacting Jack.

Liz had never felt compelled to seek out her biological parents. Unlike her siblings, Liz's adoption papers were a matter of public record from the beginning. Both of her parents were American service personnel stationed in Seoul at the time of her conception and birth. From the day she was told of her adoption, she had accepted it, no questions asked. She lived her life in similar fashion, rolling with the punches, not taking things too seriously, knowing how blessed by God she was to have her family, her health, her home.

Neither she nor Helen had ever heard David talk about his mother, a young Korean girl who came to live at the mission a month or so after he was born. He was small for his age, and colicky. Omma tried to teach the young mother how to care for the child, and they tried several home remedies to ease the colic. But after weeks of

142

nearly nonstop crying, the couple awoke one morning to find the girl gone. She left David behind.

It was Liz's gut feeling that David had never really dealt with it. She supposed it was the reason why he had put off marriage and family until later in life. But his wife Janice, twice divorced but not quite ready to throw in the towel, had seen through all his excuses and called his bluff. Now, seven years and one daughter later, Liz had never seen him happier.

This time was important for all of them, especially Helen. This would be the culmination of a lifetime of hopes and dreams for her. Liz prayed she wouldn't be disappointed.

And pity the man if Kenneth stood in her sister's way of finding this last remnant of happiness that had eluded her for so many years.

Kenneth waited with David at baggage claim for Liz. Her brother ran the last few yards to greet her. Despite their marked difference in size, he lifted her off her feet and twirled her around.

Liz let out a whoop and David set her down. Even in flats, she was at least two inches taller than him. "How have you been, *Chakun Kom?*"

Kenneth took a moment to translate the phrase—little bear. It was a favorite endearment of theirs.

"Ahhh… I'm very good, *Arumdaun Kom.*"

Some other kind of bear… fair. Fair bear because of Liz's complexion and light red hair.

"And how is our *Ch'onsa Kom?*" she asked.

David's smile faded. "Our angel bear is… different. She looks very tired and thin. But her spirits are good."

"I think she's doing remarkably well under the circumstances," Kenneth interrupted.

Liz came over and hugged him. "How are you, Kenneth? You holding up okay?"

"I'm fine. Shall we get your luggage?"

Liz raised a brow at David. "Some things never change, do they?" she whispered.

After claiming her bags, they piled into the car and headed out toward Carolina.

"I thought about flying into Greensboro and driving to Swan Quarter to catch the ferry to Hatteras," Liz told Kenneth from the back seat. "But I wanted to take the scenic route."

Plus, her doing so ensured he would be inconvenienced. Kenneth had no doubt that was her plan all along. She seemed to take great pleasure in her attempts at riling him up every once in a while.

"Is this car new?" She ran a hand over the tan leather upholstery.

Kenneth caught her eye in the rearview mirror. "We traded in both of our Lincolns a few months ago."

"But weren't those cars only a few years old?"

He shrugged. "Helen wanted a new one, so I bought it for her."

Liz stared at him. "Since when do you go out on a whim and buy two new cars?"

Kenneth squirmed in his seat. Finally, he said, "They were offering no interest, same as cash."

"Ahhh… I see. The real Kenneth Price is back amongst us." She leaned forward between the seats. "David, how long are you staying?"

"Michael and I have to leave Sunday morning."

"But that's only two days away!"

"I have to get back to the gallery. We're having a major showing next week and Vince is on vacation. Janice can't do the whole thing by herself. But we'll be back for Thanksgiving. All three of us. I promise."

Liz sat back in her seat and crossed her arms over her ample chest. "Well, you could have at least told me you were leaving early." She sulked a moment. "Can Brooklyn stay?"

"Well… I hadn't thought about it."

"David, I haven't seen that child in nearly two years. If you have to go back to New York, the least you can do is let her stay with us. I'm sure Helen would like to spend more time with her only niece. And I want to see her, too."

"What about her schoolwork?"

"She's in *first grade*, for heaven's sake! What's she gonna miss?"

David smiled. "I'll talk to Janice." He turned to Kenneth. "Is there a problem with her being at the beach house?"

"Of course not."

"Then it's settled." Liz scooted back into her seat. "You go and carry your sorry butt back to New York. Brooklyn stays."

They stopped for a late lunch in Kill Devil Hills, then got back on the road. "Looks like things are starting to shut down for the season," Liz said, as they drove past diners and breakfast houses with hand-printed signs in the windows announcing the last date they would be open for business. Most were closing the day before Thanksgiving, but a few were staying open until the first of December to catch the final trickle of tourists before Christmas.

"Except for the outlet malls," Kenneth pointed out. "They're open all year-round now."

"Price of progress, I suppose." She rolled down the window. "It feels warm. What's the temperature?"

"We're at the beginning of a warm front," Kenneth replied. "Supposed to be in the upper 60s by tomorrow and through the weekend."

"Good. Maybe we can get Helen out of the house and do some things."

"The doctor said she shouldn't overexert herself."

"It's not like we're going to make her run around a track or anything, Kenneth." She started to say something else but stopped short when she met his eyes in the mirror. "What's wrong? Has something happened?"

"Helen's stopped taking some of her medications. Against my wishes and those of her doctor, I might add."

"I'm sure she has her reasons."

"She says they make her feel worse. She says she'd rather feel better and take her chances than extend her time and feel rotten." His voice faltered on the last few words.

"Then that's good enough for me," she replied softly.

"That's easy for you to say." A flush of emotion heated Kenneth's face. "You're not the one who's going to feel responsible if a complication arises."

Liz folded her hands in her lap and took a moment before replying. "Kenneth, I know this is a difficult time for you. It's hard for everyone. But this is *her* life, not yours. She has the right to decide how her course of treatment should go. Or not go." She stared at his reflection. "You think she's being selfish, don't you?"

"No, I wouldn't say selfish. But a part of me does wonder if she's thought about how these decisions will affect others in her life who care about her."

"But don't you understand? She *is* thinking of the others around her. She doesn't want this thing to drag on, for everyone to watch her slowly waste away." Tears sprung to her eyes, and she shook her head. "You and I both know she wouldn't want that."

"What did you have in mind to do?" David asked. "With Helen, I mean."

"Whatever she wants to do for as long as she's able to do it," she replied. "Dinners out. Maybe charter a boat for the day. And I know she'd love to see Ocracoke one more time."

A moment later, Liz asked the question Kenneth had hoped she wouldn't ask. "How did things go with Karen and this Jack Dozier? Did he show?"

When Kenneth didn't answer, David replied, "Karen brought him down yesterday. He's supposed to be staying about a week."

"A week? I would say that's pretty generous of him. What's he like?"

David's eyes cut over to Kenneth. "He seems very nice. Brooklyn took to him right away."

"I plead the fifth," Kenneth grumbled.

Liz sighed. "You're impossible, Kenneth." She directed her attention back to her brother. "Do you think he believes he's Helen's father?"

"I have no idea. But they talked for quite a while yesterday when he first arrived, and when I called the house earlier, Karen said they took a long walk out on the beach today."

She caught Kenneth's eye again in the mirror. "I can see you're dying to say something," she told him. "What is it?"

He shook his head. "I just don't think this is a good idea. What if he isn't who he claims to be?"

"I wasn't aware he was claiming to *be* anyone. Have you forgotten Helen was the one who started this whole thing?"

"You know what I mean. What if he's trying to take advantage of the situation?"

"In what way? What in the world could he want from her?"

"I don't know. I just don't trust him, that's all."

"What kind of motive could he possibly have?" she argued. "He never even knew she existed until a few days ago."

"What if he isn't her real father? Have you thought about that?"

146

"What difference does it make whether he is or not? Helen's never going to know."

Kenneth did a double take in the mirror. "*What* did you say?"

"I said, what difference does it make—"

"I heard you the first time. I just can't believe you said it."

She shrugged. "The way I see it, Helen has reason to believe this man is her biological father. Maybe he is, maybe he isn't. But he's here now. And she's obviously enjoying his company. I say leave it at that."

Kenneth said nothing more, but he couldn't help poring over the seed of possibility she had planted there.

They crossed the bridge spanning the choppy waters of the Oregon Inlet. As they neared Avon, Liz asked, "Did Helen find the carousel she was looking for?"

"I uh… I haven't spoken to her about it recently," Kenneth replied.

Liz narrowed her eyes at him. "You haven't helped her at all with this, have you?"

"I told you, Liz. I have grave reservations about all of this."

"You don't get it, do you? This isn't about you or me or anyone else. This is about *Helen*." She dismissed him with a wave of her plump hand. "Forget it. I'm not going to argue with you about this anymore."

David looked back and forth between the two of them. "I think she has her heart set on the one at Coney Island."

"That's a long way to travel," she said.

For once, Kenneth agreed with her.

"Coney Island," she said. "Do you remember the monkey?" Her smile widened into a grin.

David laughed. "I remember."

"What monkey?" Kenneth asked.

Liz scooted up between the seats again. "One day Daddy took us to Coney Island. We'd never seen anything like it before. All the rides and the attractions and the people. We were so fascinated, especially Helen. The carousel was her absolute favorite. She probably rode that thing a dozen times. Then we went to this area where a traveling carnival had set up this big tent, and there were these clowns doing a vaudeville kind of skit with some monkeys."

"You mean, like chimpanzees?"

147

"No, they were little, like the kind you used to see standing on street corners with organ grinders. They were dressed up like bellhops with these little shiny vests and caps. One of the clowns was wearing huge yellow shoes, and he had a monkey named Pepper, and they came over and stood right in front of us to do their skit. You know those trick flowers that clowns use? The ones that stick out of their lapel and squirt water at you?"

Kenneth nodded.

"Well, these monkeys had them on their vests, and Yellow Shoes ducked out of the way just as Pepper sprayed him, and the stream of water hit Helen square in the face." She doubled over with laughter. "She thought the monkey had peed on her!"

Kenneth burst out laughing. "Helen never told me that story."

"She cried and cried," said David. "Mom and Dad kept telling her it was only water, but Helen didn't believe them. From then on, she would never go near the monkey cage at the zoo or watch them at the circus."

Liz wiped away mascara from beneath her eyes. "Oh Lord, that was so funny. I'll have to mention it to her while I'm here and see if she still remembers it."

"I doubt she's forgotten it," David said.

Dusk crept in as they neared the outskirts of Hatteras. The next time Kenneth looked in the rearview mirror, Liz was asleep.

20

Helen was overjoyed to be reunited with her siblings and their mother, although Liz couldn't hide her shock at Helen's haggard appearance.

"I know I've looked better," Helen whispered in her ear as she hugged her in the kitchen. "You don't have to pretend."

Liz wiped tears from her eyes. "You're still our *Ch'onsa Kom*. Always."

Helen smiled and held out a hand toward Jack. "Lizzie, I'd like you to meet Jack Dozier."

Liz stood there, staring back and forth between the two of them.

Helen could guess what she was thinking. The eyes… the nose… the widow's peak. The moment grew awkward.

"How rude of me," Liz said. "Gawking at you like a fish in a bowl." She shook his hand. "Nice to meet you, Jack. I hope you enjoy your stay here."

The atmosphere during dinner was decidedly more pleasant than the previous evening. The conversation flowed freely, and Kenneth was surprisingly civil toward Jack. Nadine had prepared a huge spread of leg of lamb with all the trimmings, including a trio of desserts to choose from.

"I couldn't decide which one to fix," Nadine explained. "Plus, we all know how much Scott loves his sweets. This stuff will be gone before the weekend's up."

"Is he going to eat all the chocolate cake?" Brooklyn asked.

"No, sweetie," she assured her. "I'll make sure he leaves some for you."

"You should lock it in cupboard then," Helen's mother remarked.

"He's not *that* bad, Omma," Helen said.

"Oh yeah?" Karen piped up. "How about the time he ate my entire birthday cake?"

Helen made a feeble attempt at defending her youngest. "That was years ago. You two were just kids then."

"He was *sixteen*, Mom."

She shrugged. "Butter cream frosting always was his favorite."

Liz laughed into her coffee cup. "When does Scott get in?"

"He's supposed to be here sometime tomorrow morning," Kenneth said.

"He's driving?"

"Of course," Nadine said. "You didn't actually think he'd leave that hot rod of his behind, did you?"

"That boy would rather tinker around with cars than breathe," Michael said.

"Isn't that the truth?" Karen stirred cream into her coffee.

"Your brother likes cars?" Jack asked.

"*Vintage* cars," Michael emphasized.

"Daddy wanted to give him a new car when he graduated from high school," Karen said. "Like a going-away present for college. But he insisted on keeping that old clunker he had. He said it was a work in progress."

"Yes, but there was a catch," Helen added. "Tell them, Kenneth."

Kenneth dropped his napkin onto his plate and leaned back in his chair. "He came to me a few days after graduation and asked me if I was serious about getting him a new car. I told him yes, that I felt he deserved it for all the hard work he'd put into his wrestling and for making the Iowa State team. So, he said seeing as I was planning on getting him a car *anyways*, could I give him the cash instead to fix up an old '65 Mustang he'd found for sale."

"A chip off the old block, I'd say," Liz said. "Did you give it to him?"

Kenneth pursed his lips. "I gave him half."

"Cheapskate," she muttered.

"Helen and I went to see him during Christmas break. We went with him to take a look at this car. Let me tell you, it was bad."

Helen shook her head. "You couldn't even start the engine. And the frame looked like someone had taken a sledgehammer to it."

Liz's eyes widened. "Oh my."

"So, I made a deal with him," Kenneth said. "I gave him part of the money for the initial purchase to get started on it. Then I told him we'd reassess things after that. When he came home that summer, we didn't even recognize it when he pulled into the driveway. He had completely restored the thing."

"It was amazing," Helen said. "Scott did almost all the work himself."

"You didn't think he could do it, did you?" Liz asked Kenneth.

For a moment, Helen thought he was going to be angry. But then he shook his head and said, "I had no idea he was that good with cars."

Jack took his dishes to the kitchen but then was shooed out. "We've got this," Nadine said. After all the dishes were cleared away, Liz asked if anyone had brought a board game. All the men, except Jack, groaned in unison.

"No games," David said. "You can count me out."

"I'll second that," Michael replied. Kenneth smiled and shook his head.

Liz arched an eyebrow. "Ladies, did you notice that once again, it's the men who don't want to play?" She turned to Brooklyn. "What do you think?"

Brooklyn straightened her back. "I think they're just being scaredy-cats."

Liz sighed dramatically. "From the mouths of babes."

Jack was completely lost.

"It's kind of a tradition whenever Liz visits," Karen explained. "The women challenge the men to a board game. The men almost always lose."

"Your odds are even better with Jack here," Liz pointed out. "You have an extra player."

"We're still outnumbered," said Michael.

Nadine stood. "As much as I would like to whup all of your butts," she said to the quartet of males seated in front of her, "I'm afraid I'm going to pass. I'm pooped." She started toward the stairs. "Don't leave too many bruises, ladies."

151

"But that still leaves you guys with five on your team," Michael said.

"Brooklyn's six years old," Liz replied dryly. "She doesn't count."

The four men looked around the table at one another. Michael's gaze landed on Jack. "What do you say, Jack? You up to this?"

He shrugged. "Depends on what it is."

"How about Tri-Bond?" Liz suggested.

They replied with an emphatic no. "You guys are too good at that one, Sis," said David.

"All right then. How about Trivial Pursuit?"

More silence. "Are you any good at history, Jack?" David asked.

"Or how about old movies and TV shows?" Michael added.

Jack thought for a moment. "I would say I'm pretty good at both."

Liz baited them further. "We'll even give you a head start with one free marker in your game piece."

Michael scooted his chair back. "That won't be necessary."

He went to the closet in the foyer and returned with a box in his hands. A gleam of merriment danced behind his wire-rimmed glasses. "I went out and bought the new Genius Edition before we left the city. Special emphasis on sports and world news." He placed the game on the table as if laying down a gauntlet. "What do you say, ladies? Are you up to the challenge?"

"Bring it on," Liz replied.

Two hours later, the women celebrated their victory with relish, much to the chagrin of their male counterparts who sat glumly in their seats and waited for the hoopla to die down.

"I thought you said these cards were harder," Kenneth said.

"They're supposed to be," Michael muttered. His face brightened. "Best two out of three?"

"Let's go," said Helen.

Not long after, Brooklyn fell asleep in Helen's lap, and David carried her into the living room and laid her down on the sofa. Ringo and Star soon joined her, curling up into twin balls at her feet. Jack marveled at how she could sleep with the racket. Finally, around midnight, the winning game was decided in favor of the women when Kim Sung correctly answered a question about a little-known mountain range somewhere along the Pacific Rim.

Michael gaped at her in amazement. "How did you *know* that?"

Kim Sung just smiled at him.

Liz started to clear the board to start another game, but Jack held up his hands. "You'll have to continue the fight without me. I'm going to bed." He bid everyone goodnight.

In his room, he found fresh towels hanging in the bathroom and the bed linens turned back. No doubt Nadine's doing. A carafe of herbal tea sat on the bureau, along with a note from Helen assuring him the decaffeinated blend would not keep him awake. He poured himself a cup. He tasted a hint of almond. Not too bad.

Twenty minutes later, as the sounds of crashing surf and muted laughter lulled him toward sleep, he realized he felt at ease in this place.

And with these people.

It had been a long time since Jack felt even remotely comfortable in the company of others. After Norma's death, he had purposely cut himself off from everyone, like a mortally wounded animal that burrows inside an abandoned cave to die. Eventually, the phone stopped ringing and friends and neighbors no longer came around.

He thought of Charlie Little, his old pool hall buddy. They had met through their wives, who were both teachers, and the two men struck up an easy friendship. For years, they went every Tuesday night to Haddie's Pub in Ghent to drink a few beers and shoot the bull while they played a round or two of pool. But that routine had stopped long ago.

The last time he saw Charlie, he was complaining to Jack about how his wife Margaret wanted to take a trip to Rome for their fiftieth anniversary. Charlie didn't want to go. Not because he didn't have great affection for his bride of nearly half a century, but because he didn't want to spend the money.

Jack told his friend he was the most tight-fisted old fart he'd ever met. The dispute was finally settled when Margaret told her husband he could keep his fuddy-duddy self at home, and she took her sister instead. Jack had a good laugh over it, but Charlie hadn't thought the incident quite so humorous.

How long ago had that been? It had to be more than a year… no… two years now. He'd heard through an old acquaintance

Margaret had suffered a heart attack a few months after Norma passed away. She'd gone through a rough rehabilitation, he was told, but was doing better now.

Maybe he'd give Charlie a call when he got home. Meet him at Haddie's for a beer or two and a round of pool.

For old time's sake.

21

Sunlight peered around the edges of the drawn shades in Jack's room, warming his eyelids and coaxing him out of a deep sleep.

The sound of raucous laughter drew him toward the kitchen. For a moment, he thought the others had stayed up all night. But when he entered the room, he saw Helen and Liz at the breakfast table with a dark-haired young man between them. He was halfway through a huge pile of scrambled eggs and a stack of pancakes.

Helen introduced him. "This is my son, Scott. He just got in from Iowa State."

Jack could tell from the blank look on his face the kid had no idea who he was.

"Looks like I'm late for breakfast," Jack said.

"Nope." Nadine pulled a pan of blueberry muffins from the oven. "My favorite godson decided to arrive at the crack of dawn and announce he was hungry."

"I'm your only godson." Scott said.

"Oh, yes. I keep forgetting that. Would you like a muffin, Jack?"

The aroma of piping hot blueberries and cinnamon permeated the room. "Sounds good." He poured himself a cup of coffee and sat down. "I hear you're a wrestler," he said, to break the ice.

Scott nodded and drank more coffee. "That's how I got into Iowa State."

"Tough sport," he added.

Scott didn't reply.

155

"We were thinking of taking a boat trip later today," Helen broke in. "Kenneth went down to the dock to see if he can set up a chartered tour. Would you like to come?"

"Sure." Jack hadn't been on a boat in years.

The talk around the table dwindled until Scott announced he was going to bed to get a couple hours of sleep. He stood and stretched his arms over his head. "Nice crib, Mom. Dad actually agreed to spring for this?"

Helen took the ribbing in stride. "Come along, you. I'll show you to your room. I think we saved you a broom closet somewhere."

Helen had to stop on the second-floor landing to catch her breath. Her face felt cold and pasty. Scott looked at her with concern. He took her by the elbow to steady her.

"You okay, Mom?"

"I'm all right," she said between breaths. "Just give me a minute here."

Scott put down his suitcase. Worry creased his brow.

By the time they reached the third-floor guest room, Helen was winded once again. Scott led her over to the bed.

"I guess I'm a little more tired than I thought."

"Mom, you're worrying me."

"I'm fine." She forced a smile. "How do you like the room?"

From the way he rolled his eyes, she supposed he knew the question was a distraction. He looked around at the antique walnut furnishings and canopy bed draped in sheer white veiling. Through the open door of the bathroom, a slice of pale mocha walls and a claw-foot tub were visible.

He shrugged. "It's a little frilly." He went over to the large expanse of windows overlooking the ocean. "But the view sure is great."

He leaned back against the sill and crossed his arms. "You gonna tell me who this Jack character is?"

Helen met her son's gaze. "Are you going to tell me what's been eating at you for the past several months?"

"Wow," he said flatly. "And here I was thinking I was the poster child for the blissfully unaware all-American college kid."

"Quid pro quo. I'll spill my guts if you do."

"Is he the man from the wallet pictures?"

"Yes," she replied.

Scott turned away. He blew out a breath. "That's pretty heavy stuff, Mom."

Helen patted the space beside her on the bed.

"I think it's time we brought you up to date on what's been going on the past few weeks."

Later that morning, Jack took a short stroll on the beach with Helen. Eyeing his khaki pants and button-down shirt, she asked if he had brought any old clothes with him. He hadn't.

"You might want to go into town and buy a cheap pair of jeans or something," she suggested. "Deep-sea fishing can be pretty messy."

When they got back to the house, he borrowed Karen's rental car to go shopping and take a look around. The immediate area near the beach house was quiet and remote, mostly residential, with few tourists milling about.

He found a strip mall with a Wal-Mart and pulled into the parking lot. Keeping in tune with the surrounding landscape, scattered groupings of potted ficus trees and sea grass softened the harshness of the asphalt terrain. The effect was spoiled, however, by a pair of palm trees at the entrance, the top third of their trunks and fronds swaddled tightly for the coming winter in what appeared to be bright yellow plastic wrap. They reminded Jack of those crinkled pieces of cellophane on toothpicks. He had never figured out what purpose those things served.

When he returned from his shopping, he found Scott tinkering with his car in the driveway. Brooklyn stood on tip-toe beside the front fender, peering over the rim of the hood.

"Hello, Mr. Jack." She was dressed all in pink today, from her Hello Kitty sweater to her sneakers. "I'm helping Scott with his car."

"I see that." He surveyed the hulking engine block exposed before him. It was spotless. "You could eat off that thing."

Scott grinned. "I try to take care of her."

Jack stood back and admired the bodywork of the classic design. "Is this a '66?"

"Close. It's a '65." Even though the temperature was mild, he had already worked up a sweat. He used the sleeve of his T-shirt to wipe his brow. "You like old cars?"

"Well, I wasn't exactly a young man when hot rods became popular back in the '50s. But I did have a '57 Chevy."

Scott's eyes widened. "Oh, man. That make was sweet. Tail fins?"

"Of course."

"What kind of engine?"

"V8, three-on-the-column stick shift with bench seats. Even had a set of fuzzy dice hanging from the rearview mirror." He glanced down at the car's tires. "You ever heard of Port-A-Walls?"

He shook his head.

"Back then, you could buy either plain black tires or whitewall tires. Of course, everyone wanted whitewalls. But they were four bucks more apiece than regular tires. So, some company came up with these white rubber strips you could apply yourself. Called them Port-A-Walls."

"What color was the car?"

"Similar to this one, but darker. More like a maroon color, actually." He ran a hand over the gleaming candy apple red paint. "How'd you get it to shine like this?"

"Three coats of a special lacquer. Sprayed it on myself. Took me almost a month to get it right."

Jack was impressed. "Same engine?"

Scott shook his head as he handed Brooklyn a wrench and reached for another. "Those old Ford engines aren't worth sh—" He glanced down at Brooklyn. "Uhh... They're not worth shooting these days."

"You were going to say the 'S' word," she said.

Scott stood to his full height and wiped his hands on a rag. He was built like his father, stout and muscular, with a broad chest that tapered down to a narrow waist. But his striking facial features and full smile were his mother's.

"Is that so? And how do *you* know the 'S' word, little Miss Brookie?"

She shrugged. "I just do." Her rosebud mouth formed into a frown. "And don't call me Brookie. That's a baby name."

He winked at Jack and hooked a thumb in the child's direction. "Six years old." He tossed the grease-stained rag aside. "You wanna hear the engine?"

"Sure."

"I wanna do the key!" Brooklyn ran around to the driver's side door and clambered onto Scott's lap behind the wheel. Jack peered inside the vehicle. The interior was as spotless as the engine, with the original Pony seats and chrome detailing on the dashboard.

"You remember how we did it last time?" Scott asked her.

Brooklyn studied the shiny silver key dangling from the ignition as if it were a priceless gemstone. "We turn it that way." She pointed toward the windshield.

"That's right. Go ahead."

She grasped the key and turned. The engine came to life. "I did it! It was even easier than the last time."

"That's because you're so much bigger now," he said.

The three of them congregated once again under the hood as Scott expounded in detail on the finer points of the car's 350 V8 engine.

"This doesn't look like a Ford block," Jack said.

"It's not. This here is a Corvette LT1 engine. Straight from the factory."

"Really? And you were able to convert it?"

"You'd be surprised what you can do with today's engines. I replaced the original 289 and made all the changes. Purrs like a kitten, doesn't she?"

Jack thought the engine sounded more like the droning buzz of a dozen B52's circling on the horizon. "I have the feeling this cat has some pounce to it."

"Oh, she can run." Scott grinned. "The old engine went zero to sixty in about twelve seconds. This one will get you there in less than six."

Jack raised an eyebrow. "Impressive."

Scott made one more minor adjustment to the engine's carburetor, then closed the hood. He squinted at Jack in the glaring sun. "You wanna go for a ride?"

"Love to."

"Can I go, too?" Brooklyn asked.

"I tell you what." Scott crouched beside her. "Why don't you go inside and tell Nana and Aunt Helen we'll be back in a little while, okay? I'll take you for a ride next time."

Brooklyn crossed her arms across her chest. "Is this about 'big people talk'?"

"Huh?"

"Never mind." She turned around and headed toward the house.

"Are you sure we should do this right now?" Jack asked. "I thought we were leaving for the boat trip."

Scott pulled on a pair of mirrored Ray-Bans and started the car. "We're not leaving until around noon. And besides, my dad hasn't gotten back yet from the marina."

Jack got in and put on his seat belt. "If you say so. But if your father says anything about us being late, the buck stops with you."

Kim Sung watched from an upstairs window as Scott's car pulled out of the driveway. She was pleased to see that her grandson appeared to be taking a liking to Jack. She heard Brooklyn's footsteps bounding up the stairs.

"Hello, Sweetpea," she said.

"Scott says he and Mr. Jack will be back in a little while. They're going for a ride in his car."

She took note of Brooklyn's sullen mood. "Is something wrong?"

Shrugging her shoulders, the child twisted a thick strand of her dark hair between her fingers, a sure sign something was bothering her. Finally, she said, "Scott calls me Brookie."

"What does he call you?"

Brooklyn let go of her hair with a sigh. "He calls me Brookie. I don't like it."

"I see," she replied. "Have you told him this?"

"Uh-huh."

"And he is still saying this name to you?"

"Uh-huh."

Kim Sung took her by the hand and led her down the hall. "I am thinking we should do something about this."

160

22

"You ready?" Scott asked.

"As ready as I'm going to be," Jack replied. They were on a nearly deserted expanse of highway, the car top down, headed toward Hatteras. He braced his feet against the floorboard and waited for the initial surge of acceleration.

Scott floored the gas pedal, and the Mustang shot forward with a squeal of tires and smoke. Jack's head pressed back into the upholstery of the bucket seat. A sense of exhilaration coursed through him as the passing scenery of sand and surf flashed by him, slowly at first, then faster and faster. The salt-tinged air whipped through his hair. He released his grip on the door handle and enjoyed the ride.

Scott topped the car out at around eighty and kept it there for several miles. Jack was concerned when they came to a sharp curve in the road, but Scott handled the wheel easily, taking the curve at precisely the right speed. He swung out across the left lane, coaxing the tires to hug the median through the bend, then swerved back smoothly to the other side.

"Isn't she something?" He raised his voice above the sound of the rushing wind.

Jack marveled at how well the car ran. With that kind of power under the hood, he had expected a rough ride. "How did you get her to run so smoothly?"

"It's all in the suspension and framework. Every car is different. You gotta know which adjustments and revisions to make."

"Well, whatever you did, it works. She rides like a dream."

As they neared the outskirts of Hatteras, Scott lowered his speed. When they came around the final curve before the ferry, a state trooper's patrol car came into view, partially shrouded by a stand of cedar trees. They passed by without incident.

"How'd you know he was there?" Jack asked. An impish grin spread across Scott's face. "Let's just say I have a nose for speed traps."

He pulled into a convenience store gas station and topped off the tank. Jack took advantage of the break to use the restroom. When Scott returned to the car, he placed a grocery sack in the back seat.

"So…" He craned his neck around as he backed out of the parking lot. "Are you my grandfather or what?"

The question was blunt, almost rude. It hung in the air between them like an unpleasant odor. "Well… you're certainly direct, I'll give you that." Jack pondered on his response as they pulled out into traffic and headed back toward the beach house. A number of possible answers ran through his head. None of them seemed quite right. Finally, he said, "It looks like it might be the case."

"You don't know for sure?"

"It's a long story."

"Seems pretty simple to me," he replied. "I mean, you either are or you aren't."

Jack considered the strapping young man beside him, so full of the misconceptions and delusions of youth, when all of life's questions can be answered by a yes or no and every scenario falls neatly into a category of black or white, good or bad. In some ways, he was envious. "You'll find as you get older that things aren't always so cut-and-dried."

Scott's jaw clenched. "With all due respect, I think I know a little bit about life. Don't assume I'm naïve about things just because I'm young." They passed the same state trooper in silence, now parked a mile or so farther inland. "The details of how my mother was conceived are none of my business. And to be honest, I really don't care. All I want to know is whether or not you knew about her and what you plan to do about it now."

Jack stared straight ahead through the windshield until the road in front of him became a flat, gray blur. "I didn't know. Whether you choose to believe that or not is up to you. But I assure you it's the truth."

A few hundred yards from shore, an old barge sat anchored, its steel hull coated in layers of rust, a dozen sagging tire bumpers hanging listlessly from either side. The sight of it made Jack feel worn, used-up. "As for the second part to your question… I have no idea what I'm going to do from here on out."

Nothing else was said until they pulled into the beach house driveway. "Don't worry about my dad," Scott said. "He can come across as a jerk sometimes, but he really is an okay guy." He offered up a half-smile. "Most of the time."

They walked into the foyer just as Karen was hurrying down the stairs, still dressed in her bathrobe.

"Ahhh… the queen of torts has arisen," Scott said dryly. Despite his teasing tone, he embraced her warmly. "How you doing, Sis? You look great." He glanced over at Michael, who was standing beside her. "Wish I could say the same for you, bud."

Michael was clearly used to his brother-in-law's ribbing. "Good to see you too, Scott." The two men shook hands.

Karen yawned. "The jet lag must have finally hit me. I slept like a log last night." She ducked into the kitchen and returned with a bagel and a glass of orange juice. "I'll be just a minute." She hurried back up the stairs. "Don't leave without me."

"You gonna do something with that hair?" Scott called after her.

Karen stuck her tongue out at him.

Jack followed Scott into the kitchen, where the aroma of onions and dill pickles filled the air. In the laundry room doorway, Star and Ringo stood on their hind legs behind a mesh gate, licking their chops and whining softly.

"Don't you ever feed those mongrels of yours, Nadine?" Scott asked. He peered over her shoulder at a large serving platter piled high with boiled eggs. "Are those the awful deviled eggs you're so famous for?"

"You mean, the ones you dislike so much that you manage to eat at least a dozen every time I make them?"

When he reached over to snag one, Nadine swatted him on the hand with a slotted spoon. "Don't you dare," she warned. "Those are for later."

"Okay, okay." He started to turn around, then feigned to the left and grabbed one. He popped the entire thing into his mouth before Nadine could react.

"You should be the size of a barn with the way you eat." Nadine shook her head. "Lord knows I wish I had your metabolism."

Scott peeked inside the picnic basket. "I see you made your special fried chicken, too."

"I may have lived in New York for the past twenty years, but I know how to make a southern meal." She turned around to face him, hands on hips. "Would you believe Michael suggested we get *take-out* chicken?" Her facial expression couldn't have been more horrified if someone had picked up one of her dogs and thrown it across the room.

Michael was sitting at the breakfast table, his laptop open in front of him. He shrugged. "I was only trying to make things easier for you."

Nadine went back to work. "I appreciate that, sweetie, but I don't want easy. I want *good*."

Kenneth came down the service stairwell to the kitchen. "We're late." He glanced at his watch. "Our charter time is for noon."

Scott winked at Jack as he pulled out two six-packs from the grocery sack and placed them on the counter. "We were out of beer. And besides, Karen's not ready yet." He turned his attention back to Jack. "You ever been saltwater fishing?"

"A few times," he replied. "Didn't catch much though."

Scott walked over to his father and slung an arm around his shoulders. "Well, stick with this guy if you decide to put out a line today. He can show you the ropes. Right, Dad?"

An uncomfortable silence followed as everyone waited for Kenneth's response. He cleared his throat. "Sure."

Scott gave him a hearty slap on the back before going upstairs.

Liz was having a tea party with her mother and Brooklyn, along with several stuffed animals and dolls propped up in chairs around the table.

Scott poked his head inside the doorway. "Well, if it isn't little Miss Brookie. Why wasn't I invited to your party?"

Brooklyn poured air into teacups. "Hello, Winston."

164

Scott's smile disappeared. He looked at Liz, but she was as surprised as he was. Omma, her hands folded in her lap, continued with her instruction in the proper manner of serving tea.

"Very funny." He placed both hands on his hips. "Now which one of you told her that?"

"Told who what?" Omma asked.

"About my middle name."

"You do not like to be called this name?"

"You know I—" He stopped short, remembering what Brooklyn had told him earlier out by the car. "I think I see where this is going."

He went over and spoke to Brooklyn at eye level. "I tell you what. You don't call me by my middle name, and I won't call you Brookie anymore. Deal?"

"Deal." The child placed her toy teapot on the table. "But why did Aunt Helen and Uncle Kenneth give you such a weird name?"

He laughed. "That's a good question."

Scott and Liz's mother left to help pack up the cars. Liz was about to join them when Brooklyn asked, "Can I ask you something, Aunt Lizzie?"

Liz sat down in her chair. "Of course you can, sweetie."

Brooklyn made a fuss of putting away teacups and saucers, but Liz could see she was thinking hard. Finally, she said, "Aunt Helen is real sick, isn't she?"

Liz's heart fell. She prepared herself for what she knew was coming. "Yes, she is."

"Like my Mr. Hamster?"

Her brow furrowed. "Who?"

"My Mr. Hamster I got for my birthday last year. One day I found him all curled up in his corner. I put my finger through the cage, but he wouldn't move. Mommy came and took him out. She said animals get sick sometimes and go away and don't come back."

"Yes, that does happen."

Brooklyn looked up at her. "Is Aunt Helen going away, too?"

"Who told you she was going away?"

"Daddy says she's going to heaven soon to be with Jesus and the angels. But I don't want her to go! I want her to stay here with me

165

and you and Uncle Kenneth and everyone else." The tears came then, and Liz pulled her onto her lap and held her.

"I know you do, Sweetpea." She smoothed her hair as the child sobbed into the crook of her neck. "But sometimes we can't stop things like this."

"God can." Brooklyn's eyes were bright beneath her tears. "God can make her all better."

A child's simple faith.

She thought back to those seemingly endless days and nights after their father's death, weeks and months spent walking a tightrope of hope as fragile as the silken threads of a spider's web. How she wished everything could go back to the way it was. Daddy would walk off the pier again, smelling of fish and the sea, his pockets brimming with small treasures for them to find. But he never did.

"Yes… God could make her better," she answered carefully.

"Then why doesn't He?" Her face crumpled again. "He's got plenty of angels in heaven. Why does He need Aunt Helen?"

Liz's own eyes brimmed with tears as she rocked her. "God isn't the one taking her from us, Sweetpea. The cancer is."

"Well then I *hate* her cancer!" she exclaimed. "I *hate* it!"

Liz held her close and let her cry until she was done, all the while knowing, like a charm taken from a bracelet, a tiny piece of this child's innocence was lost forever.

23

Helen caught sight of the *Nettie B*, sitting with its motor idling at the end of the marina dock. The others followed her and Kenneth to the pier, loaded down with picnic baskets and coolers. A man climbed down the ladder and welcomed them.

"Captain Marty Byrum," he said. "Glad to have you folks aboard." The sound of the boat's rumbling engines nearly drowned out his voice.

Helen liked him right away. Dressed in jeans and an oversized Hawaiian shirt, with a jolly face and a belly to match, he looked like an aging Beach Boy.

"Is this a forty-footer?" Kenneth asked.

"Forty-five," he replied. "You do much boating?"

"We used to have a small pleasure boat a long time ago. Nothing like this. How old is she?"

"The registration papers say twenty." Captain Byrum rubbed his salt-and-pepper beard. "But she looks so good for her age, I shave off about ten years when people ask. Just like my wife. Right, darlin'?"

A petite, middle-aged woman emerged from the cabin, dressed in a pair of dungarees and a denim work shirt. She carried a bucket filled with cleaning supplies. "I don't know what you just said about me"—she fluffed her helmet of silver hair—"but I'm sure it was charitable." She extended her hand to Kenneth. "Name's Nettie. Nettie Byrum."

She turned to Helen. "And you must be Helen."

There was nothing remarkable about the woman's face—good skin, a rather plain nose, soft gray eyes. And yet, Helen was unable to turn away.

Nettie smiled and released her hand. "Let me show y'all around."

While Nettie gave everyone a tour of the boat, Helen and Kenneth went with Marty to the helm and talked about the current fishing reports.

"A few wahoo and marlin were spotted in the Gulf," Marty said. "And striped bass and triggerfish are biting up a storm in the sounds."

While they discussed the plan for the day, Helen went below to catch up with the others.

"Here's the tackle cabinet," Nettie said. "Plenty of rods and reels to choose from, and you have your pick of lures or live bait."

She moved about the cabin, explaining the galley features and safety precautions. Brooklyn was fitted with a life jacket, the smallest they had.

She made a face as Nettie pulled the item over her head. "It smells funny."

"That's because we have to strap these onto the bigger fish when we catch 'em so they don't jump out of the boat!" Nettie winked at Helen.

Right before they were set to leave, Kenneth brought a portable oxygen tank below deck. Helen's eyes darted between the green oblong tank and Nettie. "Do you think that's necessary?"

Kenneth stowed the tank beneath the galley sink. "Just to be on the safe side, okay?" He leaned in to kiss her cheek, then went back up to the deck, leaving the two women alone.

"So much frustration," Nettie murmured. "But it stems from his love."

"I'm sorry, what?" Outside, the boat's engines revved, and the boat rocked gently against the dock. Helen reached out and steadied herself against the counter. The air inside the cabin felt close, with lingering odors of Pine-Sol and lemon-scented furniture polish.

"It's getting near for you, isn't it?" Nettie asked quietly. Helen could only stare at her. The woman reached out and placed a hand over hers. "This thing you seek. You will find it. But not where you thought."

Helen was dumbfounded. Who was this woman? And how did she know these things? She started to say something in reply, but Nettie patted her hand and quickly climbed the galley stairs to the deck.

Minutes later, as the boat pulled away from the dock, Helen saw her standing on the pier, watching them leave. On impulse, she waved goodbye, but Nettie had already turned back to the dock.

By midafternoon, the welcoming November sun lay like a glaze across the water as the *Nettie B* left the Hatteras Inlet and went around the southernmost tip of Ocracoke Island. Along Silver Lake Harbor, barnacle-encrusted shrimp boats and old fishing rigs shared the same docking space with lengthy yachts and sleek pleasure craft in an odd mix of cohabitation. Offshore, a clam boat raked the muddy bottom of the lake, leaving clouds of clay-colored sediment behind in its wake.

"That there is the oldest lighthouse in the Outer Banks." Marty pointed. "The Coast Guard owns it now."

Jack could just make out the white mortar structure of the Ocracoke Lighthouse, barely visible above the tree line.

"Can you still go inside it?" Karen asked.

"Oh, yes. It's one of the biggest attractions here in the village."

"It doesn't look very tall," David added.

Marty chuckled. "She may not be very big, but she's a trouper, that gal. Survived some of the roughest storms this area has ever known. Back in '44, she was about the only thing left standing when a big nor'easter came barreling through here. The tide flooded the area all the way up to the doorstep, but not a drop of water got inside."

"You were there?" Scott asked.

"How old do you think I am?" he quipped. "No, my granddaddy told me about it when I was just a pup."

"Does the lighthouse still work?" David asked.

Marty shook his head. "It functions as a nightlight of sorts now for the village. They turn it on every evening and off again at sunrise." He steered the boat through a break in the buoys, then headed south. "It'll take us about an hour to reach the deeper parts of Raleigh Bay," he said. "Might get a little choppy."

Jack took hold of the boat's railing with both hands and adjusted his stance to match the rhythmic rise and fall of the vessel as it crested the churning waves. His stomach lurched once, then settled in for the ride. Helen carefully made her way over to him. Jack was aware of Kenneth's watchful eye next to Marty at the helm.

"You look a little pale," she said.

Jack felt his stomach somersault once more. His mouth began to water. "I'm afraid I'm out of my usual element right now." He grasped the railing tighter, willing himself not to be sick. "It's been more than thirty years since I've stood on the deck of a boat." He felt the remains of his breakfast rise into his throat. He swallowed hard.

Helen rummaged around in her jacket pocket and pulled out a small flesh-colored patch. "Try one of these. Kenneth picked them up for me at the drugstore earlier." She removed the backing and handed it to him. "Place it behind your ear or on the back of your neck."

"What is it?"

"It's for motion sickness." She turned her head so that he could see where she had placed hers. "I didn't want to take a chance with all the nausea I've been having lately. I thought of offering you one earlier, but I figured with you being in the Navy…" She shrugged.

Jack smiled. "Rather ironic, isn't it?"

Nadine emerged from the galley. "Who's ready to eat?"

Jack clutched a hand to his stomach, and Helen laughed. "You go ahead. I think I'll wait a little while."

Nadine called up to Marty to ask if he wanted anything. He told her his wife would have dinner waiting for him when they got back. "Nonsense." She looked at her watch. "That's hours from now. We can't have a hungry captain onboard. I'll fix you up in a jiffy."

She took him a plate of fried chicken, potato salad, coleslaw, and cornbread. Despite his previous protests, the captain settled into his chair and dug in, one foot wedged between the wooden spokes of the wheel, steering the boat.

Instead of returning to the galley, Nadine came up next to Jack at the railing. She eyed him as if he were a stowaway cowering inside a lifeboat. "You're not eating?"

Jack could feel everyone's eyes on him. "Maybe in a little while."

She came closer. "You okay? You don't look so good." Her ginger-colored hair was pulled back in a tight bun. The style brought out the fiery blue of her eyes but made her face appear fuller.

"My stomach's a little queasy, that's all."

"Ahhh… I've got just the thing." She waddled away in her penguinesque stride. When she came back, she handed him a plastic cup.

Jack looked at the fizzing contents and took a sniff. "What is it?"

"Old family recipe. Guaranteed to settle your stomach."

"Helen gave me one of those patch things."

"Those things take an hour or more to kick in," she scoffed. "Go ahead. It won't hurt you."

He took a sip of the frothy concoction.

"You have to drink it all at once," she said. "That's how it works."

He finally resigned to drink the stuff and get it over with. He handed the cup back to her. "Tastes like… Alka Seltzer."

"It is. A double dose. Mixed in Sprite instead of water, with a pinch of ground ginger thrown in. It'll soak up all that acid you've got churning around inside your stomach. In a few minutes, you'll—"

Without warning, Jack let out a booming belch. Marty jerked his head around to see where the sound had come from, then let out a hearty laugh. Brooklyn giggled and covered her mouth with her hand.

Jack's face burned. "Sorry," he mumbled.

Nadine laughed. "What for? Better out than in, I always say." She wagged a finger at him. "I expect you to partake of my wares like everyone else. Can't let all this good food go to waste. I'll make sure plenty is left for you below deck."

Jack stood facing the ocean a few minutes longer, stifling a string of sodium bicarb-induced emissions that felt as though they were coming all the way from his toes. He let out one last rumble, then took a deep breath of the salt-tinged air. To Nadine's credit, he *did* feel better. And suddenly hungry, too. He went down to the galley.

The picnic baskets and coolers had been emptied of their contents, which were laid out along the galley counters. Everyone else had broken off into pairs or small groups to talk while they ate.

Nadine handed him a plate. "Here you go. Get it while the gettin's good."

Jack pulled up a chair next to the counter. He noticed Nadine wasn't eating. "Did you eat already?"

"I sampled too much of this stuff earlier while I was making it."
She reconsidered the platter of fried chicken in her hand. "Well…
maybe just one piece." She removed a breast, then eyed the other
dishes. She hesitated for a moment and then loaded up her plate.

"So…" she began as she plopped down into a chair beside him.
"What's your story, Jack Dozier?"

Jack wiped his mouth with a napkin. "I'm sorry?"

"Your story. Tell me why you're here."

When he didn't answer right away, she gave him a knowing look.
"I have a pretty good idea already. And if you don't want to talk
about it, I understand. But it doesn't take a rocket scientist to put two
and two together."

"I'm still… sorting things out," he told her.

Nadine didn't push further.

"What about you?" he asked. "Why don't you tell me about
yourself."

Nadine seemed surprised anyone would ask her such a question.
"Me?" She laughed. "What in the world do you want to know about
me?"

Jack poured himself a glass of iced tea. "How did you come to
know Helen?"

Nadine smiled. "Well, I worked as a nurse's aide for twenty years.
Mostly nursing homes and private duty. Backbreaking work let me
tell you. I was burned out, needed something different. I did
housekeeping with one of those agencies, but I hated it. No contact
with people, just going from one empty house to the next all day
long. Then I saw an ad in the paper for someone looking for part-
time help in her home. Cooking, cleaning, picking the kids up from
school—that sort of thing. I answered the ad and the rest, as they say,
is history."

Her expression grew wistful as she stared down at her plate. "That
was fourteen years ago. I have so many memories with this family."

She told him about holidays and last-minute school play costumes
and countless rainy afternoons spent baking cookies with Scott and
Karen as the two siblings argued over who got dibs on the last
morsels of dough in the mixing bowl.

"The first time I met Helen, we sat in the kitchen and talked for
hours. I was supposed to be interviewing for the job, but we barely
even talked about it. I know it sounds like a cliché, but I felt like we'd

172

known each other for years." She sighed. "Kenneth was a whole other Geraldo. He's a hard man to get to know. My granny used to say she loved all of God's creatures, but there were a few she preferred stuffed." She shrugged. "He eventually grew on me."

She laid her fork down on her plate and her eyes filled with tears. "I don't know what I'm going to do when Helen…"

"Do you have any family?"

"One sister, in Raleigh. We see each other out of obligation every few years or so. She's ten years older than me and we're not particularly close. Our parents passed away years ago."

"You never married?"

A blush spread across her face. The freckles on her cheeks stood out like splatters of brown paint against a pink backdrop. She shook her head as she buttered her cornbread. "I came close, once. When I was very young. But it didn't work out."

Jack looked down and noticed Nadine's feet, surprisingly small for a woman her size. The leather straps of her sandals cut into the soft pink flesh of her instep, and her heels were cracked and calloused. In that brief moment, Jack thought he understood this woman fully—a lifetime spent taking care of others but not herself, demonstrating her love with her baker's hands and culinary delights, content to come home to her dogs and her books and her beloved Yankees. A lonely woman. But never alone.

Brooklyn's shrill laughter outside on the deck broke the silence. The child's animated face appeared in the galley doorway. "Hurry! Come see the dolphins!"

24

Helen looked over her shoulder at Jack and Nadine as they made their way topside. "Over here!" she said.

Nadine spotted them first. "There they are!"

The cluster of bottlenose dolphins kept pace with the boat, frolicking in the water like a herd of colts nipping at one another's flanks. A pair close to the boat leaped out of the water in unison, their fluted voices calling out to one another in a language mortal man wasn't meant to understand.

"Listen to them!" Helen exclaimed.

Scott leaned out over the railing. He cupped his hands around his mouth and tried to duplicate the sounds.

Michael made a face. "That doesn't sound like a dolphin."

"I thought it sounded pretty good," he said. He turned to Liz. "What did it sound like to you?"

"Like a clam farting in a bucket."

Brooklyn was reduced to a fit of giggles. The playful voices of the dolphins seemed to mimic her. On impulse, Helen looked up at Kenneth on the bridge and called out, "I want to see them from where you are!"

"I don't think that's a good idea." He hurried across the bridge, but Helen had already mounted the first rung.

Scott went over to the bottom of the ladder. He gripped her waist with both hands and helped her pull herself up to the next rung. "Go slow, Mom."

"That's the only way I *can* go," she said dryly. She looked out over the water. "I don't see them," she said, afraid she was missing the show. On the last rung, Kenneth pulled her up onto the bridge. He started to say something, but she cut him off.

"There they are!" she said, pointing past him.

Marty cut against the tide to keep the animals alongside them. They had gone about a mile when, almost as suddenly as they had appeared, the dolphins dove deep and swam away.

Brooklyn stood on the lowest rung of the boat's railing, looking down at the water. Her father stood behind her. "Where did they go, Daddy?"

He shook his head. "I don't know, sweetie."

Marty reached over and cut the boat's twin engines. The only sound was the soft lapping of the waves against the boat. A tremor passed through the vessel. Helen sensed the presence before she saw it.

"Why'd you cut the engine?" Scott asked.

"Don't want to scare them off." He appeared to be tracking something in the water. Helen followed his gaze. There was a shadowy form just aft of the boat's stern.

Kenneth looked at Marty with mild alarm. "Them?"

"The leader is about two fathoms down." Marty motioned for everyone below to move over to the port side of the boat. "Watch right over there." He pointed to a spot about fifty feet out. "He's headed this way."

The humpback's curved dorsal fin, as large as a truck tire, cut the surface. It came toward the *Nettie B*, then swerved at the last second and followed alongside, the animal's massive arched back gliding through the water as smoothly as a brush stroke on canvas.

"That there's a male," Marty said. "You can tell by the shape of the dorsal fin. He's an old one, too." He pointed to the animal's scarred and spotted hide. "Some can live a hundred years or more."

The whale passed the boat, then made a slow, concise turn and repeated the pattern on the other side of the vessel. Brooklyn was beside herself with excitement.

"Haven't seen a humpback in these parts for quite a while," said Marty. "Must be on his way to the Caribbean for the winter. That's where they go this time of year." He readjusted his ball cap and surveyed the surrounding water. "Strange that he's surfacing alone though. Most humpbacks migrate in pods."

"What's a pod?" Helen asked.

"Group of whales, he explained. "Dolphins also travel in pods. More safety in numbers."

The humpback circled the boat one last time, then brought its massive tail up out of the water as it dove beneath the surface. The edges of its dark flukes were tattered and worn, like the hem of an old dress. In contrast, its pearl-gray underside appeared supple and smooth. The enormous appendage struck the surface of the water once with a resounding slap. Then it was gone.

Everyone on deck started talking at once. Then a collective gasp stilled the air once more as the humpback suddenly resurfaced, its head coming straight up out of the water less than ten feet away from the side of the vessel.

No one moved. The whale slowly bobbed up and down like a buoy, nose to the sky as sea water ran down its barnacle-encrusted hide in rivulets, its mouth curved in a perpetual grin while one onyx-black eye, a century's worth of images captured within its lens, viewed the boat and its inhabitants with curiosity.

Helen was awestruck. She felt an unexpected connection with this magnificent animal. This gentle, majestic creature had seen many years, had sired numerous offspring, had journeyed thousands of miles beneath the ocean depths. Age had bestowed upon it the due honors of respect and reverence from its own kind. Now it neared the final phase of its life, content and unafraid.

Tears streamed down Helen's smiling cheeks as a wave of sheer joy washed over her. Kenneth wrapped his arms around her waist as she laid her head back against the broad expanse of his chest. "Thank you, Lord," she whispered. "Thank you for this gift."

She looked down to find her mother standing alongside Jack and Karen, her hands on Brooklyn's shoulders in front of her. Jack turned away from the humpback to meet her gaze, and Helen wondered if he too had sensed a connection.

The humpback lingered a moment longer, then submerged and disappeared. From somewhere below, a sound like a lion's roar echoed throughout the depths. Then a high shrill was made in response. Other sounds soon joined in. They seemed to be coming from everywhere.

Another humpback broke the surface, blowing air through its blowhole and sending a spray twenty feet into the sky. Then another whale appeared, then another, and then another, until a pod of nine

176

humpback whales surrounded the boat, some surfacing, some spouting, others slapping the water with their pectorals in a form of play. Liz and Michael grabbed their cameras and began clicking away, trying to capture the moment on film.

Laughter mixed with Helen's tears. She felt as giddy as a schoolgirl. She turned around in circles, not knowing where to look first. She could see Marty stealing glimpses of her from the corner of his eye. *He must think I'm crazy.* She tilted her head back and laughed harder.

The whales' antics continued for several minutes, with Marty giving a running commentary on their behaviors. Then the leader dove deep, turning south away from the boat. The others soon followed. The abrupt silence following their departure seemed deafening.

"Wasn't that *amazing*?" Liz exclaimed. She took a final shot of Michael with her disposable camera. She watched as he started to tuck away his Nikon in a carrying case.

"How many shots did you take?" Before he could answer, she pulled the camera toward her and looked at the counter. "You only took *six* pictures? Michael, this was a once in a lifetime event! How could you only take *six pictures*?"

A sheepish expression crossed his face as he fumbled with his camera bag. He shrugged. "I'm particular about my photographs."

Karen sidled up next to her husband and hooked an arm around his waist. "He waits for just the right shot. And besides," she added, "I've seen your photo albums, Liz."

"What's that supposed to mean?"

"It means you take lousy pictures," Scott chimed in, no doubt getting even at her for her crack about his dolphin impersonation.

"I do not!"

"Yeah, you do, Lizzie," David said. "You have a tendency to cut people's heads off."

"And they're all lopsided and out of focus," Scott added. "Like you were scratching your butt or something while you were taking the picture. You really need to get a digital camera so you can delete the ones that stink."

Liz tucked her camera away inside her purse and tried to appear insulted. "Well… looks like I will *not* be sending either one of you ungrateful little snots any more duplicate prints."

177

Scott grinned. "You promise?"

Liz turned to Marty at the helm. "Are we going to do any fishing sometime today?"

They didn't catch much out in the deeper water. Jack was robbed of his bait twice. Kenneth got hold of something big, but his line snapped before he could reel it in. Brooklyn was disappointed. She sat on the edge of the boat deck, dipping her plump rubber worm into the water every few seconds. Before long, she lost interest and went below deck with Karen to play with her dolls.

In the late afternoon, they headed back toward the calmer waters of the Pamlico and Croatan Sounds and trolled for mackerel and amberjack. Kim Sung reeled in a small striped bass. Kenneth and Marty snagged a couple of triggerfish over by the concrete pylons of the Oregon Inlet Bridge.

Further inland, a downfall of driftwood brought a frenzy of sea bass and cobia. Jack pulled in a pair of good-sized cobias. Helen had no sooner dropped her line when something took her bait and ran with it. She let out a whoop, and Kenneth helped her reel the fish in. It was a sea bass, around four pounds. She held her prize up triumphantly. Michael took a picture of her and Jack with their catch, the silver-green scales of the two cobias gleaming dully in the fading light.

As they headed back to the marina, Helen approached Marty at the lower deck wheel. She thanked him for a pleasant trip, then looked out through the salt-streaked windshield as she tried to figure out how to say what she wanted to say. "Your wife…" she began.

"Say something to you, did she?"

"How did you—"

"I just had a feeling." Marty turned the wheel sharply and steered the boat into the channel. Another boat going in the opposite direction signaled its horn, and Marty answered back. "My Nettie has what you would call a gift. I can't explain it. Neither can she. But for as long as I've known her, she's… sensed things about people. It's been a long time since she's used it."

Helen didn't understand what he meant by that.

"When she was younger, she used to tell people things. Things she had no way of knowing. Like the time she knew old lady Percy's cat was stuck in a drain pipe down by the creek, even before anyone had gone there to check. Or the time she told Molly Draper she was carrying twins, even though she hadn't told anyone she was expecting."

He shrugged. "Everyone thought it was just a novelty, you know? A joke. 'Cept for Reverend Akins, who told Nettie's momma and daddy that seers were in danger of hellfire and that she was practicing some kind of witchcraft." He laughed. "Net's daddy about threw the reverend out on his bum, let me tell you."

"How did others react to what she told them?" Helen asked.

"Sometimes people believed her, sometimes they didn't. But I can tell you one thing. She was always right. But then she started having what she called bad visions. One day she came to me and told me her granddaddy was going to die soon. She said she could see him dying in her mind, and that he was cold and alone." He removed his cap and combed a calloused hand through his hair. "Tore her up, it did."

"What happened?"

"Two days later, her Grandpa Steller lost control of his pickup and ran it into a ditch on the side of the road, way out in the sticks of West Virginia where they lived. It was the dead of winter with at least a foot or more of snow on the ground. He was frozen solid by the time they dug him out."

Helen felt a cold finger slide up her spine.

"Ever since then, she's been reluctant to share her visions, or whatever you want to call them. I asked her about it once. She said it was too much of a burden to see so much sadness and pain and not be able to do anything about it."

He pulled back on the throttle and turned to face her. "Your husband told me about your cancer. I don't mean to pry, but whatever it was Nettie said to you, did it have anything to do with your illness?"

Helen nodded. "Yes. Yes, it did."

"Then you might want to take heed."

25

On the cusp of evening, Marty docked the boat at the marina. A brilliant autumn sunset greeted them as they walked across the pier to the parking lot. Nettie's words still resounding inside her head, Helen glanced behind her at the main building to see if Nettie was still around, but the office was dark.

A wave of fatigue settled into her legs like a pair of lead weights. The events of the day had worn her out. She wanted nothing more than to go back to the beach house and fix herself a cup of hot tea and go to bed. But then she remembered the dinner plans for Scott's belated birthday celebration—the last one she would spend with him. Sleep would have to wait.

From the marina, they drove to Harry's, a rambling Cape Cod–style restaurant and sports bar on the outskirts of Hatteras, known throughout the Outer Banks for their homemade hush puppies and clam chowder. Even in the off-season, the Friday night crowd was thick. While the others waited in the lobby for a table, Scott persuaded Jack to join him in a game of pool in the back room. Helen, Kenneth, and Michael followed.

"I tell you what." Scott retrieved the cue balls and set them on the table. "Let's break up into teams. Me and Michael against you two guys." He glanced over at his father. A smile tugged at the corners of Scott's mouth, as if he were the only one who knew the punch line to an inside joke. "How about it, Dad?"

Helen looked from her husband to Jack. Why was Scott doing this? Jack laid his pool cue on the table and started to excuse himself, but then Kenneth asked, "You any good at this?"

Jack stopped, clearly surprised by the question. "It's been a while, but I can hold my own."

Kenneth nodded. "Rack 'em up then."

Thirty minutes later, father and son were still going at it with an intensity bordering on obsessive. It was apparent to everyone the two had squared off like this before, and not just at playing pool. Halfway through the game, Jack and Michael hung up their pool cues and watched from the sidelines with Helen.

When Karen came over to tell them their table was ready, Kenneth was down to his last move, sinking the eight-ball in a right corner pocket.

Scott dropped his cue stick onto the table with a loud clatter. "Let's go eat."

Karen raised a knowing eyebrow at her mother. She sandwiched herself between her husband and Jack and looped her arms through theirs as they walked back to the dining area. A table for ten was reserved for them next to the fieldstone fireplace.

"This place smells like Easter eggs!" Brooklyn exclaimed.

Her father looked at her quizzically. "Easter eggs?"

"It's the fish and chips," Karen said. "I can smell the vinegar from here."

"I have never understood this phrase," Omma said. "You have fish, yes. But where are chips?"

Brooklyn turned her attention to her aunt. "Aunt Helen, can we decorate eggs again this Easter like we did last year? That was so much fun! Remember, Daddy?"

A lump of regret formed in Helen's throat as she thought about all the things she would never do with this child. Kenneth reached under the table and took her hand in his. The simple gesture nearly moved her to tears. She pasted on a smile. "We'll have to wait and see."

"You know what we should do this weekend?" Scott said. "Let's have a clambake."

A spark replaced Helen's sorrow. "We haven't had one of those in ages!"

"What's a clambake?" Brooklyn asked.

"Are you talking about out on the beach behind the house?" Nadine asked. "Can we do that? A bonfire, I mean?"

"I doubt it," Kenneth replied. "I think they have restrictions about things like that."

"It's a private beach," Scott said. "I don't see why not."

"What's a clambake?" Brooklyn asked again.

"I'll have to look at the lease agreement. It may be considered a fire hazard."

Scott was clearly peeved by his father's ever-present sense of caution. "What's to catch on fire? You're surrounded by miles of sand, for crying out loud."

"I said I'd look into it, Scott."

"Nobody's listening to me!" Brooklyn crossed her arms over her chest and glared at everyone sitting around the table.

"I'm sorry, sweetie," Helen said. "A clambake is like a party out on the beach, with a big fire and lots of food and dancing." She placed a hand on her husband's arm. "Please, honey? It'll be just like old times."

Kenneth's features softened. In all the years she'd known him, he'd never denied her anything she really wanted—within reason, of course. And Helen was a reasonable woman. "I suppose it would be all right."

"How about Sunday?" Scott asked.

"Michael and David are leaving to go back to New York on Sunday." Liz promptly stuck her tongue out at her brother.

"Okay. Tomorrow then."

"Can we get everything together on such short notice?" Karen asked.

Nadine was already pulling pen and paper from her purse. "I'll start a list."

Helen made it as far as dessert, but fatigue finally won out and she asked Kenneth to take her back to the beach house. He gave Scott his credit card to settle the bill while he brought the car around. Helen insisted everyone else stay and enjoy the rest of their evening, but Nadine and Liz both chose to forgo a slice of Harry's famous Black Forest Cake and head back with them.

"We've got a lot of planning to do for tomorrow," Nadine said.

182

Brooklyn had fallen asleep after dinner in Omma's lap. "I go back and put her to bed," she said.

Karen turned to Michael. "I might as well go, too."

"You don't want to stay?"

"And be the only female amidst all this testosterone? No, thank you." She kissed him on the cheek. "Stay here and do your male bonding thing. You know… play pool, drink beer. Whatever it is that you men do. I'll see you when you get back."

The pert blonde waitress, who had exchanged glances with Scott all evening, set the tab in front of him, along with a note. He looked up in time to see her smile at him over her shoulder as she walked back to the bar.

Tilting back his bottle, he finished the last of his beer. "I think I'll pass on that pool game." He scrawled his father's signature across the receipt and added a generous tip to the tab. He stood and headed toward the bar. "I'll see you guys later."

26

Karen was reading in the sunroom when she heard Scott come in. Everyone else had gone to bed hours ago. She closed her book and instinctively went to the kitchen. She found him standing in a wedge of yellow light from the open refrigerator door.

"Hey," she said.

Startled, he almost dropped a carton of milk on the floor. "I didn't know you were still up."

"I waited up for you." She lifted her chin, indicating the leftover blueberry muffin in his hand. "Are there any more of those?"

Scott placed the basket of muffins on the island and poured glasses of milk for them both. "Why'd you wait up for me?"

Karen stifled a yawn. "Because I need to talk to you."

"About what?"

She took her time removing the paper liner from her muffin. "Do you think I'm stupid?"

Scott grinned. "Is this a trick question?"

Normally, her brother's boyish charm was disarming. But not tonight. "I'm serious, Scott."

"Okay, okay." He polished off his snack in two large bites and reached for another. "Tell me what's on your mind."

"I know what you're doing, little brother. And I think it's pathetic."

"Huh?"

"This thing with you and Jack. Do you actually think no one sees through your act?"

Scott poured another glass of milk. "I don't have the slightest idea what you're talking about."

Karen leveled her gaze at him. "Get real, Scott. The car ride, inviting him to play pool, how you talked to him almost nonstop at dinner. Since when do you go out of your way to endear yourself to elderly gentlemen you just met?"

"I happen to like the old guy. He's pretty neat."

"Not to mention the fact he might be your grandfather, right? I'm sure that's what has compelled you most of all."

"Well… that, too," he stammered.

"Uh-huh. And I'll be making partner next week."

Clearly irritated, Scott replied, "Do you have a point to make here? Because it sure would be nice if you'd get around to it."

Karen took the plunge. "You're using Jack to get to Dad."

Scott made a show of shrugging off the comment. "How in the world did you come up with a crazy idea like that?"

She didn't reply. An awkward silence fell between them as Scott fidgeted in his chair. Karen knew her brother loved her dearly. But he hated it when she was right. As an awkward teen struggling to find his place in the shadow of his "perfect" older sister, he must have resented her. Ever the dutiful daughter, achieving top grades, succeeding at everything she set out to do—she'd been a tough act to follow.

Scott's wrestling seemed to change all that. He was a natural and clearly reveled in the admiration of his coaches and peers. An added bonus was a closer relationship with their sports-loving, competitive father. But most of all, Karen knew he loved wrestling because it was something she couldn't do.

"I know I get on your nerves sometimes, Scott," she said. "I don't mean to come across as a know-it-all. I know you and Dad have had your problems over the years. But I don't think now is the time to aggravate the situation." She reached for another muffin just to have something to do.

Scott started in on his third. "You're gonna get fat if you keep eating those." His eyes dropped to her waistline. "As a matter of fact, I thought you were looking a little thicker around the middle."

"I am not! I haven't—" She crossed her arms over her chest. "Quit changing the subject. We need to talk about this."

Scott rubbed his eyes and sighed. "Give me a break, will ya?"

Something in the tone of his voice made her soften her resolve. "What's going on, Scott? I know something's wrong. Mom knows, too."

"What did she tell you?"

"Nothing. Only that she knows something's been brewing with you for a while. I take it you've talked to her?"

Scott didn't answer. "Has Dad said anything?"

"No. Should he have?"

"Nope." A derisive laugh chased his words. "Dad is about as observant as a tick with its head in a dog's hide. He wouldn't notice if a tractor came up the beach and plowed through the kitchen."

Karen's brow furrowed. "You're not making any sense, Scott."

"I know." He drained the last of his milk. "I'm going to bed."

He leaned over and kissed her cheek. The stubble of his day-old beard scratched against her face. She caught a whiff of his cologne, something woodsy with a citrus undertone. When had her baby brother grown up? It was hard to believe he was twenty-one now. The last couple of years were a blur, what with Scott going away to college and her long hours at the firm and Mom's illness. She hadn't kept in touch like she should have. Neither of them had.

She recalled younger days, simpler times, before the complexities of life had stolen away their childish dreams and pastimes. "Remember when we were little how we used to make tents out in the backyard?"

Scott turned around in the doorway and looked at her quizzically. "Yeah. Why?"

Karen didn't move from where she sat. Outside, the night that lay beyond the kitchen windows was so dark it was almost palpable. She suddenly felt very lost and alone.

When she didn't answer, Scott came to her and put his arm around her shoulders. He leaned in close to her ear. "The blankets always smelled like mothballs. You would stand on that wooden stool Mom kept in the laundry room, and you'd climb onto the washer and pull them down from the shelf. We chose the old magnolia tree in the back of the yard because it was the only one with branches low enough for us to reach. I would hand you the clothespins and you'd string the blankets together."

Tears blurred Karen's vision as she nodded, remembering. Scott continued. "There were four blankets. Two pink ones, a blue one with a big hole in the middle, and an old white one. I would watch you as you put the tent together. I thought you could do anything. You were the best big sister I'd ever had."

A sob escaped Karen's throat. "I'm your only big sister, you dope."

Scott pulled her closer and kissed her dark hair. "I know. But my compliments are few and far between, so you better take them when you can."

Karen wiped the tears from her cheeks. "Do you remember the picnics we had?"

He nodded. "We'd go inside the tent to eat lunch. It was always the same. Ham and cheese sandwiches, those little boxes of raisins, and lemonade. We'd sit in front of the hole in the blue blanket and the breeze would blow in through it. Sometimes we'd play Chutes and Ladders. And then it would be time for my nap, and you would tuck me in with a sheet and a pillow and I'd fall asleep right there on the grass."

Karen felt a sudden pang of guilt. She and Scott built their backyard tents for three summers in a row. Then, during her twelfth summer, when her interests shifted elsewhere—to boys and makeup and slumber parties with her friends—Scott was left behind.

She remembered one hot summer day when he stood on the front porch of their house, watching as she left with a friend to go roller-skating. He must have been around six or so. Scott kept calling her name, but Karen ignored him. She dreaded the thought of him coming off that porch and chasing after her across the yard, making a scene. She slung her skates over her shoulder and walked faster.

"Aren't little kids the worst?" her friend said, rolling her eyes.

Karen laughed. "Yeah. The worst."

But when they reached the sidewalk, her conscience was eating a hole in her stomach. She stole a quick glance back. Scott was still standing there on the porch, wearing a pair of yellow swimming trunks still damp from the wading pool, a forgotten Popsicle dripping cherry-flavored syrup onto the concrete, his other hand slowly waving goodbye.

She knew she should go back and say something to him, but she didn't. She gave him a furtive wave, then turned back around and walked away. After that, Scott no longer hung around waiting for

Karen to play with him. He learned to build his own tents in the backyard.

Now, nearly sixteen years after the fact, Karen asked Scott if he remembered the incident.

His brow furrowed. "Can't say that I do."

She felt so ridiculous she burst out laughing. "And here I was thinking I had ruined your psyche." She pressed the heels of her palms over her eyes. "I am so *emotional* these days."

Scott stood behind her and massaged the area between her shoulder blades with his thumbs. "We're all under a lot of stress right now."

They stood that way for a long moment. Then Karen asked, "What are we going to do without her, Scott?" Tears ran down her cheeks. Then she abruptly pushed her chair back.

"Enough. I can't think about this anymore tonight."

She grabbed a tissue and blew her nose. Then she gathered their dirty glasses and washed them in the sink. Drying her hands on a towel, she started to say goodnight when Scott said, "I dropped out of school."

Karen tossed the towel on the counter and sat back down. "This is a joke, right?"

Scott assured her it wasn't.

"Does Mom know?"

"I told her earlier today."

"Does Dad?"

He gave her a look of mocking disbelief. "Now what do you think?"

Karen took a moment to absorb the news. "But why would you do such a thing, Scott? I thought you were happy there. We all did."

Scott rubbed his face with both hands. "Yeah, well… things aren't always what they seem." When he looked up, his eyes were bloodshot. "I'm too tired to talk about this anymore. I'm gonna hit the sack."

"Speaking of which…"

"What?"

She pondered how best to approach the subject. No matter how she phrased it, she knew he was going to be upset. "I don't think Dad's too happy about you staying out so late."

"Why? I had my cell phone with me."

She shrugged. "I know. But you know Dad. I guess he feels like we should be here with Mom."

"She's *asleep!*"

She held up her hands in surrender. "Don't shoot the messenger. I'm just telling you what I sensed."

Scott waved a dismissive hand in the air. "Whatever. I'm going to bed. See you in the morning."

Karen refrained from telling him it was already morning. She felt wide awake now, wired. There was no way she would she be able to sleep. The clock on the far wall showed ten minutes before three. She thought of taking a sleeping pill, but it was too late. She'd sleep for half the day tomorrow if she did.

Which isn't such a bad idea, now that I think about it.

The sound of the ocean beckoned her, and she went out onto the back deck and leaned against the railing. The moon had taken refuge behind a heavy curtain of clouds. The beach was shrouded in inky darkness. To hear the pounding surf but not be able to see it made Karen feel disconnected from her surroundings, like a blind man standing in the middle of a crowded room.

Out of the corner of her eye, she saw a light come on in the bedroom directly above her. She looked up in time to see her father's shadow pass in front of the drawn shade.

"*Please*, Lord," she whispered. "Please put a fire under my brother's hindparts and hurry him up those stairs."

Kenneth emerged from the bedroom at the end of the hallway in his pajamas and slippers.

"I guess you came out here to get on my case about staying out so late," Scott said.

Startled, Kenneth came to an abrupt stop. His voice was still rusty with sleep. "Actually, I was going downstairs to get your mother a glass of water and an extra blanket. But now that you mention it, I do think the matter needs to be addressed." He started down the steps. "Let's go downstairs so we don't wake up your mother."

"There's nothing to talk about, Dad."

Neither one moved from where they stood. Finally, Kenneth said, "I was told you picked up some girl at a bar tonight."

"Her name is Cynthia. And I didn't pick her up at a bar. She was our waitress at the restaurant."

"Do you think that's wise, staying out half the night with someone you don't even know?"

"We went for a drive and took a walk on the beach. I hardly think that's criminal."

"I think you should be here with your mother."

"I *am* here," Scott said, his voice rising.

"It's three o'clock in the morning."

"I can tell time, Dad."

He let the sarcasm pass. "I'm just wondering if you have your priorities straight, son."

Scott's jaw clenched and unclenched. "Excuse me for being human, Dad," he said quietly. "But I refuse to just sit around here, hovering over Mom like some… *vulture* or something, waiting for her to die."

Kenneth bristled. "How dare you say that!" He struggled to keep his voice down. "This is your mother you're talking about!"

"No, Dad. I'm talking about *you*, not Mom. Can't you see what you're doing? You're driving everybody in this house crazy with the way you're acting."

"Well, no one else has voiced this to me."

"They shouldn't have to! I've been here for one day and I can already sense it. Everyone avoids you like the plague."

"That's ridiculous."

Scott shook his head. "I don't think so."

He took a step toward his father, who stood below him on the stairs. "I've figured something else out, too. I think I know why you don't like Jack being here. You don't like him being here for the same reason you're acting like you are about Mom. It's about control. It's *always* been about control with you! So long as he's here, you can't call all the shots, and that's driving you crazy."

Kenneth's mouth formed into a tight line. "I refuse to listen to this." He started down the stairs.

"Have you cried yet, Dad?"

He turned around and stared at Scott. "What?"

"You know… cry. I mean really break down and cry over Mom."

"Scott, I don't see what this has to do—"

He blurted out an expletive. "Just answer the question! Is that too much to ask?"

Kenneth pointed a finger in Scott's direction. "I did not raise you to speak to me this way." He started back down the stairs.

A derisive sound escaped Scott's throat. "What can I say?" he scoffed. "I learned from the best."

Kenneth whirled around. "And what exactly is *that* supposed to mean?"

Scott had opened his mouth to reply when his mother's voice came from the master bedroom. "Scott? Kenneth? What's going on?" She stood in shadow outside the bedroom door, one hand braced against the wall for support.

Scott recovered first. "Nothing, Mom. Dad and I were just discussing the clambake."

Kenneth took his cue. "I'll be right back with your water and extra blanket."

When the sound of Kenneth's footfalls had disappeared, Helen walked over to the banister and whispered, "Is this about you leaving school? Did you tell him?"

He shook his head. "No. I haven't told him yet."

"Then what were the two of you arguing about?"

"You know how heated these debates can be, Mom."

"Debates over what?"

"Grilled shrimp versus scampi. Can get quite ugly."

"Scott, please tell me what—"

Scott placed his hands on her shoulders and kissed her forehead. "I love you, Mom. Go back to bed and get some rest."

27

"This stuff is like cotton," Jack remarked, as he and Helen crossed over the main highway toward the marsh. A dense veil of fog had arrived with the dawn, shrouding rooftops and obscuring the skyline like a thick batch of smoke. They hadn't gone far, but when he looked back in the direction they had come, he couldn't see the beach house or any of the surrounding landmarks through the dank mist. "Can we still have the clambake?"

"This'll burn off by midmorning or so," she replied. "But it won't hurt my feelings if it doesn't. A fog this low doesn't come around very often." She stopped walking and closed her eyes. After a moment, she asked, "Do you hear that?"

Jack stood beside her and listened. "The ocean, you mean?"

She shook her head. "Close your eyes and really *listen*."

The only thing he could hear was the distant crashing of the ocean waves behind them. Then the faint cry of an egret came floating through the fog from the marsh.

"Did you hear that?" she asked.

He listened more intently. After a while, he was able to block out the roar of the ocean and pick up on the more subtle sounds pulsing around him. The wind rushing past his ears. The wail of a gull passing overhead. The low bass of a foghorn out to sea.

"It's like an orchestra," Helen said. "It's easy to hear the strings and the brass. But you have to really listen for the notes of the cello and the flute."

Veering away from the shoreline, the fog lifted a bit. Clusters of cattails were turned silver with dew, and tendrils of mist threaded through the low-hanging branches of the cypress trees. With the bulk of the orchestra now behind them, new sounds joined the symphony. Jack heard the *bruuuuuup* of a bullfrog, the gentle lapping of the marsh tide, the *plop plop plop* of dewdrops falling from the cypress leaves.

When they reached the spot where Jack had stood the previous day with his coffee, he was surprised to find a pair of Adirondack chairs on a grassy knoll next to the shore.

Helen gave him a wink. "A little bird told me you liked it here."

Jack looked back over his shoulder in the direction of the beach house, vaguely aware someone had been watching him.

Helen settled herself into a chair and propped her feet up. She took two breaths in quick succession, then another.

"Are you okay?" he asked.

"It's the humidity from the fog. Makes it harder to breathe."

"Do we need to go back to the house?"

"No, I just need a little extra juice." He watched as she pulled from the pocket of her windbreaker a small rectangular box that had a line of oxygen tubing attached. She inserted the prongs into her nose and turned a dial on the box. Then she leaned back in her chair and took several deep breaths.

"That's an oxygen tank?" He marveled over the compact device.

"Cute little booger, isn't it? I found it in a medical catalogue. It only lasts for about forty-five minutes, though. Then you have to refill it from a regular tank." She turned her head to look at him. "Does this make you uncomfortable?"

Jack hadn't thought about it until she asked. "Of course not." He didn't want to admit that the device made her seem more vulnerable, frail.

They both sat back in their chairs and watched as a few remaining mallards and a pair of tundra swans paddled their way across the marsh through the rising mist. With the first frost, they would make their way south.

"When I was little, I used to think ducks walked along the bottom of the lake with their feet," she said.

Jack's brows knit together. "What?"

"I didn't know they could float on top of the water," she explained. "I thought they curled these long legs inside of them somewhere and stretched them out whenever they went swimming.

Isn't that silly?" She looked at him and smiled. "What did you believe as a child that turned out to be wrong?"

He thought hard for a moment and then said, "For the longest time, I thought babies came from angels. At least, that's what my grandmother told me. And I used to think a watermelon would start growing inside your stomach if you accidentally ate a seed."

Helen laughed. "I thought the same thing about apple seeds."

Jack started to say something, then stopped.

"What?" Helen asked.

He shook his head, embarrassed. "It seems so ridiculous now."

"It can't be any worse than my duck theory." She leaned in, a look of mischief in her eyes. "I won't tell if you won't."

"Well," he began, "our mother used to tell Charles and I to eat our vegetables and drink our milk so we would grow up big and strong."

"Sure," she replied. "I did the same thing with my kids."

"Well… that was just so puzzling to me. I couldn't figure out how that worked. I imagined that all the different vegetables went to different parts of your body. Like, maybe snap beans went to your legs to make them long, but peas were smaller, so those probably went to your toes. And milk, of course, went to your bones to make them white." Jack shook his head. "Silly, I know."

Without missing a beat, Helen asked, "What about tomatoes?"

Jack thought about it. "Your heart, maybe? To give it its red color?"

"That makes sense. How about cauliflower?"

They both answered at the same time. "Your brain!"

"What about fruits?" Helen asked.

Over the next several minutes, they took turns throwing out names of various food items, mixing together a tossed salad of sorts with their words and images as they contemplated the designated place for each item inside the human body. The humble eggplant stymied them both.

"Did you believe in Santa Claus?" Helen asked.

Jack nodded. "My brother and I both did."

"I thought the pictures of Santa were wrong."

"In what way?"

194

"Because he's supposed to be this jolly old fat man, but I knew he had to be skinny because I looked up our fireplace once and there was no way he could squeeze down our chimney if he was fat."

Jack chuckled. "Do they celebrate Christmas in Korea?"

Helen draped one arm over her chair and raked the sand with her fingers. "Yes, but in a different way. It's a national holiday, but not like it is here. Everyone takes the day off from work and families get together to eat dinner and exchange gifts, but that's about it. The traditional story of Christ's birth is relatively unheard of there. And you don't see many Christmas trees or decorations."

She smiled. "A few years after our parents were married, our dad put up a Christmas tree for the first time. I must have been around five or so. He decorated it with some shells and tinsel and set it outside on our front stoop. Omma said it was the strangest thing she'd ever seen in her life. People from the village would walk by our house and stare at it. I figure he was starting to get homesick around that time, because less than a year later we left Korea for the States."

"What was it like for your family, moving to a whole new country like that?"

"It was certainly a culture shock," she replied. "I think it was hardest on our mother. Korea is in her blood. But kids are resilient. It took a while, but we adjusted pretty well."

She looked over at him. "Do you believe what they say about childhood being the best time of your life?"

"I would say most people agree."

Helen shook her head. "I don't. I mean, I love a child's awe of the world and their innocence about things. But there's only so much of life you can comprehend as a child, you know? But to grow to a ripe old age and have all this knowledge and wisdom and life experience to draw from. I think that would be very fulfilling."

Jack knew the easy route would be to simply mutter something empty and agreeable and leave it at that. But he couldn't.

Who gives a flying frog about wisdom when you can barely hold your water in time to make it to the bathroom? My knees are shot. I don't hear so good anymore. I can't remember stuff half the time and the other half I'm trying to remember what I forgot! I let my family down. I distanced myself from my only brother. I buried the only woman I've ever loved. How's that for life experience?

195

Surprised by the volatility of his thoughts and emotions, it occurred to him that, in some ways, he'd become a bitter old man. The revelation saddened him more than he thought it would.

He emerged from his reverie to find Helen staring at him. He wondered how long she had sat there like that. He cleared his throat. "It's not always such a great thing to grow old," he said quietly.

Her eyes dropped to the gauge on her oxygen tank. "We'd better be heading back."

As they neared the beach house, the fog had lifted enough for Jack to make out the form of someone standing in front of an upstairs window, overlooking the marsh. But before he could determine who it was, the person was gone.

28

Karen stood at the kitchen counter, making a pasta salad. Nadine peeked over her shoulder at her progress. "We need to get that ham in the oven."

The kitchen looked like a minor disaster area. Every inch of available counter space was occupied. At the island, Aunt Lizzie and Nana were peeling shrimp. Out on the beach, Scott was setting up the coals and kindling for the bonfire. On the back deck, her father and Uncle David scrubbed clams and oysters while Brooklyn sat on Michael's lap and watched.

Karen looked at her husband through the window and smiled. A reluctant transplant from the central Midwest, he'd never grown accustomed to handling raw seafood.

Nadine reached around her for a spatula. "Liz tells me you're thinking of getting breast implants."

Karen whirled around. "Aunt Liz!"

Liz feigned innocence. "What? If you didn't want anyone to know, then why did you say anything in the first place?" She went over to the sink and washed her hands. "Besides, I can't believe you'd think of doing such a thing."

Karen bit her tongue. While she loved her aunt dearly, she wasn't exactly known for her discretion. "I said I was *thinking* about it. There's a difference."

"You're beautiful just the way you are."

She looked at her aunt's ample cleavage, then back again at her own humble bosom. "That's easy for you to say. You've got big boobs."

"Sweetie, having big boobs is not all it's cracked up to be." She removed a large bowl of salad greens from the refrigerator. "Your back hurts all the time, it's hot as Hades in the summer, and men are always staring at your chest."

"It's true," Nadine said. "I was a D cup by the time I was fourteen. If I had the money, I'd get mine reduced."

"Don't blame you," Lizzie agreed.

Karen looked back and forth between Nadine and her aunt. "Oh. So, it's okay to make your breasts smaller, but not bigger?" She shook her head. "That doesn't make sense."

"In our country," Nana said, "most women tend to have—how do you say—humble breasts. We do not aspire to such things. It is one's spirit and honor we focus on, not outward appearance. When we come to America, I am surprised by importance of large chests in women. I was made to feel… less, somehow. But my husband, he assure me that I am okay. He say more than handful is just waste."

Liz suddenly dropped her knife onto the island with a clatter and went over to the refrigerator. She opened the freezer door and stuck her head inside. Everyone turned to look at her.

"What in the world are you doing?" Karen asked.

"I'm okay," she replied, her voice muffled from inside the freezer compartment. "Just a good old-fashioned hot flash."

She stood there a minute longer, then closed the freezer door and wiped her forehead with a paper towel. "I am convinced that weeds and hot flashes are God's way of showing us He has a sense of humor."

Through the bay windows, Karen caught sight of Jack and Mom making their way back to the beach house. She thought her mom looked tired.

"So… what does everyone think about this Jack Dozier fellow?" her aunt asked.

"I like him a lot," Karen replied.

"I do, too," Nadine said. "He seems like a nice man."

"Do you think he's Helen's real father?" her aunt asked. No one answered. She looked from one face to the next. "Oh, c'mon. Surely everyone here has thought about it."

Nadine spoke first. "I think he is."

"The physical resemblance is amazing," Karen added. "And the dates certainly add up."

Her aunt nodded. "I'm wondering what will happen after—well, after Helen is gone."

"What do you mean?" Karen asked.

"Well… it's not like he's under any obligation to keep in touch or anything. I'm curious to see what he'll do." She sliced a tomato into wedges. "I personally don't see it happening."

"Why not?" Karen asked.

She shrugged. "I just don't. It's gotta be awkward for him, you know? I probably wouldn't if I were in his shoes."

Nana put down her paring knife and folded her hands in front of her on the counter, her eyes downcast. "Is not good to speak of someone like this."

"What did I say wrong, Omma?"

"This is not right speed. Is idle chatter, Elizabeth. You know better." She picked up her knife and resumed her work.

Aunt Liz's face turned bright red at the unexpected reprimand. "I didn't mean any harm, Omma," she said quietly. "I just wondered what everyone thought about the situation, that's all."

The subject was quickly dropped.

Later that morning, Jack took off his shoes and socks and went back out onto the beach. He rolled his khaki trousers up to his knees and waded into the surf. Just as Helen predicted, every trace of fog had burned off to reveal a seemingly endless backdrop of sun-drenched sky. A northerly breeze whipped the clouds into mare's tails. The ocean was a deep belt of blue-green, edged with a lacy trim of white foam.

A few feet away, Scott stood on the shore with his arms folded across his chest, seemingly lost in thought. Behind them, Kenneth grumbled to himself as he tried in vain to shoo away a flock of seagulls encroaching upon their camp. He didn't appear to be making much progress. He no sooner got rid of one pack when a new bunch swooped down and took their place.

Jack hadn't seen father and son speak a word to each other all morning.

"I take it your dad doesn't like seagulls."

Kenneth uttered another muffled curse as he went after a new grouping of birds that had settled onto a piece of driftwood next to the picnic tables.

"He hates 'em," Scott replied, turning around to look at his father. "Always has. He calls them ocean rats."

He turned his attention back to Jack. He lowered his Ray-Bans and looked down. "When was the last time those Q-tips of yours saw some sun?"

Jack looked down at his thin, hairless legs, as white as the underside of a fish's belly. He smiled. "I haven't been to the beach in years."

He let the rush of incoming water bury his pale feet in the wet sand, then watched as the receding tide exposed first his ankles, then his heels, and finally his toes.

"It's my understanding you and your dad had a disagreement last night."

Scott dug out a broken clamshell from the wet sand with his sneaker. "What makes you think that?"

"My room is at the bottom of the stairs."

He shrugged. "No big deal. My dad and I have been at outs with one another for a while now."

"Why is that, do you think?"

Scott remained silent. Jack knew from experience the answer was too simple and too vast to convey in words.

Finally, Scott said, "I'm really not in the mood for a lecture right now."

"No lecture," Jack assured him. "Just that what you're experiencing is nothing new."

"What do you mean?"

"All sons want to please their fathers. It's inherent."

Another shrug. "I suppose."

"It gets confusing though sometimes, doesn't it? Especially when what you want for your life isn't what others think you should do."

Scott turned and eyed Jack with new interest.

"Your dad means well. He only wants what's best for you."

"What's best for me, huh?" Scott sneered. "All he sees is what *he* thinks is best for me. But he's never once asked me what *I* want."

"Have you ever told him?"

Scott looked away. "No, I guess not."

"There's nothing wrong with wanting something different. But he can't know if you don't tell him." He turned to face him. "Your father loves you very much. Just remember that."

As Jack continued his walk, he watched as Kenneth, clad in canvas shorts and dock shoes, walked between the dunes toward the beach house, his steps precise and careful in the shifting sand. When he reached the top step of the back porch, he turned around and met his son's gaze across the expanse of sand between them.

Scott straightened his back.

Kenneth indicated the pile of kindling Scott had arranged for the evening bonfire. "That's enough wood, son," he called out. "Don't make it any bigger."

After his father had disappeared inside the house, Scott stood beside the dormant bonfire site, his hands stuffed deep inside the pockets of his jeans. Then he bent down and tossed two more driftwood logs onto the pile.

It took several trips to bring everything down to the picnic site. The seagull problem was resolved when Nadine brought Ringo and Star to the beach and let them romp at will on the sand. The dogs ran around in frenzied circles, not sure which direction to take first, chasing after the squawking, flapping birds as fast as their diminutive legs could carry them.

"Those mutts are as fidgety as a skillet full of ants," Liz remarked.

"They won't hurt them, will they, Aunt Helen?" Brooklyn asked. Yellow was her color of choice today.

"Don't you worry, sweetie," she assured her. "They put on a good show, but they don't stand a chance at catching one of them. Those birds are too fast."

"No, I meant Ringo and Star! Uncle Kenneth says those birds are mean. I'm afraid they'll peck their heads or something."

The dogs soon grew tired of chasing gulls and rolled around in the sand beneath the picnic tables while everyone ate lunch. Both the food and the talk were plentiful, and the afternoon fled by.

A few hours before sunset, the bonfire was lit and left to smolder. Helen went back to the beach house to take a nap, although her rest was fitful at best. Not able to find a comfortable position, she tossed and turned for what seemed like hours before she finally drifted off.

She awoke with a start, unable to catch her breath. The air around her felt thick, cloying—as if someone had placed a wet blanket over her face. She reached up to find the bandana on her head soaked with sweat. She yanked it off.

Panic filled her throat and reached down with icy fingers to squeeze her lungs even tighter. Fumbling for her oxygen tubing, she sat upright on the side of the bed and took in great gulps of the concentrated mixture as she waited for her racing heart to slow its frantic pace.

She focused her attention on a large nautilus shell on a bookcase across the room and began counting. *One ... two ... three ... keep breathing! ... four ... five ...*

Was this what the end would be like for her? Common sense and years of experience as a physician told her that the chain of events taking place inside her body was to be expected. She clung to those sensible thought processes like a drowning man straining to grasp an outstretched hand.

My red cell counts must be low again, that's all. Less red blood cells means less oxygen to the body. That's why I can't get enough air. Keep breathing. Just keep breathing.

But no amount of reasoning could dispel the morose images that had taken root in Helen's mind. She had hoped that, when the end came, she would slip away into a coma, peaceful and devoid of pain. But instead, she saw a woman she barely recognized, wide-eyed with panic, her hands clawing at the bed sheets as her burning lungs struggled to draw in more air.

"I'm not ready for this, Lord," she whispered. "I thought I was, but I'm not." Her next train of thought followed quickly on the tails of her panic.

I'm running out of time. I've got to talk to Jack soon.

Quick tears spilled from her eyes. "Please help me get through this, Lord," she prayed. "Please."

She made her way to the bathroom and chased two Xanax tablets with water from the tap. Then she went back to the bed and sat on the edge. She held the oxygen mask to her face and closed her eyes. She listened to the silence of the house as she filled her lungs with slow, deep breaths. Her heart and breathing gradually slowed.

Her thoughts wandered to the patients she'd treated over the years. She thought of all the times she had sat in her office, going over dreaded lab results or biopsy findings with those who had placed their trust in her. She witnessed the gamut of emotions as they struggled to digest what they were being told: fear, anger, regret, sorrow. Occasionally, there was relief. She marveled at the ones who had accepted their fate with uncommon grace, knowing that this earthly home was only temporary and that something far greater awaited them.

She wondered how she would be remembered. Helen knew she had been a good doctor, a good wife, a good mother.

Not always such a great servant, Lord. Sometimes I didn't listen when You tried to tell me things.

"But I tried," she whispered. "I tried."

It occurred to her, not for the first time, that she would soon come face to face with the One who had bled and died for her, who loved her unconditionally from the moment she was conceived. What would that moment be like? To see not only her Heavenly Father, but also her earthly father, and the dear friends and loved ones who had gone on before her. And what of her birth mother, the one who had placed her on that stoop in South Korea so many years ago? Would she be there? Would Helen even know who she was if she saw her?

Tears filled her eyes again. She couldn't begin to comprehend it.

Her thoughts turned to those she was leaving behind. Her heart ached. She felt as if she were standing over a great divide, with one foot on either side. The pull of her earthly home was so strong. She thought of the things she would miss—her son's mischievous eyes and Omma's gentle smile; the sheen of Karen's hair turned auburn in the sun; the feel of Kenneth's hand on the small of her back when they entered a room; the brilliance of purple morning glory vines in September and the silence of falling snow.

She allowed herself to cry then—a cathartic, cleansing effort that left her feeling both drained and renewed at the same time. Then, taking her oxygen with her, she went into the bathroom to make herself presentable for the evening.

29

Following the sound of '60s beach music, Helen walked with Jack to the bonfire site at dusk, when the setting sun had turned the placid surface of the ocean a rosy gold. The smell of roasting meat and Old Bay anointed the air.

She could feel Jack's eyes on her as they slowly made their way along the sand. "Did you get some rest?" he asked. He looked down at her portable oxygen tank.

"I did." She forced a smile. "Should be nice weather tonight for the bonfire." She chose a spot next to her husband and mother. Kenneth didn't say anything when she set down her oxygen tank, although he looked over at her every few minutes or so, as if he were silently assessing her.

The oysters and clams were buried whole in the glowing embers, and everyone sat on blankets around the fire, waiting for the telltale *snap!* of the shells as they burst open from the fiery heat. Brooklyn sampled her first oyster but didn't find them to her liking. She gave the bite-sized delicacy to Star and Ringo.

Scott laughed. "That's some expensive dog food."

Helen suggested roasting hot dogs instead, and Brooklyn went with her father in search of a stick. When she came back, she sat on Helen's lap in the sand and listened carefully to her aunt's instructions on turning the hot dog so it would cook on all sides and not letting it get too close to the fire.

The frankfurters were a success. But the marshmallows didn't go quite as well, and Helen helped her pick off the charred parts to get to the soft, gooey center. Holding her close, she breathed in the scent of Brooklyn's hair, which smelled of smoke and moon-sweetened tides. She looked around at her family, listening to their conversations and laughter, their smiles glowing like iridescent pearls in the fading firelight. She turned to Kenneth and said softly, "Surely heaven must be made of moments like this."

He took her hand in his and kissed it.

Jack couldn't remember the last time he'd been to a clambake. Michael went over to the CD player and put in a disc of slow R&B tunes.

"Why'd you do that?" Liz asked.

"Because I want to dance with my wife." He pulled Karen up from their blanket and led her to a spot just within reach of the fire's glow.

Jack watched as they spoke to one another in hushed tones, the fusion of moonlight and fire transforming their joined shadows into flickering silhouettes. Michael buried his hand in the spill of Karen's hair, while his other caressed the small of her back. When he leaned down and whispered something in her ear, she smiled and wrapped her arms around his neck and drew him closer.

Unable to turn away, Jack watched as the two swayed slowly to the music, recognizing the unspoken message of love and desire in the subtle movements of their bodies and in their eyes. While the song and the participants may have changed, he still remembered the dance. For the first time since Norma's death, the memory of his wife didn't bring him sorrow.

"All right, you two," Liz announced dryly. "Go get a room."

She went over to the stack of CDs and perused the available tracks. "What this party needs is some good old-fashioned swing tunes!"

Jack found his spirits further lifted as the trumpet-laden strains of an old Benny Goodman tune rang out into the night air. He looked up to find Liz standing over him, hands on hips.

"What do you say, Jack? Are you up for this?"

Looking back at Michael and Karen, he saw the couple had already switched gears into some high-energy dance steps. Not exactly swing, but close enough. On the other side of the bonfire,

Kenneth was teaching Brooklyn a few basic dance steps while Helen and Kim Sung watched.

"I used to be pretty good at this, if I say so myself." He brushed sand from his knees as he stood. He wondered if his stubborn, inert joints were going to cooperate or, if after the first few minutes, they would remind him loud and clear that eighty-year-old men aren't supposed to participate in such activities.

Liz reached out and took his hand. "Let's show them how it's done, shall we?"

They started out slowly with a few breezy West Coast Shuffle moves, then increased their paces into some lively shag and jitterbug steps. Jack felt the familiar burn in his hips and knees, but he dug his toes deeper into the sand and kept moving, determined to match his partner's enthusiastic moves. They soon drew the attention of the others, who stopped what they were doing to watch.

"You *are* good at this!" Liz exclaimed.

"Years of experience." He raised his voice to be heard above the music. "My wife and I used to do this all the time. Where did you learn to dance?"

"From an instructor years ago. I told my husband we needed to find something we could do together. It was either dance lessons or the gardening club. He chose dancing."

"Smart man."

"Can you Charleston?"

"You bet."

She took her place beside him. "Let's do it, then!"

It took them a minute or two to synchronize their steps. But by the start of the next song, they had perfected their timing, and they began kicking up the surrounding sand with gusto. Michael and Karen copied their moves. Kenneth switched partners to Nadine, who proved to be a quick study, and she whooped and hollered her enthusiasm.

Out of the corner of his eye, Jack saw Scott go over to Kim Sung and ask her to dance. At first, she shook her head no. Then Helen leaned over and said, "Go for it, Omma!"

Her grandson pulled her to her feet. "I not know this dance," she argued. "Is too complicated."

"Neither do I." He laughed as he led her toward the bonfire. "We'll just fake it till we make it."

206

Clearly puzzled, Kim Sung replied, "I not understand this phrase."

He pointed to the others. "Just do what they do, okay?"

Kim Sung didn't falter too badly. She had natural grace and fluidity of movement. Scott, however, proved to be an awful swing dancer. Jack and Liz tried to help, but it was no use. On the sidelines, Helen laughed until she was reduced to tears.

Nadine took a break and plopped down beside her, shaking her head. "He looks like a drunk orangutan."

Helen burst into laughter once more.

Jack finally had to give up. "These old bones can't take anymore." He handed Liz off to David, who had joined in on the fun.

Much later, after the bonfire was doused and everyone headed back to the beach house, Liz caught up with Jack. "I was planning on going to church in the morning. Would you like to go with me?"

Jack had forgotten the next day was Sunday. He didn't remember seeing any churches nearby.

"I know a little place," she said. "Are you an early riser?"

"Yes."

"Let's go to the sunrise service, then."

Jack wasn't sure he wanted to go. Except for Norma's funeral, it had been well over a decade since he'd set foot inside a church.

Liz must have sensed his growing hesitation because she said, "Dress casual. And don't worry. No one's going to force you to speak in tongues or handle any rattlesnakes." She gave him a wink. "At least not on the first visit."

30

Jack awoke feeling as though he'd aged twenty years overnight. His hip and knee joints throbbed like bass drums, and the muscles in his legs felt as tight as guitar strings. He inwardly cursed himself for his foolhardy actions the previous evening. What in the world had made him think he could carry on like that and be able to stand up straight the next day? He closed his eyes and grimaced. What a foolish old man he must have looked to everyone.

He glanced at the glowing numbers of the digital clock on the nightstand. Almost six o'clock. Dawn was nearing its threshold. Maybe Liz had overslept or forgotten about their scheduled meeting. He started to drift off back to sleep.

No such luck.

A light rap sounded at his door. "You awake?"

He uttered a mild oath under his breath. He cleared his throat. "Yeah," he replied, his voice thick with sleep. "Give me ten minutes."

He lay in bed a minute or two longer, steeling himself for the onslaught of discomfort to follow. After hobbling to the bathroom, his joints stabbing him at every step, he took two Percocet pills from the bottle in his shave kit and turned the shower on full blast, as hot as he could stand it. His muscles slowly began to loosen up, and the pain in his joints subsided a little.

When he walked into the kitchen, Liz was waiting for him. He was surprised to find her dressed in walking shorts and a light windbreaker. His corduroy trousers and loafers seemed almost formal in comparison.

"Do we have time for coffee?" He hoped a jolt of caffeine would wake him up.

Liz held up a large silver thermos. "Already made some. We'll take it with us."

Jack had never heard of a church that allowed you to drink coffee in the pews, but he didn't argue. He followed her out the door.

A few miles up the road, Liz pulled over onto a sandy embankment and cut the engine. Jack looked around. There was no sign of anything that looked like a church. The only thing he could see in the pre-dawn light were rolling sand dunes topped with thick tangles of trumpet vines and stands of sea grass shrouded in mist. The sound of the ocean, almost a half-mile away, was barely audible.

"Where are we?"

"I found this place the other day," she replied, as if that answered his question. She grabbed the thermos and a blanket from the back seat and got out of the car. Jack retrieved his cane and followed her.

On the far side of the nearest dune, a long boardwalk twisted and turned toward the beach, ending in stairs that led down to the shoreline. The mere thought of walking that far made Jack wince. He started up the incline. It wasn't quite as bad as he expected. Rest stops were positioned every hundred yards or so. Liz didn't seem to mind. Below them, tall stands of copper-colored grass rustled like coarse silk in the light breeze. A small bobwhite, with its striated brown and white markings, pecked around in the sand.

Near the end of the walkway, Liz went on ahead to pick out a spot. Jack took his time. When he found her, she had already spread out the blanket, a red and green plaid which stood out in stark contrast against the pale sand. She handed him a steaming cup of coffee and then sat down on the blanket, facing the ocean, and sipped slowly from her cup, taking in the view.

By this time, the sun had announced its arrival as the final remnants of night gave way to the start of another day. Along the shoreline, whitecaps appeared as a northerly breeze pushed the tide forward.

"I bet you thought I was going to drag you into some church building, didn't you?" She tilted her head back to watch an osprey as it flew overhead, then turned her attention back to the sunrise. "As far as I'm concerned, we *are* in church."

They sat together in silence, drinking in the scenery and the hot coffee. Below them, a man walked along the deserted beach with a black Labrador at his side. Occasionally, the dog raced off from its master to chase after a tern or to dig holes in the sand. The man stopped and removed a tennis ball from the pocket of his windbreaker. He tossed it out into the water, and the dog bounded after it.

Jack and Liz watched as the game progressed. The Labrador paddled out against the current, its dark head the only part of him visible above the water. Then the dog returned to the beach and dropped the sopping wet ball at the man's feet, showering him in a spray of seawater as he shook himself from head to tail. The sound of the man's laughter carried up to them.

Liz said, "I once heard someone say God is happiest when His children are at play. I think that was a pretty smart person, don't you?"

Here we go. Jack braced himself for the dreaded conversation about God. Or a higher power. Or whomever it was people referred to when talking about organized religion these days.

But to his surprise, Liz said nothing. She sat cross-legged on the blanket in her worn Birkenstocks, a small New Testament open on her lap, occasionally moving her lips in silent prayer or humming a chorus to a song Jack didn't recognize. It was the most unpretentious act of worship he'd ever witnessed.

"Have you ever lost sight of your faith?" he asked.

Liz was silent for a long time. "Once," she replied. "A long time ago." She sighed, a sound that seemed to resonate from a place seldom touched. "My husband and I lost a child. It was our first. We were young. Dan had just graduated from seminary and taken a position at a small church in Oregon. We'd only been married a little over a year when I found out I was pregnant.

"I was so homesick. I'd never been that far away from my family, and I didn't have many friends. I couldn't seem to fit in with the other women at the church. I hated my secretarial job. Long hours and lousy pay. I'd call Helen or Omma and bawl my eyes out. I didn't want to burden Dan because he already had enough on his plate. The church had a lot of elderly members and there were a lot of needs."

Her tone grew wistful, and she smiled. "The pregnancy was a complete surprise. But Dan and I both were thrilled. From the day I

210

found out, everything changed for me. It was like I had discovered a new purpose. I read all the literature. We went to birthing classes. I was the picture of health. The doctor said the baby was developing perfectly."

She paused. "Then I woke up one morning and found blood on the bedsheets. I was in the middle of my seventh month. By the time Dan got me to the hospital, I had already begun to dilate. I was in premature labor. They gave me drugs to stop it, and I stayed in the hospital for a week. I was sent home on strict bedrest, and Omma flew out to stay with me. I did everything I was supposed to. But two weeks later, I went into labor again. This time they couldn't stop it."

Liz placed her empty coffee cup on the blanket and laced her fingers around her knees. "I gave birth to a baby girl. Amy. She weighed three pounds. The doctors said her lungs were working at a quarter of their capacity. But she held on for a week."

She told Jack about the long days and even longer nights she and Dan stood watch over their daughter's incubator in the neonatal intensive care unit, her tiny body connected to a seemingly endless array of tubes and wires and machines. Keeping her alive.

"She didn't move or cry much, and a thick layer of ointment kept her from opening her eyes so that she wouldn't be blinded by the lights. That's what bothered me the most. That she couldn't see me. But I would talk to her through the plastic, and we put on gloves and reached through slits in the side of the incubator to touch her. When the doctors finally said it was only a matter of hours, they let us hold her for the first time. She died in my arms."

Jack's mind flooded with memories of his own unfortunate attempts at parenthood and Norma's subsequent grief. But neither of them had experienced the thrill of their baby's movements within Norma's belly, never held their newborn child in their arms.

"After the funeral, people from the church would say Amy was in heaven with the Lord, and we can't always understand God's will. I wanted to strangle them. I was so *angry* at God for the longest time. I didn't understand why this child was taken from us."

She met Jack's eyes. "I finally realized that things simply happen sometimes. It's no one's fault. Not God's, not anyone's. Our daughter's lungs weren't strong enough to sustain life. That's why she died." She turned her gaze back to the ocean. "To hang on to that anger was just an excuse. It was eating me alive, destroying my marriage and everything around me. I had to let it go."

Jack pondered her words for a moment. "Do you believe God causes bad things to happen?"

"What do you mean?"

"Well… growing up, I used to hear preachers talk about the wrath of God and how He brings tragedy in people's lives simply because He can." He was quiet for a moment, lost in thought. "A twister came through our area once. Did a lot of damage to the crops and trees. There was a house right in its path, the old Johnston place. Leveled it to the ground. The pastor said he believed God had intentionally destroyed their home because the Johnstons had stopped coming to church." He looked over at her. "Do you believe God works that way?"

Liz shook her head. "I have a hard time with that. I certainly don't have all the answers. And I can only draw from my own experiences. But if you were to ask me if I thought God deliberately took Amy from us or reached down and touched Helen's body with cancer, I would have to say no. I believe God uses life's circumstances to speak to us, draw us closer to Him." She shrugged. "It's up to us as to whether or not we listen."

"And if we don't?"

She smiled. "That's the beauty of God's love. He's given us the freedom to choose."

"I never thought of it that way."

She poured more coffee. "Any particular reason why you're bringing these things up?"

Jack couldn't put into words what he was feeling. It felt like he was treading water in a deep, dark place with no rescue in sight. As a young boy, he had embraced the idea of God as he understood Him to be, a caring and loving entity who forgave all sins. But as he grew older, he found it difficult to discern between the God he had known as a child and Pastor Tucker's caustic, fire and brimstone version.

His father had instilled in him the importance of honesty and character. But his mother wielded a far more spiritual influence with her busy hands and charitable heart than any amount of shouting from behind a pulpit.

It was during the time he spent in Korea, at the height of the war, that he first felt his faith begin to waver. Witnessing the carnage and violence that surrounded him like a dark stain, he pondered more than once whether God even existed. How could man's soul mirror God in the midst of such atrocities? The question needled his conscience for many years.

After returning home, he continued to attend church with Norma, but after a while, he didn't see the point in it, and so she went without him.

Decades later, as Norma lay dying, he fell to his knees and begged God for a miracle. He would do anything—go back to church, fund a missionary, feed the poor. He knew he was bargaining. But he hoped God would forgive him for that.

She died anyway, along with what felt like the final remnants of Jack's soul.

He felt the touch of Liz's hand on his. He hadn't spoken a word, yet her pale gray eyes seemed to register understanding. "I think we all get a little lost along the way sometimes, don't you?"

He cleared his throat and turned away. "Yes, I suppose we do."

She patted his hand and turned her attention back to the Labrador and the man on the beach. "But the good thing is, we can always come back home."

31

Helen believed autumn on Ocracoke Island was a unique time to either enjoy or endure, depending on one's perspective. For those summer people returning home after a fun-filled vacation on the island, it was a melancholy time as they packed away their souvenirs and seashells and rolls of film to be developed and later forgotten, tucked away inside dusty photo albums on a closet shelf.

But for those steadfast folks who remained, a certain feeling arose within their breast when that first nip of cooler weather was felt in the azure September air—a sense of anticipation, knowing they'd soon reclaim their quaint village and pristine beaches.

Not that anyone would confess these thoughts to an outsider. The year-round residents knew the importance of tourism to their little haven.

A remark or two might be said around town when the first leaves began to turn color, or when the cool night mist lifted off Silver Lake and twined its way into the space left between sleeping couples, prompting them to snuggle deeper beneath the blankets. Shopkeepers might comment about how quiet the village streets were without all the bicycle traffic. And it was always a sure sign of coming change when Powell's Grocery put out plump, ripe pumpkins and bright pots of mums.

In September, shopkeepers began marking down their summer inventory in anticipation of the Labor Day weekend rush. By mid-October, beach rentals were given a final cleaning and locked up tight. And by the first of November, most retail businesses shut down for the winter, with the exception of a few upscale shops and restaurants that catered to off-season vacationers and the locals.

As a result, every fall Ocracoke was transformed from a quietly bustling village to simply quiet. Very little traffic, few lines at the post office, and nearly deserted beaches. It was in that tranquil setting Helen wished to revisit the place she and her family had spent so many summers.

"Let's take the ferry over to the island for the day," she suggested over breakfast. David and Michael had left earlier that morning for New York, with a promise to return in time for Thanksgiving.

Liz jumped at the idea. "I want to buy a set of salt and pepper shakers."

Scott downed the last of his coffee. "You must have over a hundred of those things by now."

"One hundred and two, to be exact."

"What do you want a bunch of salt and pepper shakers for?"

"Because I *collect* them." She enunciated each word as if she were addressing a small child having a hard time following directions.

"Do you use them? Like in cooking?"

"No. They just *sit*. In a curio cabinet in our living room."

He shook his head. "I don't get it."

Liz laid her newspaper on the table. "Didn't you ever have a shoebox full of baseball cards when you were a kid?"

"No."

"How about marbles? Or rocks? Something like that?"

"No."

"Toy soldiers? GI Joes?"

"Nope."

"Never mind. I give up then." She turned her attention to Helen. "I'd like to find a lighthouse set. Preferably handmade by a local craftsman. You know what I like."

"That shouldn't be too hard to find." She toyed with the remains of her breakfast. "Do you think our old cottage is still there?" she asked Kenneth.

He pursed his lips. "Hard to say. But we can go by and see."

215

They arrived at the Hatteras ferry parking lot with twenty minutes to spare before the next transit to Ocracoke Island. Kim Sung felt a quickening in her chest at the reality of her daughter's steady decline. The short walk from the parking lot to the ferry landing had left Helen pale and winded. She sat on a bench between her and Kenneth, trying to catch her breath. Kim Sung felt useless, ineffective.

While they waited, Jack ambled over to the water with Brooklyn. Along the dozen or so creosoted pylons lining the dock, brown pelicans with their canvas sail gullets stood sentry, while flocks of laughing gulls and terns played a waterfowl's game of musical chairs.

Jack showed her how to tell the different birds apart by their markings. Brooklyn gestured to the thick paste of white droppings smeared across the tops and sides of the wooden pylons. "Those birds sure do poop a lot."

Jack laughed. "They're noisy, too, aren't they?"

The screeching cries of the gulls and terns scratched across Kim Sung's eardrums like a nail.

Minutes later, the ferry docked, and Kenneth and Scott parked their cars on the deck. Brooklyn darted about, wanting to see the view from all sides. "I've never been on a ferry before, Nana!" She dragged Kim Sung by the hand toward the bow.

"I see you are very excited."

She stole a look over her shoulder at Helen as Kenneth helped her out of the car and found a seat. She never thought she would bury one of her own children. The parent should be the first to leave this world, not the other way around. More and more lately, she found herself reliving the past, leafing through photo albums and scrapbooks, remembering those early years of their marriage, when her husband and children were young and carefree and vibrant with health.

How she wished John were here. It was at times like these she missed him the most. She could still recall the sound of his voice and the familiar fit of his embrace, like a soft leather glove, unlike any other. Here, now, he would have known exactly what to say to restore her faith and calm her fears. No one, not even her own family, could identify with what she was going through.

"Did you hear me, Nana?" Brooklyn tugged her arm.

Kim Sung looked down at her. The child was jabbering on about something, but she hadn't heard a word.

"You're not listening to me!" Brooklyn crossed her arms and stood by the railing, pouting. Her emotions had been unusually erratic over the past few days, spinning out of control. Just this morning, she had thrown a temper tantrum over an outfit her father had laid out for her to wear.

When Kim Sung was her age, such behavior was not tolerated. Indeed, the mere thought of acting out in such a way never crossed her mind.

But times had changed. *She* had changed. Her children were raising their offspring in a very different world than the one she had grown up in. Giving Brooklyn space to work things out for herself, she turned her attention back to Helen as she joined her daughter and son-in-law.

The captain signaled their departure with three throaty barks of the ferry's horn. As they pulled away from the dock, the water churned and foamed, stirring up sediment from the murky depths. Leaving their posts, the pelicans followed behind in the boat's wake, diving headfirst into the water, only to break the surface again seconds later and take to the sky, their swollen gullets filled with seawater and wriggling silver minnows.

Further out, stately mansions were set out like chess pieces along the distant shoreline. Helen leaned against the railing and looked through Kenneth's binoculars to get a better view. "I don't remember any of those homes," she said. "This area has really built up since we were here last."

Passing the last of the inland buoys that acted as driving lanes for local boat traffic, the captain picked up speed and made a slow, wide turn in the direction of Ocracoke Island.

"How long does it take to get there?" Liz asked. The sound of the wind and the roar of the boat's engines made it difficult to carry on a conversation.

Karen's dark hair swirled around her head like a wreath. "About thirty minutes."

Liz pulled out a scarf from her bag and tried to tie it around her head, but the stiff breeze kept the sheer material from cooperating. "Oh, I give up. Guess I'll be having a bad hair day."

They disembarked from the ferry at the Ocracoke dock and drove the twelve-mile strip of highway leading to the village proper, the Atlantic pressing in on both sides of the road. When they reached the outskirts of the town, Helen asked Kenneth to drive toward the west end of the island to see if their old cottage was still there. It wasn't. In its place was a sprawling brick and steel condominium that stood out like a flamingo in a snowstorm amongst the small clapboard homes and businesses.

"They must have torn down twenty houses to build that thing." Helen was surprised the surrounding neighbors had sold their homes. Most had adamantly declared they would never sell.

The car rounded a sharp bend in the narrow road.

"Mom, isn't that our old place?" Karen asked.

Kenneth stopped in the middle of the road, and Helen turned to look out through the back window. She drew in a breath. There it was! But... how did it get *there*?

Kenneth put the car in reverse and stopped in front of the house. It was a near miracle Karen had even seen it. The sandy patch of yard was overgrown with tall weeds and tangles of morning glory vines. The cottage itself, propped up on concrete block stilts and canting slightly to the left, was in a state of disrepair with peeling paint and a sagging roofline. Along the small front porch, there were gaps in the spindles like missing teeth, and thick sheets of opaque plastic covered the broken windows like cataracts.

Up the street, an older woman dressed in a pair of plaid Bermuda shorts and a sweatshirt was walking toward them. A large English bulldog preceded her, straining at its leash.

Helen rolled down her window. "Excuse me!"

It was hard to tell who was walking who as the bulldog bounded forward on stout, powerful legs. When they reached the car, the dog began darting back and forth, sniffing the tires. A wet *whuffing* sound came from its drooping jowls.

"Heel, Buster." The woman tugged on the leash. The dog immediately quieted and sat back on its haunches.

"Are you from around here?" Helen asked.

"Yes, I'm a Banker."

"I was wondering if you knew anything about this cottage here."

The woman turned to face the dilapidated structure. "You mean the old Peterson place?"

Helen recognized the name at once. "Yes. We used to rent it from them in the summer, a long time ago."

"Well, I know it used to be back there"—the woman pointed behind her—"around the bend. But that was years ago. A bunch of real estate brokers came in and bought out most of the homes along the water here. Paid out some big bucks, I can tell you that. But Mr. and Mrs. Peterson and a few others refused to sell, so negotiations were stalled." She peered over her sunglasses at the looming condominium complex. "Ugly old bird, ain't it?"

She pushed her sunglasses back up. "Anyway, I heard both of them up and died. Not at the same time, but within a few months of each other or something like that, and there was no one left to handle the estate. The developers worked around the place, tearing down all the other houses and clearing the ground until they couldn't go any further. The house stayed put where it was for the longest time. Then one day a big transfer vehicle came and moved it over here and that's where it's been ever since."

Helen studied the rundown cottage, trying to see it as it used to be, with pots of red geraniums on the porch and a pair of wicker rockers flanking the front door. The inside of the house was sparsely furnished and airy, each room painted a different color, and handmade patchwork quilts covered the beds.

The kitchen had been Helen's favorite room in the house—butter yellow, such a pretty color—with sheer lace curtains covering the windows and racks of copper pots and pans hanging from the ceiling. For an hour or so each morning, as the sun passed over the east corner of the house, the room was ablaze with light, so bright it almost hurt her eyes as she sat there with her morning coffee.

She remembered the sounds: of foghorns out at sea, the back door slamming as Karen and Scott came running in from the beach, how the iron bed in the loft creaked whenever she or Kenneth rolled over in their sleep.

Helen could see no resemblance whatsoever to the place that had once housed so many memories. She wished Karen hadn't found it.

"You've been most helpful. Thank you." She rolled up her window and the woman moved on, with Buster once again taking the lead. Helen reached over and took Kenneth's hand.

"Let's go."

Traffic was light as they drove around the island, stopping at familiar places so Liz could take pictures. So much had changed, and yet everything was the same.

Powell's Grocery was still there on the corner, and the coffee shop next to the hardware store remained open for business, although the sign outside bore a new name. The post office was now open five days a week instead of three, and a chiropractor had set up shop next door. The island's only gas station, with its silver-handled pumps and red tin roof, was still there next to Till's Bakery at the end of Cobbler Street. The smell of fresh-baked bread and doughnuts cast a heavy golden aroma around everyone who walked by.

"You gotta try one of these." Helen handed Jack a glazed bowtie. "They're the absolute best. Krispy Kreme, beware." She ate half of the pastry, then offered the rest of it to Scott, who gladly wolfed it down, along with two lemon-filled doughnuts and the other half of his grandmother's bowtie.

Karen licked the glaze from her fingers as she polished off the last of hers. "I'd forgotten how addictive these things are." Scott just looked at her and grinned. She straightened her back and sucked her stomach in. "Shut up." She punched him in the arm.

Their next stop was the Ocracoke Lighthouse. The flight of steps to the top was too steep for Helen, so Jack waited with her at the bottom while Liz went up and snapped away with her camera. Pigeons and gray squirrels, long accustomed to people, came within a few feet of their park bench, pecking and chattering for food. Helen tore a leftover doughnut into small pieces, and they took turns feeding them.

"I wonder where the squirrels came from," Jack remarked.

Helen looked over at him. "What do you mean?"

"Well, we're on an island, right? The pigeons I can understand. But how did the squirrels get here?"

"I don't know." Helen pondered the question for a moment. "Maybe someone brought a pair or two over from the mainland and set them free?" She shrugged. "Or maybe they smuggled over on a ferry?"

"Your guess is as good as mine."

When Liz came down, she announced she was ready for some "serious shopping." They drove to the center of the village where the specialty shops and stores were located. Scott said he would rather drive around the island and have a look around. They decided on a time to meet back.

Before they had reached the end of the parking lot, Helen stopped and grabbed hold of Kenneth's arm for balance. She suddenly felt dizzy and feverish. She pasted on a smile. "Honey, I think I'll be needing my chariot." Without a word, he hurried back to the car and retrieved her wheelchair from the trunk.

As she settled herself into the seat, Brooklyn chattered nonstop about the chair's big shiny wheels, and why did she call it a chariot, and could she push Aunt Helen herself.

"I have an idea," Helen said. "Why don't you ride *with* me in my chariot, how does that sound?"

Most of the shops were located along the perimeter of Silver Lake Harbor. Small fishing boats and wood ducks bobbed in the shallow water like corks. Empty fish nets hung along the sides of the vessels like curtains of Spanish moss. A group of teenage boys, their jeans and baseball caps hung low on their hips and foreheads, eyed Karen as she walked by. Kenneth looked at them as if he'd stepped in something foul along the sidewalk.

It wasn't long before Brooklyn grew restless. Leaving a gift shop where Liz found the perfect set of lighthouse salt and pepper shakers, she hopped down from Helen's lap and began jumping over the cracks in the sidewalk.

"Why don't you take her for a walk," Helen suggested to Kenneth. "Let her burn off some of that energy."

His reluctance to leave her was apparent. "I don't know…"

"You said you wanted to stop by that cigar shop you used to go to. Didn't you tell me you were out of cigars?" She knew he was down to his last two Bolivars in his humidor.

"Well… yes… but that place is clear over on the other side of the village."

"Right. So?"

"I'd be gone for probably an hour or more."

She softened at his concern. "I'll be fine, honey. Really."

"Dad," Karen chimed in. "I'm perfectly capable of carting Mom around, okay? Don't worry."

Liz and Nadine each grabbed an arm. "Come on, you," Liz said. "We'll tag along. You haven't spent enough quality time with your favorite sister-in-law. Let's scoot."

Before he could protest any further, Brooklyn took him by the hand and started pulling him toward the candy shop across the street. "Let's *go*, Uncle Kenneth!"

As soon as they left, Karen turned to her mother and asked, "You ready?"

Helen smiled. "Yes. I already called, and they're open."

32

The place was small, overlooking the ocean and Silver Bay Harbor, sandwiched between a shoe repair shop and an upscale clothing boutique, both of which were closed. A weathered, wooden placard with the name *Carousels By The Sea* greeted them as they approached. A full-size antique carousel horse stood on display behind the mullioned bay window.

A set of silver carriage bells jingled when Karen opened the door. Nearly every inch of wall space was taken up by framed prints and photographs, except for a painted mural on the back wall depicting a fairground scene with a carousel as its focal point. The limited floor space was filled with shelves and display cabinets containing an eclectic array of horse and carousel items: ceramic and porcelain figurines, music boxes, books, clothing, and hand-crafted jewelry. Overhead, faint strains of classical waltz music wafted down from hidden speakers in the ceiling.

Helen was admiring the antique carousel horse in the window when the proprietor approached them. A plump, pleasant-looking woman in her fifties, she was dressed in an emerald green knit ensemble and matching flats. A pair of tortoiseshell glasses hung from her neck on a beaded chain.

"Isn't she beautiful?" she said.

"Exquisite." Helen took in the elaborate ornamentation and impeccable craftsmanship. "The Internet pictures don't do it justice."

The woman's brows lifted. "You must be the person I talked to earlier." If she was put off by the sight of Helen's wheelchair and portable oxygen tank, she didn't show it. She held out her hand. "I'm Carolyn Boyce, the owner."

After shaking the woman's hand, Helen stood and went over to the horse. "Tell me more about this particular beauty."

"This here is our pride and joy," Carolyn replied. "We call her Ariana. My husband and I acquired her about four years ago, such as she was. We completely restored her. It's become something of a hobby for us, especially my husband."

Helen viewed the prancer from every angle. "Your website said this is an original Stein and Goldstein horse, is that correct?"

"Yes."

"By chance, was it carved by Carmel?"

The woman smiled. "I see you know your carousels. I am proud to say this is one of the last remaining wooden carousel horses created by George Carmel." She put on her glasses and bent down to view the underbelly of the horse. "Here's his carved signature, along with the manufacturing mark and number."

Holding on to Karen for balance, Helen read the faded script. "Right where he always signed. Do you know where this one originated?"

"Hard to say." The woman removed her glasses. "Mr. Carmel carved for several different carousel companies during the nickel-and-dime empire of the late '20s. But we have reason to believe this particular horse started out as a prancer on one of the Coney Island carousels in New York City."

Helen's face lit up. "Omma!" she exclaimed, barely able to contain her excitement. "Can you believe it? I could have *ridden* this horse! I wish Liz and David were here to see this!" She looked out through the window at the street, as if willing her two siblings to suddenly appear there.

She noticed Carolyn eyeing her curiously. "My parents used to take us to Coney Island when we were children," she explained. "My favorite thing to do was to ride the carousels. There were probably six or seven of them back then. I would beg to go on them, over and over and over." She tilted back her head and laughed at the memory. "I used to clean Omma and Daddy out of their pocket change."

Her mother nodded in agreement. "Many, many quarters," she said.

"When would this have been?" Carolyn asked.

"In the late '50s, early '60s. Does that time frame fit? Do you think this horse was there then?"

Carolyn smiled. "It might have been."

Helen beamed, reaching for her camera. "Would you mind if we took a few pictures?"

"Not at all. I'll be in the back if you need help with anything."

Karen took several shots of her posing beside the horse. Helen hammed it up a bit, enjoying herself. Watching from the sidelines, Jack smiled.

After she settled back into her wheelchair, Helen said, "Jack, would you mind taking me to the back of the shop? I'd like to see the music boxes." Her mother and Karen wandered down another aisle.

"When I was a little girl, my father bought me my first music box." Her eyes took in the delicate porcelain figurines on display behind glass doors. "It was a carousel. He knew how much I loved them. It had six tiny horses on it, and it played 'Blue Danube' as they went around in a circle. I still have it, even though two of the horses are broken off and it doesn't play music anymore. I brought it with me from New York."

She asked him to take down two of the music boxes for her, and she listened to them both. One tune she didn't recognize; the other played 'Moon River.'

"I think I like this one," she said. "You can see the horse's faces better."

Jack looked from one to the other. "You're right. You can."

With a final nod, she decided. "I'll take it." She didn't bother to look at the price tag. He wheeled her down the aisle. "You must think I'm foolish, buying something frivolous like this now, when I won't be able to enjoy it for very long."

"But Karen will," he replied.

At the register, she leaned over to retrieve her purse. Jack's voice held a note of quiet urgency. "Helen?"

She looked up. "What?"

He pointed at her arm. There were several large drops of blood on her sleeve. Before she could respond, a stream of bright red gushed from her nose. "Oh!" She fumbled for tissues in her purse. She didn't have any.

Jack handed her his handkerchief. She leaned forward and held it to her face. Within seconds, it was saturated.

"I'll go get your mother and Karen," he said. The cashier paged Carolyn to the front.

Up until this point, Helen had been able to avoid drawing any attention to her situation. But as soon as Karen saw the blood-soaked handkerchief she exclaimed, "Mom!" and ran over to her.

A prim-looking woman standing in front of them at the register turned to see what was going on. She backed away from Helen as if she were a leper.

A crowd started to gather. "Please," Karen said, alarm transforming her voice into a shrill, harsh sound. "Does anyone have any Kleenex?"

"I have a roll of paper towels in the bathroom." Carolyn hurried off to retrieve them. Someone passed Omma a travel-size package of Kleenex. She pulled out the entire packet and held it under Helen's nose.

"Karen, please," Helen pleaded. "Get me out of here."

The woman in front of them turned to the person standing beside her and said, loud enough for everyone to hear, "I hope it's not *AIDS* or anything *contagious*."

Karen pushed past the woman and wheeled her mother outside. Jack and Carolyn followed. As soon as they were clear of the storefront, Helen bent forward over the side of her wheelchair and allowed the blood to flow freely. A large pool formed on the sidewalk. Karen burst into tears. Omma knelt next to Helen and spoke softly to her.

"Shouldn't you pinch your nose and tilt your head back or something like that?" Carolyn said.

"I'm a doctor. I know what to do." Helen's head was pounding, and her face was hot with fever.

Pressing a wad of paper towels to her nose, she fumbled for her cell phone and handed it to Karen. "Call your father." She turned to Carolyn. "Do you have 911 here?"

33

Helen timed the fat red drops as they made their slow, steady descent into her body.

Drip…

Drip…

Drip…

Approximately one drop every two seconds. Like another heartbeat, separate from her own, pulsing life back into her veins. *How ironic. A stranger's blood is sustaining me while my own is slowly killing me.*

The stiff plastic of her pillow crinkled beneath her head as she turned to look at the clock on the wall. It was after midnight. She wasn't sure how long she had slept. She was halfway through her second bag of packed red blood cells with one more to go, then a transfusion of platelets. At this rate, she would be here all night.

Kenneth sat upright in the reclining chair next to his wife's hospital bed. "Hello, sleepyhead. How do you feel?"

"I hate this pillow. Where is everyone?"

"Karen and Scott are with your mother in the waiting room. She's asleep. Jack, too. The others went back to the beach house."

"Jack's still here?"

He nodded. "He insisted on staying."

"Oh." She watched her husband for any sign of animosity, but none was forthcoming.

"Jack was… quite helpful today," he said. "Brooklyn was upset and crying because she didn't understand what was happening. He took her for ice cream and kept her entertained while we straightened out the details of getting you transported here. And he offered to donate blood if you needed it. Apparently, the two of you have the same blood type."

Helen was the only one in her immediate family with type O blood. Everyone else was either type A or AB.

Kenneth sat on the side of the bed and stroked the back of her hand with his fingers. "Liz talked to David in New York. He tried to call earlier, but you were asleep."

Helen was quiet for a long moment. "I guess I scared everyone."

Tears brimmed in Kenneth's eyes. "When I saw all that blood…"

Helen placed her hand over his. "I'm so sorry. You were right. I should have listened to you and Laura about the injections. I wouldn't be here now if I had."

"We don't know that for sure," he replied. "But it's Laura's opinion that you should start back on them right away. But, of course, the decision is up to you."

Despite his words, she knew Kenneth wasn't ready to let go yet. And neither was she. She sighed and closed her eyes. "I'm so tired," she murmured.

Jack paused in the doorway. Helen was asleep. Kenneth looked up at him. "Sorry. Didn't mean to intrude," Jack said. He turned to leave.

Kenneth stood and motioned him over toward the window. Outside, the dark skies were overcast with no moon.

"How is she?" Jack asked.

"She's stable for now," Kenneth replied. The lines around his eyes were deeper now, no doubt brought on by stress and fatigue. Jack hadn't seen him sleep.

"The doctor is talking to the others in the waiting room," Jack told him. "He said he would come by when he finished his rounds."

Kenneth nodded. "I spoke with him earlier. There are… some things Helen doesn't know about yet, some changes that are being recommended."

"What kind of changes?"

He swallowed hard. "Her condition is worsening. Quicker than we expected." He looked over at his sleeping wife with such tenderness, Jack had to turn away.

"I don't know what I ever did to deserve her," Kenneth blurted out. "From the moment I laid eyes on her, I thought she was the most beautiful girl I'd ever seen. She was so vivacious, so full of life, and I was just… well, I was just me." He shrugged his shoulders and turned back toward the window.

"I came from nothing," he continued. "I was quiet, a loner, with a head full of dreams. I was going to take over Wall Street and amaze the world with my brilliant business savvy." He shook his head. "Helen never cared about any of it—the money, the prestige. It took me twenty years of marriage to finally realize what she saw in me, what she really wanted, was someone who would simply stay."

Jack stood in silence, waiting. If Kenneth meant to pass judgment on him by that statement, he didn't show it.

"Did Helen tell you how we met?" Kenneth asked.

"She said you met in college."

"She was a sophomore, I was a senior. We used to see each other in the library a lot in the evenings. I wanted to ask her out but couldn't work up the nerve. So, she asked me out instead. Six months later, we were engaged."

"Who proposed?"

Kenneth smiled. Jack thought it was the first genuine smile he'd ever seen from him. "I did the asking that time."

"Are you two talking about me?"

Kenneth returned to Helen's bedside. "I'm sorry, sweetheart. I didn't mean to wake you."

"It's okay. I've slept enough today." She smiled when she saw Jack.

"How are you feeling?" he asked.

"Better." She sat up in bed and adjusted the oxygen tubing in her nose. "Looks like I was a little low on blood." She indicated the IV bag.

Jack followed the path of the tubing, but he didn't see an IV site on her arm.

"It goes in here." She pulled back the collar of her hospital gown to reveal a small transparent dressing beneath her collarbone. "It's

229

called a portacath. It can be accessed any time I need an IV. It was put in when I first started chemo."

Jack nodded. "My Norma had one of those."

A man walked briskly into the room, his white lab coat flapping behind him. A medical chart was tucked beneath his arm.

"I'm Dr. Steir." He extended his hand to Helen. His dark hair was damp, as if he'd just stepped out of the shower, and his tie was covered with dancing cartoon turkeys. "You probably don't remember me from when you were brought in earlier."

"I was pretty out of it," she replied.

"So you were. And for good reason."

He noticed her staring at his tie. He fingered the end of it. "My kids."

Helen smiled. "You're the ER physician?"

"Internal medicine, actually. But our facility here is rather small, so we all rotate shifts in the emergency department."

He pulled up a chair. Jack and Kenneth did the same. "Dr. Price, there are a few things we need to discuss." He glanced briefly at Kenneth. "I spoke at length with Dr. Kirkson earlier." He opened her chart and flipped through the pages. "As you probably already know, your red cell counts were extremely low. And your iron and platelet stores were virtually depleted. The transfusions should help with that."

He closed the chart. "But what concerns me most are your kidneys. You have a massive bladder infection, and your labs indicate a possible early onset of sepsis."

"An infection in the bloodstream," Kenneth translated for Jack.

Helen didn't seem surprised. "I suspected as much. I've been taking an antibiotic for the past few days for burning during urination. And I've been running a low-grade fever at night."

"For how long?"

"About a week." She offered up a conciliatory smile. "I know. Doctors make the worst patients."

Kenneth was clearly flustered. Jack figured Helen hadn't made him aware of the changes in her condition.

"This crisis with your platelets may have been a blessing in disguise," Dr. Steir continued. "Had you waited much longer, you probably would have gone into full-blown sepsis."

He opened the chart again to a blank page and began writing. "You're going to need ongoing IV antibiotic therapy. And I'm afraid you'll be needing more frequent transfusions from here on out. That will be handled per Dr. Kirkson. I've already ordered the first round of antibiotics to start tonight." He shot a cuff and looked at his watch. "Excuse me, this morning. You'll be on two different kinds. One for the bladder infection and one to prevent sepsis."

"Can I do these at home?" Helen asked.

Dr. Steir jiggled the end of his ballpoint pen with his thumb. "It's my understanding you'll be staying here in the area indefinitely."

"Yes, that's correct."

More jiggling. "I don't see why not." He closed her chart and stood. "I'm aware of your prognosis, Dr. Price. I know you'd rather be home with your family. I'll consult with our pharmacy and see what we can do. They'll talk with your insurance and we'll go from there. But the first doses of both medications will have to be administered here, in case of a reaction."

"Of course."

"And I insist that everything be set in place before you leave."

"I understand. Thank you, Dr. Steir."

He was almost out the door when he abruptly turned back around. "You might want to consider harvesting blood from your family over the next couple of weeks, if they're compatible. We've had a run lately on type O blood, and our stores here are quite low. Just a thought."

The upholstery of Jack's chair gave an audible sigh as he stood. "I guess I need to start taking those iron pills right away." Helen smiled, but the joke was clearly lost on Kenneth. He bustled about, making notations on a piece of scrap paper concerning the details that needed to be taken care of before his wife could go home.

"Kenneth, I want you to go back to the beach house and get some sleep."

"I'm fine."

"Honey, my mother is sleeping on a couch in the waiting room. That can't be comfortable for her. It'll be noon or later before I'm released. There's no sense in sticking around here." She shooed him toward the doorway. "Go round up the others and take them back."

He hesitated by her bedside.

"Please," she added.

Kenneth reluctantly agreed. Jack started to follow him.

"I'd like to speak with you for a moment, if you don't mind," she said.

He returned to his chair. Helen stared at her folded hands for a long moment. Then she said, "I think it's time I told you about that favor I have to ask of you."

While Helen grasped for the right words, Jack waited quietly. Now that the time had come for her to reveal her wish to him, she suddenly found herself drowning in doubt. It all seemed so silly, even childish, to her now. What had she been thinking? How in the world could she explain this to him?

She cleared her throat. "When I was six years old, I rode a carousel for the first time at Coney Island."

The mere mention of the place immediately transported her back in time to her first summer in the States when Dad had taken the family there for the day. Even now, more than forty years later, she could still hear the rousing strains of carnival music and the smell of roasted peanuts and buttered popcorn as she wound her way among the sights and people along the boardwalk. Helen and her siblings had never seen or experienced anything like it. When she spotted the carousel, she stood at the end of the boardwalk, transfixed.

"I couldn't take my eyes off it," she said. "Daddy took us for a ride and I've been in love with them ever since." She shrugged. "I can't explain it. There was just something about riding that carousel horse that made me feel special, that made me feel… *free* somehow."

Helen had many good memories of her childhood. But few were etched in her mind as clearly as this one. How *alive* she had felt that day! For just a little while, on that long-ago summer afternoon, she forgot she was a confused, homesick girl in a strange new land of towering buildings instead of beach cottages and rough concrete beneath her feet instead of sand.

She closed her eyes and relived that moment again—the salty sea breeze in her hair, the rocking movement of the pretty, painted horses surrounding her, the whimsical sound of waltz music floating in the air as the galloping wooden steeds rode around and around in a circle.

Hot tears burned her eyes behind her closed lids. How she wished she could feel that way again. No worries or thoughts about cell counts, or funeral arrangements, or food tasting like metal, or how her family would cope after she was gone.

When she opened her eyes again, Jack was watching her with a wary expression. She smiled at him through her tears and covered his hand with hers. "Will you ride a carousel with me?"

Jack entered his bedroom and quietly closed the door behind him. The space was pitch-black, but he didn't bother turning on a light. Holding out an arm for balance, he felt his way around the furniture to the bed and sat down. He couldn't remember when he had felt so tired. Above him, he heard the muffled sounds of footfalls, of doors being eased shut, of running water trickling through the pipes in the walls.

Then silence.

His aching joints and body begged for sleep, but his brain refused to shut down. His mind kept returning to all the events that had transpired over the past few days.

The man and the dog on the beach...

The good thing is, we can always come back home...

The crimson drops of blood on Helen's sleeve...

Will you ride a carousel with me?

Sitting on the park bench, feeding the squirrels and pigeons...

Helen posing by the carousel horse...

We can always come back home...

The sound of seagulls squawking overhead on the ferry...

Will you ride a carousel with me?

A heavy weight sank on his chest. *I've been a selfish old man.* So many months he had grieved over Norma, oblivious to everyone and everything else around him, when there were others hurting just as much as he was. How must Helen feel, knowing she would soon leave behind a husband and two children, along with her many family members and friends?

When was the last time you did something for someone else? Reached out and helped a friend in need? He thought of his old pool buddy, Charlie Little.

233

Where had he been while Charlie was nursing his wife Margaret back to health after her heart attack?

I'll tell you where. You stayed right where you were and did nothing, that's what you did. Not a phone call, not a visit, nothing. Charlie and Margaret had been good friends. They'd stayed by Norma's side to the end. But in Charlie's time of need, when he would have welcomed an ear to listen or a comforting word, Jack was nowhere to be found.

His thoughts returned to Helen and what she had revealed to him. *Such a small thing to ask. Whether she's my daughter or not, surely I can do this one thing for her.*

Jack eased himself down onto his knees beside his bed and for the first time in a very long while, he began to pray. Not for himself, but for Helen. Not for the gift of healing, but simply for enough time to fulfill her request.

Somewhere in the night, as he lay awake in the quiet of his room, Jack made his peace with God. When he finally slept, his dreams were untroubled.

34

Kenneth slipped into Scott's room early the next morning and shook his shoulder. "Wake up, Scott."

"Huh?"

"I want you to go with me to pick up your mother."

Scott sat up in bed and rubbed his eyes. "What? What time is it?" He looked at his watch.

"I want you to go with me to pick up your mother."

"I heard you the first time." He closed his eyes and flopped back down onto the bed, arms outstretched.

Kenneth stood where he was and sipped his coffee. "Scott?"

"All right, Dad! Give me a minute, okay?"

Kenneth turned to leave. "There's coffee downstairs if you want it. We'll get something to eat on the way."

Ten minutes later, they pulled out of the driveway, headed to Nags Head. Kenneth drove Scott's Mustang.

"Why'd you want to take my car?" Scott mumbled.

"Just wanted to see how she runs."

Overhead, the sky was low and leaden, with the promise of rain. Colder, too. The temperature had dropped a full ten degrees since the previous day. Scott stuffed his hands in the pockets of his letter jacket and slid down in his seat. Within minutes, he was out.

On the outskirts of Hatteras, Kenneth stopped at a McDonalds to get breakfast. When he returned to the car with the bags of food and fresh coffee, Scott was awake. Yawning, he stretched his arms over his head and then dove into the bag. "Is Mom being discharged this early?"

"Probably not until after lunch."

"Then why are we going to the hospital now?"

Kenneth shrugged as he removed the wrapper from his sausage biscuit. "I thought we could sit here and eat, maybe talk along the way."

Scott rolled his eyes. He took a gulp of hot coffee and then yelped, spilling half the contents down the front of his jacket. Muttering an oath, he grabbed a stack of napkins to clean up the mess.

Kenneth stared at him. "Is there anything you'd like to talk about, son?"

"What do you mean?" He gathered up the soiled napkins and stuffed them in the empty food bag.

"When were you going to tell me about quitting school?"

Scott slumped back against his seat and dropped the bag onto the floor. He looked out the window. "How did you find out? Did Mom tell you?"

Kenneth sipped his coffee while the early morning traffic out on the highway began to thicken. "I wasn't aware your mother knew."

"Dad, I—"

"I put in a call to Coach Martin before you left. I was worried about you. He told me." He felt the flash of hurt all over again. "You tell your coach you're leaving school, but you don't tell *me*, your own father?"

Scott stared out the passenger window. Finally, he said, "I don't want to wrestle anymore, and I don't want to be a business major. In fact, I don't want to go to college at all."

Kenneth was stunned by the finality of his words. "But… why would you want to throw all that away, son? You've worked so hard."

"Because I don't *want* it, Dad. It's not me. It never was."

"What's not you, Scott? Please explain this to me."

"All of it." He made a sweeping gesture with his hand. "The whole college thing in general. I can't see myself three years from now stuck in an office wearing a suit and tie, staring at a bunch of company stock reports I care nothing about."

"What about your wrestling?"

"So I'm a good wrestler, Dad. So *what*? You're the hot jock on campus while you're in college but afterward, it doesn't mean anything."

"That's not true, son. Later, when you go to apply for corporate positions, your athletic record will show you're disciplined, dependable. That you'll do what it takes to help make their company a success."

Scott stared at him. "Are you even *listening* to me? That's *not* what I want to do!"

A man parked two spaces over from them opened the driver's side door to his pickup truck and climbed in behind the wheel. His head swiveled around at Scott's words.

"Keep your voice down," Kenneth muttered.

Scott rolled the window down and said to the stranger, "Me and my dad are having an argument here, but he doesn't want anyone to know." The man looked from Scott to his father as he started his truck. He locked his door before pulling out.

Kenneth gave his son a look of frosty annoyance. "That was extremely immature, to say the least. After seeing behavior like that, I'm supposed to feel confident you know which direction your life should go?"

Scott stared at his father. Then he lifted his chin and said, "Yes, Dad, I do." He reached across and pulled the keys from the ignition. He got out and went around the back of the Mustang to the trunk. When he came back, he tossed a magazine into his father's lap. "*This* is what I want to do."

Kenneth wasn't familiar with the glossy periodical. On the cover was a showroom photograph of a canary-yellow fully restored Corvette.

"What? You want to sell cars?"

Scott snatched the magazine from him. "No, Dad." He thumbed through the pages. "There's this guy in California who runs an automobile restoration shop. He specializes in old cars, most of them antiques, and his crew completely restores them." He handed the magazine back.

Kenneth skimmed over the article and pictures, barely able to conceal his disdain. "You mean to tell me, you want to throw away an athletic scholarship and college education to be a... a *grease monkey*?"

"That's not what this is!" Scott closed his eyes and sighed. He lowered his voice. "These are highly trained professional detailers and engine experts. There are only a handful of these shops around the country."

"We're still talking about being a mechanic, Scott. There's not much of a future in that."

"You don't understand, Dad. These guys have clients all over the world. Car hobbyists, antique dealers, collectors. This is *big* business. Last year, the company grossed over ten million dollars."

Kenneth blinked. "You're kidding me."

"I've talked with the owner, Gil Klein. And I've sent him pictures of some of the bodywork and detailing I've done. He likes my stuff."

"Does your mother know about this?"

Scott shook his head. "I haven't talked to anyone about it." He took a deep breath. "The owner is interested in taking me on as an apprentice, see how it works out. I was thinking maybe I'd go in the spring. I've saved up the money for it. I have enough to get by for a few months. I'm going with or without your blessing. But I would feel a whole lot better if I knew you were backing me on this."

Kenneth closed the magazine. At a loss for words, he looked down at his half-eaten breakfast. He wrapped up the remains and threw it away. "I don't know what to say, son."

"Just tell me you'll support me in this," he replied. "That's all I want."

"How long have you felt like this?"

"Quite a while."

"Why didn't you tell me?"

Scott laughed. "I'm sure you'll find this hard to believe, but you're not exactly the easiest person in the world to talk to sometimes."

Kenneth took the criticism without comment. He looked at his watch. "We need to get on the road. We'll talk about this later." Then he started the car and drove out of the parking lot.

An hour later, Kenneth parked the car in the hospital lot and looked over at his son. He was asleep again, slumped against the passenger window. Scott had always been a deep sleeper, like his mother. Both were slow to wake up and weren't particularly pleasant to be around until they showered and had their first cup of coffee.

Karen, on the other hand, was like him—a light sleeper and a morning person.

In many ways, Scott was his mother's son—in their mannerisms, their personalities, their outlook on life. Karen's personality favored Kenneth's. Driven and ambitious, she was a perfectionist determined to succeed at anything she tried. Although steadfastly proud of both his children, he secretly wished Karen would slow down, maybe quit work for a while and start a family. He could only imagine the look on her face if he were to ever voice those wishes.

I'd never think of asking Scott to do something like that. Be a stay-at-home dad while his wife went out and worked? The concept was much more common these days, but he couldn't quite wrap his head around the idea.

He knew he was a product of his own gender bias. Even with Helen, there was friction at first over her being a working mother while Karen and Scott were growing up. But Kenneth eventually saw that, despite her hectic schedule, Helen's first priority was always her family.

Watching his son sleep, he could see that Scott's facial features had changed a little over the past year, become more defined. He hadn't noticed before. With Scott away at college, Kenneth was so preoccupied with his own thoughts and fears he hadn't stopped to consider how all of this was affecting his son.

I'm losing my wife. But he's also losing his mother.

He thought back to what Scott had said to him earlier about not being an easy person to talk to. He hadn't said anything then, partly because he didn't want to argue, but mostly because he knew it was true. Sitting behind the wheel of his son's car on that chilly November morning, he realized there were a few things he wished he'd done differently concerning his family, especially his son.

A delivery truck in the parking lot backfired, and Kenneth jerked at the sound. He looked over at Scott. He hadn't budged.

"Typical," he muttered, smiling. He reached over and shook his shoulder. He had to repeat the gesture several times before Scott finally roused.

"Are we there yet?" He yawned, looking around.

"We're at the hospital."

"Can we pick Mom up now?"

He shook his head. "Not for a while." He looked out through the windshield and tried to think of the best way to convey to Scott the things he was thinking. Words evaded him.

"Dad? Are you okay?"

Kenneth looked over to find his son watching him, a guarded expression on his face. He looked away and took a sip from his coffee cup, but the contents had grown cold.

"What you were saying to me earlier—about the car thing?"

"Yeah?"

"I hear you. I'm not saying I agree with the whole thing yet, but I'm trying to understand where you're coming from, okay?"

Scott shrugged. "That's all I'm asking you to do, Dad."

In an uncharacteristic show of emotion, Kenneth wrapped his arm around Scott's neck and pulled him close. "I'm already losing your mother." His words were muffled by the thick leather of Scott's letter jacket. "I don't want to lose you, too."

35

The storm came up from the Gulf, unusual for that time of year, cutting across the Florida panhandle and continuing inland along the East Coast, drenching Atlanta and Charleston with torrential downpours before taking an abrupt northeasterly turn late Sunday night in the direction of the Outer Banks.

The first bands of light rain began falling soon after Helen came home on Monday afternoon. A local pharmacy had delivered her medications and IV supplies earlier that morning, and Karen and Kenneth spent most of the overcast afternoon learning how to administer the antibiotics, which had to be done three times a day. Liz sat in a nearby wing chair and watched.

"You'd think they could come up with something that could be given less frequently," Helen grumbled. She was stretched out on the sofa in the living room, waiting for the last twenty minutes of her current infusion to be completed.

Kenneth peered over his bifocals at her. "Would you rather be back in the hospital?" He labeled a large plastic container of her supplies with a permanent marker.

"No," she sighed. "I just feel hemmed in by all of this." The inclement weather wasn't helping matters. The rain was coming down harder now and the wind was starting to pick up, causing the hanging baskets of purple pansies on the front porch to sway to and fro in the stiff breeze.

"I do feel better," she admitted.

"Your color looks really good, Mom," Karen said.

"My appetite is better too. I have a sudden craving for a thick cheeseburger with extra tomatoes and a dill pickle on the side."

Her mother came into the room. "There is bad storm coming. It was told on the news."

They looked out through the large plate glass windows. The late afternoon light was quickly fading as the rain beat out a steady rhythm on the roof. The horizon boiled with purple-black clouds. "I think you're right," Kenneth said. "We better get the chairs and baskets off the porches."

The height of the storm hit Hatteras an hour or so before dusk. Pelting rain pounded the shoreline, and thunder rumbled like hoof beats as storm clouds scudded across the angry sky. Over by the marsh, the wind snapped the branches of the water oaks like broken bones, and a sudden gust blew an abandoned osprey nest from its perch. It rolled across the sand like a tumbleweed.

In the middle of dinner, the power went out. Nadine found a box of utility candles in a kitchen drawer and everyone congregated in the living room to watch the passing storm through the windows.

"I've always loved thunderstorms," Helen told Jack, as Brooklyn lay asleep on the couch with her head in her lap.

"Why?"

"It's hard to explain. I think the beauty of it is in its power. How the forces of nature collide and you can't do a thing to stop it." She shrugged. "That kind of power is beautiful to me."

Jack nodded. "My Norma used to tell me the world seemed fresh and new after a storm, like the clouds and sky were scrubbed clean by the rain."

Helen leaned her head back and smiled. "I like that." In the dim light, Jack's lined face appeared softer, more vulnerable. "You miss her."

"Every day," he replied, a faraway look in his eyes. He cleared his throat. "You probably think I'm a foolish old man, still pining over my wife after all this time."

"Not at all." She stroked Brooklyn's hair. "I think it's a testimony to your marriage that you still think about her as much as you do. You were blessed to have found someone you felt such a kinship with. Not many people can say that."

"She was truly the best thing that ever happened to me." Haltingly he added, "I wish… you had known her."

242

Savoring the moment, Helen replied, "Me, too."

Later that night, as they were getting ready for bed, Kenneth showed Helen a copy of an e-mail he'd printed off earlier in the day.

"What's this?" she asked.

"Before the power went out, I went online and found a phone number for the manager of that carousel you had your heart set on at Coney Island. I gave him a call. The place is already closed to the public for the season, but he's agreed to let us have the carousel to ourselves for as long as we want on Thursday. We just have to meet him at the gate and he'll let us in."

Helen couldn't believe what she was hearing. She tried to read the e-mail, but the words were blurred by her tears. She wrapped her arms around her husband and buried her face in his neck. "This means so much to me."

"I know it does, sweetheart. We'll leave on Wednesday. We'll take our time driving up there, spend the night wherever you want, and then go to the park on Thursday."

She pulled a tissue from her robe pocket and blew her nose. "But you were so against this. What made you change your mind?"

Kenneth wrapped both of her hands in his and kissed them. "People can change, you know."

She decided not to argue.

Kim Sung stood in front of the kitchen window the morning after the storm, filling a kettle with water at the sink. She spied three boys out on the beach, poking at two large objects half buried in debris near the surf. "Scott, what are these boys doing?"

He got up from the breakfast table and joined her at the window. "I don't know." He shrugged. "Maybe it's a dead seagull or something."

Kenneth and Helen came down the back staircase into the kitchen. "What's going on?" he asked.

They went out on the back deck to get a better look. The two objects were a pair of hawksbill turtles. One lay still. The other had retreated into its shell to get away from its attackers, who were kicking sand in its face. When one of the boys raised his stick over his head and struck the turtle's back, Kenneth hollered, "Hey! What do you think you're doing?"

The boys dropped their sticks and fled.

Scott followed his father out onto the beach. Karen and Kim Sung brought up the rear. As they drew near, the larger turtle raised its head and hissed at them, its hook-like beak snapping several times in warning. It scrambled back to its smaller, inert mate and covered her head with its body, shielding her.

"You think a boat propeller got them?" Scott asked.

"Looks like it," Kenneth replied. There was a deep cut on one of the male's hind legs, and part of its tail was missing, severed cleanly at the tip. "The female's dead." He took one of the sticks and cleaned off the seaweed and debris from its brown-spotted shell. A large, gaping crack went all the way down to the soft body.

"How do you know it's the female?" Karen asked.

Poking around in the debris, Kenneth uncovered a large hole dug in the sand. At the base was a small mound of white, gelatinous forms. In the throes of death, instinct took over and the female had struggled to make it to shore, where her body purged itself of its immature, unfertilized eggs.

Karen gagged. Staggering backward, she clamped a hand over her mouth and hurried back toward the beach house.

"What is it?" Helen called out. Before anyone could answer, she came down the deck steps and slowly made her way across the sand. She stopped short when she saw the turtles. "Oh, Kenneth," she breathed, placing her hand on his arm. "Isn't there anything we can do?"

Kim Sung carefully approached the male from behind. The turtle turned its head in her direction but didn't hiss. She bent forward from the waist and studied the animal's injuries. "This one will die here. I see many turtles like this in Korea. They choose mate for life. He will not leave."

"Maybe there's an animal rescue service out here," Scott suggested. "Or at least a veterinary hospital."

"I'm positive we passed by an animal hospital on our way down here," Kenneth said.

"But do they take wild animals?" Helen asked.

"We can call and find out."

Scott started to turn back toward the house. "I'll go find something to put him in."

"Is not what nature intended for this creature," Kim Sung said. Everyone turned to look at her.

"What do you mean, Omma?"

She indicated the turtle at her feet. "It is this creature's time to die. This is the path laid out for it. To interfere is to disrespect the balance of life and death."

Kenneth shoved his hands into the pockets of his jeans and looked away while Scott toed the sand with his shoe. Helen was silent. The moment grew awkward.

Kim Sung hung her head and clasped her hands in front of her. "It is not my place to pass judgment," she said quietly. "I apologize. Please do as you see fit."

"There's no need to apologize for your feelings, Omma," Helen said.

Kim Sung acknowledged her daughter's words with a bow. "I go and help make breakfast now."

Kenneth met the Hatteras Beach Patrol car in the driveway and waited as the officer donned his hat and gathered up the necessary paperwork. Tucked in behind the wheel, the young man's gangly frame was too long for the cramped squad car. He looked like a stork packed inside a crate.

The man emerged from the car and introduced himself. "I'm Officer Hal Doogan," he said, shaking Kenneth's hand. Dressed in a liver-colored uniform which stood out in stark contrast to his copper-colored hair, the man wore a badge but no gun, and the patch on his sleeve wasn't official police issue.

Rent-a-cop or real cop, Kenneth didn't care, so long as the problem with the injured turtle was taken care of. He led the young man around the side of the beach house. "You get many calls like this?"

"No, sir. This is a first for me."

As they crossed the beach, their progress was slow because Officer Doogan kept stopping every twenty feet or so to shake the sand from his shoes.

"He hasn't moved," Helen said, as they neared the site. She had returned to the house only long enough to get dressed and complete her morning dose of antibiotics.

"We called the animal hospital in Kitty Hawk," Kenneth explained. "We were told to call animal control, but they said the only thing they can do is remove the turtle from the beach. They can't treat it."

Officer Doogan gave a noncommittal grunt. He removed his hat and scratched his head. "Tell you the truth," he drawled, "I don't have the slightest idea what I can do here. There's no protocol for this kind of situation."

"Could you at least make a few calls?" she asked.

"I wouldn't know who to call, ma'am."

Helen paused a moment. "Isn't there a nature refuge around here?"

He nodded. "There's one out on Pea Island."

"Well… don't some of those places have animal rescue teams?"

"It's a bird sanctuary. They only take injured birds."

"Maybe they could make an exception."

Another scratch to his head. He put his hat back on and took a long look at the injured turtle. "I suppose I could make a few calls."

An hour later, he had the okay from the Pea Island Bird Refuge to bring the turtle in. A marine biologist from Virginia Beach had agreed to drive down on Tuesday and take a look at it.

"I'll take him in," Officer Doogan offered. "The only thing I have on my agenda is a bunch of paperwork back at the station. I'd rather make the drive." Nadine loaded him up with coffee and homemade muffins for the trip.

The turtle offered no resistance when he and Kenneth picked him up and placed him in a large cardboard box. The injured hind leg was starting to turn black. "We might be too late," Helen said.

Kenneth put his arm around her shoulders. "At least we tried."

After the officer left with the turtle, Kenneth and Scott took a pair of shovels from the garage and buried the dead female and her eggs in the sand. On their way back to the beach house, Kenneth told him about the planned trip to Coney Island. Helen had already talked to Jack, and he was agreeable to whatever she wanted to do. Nadine, in her usual fashion, was busy preparing food and snacks for the trip.

"That's very cool of you, Dad," Scott said.

"Well… you know… we'll save David a trip back down here by taking Brooklyn home while we're in New York."

Scott smiled and shook his head.

Kim Sung dropped the pasta into the boiling water. Kenneth and Scott were cleaning up at the kitchen sink when the doorbell rang. A minute later, Liz came into the room with a FedEx package. "It's for you, Helen," she said. "It looks like it's from David."

"Oh!" Helen exclaimed. "I'd forgotten I asked him to overnight this to me when he got back home."

"What is it?" she asked.

"My photo albums. I thought I had asked Omma to pack these for me, but I guess I forgot. I have some old pictures I want to show Jack."

Kim Sung stopped what she was doing and turned to look at her daughter. Her heart fluttered in her throat. "What pictures?" No one heard her.

Helen tried to open the box, but she didn't have the strength to pry the taped flaps apart.

"Let me do it, Mom," Scott said. He opened the box and handed her two large photo albums.

"Where's Jack?" she asked.

"He's taking a nap," Nadine replied. "Karen said she would wake him up when lunch was ready."

The disappointment in her eyes was apparent. "I guess it'll have to wait."

Kim Sung suddenly cried out in pain. She had forgotten about the pot of pasta she was stirring. The contents boiled over and the scalding water burned her hand.

Kenneth quickly came over and removed the pot from the burner. Liz led her over to the sink and ran cold water over the burn.

"*Orisokun, orisokun,*" Kim Sung murmured, shaking her head.

Helen said the injury wasn't serious, and she applied antibiotic ointment and a Band-Aid. "No more cooking for you today, Omma. Why don't you go relax. Nadine can finish up here."

As she headed toward the living room, Kim Sung's gaze settled once again on the photo albums lying on the island.

Orisokun.

Foolish.

36

"This one here is of Mount Hallersan from the base," Helen said.

Jack sat beside Helen on a wicker sofa in the sunroom. They were looking through her photo albums while her afternoon dose of antibiotics infused. Faint strains of a college football game filtered in from the other room. They had already leafed through the first album, which was filled with baby pictures of Scott and Karen and early photos of her and Kenneth in college and of their wedding. Now they were looking at photographs of Helen's childhood home in Korea.

"And this one is a view from the peak overlooking the north bluff. You can see all of Cheju Island from there." She turned a page. "And this is '*Nulgan Sonbae,*' the rock formation we were talking about on the beach."

Jack brought the album closer to his face. "Old Man River," he murmured. "I remember this."

"It had to be low tide in order to see his entire head." She pointed to a hooked area of jagged rock which served as the elder's nose. "Folklore said when the rainy season or high tide came, he held his breath to keep from drowning."

He flipped through pages of wildlife shots and photographs of John Gable and Helen playing along the shore with her siblings. "Who took these pictures?"

"My mother. Once my father taught her how to use a camera, there was no stopping her. Omma took pictures of anything that would stand still."

He came to a photo of John standing on the stoop of their small clapboard home, holding up a freshly cut evergreen tree. David and Helen and Liz gathered around him with gap-toothed grins.

"That was our very first Christmas tree," she said. "We went with him to the base of the mountain to cut it down."

"Liz's hair sure was red." He smiled. "And look at all those freckles."

Helen laughed. "Liz hated her freckles. When she was little, she used to try to scrub them off with soap. And as soon as she was old enough, she colored her hair. She's been doing it ever since."

"I think the color suits her."

She hesitated. "In Korea, it made her stand out too much, I think. Actually, all three of us stood out. Not so much David and I, because our coloring was a little darker, but Liz had a harder time fitting in."

"Where is your mother?" he asked. "I don't see any pictures of her."

Helen took the album from him and leafed through the pages. "When she was younger, Omma didn't like having her picture taken. There's an old superstition that says you forfeit a part of your soul when someone takes your picture. She no longer believes that. But I have very few photographs of her when she was young."

After flipping through a few more pages, she stopped. "Here." She set the album on Jack's lap. "This is the earliest photo I have of her."

The young girl staring back at him could have been any age. Dressed in layers of threadbare clothing that concealed any hint of breasts or feminine curves, she faced the camera with her shoulders thrust forward, as if her tiny frame were caving in on itself. Her dark hair hung in a dull sheet down her back. Her mouth was set in a thin, solemn line.

But what drew Jack in was the young woman's haunted world-weary eyes. He felt a turning deep within his chest. He had seen those eyes before.

"When was this photo taken?"

Helen removed the picture from the plastic sleeve and turned it over. Written at the top in faded ink was a date of June 1953. "This was taken when Omma and her sister first came to Cheju Island.

Their village had burned down, and my mother was quite ill. They were seeking refuge. My father took them in."

Helen replaced the photo in its sleeve and showed him later photographs of a healthy and smiling Kim Sung with John and the children. Jack offered up the occasional nod or comment, but his mind was elsewhere, five decades and several thousand miles away in a crowded smoke-filled bar in Inch'ŏn.

Kim Sung stood alone on the narrow widow's walk that wrapped around the back of the beach house on the top floor. The brisk November air nipped at her body through her loose denim pants and cotton sweater, but she made no move to go back inside. She pondered how unpredictable this life could be, with its unexpected twists and turns, how it forced one to come to grips with their sorrow and their past, even when they try with all our might to forget.

Her thoughts ran to her *omma* and how much she missed her. Her *aboji* and *haraboji,* too. The latter had become only a distant memory now. But the memory of her mother, her life cut down in front of her, still haunted her.

When she arrived in the States, Kim Sung was very young, with no idea what to expect of this free America she had only heard about, with its tall buildings and white bread and one-color money. Over time, she learned to adapt to the American lifestyle. But even now, echoes of her childhood and her homeland resounded in her heart and mind, forever shaping who she was and what she believed. She was Korean first, an American citizen second.

Over the years, she had aged quietly, with a sense of serenity and wisdom borne from years of hard work and life's lessons learned, content knowing she had raised three good children who loved her. That was all she had ever asked for.

She wasn't surprised when she heard Jack's voice through the open French doors behind her.

"I knocked on your bedroom door but no one answered."

When she didn't reply, he went over to the railing and looked out at the view of the shoreline. Stuffing his hands in his pockets, he said quietly, "If you don't know why I'm here, please tell me now and I won't say another word."

A long moment passed before she spoke. "I know why you are here."

He reached behind him and sank into a deck chair. Kim Sung followed suit. Perched on the edge of her seat, she bowed her head and folded her small hands in her lap.

"Is Helen my daughter?" he asked directly.

"She is."

"But she doesn't know you're her real mother, does she?"

Kim Sung closed her eyes and shook her head. "I tell you this now because my daughter is dying." Her voice broke. She quickly composed herself. "And because I wish to ask your forgiveness for being dishonorable to you."

Jack's brow furrowed. "I don't understand."

"My actions caused this to happen. I was the one who approached you that night. I knew you had much to drink. I led you to that room. I stole your money and wallet. I tell my sister to give Helen away."

He held up a hand to stop her. "Wait. Why don't you start from the beginning."

After so many years of keeping her story locked up deep inside her, Kim Sung thought it would be difficult to speak of the past. But to her surprise, the words flowed from her mouth.

"My real name is Song Min. I come from small family with long history of rice farming. We live in very beautiful village in the foothills of South Korea where the rice grow well and the rainy season is short. When I am thirteen, the Red Army invade our village. This was a most bad thing. They burn down all our homes and take away many villagers. I hide inside root cellar underground with my sister, Joo Hee. An enemy soldier kill our *omma* right in front of us. We do not know what become of our father and grandfather."

She described how she and Joo Hee had come to stay at the American orphanage until it closed. "The priest was a most kind man. He give us money, and Joo Hee and I go to Inch'ŏn. Is a very big place with many Americans, but we cannot find work. We go to bed hungry most nights. Some nights we sleep on the streets. We wash and iron clothing and we unload vegetables from wagons. But we can't get good work because we do not have proper papers."

252

A hot flush spread up her neck and across her face as she explained how she and her sister were forced to sell their bodies. She turned away, unable to look at Jack. "It... did not happen many times," she said. "But it was most dishonorable thing."

Jack was silent for a long time. The wind shrieked through the eaves of the beach house, reminding Kim Sung of the whistles that resounded throughout their village the day the Red Army invaded. Finally, Jack said, "You did what you had to do to survive. I find no fault in that."

She nodded. "This may be so. But I cannot excuse what I did. Then I make things worse. When I was... with you that night, you pass out asleep. I find your wallet and money. I see opportunity for me and my sister. I tell myself it is gift from the fates. So, I take it and leave. This was dishonorable thing. I not act with right action. And now that you are here, I ask your forgiveness."

"There's nothing to forgive," he said softly.

Tears stung Kim Sung's eyes. She bowed her head to him in honor. Jack returned the gesture. "But there's something I need to ask you," he said. "How do you know I'm Helen's father?"

"I do... what I must sometimes, but not often. For months before you, none. And after you, none. So... I know."

"Is that why you kept my wallet?"

Kim Sung pondered the question for a long time. "I do not know," she replied. "At first, it was good place for my sister and I to keep money. Is easy to hide in folds of our *hanboks*. And sometimes, I take out pictures of you and the woman smiling. I look at them and dream of a place where people are happy like that. Later, when I find I am going to have baby, I want to burn it. But something tells me not to, that it is important. I give it to my sister for safekeeping."

Jack urged her to continue.

"After that night, Joo Hee and I find better place to live and use some of the money to get fake papers so we can work. We pay much money for this, but many Americans leave Inch'ŏn after the war and much work is gone. Then we learn I am carrying baby. I pray and pray to the gods to remove this curse from my body, but I keep getting bigger. I try to work, but as time goes by, I am mocked everywhere I go because I not have husband. When my belly is big, no one will give me work. I stay at home and weave baskets and make pots for Joo Hee to sell at market."

She remembered the dark, dank smell of that cramped hut, with its packed dirt floor and mud walls. Day after day, week after week, she kept her hands and mind busy so that she didn't have to think about the unwanted child growing inside her or how afraid she was. Those months were the loneliest time of her life.

"Then one day, my sister hear about a white man on Cheju Island who is very wealthy. He hire many Korean with papers for farming and fishing. Every day, she go on the boat to the island to work and then come home to the mainland. It is hard work, but after many months, she is asked to come live in the white man's house and work as a washwoman and housemaid. She stay there and only come home when she is allowed. She tell me that after I deliver the baby, maybe I come work there too. We find place in Inch'ŏn that take Korean babies with American fathers that nobody want. We make plans to take the baby there. So I sit and wait for the baby to come so I can give it away and go to Cheju Island to be with my sister."

Her voice grew softer, and Jack leaned closer to hear her. "I send for Joo Hee when it is time. The labor is very bad. We have no money for real doctor, so my sister take me to baby woman—how do you say—middle wife?"

Jack didn't correct her.

"She is white woman, but kind. She not turn us away. But the labor is long and with much pain. And then something go very wrong. There is much blood and after Helen is born, the pain does not go away. Something tells me my spirit is leaving my body. I sense I am going to die. And I see my baby and I know she does not belong here. She belong in America. I make my sister promise she will find a way for her to go there.

"After she promise me, I fall asleep for very long time. When I wake up again, it is many days later and I am in hospital. They send for Joo Hee and tell her she must take me out of hospital because we have no money to pay. I am still very sick, but she bring me home to our hut and try to take care of me. Is very hard for her because she still work. Then one day she come up with plan. She take me to Cheju Island and John take us in. She tells him our village burn down and our family killed in the fire. I stay there while I get better and my sister go off to work."

Kim Sung clasped and unclasped her hands. It felt like a colony of ants were scurrying beneath her skin. She took a breath before continuing.

"Joo Hee tell me this is place she take my baby. But I not see her at first. John is very kind to me. There is good food to eat every day and he give me vitamins and powdered milk and nurse me back to health. He do not know I have given birth. He try to talk to me, but his Korean not very good. He calls me name I do not understand. Then I see he is saying name written on my papers. He call me Kim Sung. They give me false name because I not old enough by law to work. But Joo Hee old enough, so she get to keep her name.

"Then one day I see Helen." She could no longer stop her tears. "Her hair and eyes are dark like mine, and she is so beautiful. I did not think she would be, but she is. When I stand over her crib, she look at me as if she know me. When I am better, I help take care of her. John tell me about the wallet and how he find her on his stoop. But I tell no one Helen is mine. Joo Hee also say nothing. We are afraid if John know, he will send us away. I go to lessons and learn to speak English and play with Helen and other children that John take in. I cook and clean for them and for John. This go on for very long time."

Pulling a tissue from her pocket, she wiped her nose. "Then one day I find I have very strong feeling for this man. I feel love for him. I trust him. He is kind to me and my sister and to the children. When I came there, I have no faith. I not believe anyone hear my prayers. But John, he help me understand that God loves me. He bring me to Jesus. And later, he tell me he loves me too. This make me very happy. He ask me to marry him, and I say yes.

"We have wedding at foot of Mount Hallersan in old Korean custom. Is very beautiful ceremony. We are very happy together and I adopt Helen. We try for baby of our own, but… my womb is closed and I cannot carry child." She turned away, embarrassed to be sharing something so personal with a man. "We adopt David and Elizabeth and then leave Korea to live in America."

"Why did you leave?" Jack asked.

"America have much better opportunity for children. Good education. That is why we leave."

"I don't believe you."

Kim Sung's head jerked up.

"You said your family was happy there," he continued. "And Helen tells me the same. Your husband had his ministry. Korea was your homeland. So, what was the real reason?"

Kim Sung's shoulders sank. "You are very astute man." She stood and went over to the deck railing, her back to him. "Our children... is very hard for them to fit in because they not full Korean. Especially for Liz. Is hard for me as well because I marry white man. Korean custom very strict back then about who you marry. Most marriages arranged. The villagers on the island, most are kind and accept us. But I am mocked when I go to the mainland and take the children to market. There is much—how do you say—hard emotions toward Americans after they leave when war is over. Many women are left behind with babies, and the war put the economy in very bad state. Many Koreans blame Americans and have much anger toward them."

Jack nodded. "What happened to make you leave?"

Kim Sung felt as though an invisible wing nut was being tightened between her shoulder blades. "One day I take the children to market. John is not with us. When we leave the square, many villagers come out of their huts and say many hateful things. They call my children *honhyol* and pick up rocks and throw them at us. David and Liz and Helen cling to me and are very frightened. We start to run down road, but they follow us. They tell us not come back because we bring bad luck to their village."

"What is a *honhyol*?"

She turned to look at him. "*Honhyol* means half-breed in Korean. It is most shameful word. I knew my children would never have chance of normal life there. Not as long as old customs and beliefs remained."

After the incident, Kim Sung determined in her heart to leave Korea, a homeland that was in her blood but was no longer the place of her birth. When John made the decision to come to America, she had readily agreed.

"How old were the children when this happened?"

"They were very young," she replied. "I not think David remembers. I not sure about Helen and Elizabeth. We have never spoken of it."

"What became of your sister?"

256

She smiled for the first time. "She live in Florida with her children and grandchildren. I use some of the settlement money from John's accident to bring her to America. Later, she marry and have three children. Her husband died few years ago. Now she live with oldest daughter."

"Do you see her often?"

"We are still very close," she replied. "More than close. After what we went through together—is hard to explain. We are like one sometimes, no?"

Jack nodded. He sat back in his chair and sighed. "I'm so sorry what you and your sister had to go through."

Kim Sung's brow furrowed. "Is not your fault. You not one who invade our village and kill our family."

"No. But I knew what I was doing that night. Drunk or not, I could have stopped it. I could have left." He turned to face her. "I'm sorry for what happened that night. I'm sorry I caused you so much grief."

Kim Sung placed her hand over his. "No." She shook her head. "If I not meet you, I not have my daughter. I not meet John or have David and Elizabeth. I never have chance to come to America and have better life." She squeezed his hand lightly. "You have given me much. There is nothing to say sorry for."

They sat in silence for a long time. Jack leaned back in his chair and pondered all that King Sung had told him. He now saw this quiet, reserved woman in a completely different light. But there was one final question he felt compelled to ask.

"Why have you never told Helen that you're her birth mother?"

Kim Sung shook her head vigorously. "You not understand about honor and disgrace. The things I did... is in the past. Is better not to speak of them. There was much dishonesty after I come to Cheju Island. Even John not know the full truth. Now it is too late. This would only bring Helen more pain." She sat forward on the edge of her deck chair, her eyes imploring. "Please do not reveal this to her."

"It's not my place to say anything," he replied.

She bowed her head once again. "Thank you."

257

"But I do want you to consider something," he added. "Were you aware that some years ago Helen went searching for her birth mother?"

Kim Sung's eyes widened, clearly surprised by the revelation. It occurred to Jack that within the framework of every family— traditional or not, broken or whole, close or distant—there are secrets and stories, half-truths and deceptions that for reasons good or bad are never revealed.

This time, he was the one who reached out and covered her hand with his. "Do you want Helen to leave this life not knowing her real mother was right here with her all along?"

37

Kenneth hung up the phone and went in search of his wife. He found her in the master bedroom with Karen, packing for their trip to back to New York.

"I'm afraid I have some bad news," he said. "I just got a call from the owner of the carousel out on Coney Island. They had a major problem with one of the engines today and they had to shut it down. He has no idea when they can fix it."

Helen tossed a pair of socks into her suitcase and sank down onto the edge of the bed. "So, what do we do now?"

"Did you have another place in mind, Mom?" Karen asked.

"The one I wanted was the one at Coney Island, but I guess that's not going to happen."

"Surely there are other carousels," Kenneth suggested. "Like at an amusement park or something."

"I don't want one that's so... modern," she replied.

"What do you mean?" Karen asked.

She sighed. "I know it sounds silly. But I had my heart set on an antique carousel in a park somewhere, like the kind I used to ride when I was a child, with the real wooden horses and the brass ring and all the bells and whistles. It's very special to me."

Karen went over to the bed and sat next to her. "There's nothing silly about that, Mom. We just have to figure out a way to make it happen."

"Do you know of any other antique carousels that are still operating?" Kenneth asked.

She shook her head. "Not that I know of. But I wouldn't know where to start looking."

Karen stood. "I do. Let's go boot up the computer downstairs."

Two hours and several containers of Chinese takeout later, everyone in the household was still gathered around the desk in the study, throwing around ideas as to how to find an antique carousel within a reasonable driving distance. Jack marveled at how they all threw themselves into making Helen's dream come true.

Karen found two restored carousels on the Internet that were still operating on the West Coast, but those were quickly ruled out because of the time it would take to drive there.

"Why don't we take a plane?" Jack asked.

"Helen can't fly because of the risk of blood clots," Kenneth explained.

"And those are the only ones?" Helen asked.

"No, there are others," Karen replied. "But most of them are shut down for the season. There's one near Chicago and another in Florida that appear to still be open, but there's no contact information given for me to call or e-mail."

She fiddled with the computer mouse. "There are plenty of commercial carousels, though. Around this area there are two—one in Virginia Beach and one in Hampton. I know that's not what you wanted, Mom. But I can't find anything else."

"What about the woman who owns the carousel store?" Liz suggested. "Maybe she knows of a local one."

"That's a great idea, Liz!" Helen said. "What was her name again? Do you remember, Omma?"

Kim Sung sat alone on the sofa, her dinner untouched. Helen had to ask her twice before she realized someone was speaking to her. "I do not recall," she said.

Helen frowned. "Omma, are you feeling—"

"I think her name was Carolyn," Karen said. She set down her container of chow mein. "Let's go look her up and give her a call."

Scott took his sister's place behind the desk and began pulling up sports scores from several different websites. Looking over his shoulder, Jack was amazed at the vast amount of information that

260

could be garnered from the Internet. A few years ago, one of the charity organizations Norma worked for gave her one of their older computers. Frank came by and set everything up for her, but Jack had never been interested in learning how to use it. It still sat on Norma's desk in the living room, collecting dust. "How does this Internet thing work?"

Scott tried to explain it to him, but the intricacies were quickly lost on him.

"I tell you what," Scott said. "If you want, I can help you set up an account and I'll show you the basics of how to log on and everything. Then when you get home, you can have an Internet provider hook you up and you'll have access to the web, e-mail, all that good stuff. And you can transfer it to your phone if you want."

"You mean a cell phone?" Jack shook his head. "Don't have one."

Scott looked at him as if he had sprouted a second head between his shoulders. "Really? Wow. Well… we can just set up the e-mail thing then."

"This e-mail. Does it cost a lot?"

"No, it's free. It's a great way to keep in touch with people and it's a heck of a lot cheaper than long-distance phone calls."

For the first time in several days, Jack thought about the noose stashed away in his kitchen drawer. "Let me think about it." Scott went back to looking at football stats.

Liz and Karen returned. "We got a recorded message," Karen said. "She's closed up shop for the season."

Helen folded her arms across her chest and stood looking out the window for a long moment. Then she turned around and said, "Let me try one more thing." She picked up the portable phone and left the room.

Nettie Byrum answered the phone at the marina office on the fourth ring.

"I don't know if you'll remember me," Helen began. "My family chartered a boat from you and your husband last week."

"Oh, yes. Helen, right?"

"Yes. I'm… well, when we spoke below deck, you said I would find what I was looking for, but not where I thought I would, and

261

well, that's exactly where I'm at right now and I seem to be stuck and I was wondering if you could help me." She sighed. "I'm probably saying this all wrong."

"Why don't you start from the beginning," Nettie suggested. "What is it that you're looking for?"

Helen told her the whole long story.

She could hear the smile in Nettie's voice. "You don't need me. Hold on a minute while I go look up a phone number for you."

38

The remains of the old fairground were located on a deserted strip of beach along the southernmost curve of Roanoke Island. Dense patches of live oaks and scrub bushes grew parallel to the road, obstructing the view of the ocean. Kenneth and Scott parked their cars on the shoulder in front of a rusty locked cattle gate.

Helen looked out through the windshield at the stretch of sand and surf behind the gate. Not a single person or building was in sight. "Are you sure this is it?"

Kenneth folded a piece of paper into fourths and stuffed it in his shirt pocket. "Positive." He looked at his watch. "We're a little early. We still have about fifteen minutes."

Moments later, a silver Honda Accord pulled in behind Scott's Mustang, and a middle-aged couple got out. Helen was surprised when Carolyn Boyce reached through the passenger side window and shook her hand.

"When Nettie gave me your phone number," Helen said, "she mentioned your husband's name, but I didn't connect it to you. We tried to call you yesterday at your shop in Ocracoke."

Carolyn nodded. "Sorry I missed your call. Nettie filled me in on the details. This is my husband, Ted. He's the one who does the restorations I told you about."

At first glance, one could have mistakenly thought they were brother and sister. Both had the same fair coloring and light green eyes.

"How are you feeling?" Carolyn asked.

"Much better. Thank you for your help the other day."

"Glad to have been of assistance," she replied. "But I didn't really do anything."

"How do you know the Byrums?" Helen asked.

"We've known Marty and Nettie for years," Ted replied. "Good people. We used to have a pleasure boat we kept docked at their marina. We sold it to them several years back. Marty uses it for tours and deep-sea fishing. As a matter of fact, you may have boarded it."

"Forty-five footer?" Kenneth asked.

"Yep. Only one there at the marina."

"Nice boat. Why would you ever want to sell it?"

A knowing look passed between Ted and Carolyn. "Change in priorities, you might say," he replied. "C'mon and I'll show you."

Both cars followed Ted as he drove through the opening in the heavy iron gate. He proceeded along a network of meandering narrow asphalt roads that led toward the water. As they got closer to the shoreline, Helen noticed piles of dry-rotted wooden planks scattered across the sand and what appeared to be the remains of an old swing set and teeter-totter. Corrosion from the salt air had taken their toll on the metal objects until only the framework and a few dangling chains remained to the swings. The seats on the teeter-totter were rusted through.

"This must have been a children's playground at one time," Helen said.

"Sure looks like it," Liz added.

When they were a hundred yards or so away from the shoreline, Ted took an abrupt turn onto a long concrete strip that ran parallel to the water. Gulls and terns followed alongside them, dipping to and fro in the brisk air.

"I think this used to be an amusement park of some kind." Jack pointed in the distance at a low-slung outcropping of dilapidated wooden stalls. "My guess is we're driving along what used to be the main walking area. And that up there is what's left of the arcades."

"I think you're right," Kenneth said.

They followed as Ted took another abrupt turn and headed back inland along another narrow strip of asphalt. "This is like a maze," Liz said.

The road soon gave way to hard-packed dirt and sand, and the going was slow as they made their way across the open space, buttressed on two sides by towering sand dunes. As they followed the car around a final curve, a huge white canvas tent loomed in front of them, with the distant shoreline and ocean as its backdrop.

"What in the world *is* this?" Helen asked.

Kenneth opened his car door. "Let's go find out."

"All of this"—Ted stretched out his arms to indicate the beach and surf—"I inherited from my father and grandfather. At one time, believe it or not, this used to be a popular theme park back in the '30s. Roanoke Island also used it as fairgrounds in the '40s and '50s. This is all that's left."

"Looks like you were right, Jack," Liz said.

"You're probably too young to remember such places," Ted said to Helen. He turned to Jack with a smile. "But I bet you do."

Jack nodded. "Sure do."

"Over there," he continued, "used to be the Skee-Ball and penny arcades. At the front were the food stalls and a park area and playground. And next to that was the Ferris wheel." He turned and faced the ocean. "And here, right in front of the water, was a huge wooden roller coaster. Not anything like the ones you see today, but it was solid. Took several sticks of dynamite to demolish it."

"Why'd you tear the place down?" Scott asked.

"Wasn't my idea," Ted replied. "I was just a kid then. When the park went belly-up back in the '70s, my grandfather sold off all the equipment and anything else he could find a buyer for and sold the land to a development company who wanted to build high-rise condos." He shook his head. "Broke his heart to do it. This beachfront property has been in the family for generations. But they needed the money, so he did what he had to do."

"Doesn't look like anything was ever built," Scott said.

Ted smiled. "Funny thing about fate. The development company went bankrupt and the deal fell through. My dad knew how much Granny and Pappy wanted to keep this land, so our family piled our money together and moved our grandparents in with us and paid the taxes on the property every year. They both died a few years after that and the land was passed down to my dad. Now it's mine and Carolyn's."

"What will you do with it now?" Jack asked.

Ted paused a moment before replying. "We're working something out with the authorities here on Roanoke Island." He didn't say anything more.

Helen pointed to the looming canvas tent. "What is that for?"

"That's our work tent."

Helen looked around but didn't see any evidence of construction. "Work tent? For what?"

Ted winked. "Let me show you." He turned and walked off in the direction of the tent and the distant shoreline.

Helen looked over at Kenneth, but he only shrugged. She took his arm to steady herself, and the group slowly made their way across the hard-packed sand. As they rounded the right side of the canvas structure, they found the entire back side open. Helen stopped midstride and gasped as she let go of Kenneth's arm and covered her mouth with both hands.

"Oh, *Kenneth*," she whispered.

Standing before her, completely restored to its original glory, was an antique carousel.

The platform sat on what appeared to be a new concrete pad, which accommodated both the carousel and the work tent. Mounted to the deck platform were three rows of gleaming carousel horses and other animals, including a rabbit, lion, tiger, deer, and two chariot seats. Behind the rows were hand-painted panels depicting old carnival scenes and characters. Above the panels and circling the outer perimeter were Victorian-style rounding boards with beveled glass mirrors in the middle and intricately carved corbels beneath. At the carousel's peak was a wooden painted mermaid, her smile and open arms beckoning all to come take a ride.

Helen walked slowly around the carousel in wonder. It was the prettiest carousel she'd ever seen. Each piece was lovingly restored, and everything appeared to be in working order, from the brass ring to the organ. When she circled back to where everyone was gathered, she looked at Ted.

"How did you *do* this?"

"It's been a labor of love." He smiled and put his arm around his wife. "Carolyn has always loved carousels, and my dad and

266

grandfather passed down their carpentry skills to me. They were both master carpenters, and my father was also a pretty good wood sculptor. One day I found an antique carousel horse at an estate sale and convinced myself I could carve one." He shook his head, laughing. "It didn't turn out so good. But I was hooked. I turned my attention instead to the original horse and did my research and restored it, all the way down to the original paint colors. That was twenty years ago, and I've been doing it ever since."

Helen was confused. "But... why did you build a carousel *here*."

"Well, as you can imagine, after a while we started accumulating quite a collection of carousel horses and pieces. Carolyn opened her shop and we came up with the idea of starting a business selling restored carousel pieces." He shrugged. "We found out real quick there isn't much demand, except among other collectors like ourselves. Most modern carousels are owned by corporations, and they've gone to the cheaper fiberglass horses and parts. Easier to tear down and put back up quickly, like at circuses and carnivals."

"Then Ted came up with the idea of restoring his own carousel," Carolyn said.

"We used private funds from the sale of the boat and a grant from the Outer Banks Tourism Board," Ted explained. "Our goal is to turn the property into a public park, with the carousel as its centerpiece. We had to build it here first, to make sure it would actually work. I brought some carousel restorers down from New York and Canada to help out. It runs like a charm. Once we get the go-ahead, hopefully by next spring, the carousel will be housed in a glass-enclosed space with a connecting museum containing artifacts and history about the origin of carousels and how this one was rebuilt."

"I'll be running the museum," Carolyn added with a smile.

Helen gestured toward the platform. "May I?"

"Of course!" Ted and Carolyn replied in unison.

Kenneth helped Helen step up onto the platform. She took her time admiring the menagerie of carved horses and animals. The work was exquisite. She was pleased to find that Ted had restored pieces by several different carvers. She found two huge Stein and Goldstein prancers on the outermost ring, with their trademark flower garlands and large buckles. On the other side, she found a stander by Looff and a pair by Carmel in the Coney Island style, with gold leaf details and flamboyant jewels on the bridle and saddle. The playful runners and animals on the inside ring were from an eclectic assortment of artists, including a Dentzel tiger.

She stopped short when she came to a pair of Philadelphia-style prancers in the middle ring. "Oh, my goodness," she whispered. She had never seen a more beautiful pair of carousel horses. One was a Daniel Muller military-style horse, dapple gray, with iridescent fish scale armor and a black, flowing mane. The other was a Dentzel, chestnut in color, with deep-relief flowers carved into the saddle and glass eyes so expressive they seemed to follow her. Both prancers had black horse-hair tails that nearly reached the platform.

She heard Ted's voice behind her. "You like that one?"

Helen nodded. "She's just beautiful. And that one, too." She pointed to the other horse. "Dentzel and Muller have always been my favorites."

"They were the best carvers."

"This is the one." Helen placed her hand on the chestnut's saddle. "And I think Jack will love the Muller."

"Then let's do this," Ted said.

Helen walked back around to the other side of the carousel and looked out at her family gathered there, waiting. She held out her hand to Jack, and he stepped up onto the platform.

The first ride was for Helen and Jack alone. Nothing was said between them as the carousel made its leisurely circuit, accompanied by lively organ music. Even Brooklyn seemed to understand the significance of what was happening as she waited patiently by the platform, holding her grandmother's hand and watching as her aunt and Mr. Jack went around in a circle.

Helen couldn't stop smiling, even as tears rolled down her cheeks. After several minutes, she motioned for Ted to stop the carousel to allow everyone else to take a ride.

By late afternoon, everyone had taken a spin on the carousel numerous times. Brooklyn tried out every animal on the inner ring. She decided the rabbit was her favorite. Nadine and Liz rode several different horses. Scott was the only one who was able to grasp the brass ring, although Karen and Kenneth were able to grab a couple of iron ones.

When Helen grew tired, Kenneth and Jack helped her down from her horse, and they went over to one of the chariot benches. Jack sat across from her. Kenneth had just started to sit down next to Helen when she noticed her mother several horses away, standing next to a small runner Brooklyn had chosen.

"Omma!" she called out. "Come over here and sit with us."

Kenneth said, "I'll sit this one out." He kissed Helen lightly on the lips. "But I get the next dance, okay?"

Helen smiled and looked back at her mother. "Come on, Omma! It's about to start up again!"

Her mother looked down at the platform, then slowly made her way over to her daughter.

39

Over the next several days, Jack spent time with Helen, taking leisurely walks along the beach, engaging in long talks over anything and everything. She was surprised to find she liked old westerns and backgammon. Jack discovered he enjoyed Uno and herbal teas.

On Thursday, the day before he left to go home, he went to church one last time with Liz, and was a guest at one of Brooklyn's tea parties. He tinkered with Scott under the hood of the Mustang and helped Nadine whip up a batch of homemade strawberry ice cream, something he hadn't done since his youth. Everyone agreed the treat was a big hit.

That evening, Kenneth took a call from the Oregon Inlet wildlife refuge. The turtle they rescued from the beach was doing just fine, despite losing his injured leg, and the animal was scheduled to be released back into the wild in a few weeks. The staff at the station had affectionately named him "Tripod." Jack had a good laugh over that one.

On Friday, Karen drove Jack home. There wasn't a big fanfare when he left. Jack had said goodbye to everyone else the night before. Kenneth shook his hand on the front porch and then left him alone with Helen to say their goodbyes.

Helen hugged him warmly. "Thank you again for... everything."

She didn't invite him back for Christmas. Jack didn't expect her to. By that time, Helen's condition would be worse. He knew she wanted him to remember her the way she was now.

As they pulled out of the driveway, he saw Kim Sung standing alone in front of an upstairs window. Something in the solemn lines of her face, her form so small and frail against the backdrop of the huge house, made his heart ache. She placed her hand to the glass, only for a moment, and then she was gone.

Karen was unusually quiet during the drive back to Norfolk. She told Jack she wasn't feeling well. On the outskirts of Corolla, she swerved into a McDonald's parking lot and hurried inside to the ladies' room. She barely made it into the stall before she lost her breakfast.

As she washed up afterward, she looked at her reflection in the mirror above the sink. Her complexion was pasty and dark circles ringed her eyes.

She returned to the car and dropped her keys in her lap. "It looks like I didn't have jet lag after all, and it wasn't the sight of that dead turtle that made me so sick." She let out a breath. "I'm pregnant."

Jack smiled. "Congratulations!"

Karen covered her face with her hands and burst into tears.

Jack clumsily patted her on the shoulder, but that only made her cry harder.

"What's wrong?" he asked. "You're not happy about this news?"

Karen shook her head as she scrambled for a tissue in her purse. She couldn't find one. Jack gave her his handkerchief from his coat pocket. "No, it's not that." She wiped her nose. "Michael and I are both thrilled. It's just that—I don't know. I'm guess I'm feeling a little confused right now."

In truth, Karen felt overwhelmed, inadequate for this complex profession of motherhood. Who would she talk to about sleeping and feeding schedules? Should she breast feed or bottle feed? What if the baby was colicky? And what about the "terrible twos," the preschool years, the first day of kindergarten? She was getting ahead of herself, but she couldn't help it. How would she ever get through any of this without her mom's sure, gentle guidance?

I'm about to become a mother just as I'm losing my own.

"Does Helen know?"

She shook her head and wiped her eyes. "Not yet. You and Michael are the only ones I've told."

"Are you going to tell her?"

Fresh tears started again as she thought about the fact that her mother would not live to see her only grandchild. At least not on this earth. She had briefly entertained the idea of not telling her to spare her any further pain, but she knew she couldn't keep something like this from her.

"I will, I promise. I just need a little time to adjust."

Neither one said anything for several miles as they got back on the road and headed north toward Virginia. Then, as they were nearing the state line, Jack turned to her. "You know that music box your mother bought the other day? Wouldn't it be perfect for the baby's room?"

Jack pulled his suitcase and overnight bag from Karen's rental car trunk.

"I can carry that up to your apartment," she offered for the second time.

"No, no. I can do it myself."

She hugged him. "Thank you so much for doing this for my mom. I'm so glad I got the chance to meet you."

A pressing question burned on his tongue, but he had no idea how to voice it. "Will you call me when—" He couldn't get the rest of the words past the sudden lump in his throat.

Karen took his hand as tears brimmed her eyes. "Yes. I'll let you know when Mom passes."

Jack could only nod in response.

As the elevator made its ascent to the third floor, he wished he had said more, done more. Not just with Karen but with everyone else at the beach house. He wished he had told Karen and Scott what fine young people they were, and that Karen and Michael would make wonderful parents. He wished he had told Liz and David how much he admired their steadfast support of their sister. He wished he had played one more game of Candyland with Brooklyn and told Nadine she made the best blueberry muffins he'd ever tasted. He regretted the ugly scene in the den with Kenneth and not telling Kim Sung how much he admired her quiet strength and courage.

But most of all, he wished he had met Helen sooner.

By the time he reached his apartment door, Jack felt utterly drained, physically and emotionally. He had no sooner placed his luggage inside when he heard a voice behind him.

"Hey, Jack. Glad you're home."

It was Frank DeMarco, his neighbor from the second floor. Jack looked at his watch. "Thought you'd be at the precinct by now."

"Took the day off." Frank shifted his weight from one foot to the other. "Okay if I come in?"

The last thing Jack wanted to do was socialize. "Uhh … this isn't a good time, Frank. I'll call you later, okay?" He started to close the door.

"I need to talk to you for just a minute," he insisted. "Won't take long."

Jack ran a hand over his eyes and said, "I'm really not up to this right now. I've been traveling all day and I—"

"I know about your plans, Jack."

Jack's brow furrowed. "What are you talking about?"

Frank didn't respond. After a long moment, Jack sighed and gestured him into the apartment. Frank walked over to the sofa in the living room and sat down.

"By all means, make yourself at home," Jack said.

Frank ignored the sarcasm and cut to the chase. "I know you were planning to kill yourself."

Jack started to argue but stopped short. His shoulders sagged, and he looked away. "How did you find out?"

"I was worried about you when you came by my apartment and picked up that envelope. I knew something wasn't right. So, I did a little detective work."

Despite his previous statement of not wanting to talk, Jack was intrigued. He sat down on the sofa across from him. "What kind of detective work?"

"The next morning, I saw you carrying your luggage to that woman's car. I'd never seen her before, so I got a little suspicious. As you were driving off, I wrote down the license plate number and ran it through DMV. Came back as a rental. I contacted the car agency and got the name and number of the person who rented it. Came back to a woman from New York by the name of Karen Cochran and an address for a place in Hatteras, North Carolina."

Jack's anger simmered, but he held it in check. "Go on."

"I didn't do anything with the information at first. But that envelope kept bugging me. Whatever was in it, you meant to give it to me, didn't you? Not a mistake like you said it was."

He didn't answer.

"I hadn't seen you for at least a couple of months," Frank went on. "I knew you were in a bad way over Norma. I know how much you miss her. I started to worry maybe you were more than just depressed—that maybe you were thinking of doing something drastic. After a day or so when you didn't come home, I let myself in and took a look around."

"How did you get in?" Jack demanded.

Frank fished in his pants pocket and pulled out a key to Jack's apartment. He placed it on the glass coffee table. "You gave me a key when Norma was sick, remember?"

Jack had completely forgotten about the extra key. "You had no right to come in here and—"

"I found the noose and papers in your kitchen drawer."

Jack stared at him, dumbfounded. Then he went into the kitchen and yanked open the drawer next to the sink. The papers were still there, but the noose was gone.

He came back into the living room and glared at Frank. "Where is it?"

"Someplace where you won't find it."

Jack paced, cursing under his breath. "Get out, Frank. I don't want you here."

When Frank made no move to leave, Jack shouted, "I said get out! I know my rights and I'm telling you to leave!"

"Don't you want to know how I knew you were coming home today?" He didn't wait for an answer. "I asked Karen's father to let me know when she was bringing you home. He called me last night. That's why I took the day off."

"You—you talked to *Kenneth*?"

Frank nodded.

Deflated, Jack sank onto the sofa again and stared at the floor. He didn't want to know the answer but he asked anyway. "What did you tell him?"

"Pretty much everything." He explained that after he found the noose and papers, he called the contact number on the rental car agreement—Karen's cell phone. When he didn't get an answer, he

274

called the alternate contact number—the house in Hatteras. Kenneth answered and confirmed Jack was staying there. Frank explained why he was calling and that he suspected Jack was in danger of harming himself.

"I told him about Norma," he added.

Jack closed his eyes. He felt raw, exposed. "When did you make this call?"

He thought for a moment. "Two—no, three days after you left."

It all made sense now. That was the day after their confrontation in the den, when Kenneth's demeanor toward him had suddenly started to soften.

A derisive sound escaped his throat. "How ironic."

Frank sat forward on the sofa. "Jack, I care about you. You've been a good friend and neighbor. Promise me you're not going to kill yourself."

The words were out before he knew he was going to say them. "I promise you I won't do it today. That's all I can promise at this point." He stood up. "Thanks for coming by, Frank. I appreciate your concern, I really do. But I have a lot of thinking to do."

After Frank left, Jack went into the kitchen to make a pot of coffee. He was waiting for the coffee to start dripping when he noticed the red "on" light wasn't working. He turned the switch twice. Nothing. He unplugged the appliance and used a different electrical socket. Still nothing. He flipped the kitchen light switch, but the ceiling fixture remained dark. He tried a lamp in the living room with the same result.

Thinking he had blown a fuse, he took a flashlight into the utility room and checked the circuits in the fuse box. They all seemed to be in order.

He went back to the kitchen and picked up the phone to call the power company about the outage. The line was dead. He checked the connection, but the cable was grounded.

"What the—"

Then he remembered. He had called the power company and the telephone company to terminate his service. Still holding the phone receiver in his hand, Jack tilted his head back and laughed.

40

Jack's funeral was held on a brisk but sunny February afternoon, the last day of the month. He was laid to rest next to Norma.

The memorial service was held earlier that day at a small Presbyterian church in nearby Ghent, not far from Jack's home. Pastor Martin told Karen and the other mourners that the turnout was one of the largest he'd ever seen in the twenty-some years he'd been there.

Clusters of crocuses pushed their lush purple heads through the thawing ground, and bright yellow daffodils lined the cobblestone pathways as Karen made her way across the cemetery to the gravesite. A gentle breeze made the bare limbs of the oaks and maples dance in a slow waltz, swirling around the tight, swollen leaf buds that were just beginning to emerge from their slumber. Spring would be here soon.

The area surrounding the casket and open grave was alive with color from the numerous flower arrangements placed there. Jack's family and friends stood in silence as the incantations and scripture verses were read. The passages from Psalms and Ecclesiastes were chosen by Jack's wife, Doris, whom he had wed the previous April, and Charlie Little, Jack's old pool buddy.

Pastor Martin concluded the service, and the crowd of mourners trickled out through the back gate. Karen hugged Doris warmly and promised to keep in touch.

"I'm so glad he found you and your family before he left us." Doris lingered over her husband's grave a few minutes longer. Then

Charlie gently took her by the arm and escorted her to his car. Karen stayed behind.

The grounds crew stood a respectable distance away from the gravesite and waited for the crowd to disperse before starting their work. Karen watched as they lowered the oak casket into the ground and filled the hole with dirt. As the crew tamped the mounded earth with their shovels, one of the workers asked why the headstone was already in place.

"Some bigwig from upstate New York put in a rush order to the monument company," the supervisor answered. "Paid big bucks to make sure it was done today."

Karen smiled.

Their work finished, the grounds crew stowed their shovels and equipment away into the back of a pickup truck and drove away. Karen walked over to the grave site, the heels of her pumps sinking into the soft earth. She stood in front of the plain marble headstone. Only the dates of Jack's birth and death and a small American flag were inscribed on its surface. Just as he had wanted.

Wiping away tears, Karen removed three small framed photographs from her purse and placed them across the top of the headstone. The first one was of Mom, her face in profile as she sat on a chestnut-colored carousel horse, a glimpse of the gray-green Atlantic in the background.

The second photo was of Mom and Jack sitting in a chariot seat with Nana, all three smiling for the camera.

The last photo was taken only a few months ago, when Karen and her husband made a trip to Norfolk to visit Jack and Doris. It was of their three-year-old, Matthew, a huge grin on his face, clutching the pole of a carousel pony with both hands as Jack and Karen stood beside him.

Acknowledgements

If the process of writing this book could be compared to Dorothy's journey on the yellow brick road, I never could have made it here to Oz without the help of some very good friends.

I want to thank my husband, Jerry, for your support and encouragement every step of the way. Thank you for always letting me be who I need to be, and for believing in me even when I didn't. I love you to the moon and back.

To my son, Brandon, thank you for inspiring me to move out of my comfort zone and try new things.

To my wonderful editor, Kristen Stieffel, you took a lump of coal and found the diamond within. It's so hard to kill our darlings! Thank you from the bottom of my heart for your honesty and incredible eye for detail.

Thank you to all my dear friends and fellow writers who have been my cheerleaders from the very beginning and kept at me to get this book published. You know who you are.

To my readers at www.cheryllsnow.com around the globe, thanks so much for reading and sharing my blogs and stories. Your support means more than you know.

A big shout-out to my writers' group, Calhoun Area Writers (CAW). You guys make me a better writer!

To author extraordinaire, Cassie Dandridge Selleck, you came along just when I needed a swift kick to my hindparts. Thank you for stoking a fire from a smoldering pile of ashes, and for answering my endless list of questions about self-publishing. As they say here in the South, you're a peach!

Most importantly, I want to thank my Lord and Savior, Jesus Christ, for His love and mercy, and taking whatever ability I have and using it for His glory. Thank goodness God still uses broken vessels.

Note from the Author

To any military history buffs out there, I apologize for fudging the dates and details a bit concerning Jack's time spent in the United States Navy and in South Korea during the Korean War.

While this book is a work of fiction, there were several resources that proved very helpful to me as I painted my story.

For stunning photos of South Korea and vast information on Korean culture: *Korea: As Seen by Magnum Photographers* by Magnum Photos and Bruce Cummings, Ph.D. (2008); and *The Discovery of Korea* by Yoo Myeong-jong (2005). For a thorough history of the Korean War: *The Forgotten War: America in Korea, 1950-1953* by Clay Blair, Jr. (2003).

The Outer Banks of North Carolina is one of my favorite places in the world. While writing this book, I drew inspiration from my personal photos and from two books I feel capture the essence of this special place: *Coastal Wild: Among the Untamed Outer Banks* by Steve Alterman and Mark Buckler (2010); and *Outer Banks Edge: A Photographic Portfolio* by Steve Alterman (2001).

About the Author

Cheryll is a wife, mother, grandmother, author, and RN. Although writing is her passion, she also enjoys traveling, gardening, photography, puzzles, and projects that stretch her creative boundaries. Her work has appeared in numerous publications, and she is a regular contributor to the Chicken Soup for the Soul series. *Sea Horses* is her first novel. She lives with her husband, Jerry, and their rescue pets, Sadie and Callie, in the Chattanooga area of Tennessee. You can contact her via her website at www.cheryllsnow.com

Made in the USA
Columbia, SC
19 December 2020